A
GRAVE
DIAGNOSIS

35 Stories of Murder and Malaise

A Carrick Crime Anthology

Editor: Donna Carrick

A Grave Diagnosis

35 Stories of Murder and Malaise

CARRICK
PUBLISHING

Copyright Carrick Publishing 2020

Editor: Donna Carrick
Copy editor: Rosemary McCracken

Cover Art: Sara Carrick

Print Edition 2020

ISBN: 978-1-77242-125-5

Dedication

This anthology is dedicated to the countless heroes who have worked endless hours to ease our global suffering throughout this 2020 Coronavirus pandemic.

The doctors, nurses, paramedics, personal support workers and medical support staff, all of whom so bravely risk their lives and families daily to help our world, deserve our deepest gratitude.

At the time of this writing, in the United States alone, over 1,200 medical workers have died due to COVID-19.

On October 28, 2020, global pandemic deaths have topped 1,117,562. In the U.S., over 226,000 deaths due to Coronavirus have been reported. Canada has suffered 10,000 deaths, and cases are once again on the rise.

These front line medical workers are not alone in their commitment to serve an ailing world. They are assisted by grocery workers, retailers in essential services, delivery staff, and far too many others to name, who often toil in low-paying jobs for the greater good of society.

To all of these front-line workers, both in medicine and in essential services, you are an inspiration. May your contribution be never forgotten, and may you be honored by us all, long after wellness has been restored to our planet.

To our readers, we wish you good health and safety. Be well, and may we all survive this crisis to share our COVID-19 stories with future generations.

We hope our small attempt to entertain will bring you peace, and offer some relief from the worries of this stressful time.

Donna and Alex Carrick
Carrick Publishing
October, 2020

A GRAVE DIAGNOSIS

Donna Carrick

Donna Carrick is a thriller author, host of the Dead to Writes podcast, an Indie publisher, (Carrick Publishing,) former treasurer of Crime Writers of Canada and a long-time member of Sisters in Crime. Her novella The Noon God and novels The First Excellence and Gold And Fishes have all, at various times, topped Amazon's Bestselling Thriller charts. Her story "Watermelon Weekend" (Thirteen) was a finalist for the Arthur Ellis 2014 Best Short Story Award.

Oh, how I loved him! I loved him with that embarrassing, gut-wrenching poignancy that can only be mustered by the very young. That searing, all-consuming attention to his every gesture, smile or flicker of the eye…

But enough of that. He wouldn't know me now. Not that I could fault him, hidden as I was behind my medical mask, hair covering, scrubs and white coat. And with the ID strung around my neck which displayed my married name: Dr. K. McDougall.

He'd known me as someone else, someone quite different.

Even without my excess hospital gear, I doubt he would have recognized me. I was no longer the willowy blonde who'd shared a joint with him under the apple trees on Lakeshore Boulevard. My hair had darkened over time, another measure of the passing years, marking a distance we could not have bridged, even if we wanted to.

I was now, as the ancient meaning of my married name McDougall suggested, "a dark stranger". Unknown to him.

Besides, he was in no frame of mind to notice me beyond the trappings of my profession. He was distraught, fear widening those dark eyes I remembered so well. His body had the familiar still composure, that cool element that had once commanded my devotion, but his pupils were dilated, revealing panic.

And who wouldn't panic, under those circumstances?

I studied his daughter, the painfully thin, blue-eyed blonde who lay barely conscious on the bed before me. Only 22 years old, according to her chart. Still living at home with her father, my former lover, Djoser Kamel, and her mother, the still-beautiful, in a fragile, childish way, Shelly Hampson Kamel.

Shelly hadn't changed much. We'd never met, but I'm ashamed to say that after I learned of her existence I went through a brief period of obsession, during which I followed her for several weeks. So I was familiar with her smooth, heart-shaped face, her Danish-blue eyes, the tender curves of her body.

Once I'd satisfied myself all those years ago that Djoser was telling me the truth—that his then four-year-old daughter was sick, and that he could not, would not leave Shelly to manage on her own—I pulled myself together. My memory of watching from afar as Shelly held that tiny girl, comforting her in the courtyard of a Toronto medical center, was enough to appeal to my sense of morality.

I removed myself from the equation. I'd been holding back on accepting a place in a pre-med program at another university, preferring to stay at York with the man I loved. But I realized he would never love me enough to leave his child, nor would I want the cast-off love of a man who would do such a thing.

Oh, he tried to work it out with me. He called so many times, and left messages, but I never returned his calls, and I gave strict instructions to my family not to divulge my whereabouts.

To this day, I'm thankful for the understanding and support of my darling mother and father. Without their love, I'm not sure I would have found the strength to go on. Those were dark days.

But that was then.

Djoser stared at me over his mask. He was still a handsome man. He'd clearly made an effort to stay trim and healthy. The only hint of time's cruelty was in the lines at the corners of his eyes.

"When did she last eat?" I asked.

He turned to his wife.

"She hasn't been keeping anything down since Wednesday," Shelly said. She straightened her mask, and ran her fingers through her corn-silk hair. "Djoser was at one of his meetings, so it was only Kelly and me for dinner.

"At around midnight, she started vomiting. The usual symptoms. Diarrhea, stomachache. I called our doctor in the morning. He said to keep an eye on it, and if it didn't improve, bring her in."

"You did the right thing," I said. "We'll isolate her in a private room, away from other patients. I want to run some tests, keep her under observation for a few days."

"We were worried," Djoser said, "about bringing her in, under the circumstances. The hospital is a scary place during a pandemic."

"You were right to worry," I said, and wondered whether something in my voice might trigger a memory, but he was too distraught to think of anything but his daughter. "With COVID-19 rules in place, you won't be able to visit. You can tele-visit once she's well enough. If you bring her tablet in, our people will disinfect it so you can FaceTime every day. But for now, she needs rest. You'll both have to say goodbye. You can call my office tomorrow morning for an update."

Djoser kissed his daughter on the forehead. I was reminded of the cool sweep of his lips, the brush of his warm breath.

Shelly hugged Kelly, stroking her fair hair away from her face. I began to think she would put up a fight, and insist on staying with her daughter.

But Djoser said, "Shelly, we have to go." His voice was soft and kind, but firm, as if he was used to dealing with an emotional wife.

She whispered briefly into Kelly's ear, and followed Djoser out of the room.

I stood there for a moment, alone with their critically ill daughter. Kelly. I allowed the shock of the past half hour to have its way with me. It left me feeling drained. After all these years. After all the changes, the path I'd chosen, I never expected this.

She was so very thin. Obviously, this was not her first brush with illness. No one becomes this emaciated after a few days of vomiting.

If she were filled out a bit, she would resemble her mother. I saw nothing of Djoser in his daughter. Her eyes, when I shone my light in them, were Danish blue like Shelly's, and her hair, if it were clean, would be that same frosted gold as her mother's. Only illness had dimmed its shine.

Kelly hadn't been well the last time I'd seen her. That was 18 years ago. I wondered if she'd ever been well. If she had, you wouldn't have guessed it by looking at her now.

***

It was a Friday night. Djoser and I had cut our last two classes, knotting up the sheets on the single bed in my dorm. Then we walked together in the fading September sunlight, fingers intertwined, hips and thighs touching, more in love than I'd ever been, drunk with the wild colorful sights and sounds of our own passion.

When we reached the bus stop, I tried one more time. "But it's pub night. David and Moira will be there. Curtis is coming."

"You'll have fun, Kenzie. You and Curtis will dance all night."

"I want to dance with you."

He laughed, in that infuriatingly dismissive way of his. "Sorry, K, I have to get home. My friend is waiting for me."

Friend? What friend? I froze in place, unable to breathe.

We were nearly a year into our relationship. We'd met in class the previous October, and then later with friends at the pub. Since then, we'd been together nearly every day, passionate stolen moments between classes, early morning trysts and enthusiastic afternoon encounters.

Even now, a year later, whenever our fingers touched, I felt it, that electric shock, that sensation of one-ness that I could not deny.

Friend?

The way he'd said it. And immediately after it was out of his mouth, the look in his eyes, as if he was ticked at his own slipup.

Somehow I found my voice. "You're married, aren't you?"

His silence was my answer.

"Kenzie, I love you," he finally muttered.

I turned and ran blindly back to my dorm. He followed. I slammed the door, locking it against the pain, the bile in my own throat that I was sure would choke me.

"Please, Kenzie. Let me in. Let me talk to you."

After a while I realized the futility of refusing to hear him out. I opened the door, waving my hand to indicate he should sit on the bed, while I took the only chair, the one at my workstation.

"Kenzie," he began, "we were married right out of high school. We have never been in love. It was a marriage of convenience, we both knew it. I needed to stay in Canada. Shelly was my best friend at the time. We married…"

I struggled to focus on his words, to hear him over the rush of betrayal in my ears.

"Can you leave her? Can you get a divorce?" My voice sounded pathetic, but I had to ask.

6

"I *was* leaving her. Last March. I put a deposit on a place. I packed and booked a truck. Then Kelly got sick."

"Kelly? I thought her name was Shelly?"

"Kelly," he said, twisting the dagger deeper into my heart, "is our daughter."

"Oh."

We sat in silence for a moment. My energy was gone. I let him hold my hand, barely aware of his touch.

The sun was low, peeking into my dorm window from behind a depressing gray building nearby.

"Kenzie," he finally said, "I have to go. Kelly is home. She's been in the hospital all week."

I won't pretend it was easy to pull my thoughts away from my own unhappiness, but somehow I found the decency to ask, "What's the matter with her?"

"We don't know," he said. "It started last March. Stomach problems. Pain. Vomiting. It got so bad we had to put her in the hospital for a week. They ran all kinds of tests, but couldn't isolate it. Then she improved. We took her home. She's been OK since then. Until this week."

"How old is she?"

"Four," he said. He fumbled for his wallet, pulled out a photo of an apple-cheeked child with a smile that covered her whole face, pigtails flying in every direction as she ran toward the photographer.

Toward her father, I supposed.

Djoser.

"You'd better go," I said.

"We'll talk tomorrow."

"Yes. Call me tomorrow."

"I will."

He wrapped his arms around me, as if his perfect body could somehow restore the trust, the love, but it couldn't. I endured his embrace, waiting for it to end.

And then it did.

***

That night, I cried for hours at the kitchen table of my family home, my mother forcing tea and ice cream down my throat while my father occasionally looked in on us, his face full of worry.

The next morning, they drove me to my dorm, packed my things and took me home.

By Monday, I'd applied to transfer from York to the University of Toronto. I had long dreamed of becoming a doctor, and this move would allow me to pursue the right program.

Yes, I tracked Shelly down. Yes, I followed her over the next two weeks, while I waited for my transfer to be confirmed.

I'm glad I did. Seeing Shelly with her young daughter made it clear that I could never have Djoser. He wanted me to believe there was no life left in his marriage, but I could tell that Shelly wasn't aware of our affair. Her innocent face, those blue eyes…she was just a young mother who loved her husband and her child, and who didn't deserve the treatment to which she was being subjected.

I thought I would die of shame.

Instead, I moved into a new dorm at the downtown campus. I met Nathan McDougall, the good-looking student with the serious smile, who was instantly taken with me, I could tell.

We talked for hours, studied together, but I told him from the start that I wasn't looking for a relationship. I was there to study. Nothing more.

He agreed that we would be friends.

When I missed first one cycle, then another, I started to panic. Nathan drove me to the medical center, and waited while they drew my blood. The pee stick had been positive, but I wanted to be certain before I told my parents.

"We're with you, whatever you decide," my mother said.

I considered abortion, but only briefly. The idea hurt too much. When the ultrasound revealed I was carrying a boy, I resolved to name him Joseph.

And then, a funny thing happened. I thought Nathan would pull away from me, as my pregnancy developed. Instead, he stayed by my side. In fact, he came to every medical appointment, every prenatal class. And, finally, it hit me one morning, as I was waiting for him outside our classroom: I'd fallen in love with this young man. Dark of hair, with flashing, fun-filled eyes, quiet by nature, unassuming—Nathan had begun to fill the holes in my heart left there by the Djoser debacle.

I knew he was infatuated with me. But did he love me? Enough to claim a child who wasn't his blood? Enough to be a real partner, a real parent?

It was too much to ask. I tried to put the notion out of my head.

Then, one afternoon in the library, he looked up and said, "I'm here, Kenzie. Let's do this thing, together."

And that was that. I've never looked back.

Nathan was a father, in every important sense of the word. And a husband, a truer one than I deserved. Our love was not the kind that could be destroyed in a moment of betrayal. It was strong, resilient, the kind of love my parents shared. I was blessed to be his partner.

Then came the real test of our bond. When Joseph was eight, we learned he had leukemia. We fought, we cried, we went to specialists, we cried some more, and in the end, we lost our precious, beautiful boy.

We put our darling in the ground, and later, buried my parents beside him. Don't ask me how I survived. I don't know the answer, but I know it had something to do with the constancy of Nathan's love.

***

"Kelly" I said, stroking her forehead, "are you awake?"

She moaned.

I studied the roots of her matted hair. They were slightly discolored, like those of a much older woman. I could tell she didn't use dye. The texture and color were natural, like my own. And yet, judging by the roots, you'd think a color job was growing out. They were slightly darker than the corn-silk shade of the rest.

"Kelly," I repeated. I lifted her wrist. Gloved as we all were in the face of this pandemic, taking a pulse manually was difficult. I studied her hands. They were slender, not unexpected given her underfed appearance. Their skin was taut and dry. The nails had been painted, but were growing out. At their naked base, near the cuticle, I saw yellowed half-moons. Was Kelly a smoker?

I checked the chart. *No.*

"Doctor," she said, and I almost didn't hear her at first. "Please. Let me stay awhile."

"Don't worry, dear. You're not going anywhere for at least a week. We have a lot of tests to run."

She smiled. "Thank you."

"Can I ask you a few questions?"

"I think so."

"Do you smoke cigarettes?"

"No."

"Any drugs? Marijuana? Hashish? Anything?"

She gave a weak little laugh. "No, doctor. Nothing. To smoke pot, you'd have to have a life. I have no life."

"What do you mean?" I studied her. She was giving way to sleep, to the comfort of the glucose IV drip, the clean white pillowcase, the warmth of her private room.

She closed her eyes, then opened them again, looking at the window, where the last of the sun's light was filling the room, its UV rays filtered and cooled by the treated glass.

"I have no life," she repeated, before closing her eyes once more.

I let her drift into the mercy of sleep.

Poor child. Whatever demons she was battling could fuck right off for the moment. She needed rest. I would see to it that she recovered.

***

That night, as we did every night, Nathan and I half-worked, half-watched our shows, dressed in our pajamas, sipping tea and answering e-mails during the commercial breaks.

I opened Kelly's file on my tablet. Maybe it was my own grief rearing its head once more thanks to the shock of seeing Joseph's biological father. I'd almost forgotten how closely my son resembled my former lover. That languid smile, those knowing deep eyes, flawless skin and full dark mouth.

For whatever reason, Kelly's words haunted me. "I have no life," she had said, and despite the well-documented theatrics of young women, I felt the weight of her words in my soul.

Joseph had lived only eight short years, but oh, what years they had been! I glanced at my husband, remembering the camping, the beaches, the road trips, the three of us singing ridiculous lyrics to songs we hated. Those first school years, the report cards which were now tucked away in a keepsake box under our bed...

"You're awfully quiet," Nathan said.

And, just like that, the tears were streaming down my face and the words, mangled and barely intelligible, poured out of my mouth.

I told him everything. About seeing Djoser, Shelly and their invalid daughter, Kelly, at the hospital that day. I told him about my concerns, and how I doubted my judgement, given my previous relationship with Djoser.

And I told Nathan for the first time how much our Joseph, our treasure, resembled his father.

Had I done the right thing, not telling Djoser that he had a son?

I could be excused, at the age of 21, for running, for hiding away with my broken heart. But what excuse did I have, as the years began their glacial melt, for withholding that information? Whatever else Djoser might have been, and he was a heel, no doubt about it, he seemed to be a devoted father to Kelly. His fear had been genuine. He felt the terror of possibly losing his child.

10

"You have to pass this case to another doctor," Nathan said, stating the obvious. With my previous connection to the parents, it was unethical for me to treat their child.

And yet...I hadn't been able to save our son. In my heart, I knew I owed Djoser something. A part of me would always love him, or at least the memory of him. I would do whatever I could to keep his daughter alive.

"What about the hair?" I asked Nathan.

"Long-term illness will do that."

I nodded.

"Talk to Daniel," he said, referring to my colleague and our friend, Dr. Daniel Stern, a leading toxicologist at my hospital.

"I'll call him now."

***

I was at my office early the next morning, before my assistant arrived. One of my favorite things is to enjoy a few moments of peace before the day unfolds with its endless parade of the sick and the weary. In normal times, I would have my coffee and toast in the tiny lunchroom, but due to the coronavirus pandemic, Cindy, my assistant, was keeping reduced hours. When she wasn't in the office, she normally forwarded the office phone to my cell. In those moments of solitude, I was free to sit in my private office, door closed, and watch the city come to life outside my fifth-floor window.

At 8 a.m. my cell phone blipped to life. My heart leaped into my throat. It was Djoser Kamel, calling for an update on his daughter's condition.

Should I tell him he'd lost a son to leukemia? Might that have a bearing on Kelly's situation?

I doubted it, but you never knew. In any case, I'd leave the full medical briefing to Daniel, Dr. Stern.

For an instant, I considered letting Djoser's call go to voice mail, and asking Daniel to call the worried father back. But, even as I weighed the idea, my hand reached for the phone of its own accord.

"Hello, Dr. McDougall here," I said.

"Doctor, it's Djoser Kamel, Kelly's father. How is she? Did she sleep well? Is there any improvement?"

Best to say as little as possible, I thought. Let Daniel tell Djoser about the tests scheduled for that morning.

"I haven't seen her yet today," I said, "but I called the ward, and they said she slept well. The vomiting has stopped and she seems comfortable. The pain is being managed."

"Can I see her this morning?"

11

"No," I said, too quickly. "I mean, I know how much you want to, but the pandemic rules forbid visitors. She's being very well taken care of, I promise you, and once she's fully conscious again you'll be able to FaceTime with her."

"Will you call me if there's any change?"

"It won't be me. A family situation has come up," I lied, "and I have to leave town for a couple of weeks. But I've referred Kelly to my colleague, Dr. Daniel Stern. He'll stay in touch with you as the tests progress."

"How can I reach him?"

I gave him Dr. Stern's office number. I knew Daniel wouldn't be there—he was already at the hospital running a battery of tests. There was no time to lose. We could justify keeping Kelly for a week without visitors, due to COVID-19, but after that, if she was fully recovered, what then? Send her home?

"Mr. Kamel," I said, "I have a couple of questions." I was using my best doctor voice, the one with full authority, not to be denied.

"Of course."

"Kelly's file says this isn't the first time she's been hospitalized with similar symptoms. Stomachache, vomiting, and diarrhea, all acute enough to keep her in a hospital bed for up to 14 days. From what I see, she's suffered from this since childhood with no diagnosis. How many times has she been sick like this?"

He was quiet for a moment.

"Sir?"

"Yes," he finally responded, "I heard you. I'm trying to calculate…I think maybe…well, I think she's had this or something like it every year since she was four, so maybe 18 years. As for being hospitalized, maybe eight or nine times."

"Always the same symptoms?"

"Yes, to varying degrees of intensity."

"Has Kelly been under any particular stress lately?"

"We keep her as quiet at home as possible. She hasn't been well for years, not well enough for the pressures of university. She doesn't work. And as far as I know, she doesn't have many friends. She is very close to her mother."

"Is she close to you?"

"Yes, I think so, in our own way. I can't spend all day with her, as her mother does. Shelly has been her caregiver all her life. But I think we're close, as fathers and daughters go. We get along well, and I take her out often, shopping, dinner when she can eat, that sort of thing."

"But she doesn't study? Has she been depressed?"

"I think so, but you're not suggesting this is psychosomatic, are you? I don't think my daughter is the silly type."

"I'm sure you're right, but I promised Dr. Stern I'd get a few things checked off his question sheet before you talk with him. I hope you don't mind. Now, has anything been happening recently that might be upsetting to Kelly?"

Again, he was quiet, gathering his words, the way I'd seen him do so many times. Trying to lay them out and choose the best ones.

"Her mother, Shelly, and I are not close," he said. "We haven't been for a long time. I told Shelly last week that I was leaving her. I'm seeing someone, and I want a divorce."

He said it without malice, without passion, just as a matter of fact, and even though my life is settled exactly where it should be, even though I love Nathan with all my heart and always will, still, I felt that familiar dagger. Betrayal. I think it was a conditioned response to Djoser.

"I see. And the other times, when Kelly was especially sick, were there any underlying stressors in place then?"

"I don't...um...maybe. The first time Kelly ever got sick, when she was four, I was leaving Shelly then. I was seeing someone, and I'd asked for a divorce."

I tried to ignore my breaking heart. That someone had, of course, been me.

"The other times?" I pressed on.

"I'll have to think about that," he said, but I knew he was lying. He'd already understood my meaning, and I could feel the cold sting of his quiet anger coming through the phone's speaker.

"I'll be sure to let Dr. Stern know we've spoken, Mr. Kamel. I'll ask him to call you the first chance he gets."

"I want to see my daughter," was all he said before we disconnected.

***

"How did you know?" Daniel asked over dinner that evening. His husband, Bob, reached for the salt, and Nathan poured more wine for us all.

"I didn't," I answered. "I just had this gut feeling, like an instinct, the moment I saw Shelly Kamel up close. She has this look... And when I noticed the discoloration of her daughter's hair and nails, well, that added to my suspicion."

"I know," Daniel said, waving his fork, "such a good mother, so innocent, like butter wouldn't melt in her mouth. Right up till the results came back, playing the frantic mother hen, cluck-clucking that she wanted to see her chick, bringing food, which wasn't allowed, and showing up at the front desk, which wasn't allowed. As if the hospital's pandemic rules applied to everyone but her."

"I bet the COVID-19 restrictions put a damper on Shelly's love of theatrics," Nathan said.

Daniel gave a maniacal laugh.

Bob looked shocked. "What's all this?" he said. Clearly Daniel had not filled him in on the poisoning of Kelly Kamel.

"A real live case of FDIA!" Daniel shouted, brandishing his steak knife.

"Huh?" Bob said.

"Munchausen syndrome by proxy! That's what we used to call it. Very rare. I've only seen one other case, and it was nowhere near as pronounced as this one."

"Don't look so smug," Nathan said. "It was Kenzie who caught it. She saved the girl's life."

I smiled at my husband.

Daniel gave me a sly look. "But how," he asked, "did you know?"

***

A week later, during my early morning coffee ritual, my cell phone blipped again.

"Dr. McDougall here."

"Kenzie, thank you for saving my daughter."

I didn't reply. Djoser must have recognized my voice. Disembodied as it was over the phone, it was much easier to identify without the distraction of visual cues, and without the muffling effect of a face mask.

"How did you know Shelly was…I can hardly think it, much less say it…poisoning Kelly?"

"It was just a guess," I said, offering a peso of truth to a man now rich in freedom—freedom at last.

***

Like most medical doctors, I am a scientist at heart. I don't believe in coincidences. Djoser announced that he was leaving Shelly. Then Kelly, an otherwise smart, healthy child, suddenly faced a grave, undiagnosed but life-threatening illness. Shelly's marital problem was solved, at least for the moment. Marriage bond secured.

That should have been the end of it. But Djoser continued to feel trapped, and tried to escape again and again, each time resulting in his daughter's illness.

14

The common denominator?

The desperate wife. Shelly.

Djoser was a heel, but he loved his daughter. He didn't deserve to lose her. And what about Kelly? She didn't deserve a life of abuse, manipulated and poisoned by a controlling mother, who used her own daughter to punish and imprison her errant husband.

A part of me would always love Djoser. I would have to learn to accept that truth. That a broken part of my heart would likely never heal, inextricably tied as it was to the loss of the son he'd never met.

I hadn't been able to save our boy, our darling Joseph.

But I could, and did, save Djoser's daughter.

HOOKED

Rosemary McCracken

Born and raised in Montreal, Rosemary McCracken has worked on newspapers across Canada as a reporter, arts writer and reviewer, editorial writer, and editor. Rosemary's reporting in recent years on personal finance and the financial services industry sparked the character of Pat Tierney, the protagonist of her four mystery novels.

Safe Harbor, the first Pat Tierney novel, was a finalist for Britain's Crime Writers' Association's Debut Dagger Award in 2010. It was followed by Black Water (2013) and Raven Lake (2016). Uncharted Waters was released in 2020. "The Sweetheart Scamster," a Pat Tierney short story in the crime fiction anthology, Thirteen, was a finalist for a 2014 Derringer Award.

My life took a sharp turn when I headed up the Laurentian Autoroute on a rainy June afternoon in 1968. I was a 23-year-old reporter at the *Montreal Star*, hot on the trail of a career-making story. My destination was a cabin on a Laurentian lake, where I was determined to land an interview with Night Shift.

The band's four rock stars had rented the property for the summer, and sightings of them were being reported daily in the area. Fans were flocking to Sainte-Félice-des-Monts, the town closest to their retreat, hoping to spot their idols stocking up on groceries and beer on Rue Principale.

I had just passed my probation at the newspaper, and I was being assigned the small stories. With some trepidation, I'd approached the entertainment editor, asking him if I could write a feature article on Night Shift. He told me the rock critic hadn't been able to get an interview, but if I could, I was welcome to write a story. I got the brush-off when I called the band's publicity manager in New York, so I took matters into my own hands.

I deliberately chose a rainy day for the 75-minute drive from Montreal. I figured the guys would be at home because of the weather. But bouncing down the rutted lane to Lac Blanchet in my aging Chevy, with Cream singing "Sunshine of Your Love" on the radio, I wasn't sure what I would find. Maybe locked gates or a security guard at the end of the lane. Instead, I found a handsome cabin, its honey-colored logs gleaming in the rain, and a green boathouse on the edge of a private lake.

A red Ford Mustang was parked beside the cabin, and I pulled up beside it. Peering into the rearview mirror, I smoothed my blond hair. Then I jumped out of the car, slamming the door shut. "Anyone home?" I called out.

"Yeah?" A wiry guy with a mane of dark hair looked down at me from the cabin's screened-in porch.

My breath caught in my throat. Simon Donahue, Night Shift's lead guitarist, was standing right in front of me. I knew all about him: 33 years old, born and raised in Camden, New Jersey. The man who had written all the band's hits, and some of rock's most iconic songs.

"I'm Katie Kovac from the *Montreal Star*." I was trying to keep my voice steady.

He grimaced, and turned to go into the cabin.

"Wait!" I said. "I'd like to interview you for a feature for our weekend edition."

He turned, and shook his head. "Groupies. You'll do anything to lay us."

"No! I'm a reporter. Really." I took my press card out of my handbag, and held it against the screen.

He studied it—and me—for a few moments. "OK, Katarzyna Kovac." He stumbled over my name. "What would you like to know?"

"Call me Katie," I said with a smile. "What songs you're working on? What you think of…Canada?"

"We've only been here a week, so I haven't seen much. But—" his face broke into a grin "—from what's right in front of me, I'd say Canada has some wicked women."

Corny, but I ate it up.

He held the screen door open, and I stepped into another world.

The cabin was a luxury vacation home with vaulted ceilings, golden pine floors, and a kitchen with all the modern conveniences.

One living room wall was made entirely of glass, offering a panoramic view of the lake and the hills beyond it. A massive stone fireplace took up another wall. It was flanked by a semicircle of comfy leather couches, two guitars propped against them. More guitars were scattered around the room, and a saxophone lay on the mantle.

"This is where you make your music?" I asked.

Simon shook his head. "Studio downstairs."

"The other guys are down there?" I couldn't hear music, but I figured the studio would be soundproofed.

"They're in Montreal for the day."

We spent three hours in front of the fireplace, rain pinging on the metal roof. Simon got up every so often to throw another log on the fire or to refill our wineglasses. Up close, he looked older than in the photos. Years of touring and fast-living, I supposed. But his heavy-lidded gray eyes were as mesmerizing as in his pictures.

I scribbled notes as he told me about growing up in a working-class neighborhood in New Jersey. How he'd met Caleb McHugh, the bassist, and Mike Pedicelli, who played rhythm guitar, in shop class in high school, and how they honed their skills as a garage band. How they heard Jimmy Sutton drumming with a local band, recruited him, and crafted their distinctive rock sound, laced with country and blues. How they'd hooked up with a rock 'n' roll legend, toured with him for a few intense weeks, and skyrocketed to fame. I already knew Night Shift's story, but it was thrilling to hear it firsthand from this amazing man.

When I asked how he felt about the band's success, Simon shrugged and said success had nothing to do with happiness. "I want to be happy when I wake up in the morning."

I recognized that line from one of the articles I'd read about Night Shift, but I played along. "Are you happy when you wake up in the morning?" I asked.

"I would be," Simon said, looking into my eyes, "if I had a lady like you beside me." He inclined his head in the direction of the bedrooms behind us. "Want to make me happy?"

My heart was pounding so loudly I was sure he could hear it. He went over to the stereo and put on "Winterdust," their latest hit with its instantly recognizable four-note riff and swooning strings. He touched my shoulder as he passed me. I could feel the heat of his hand all the way down to my toes.

"Well?" he asked, opening a bedroom door.

I followed him inside.

***

I wrote the article—slanted toward Simon because I hadn't met his three mates—when I got back to Montreal late that evening. The words seemed to flow from my fingers right into the typewriter. It was the cover spread in the entertainment section that Saturday.

I was dancing on air. The day before, the entertainment editor had told me he was pitching to bring me into his department as a feature writer. I was on my way!

The telephone rang as I was getting out of the shower on Sunday morning. "Not a bad piece. In fact, one of the better ones we've had." Simon's voice was rough-edged with sleep, no doubt because it was just after nine.

I was stumbling through my thanks, when he interrupted me. "We're having a party here tonight. I hope you can come."

He was asking me back to Lac Blanchet. *Me!*

"Still there, Katie?"

"Ah…yeah! I'd love to come to the party."

"Great." His voice was a warm caress. "But Katie…"

"Yes?" Had he changed his mind?

"Off the record tonight."

***

I spent every weekend that summer at Lac Blanchet. We were all on highs of some kind. I'd been getting better assignments at the *Star*, and I was head over heels in love with Simon. He and his mates were flying high on the music they were making. In the evenings, they played their new songs around the outdoor fire pit. Other songs, too. "Lucy in the Sky with Diamonds" was a favorite of theirs. I liked it, too, especially when I was feeling mellow from the weed we were smoking. There were other drugs around the cabin, but I pretended not to notice the bent spoons, the razor blades and the dustings of white powder.

Most of the time, I was the only woman at Lac Blanchet. Mike had just broken up with his longtime girlfriend. Cal's wife and their two kids spent a weekend at the cabin that ended in tears and a shouting match. I never did meet Jimmy's guy, Raul. He lived in San Diego, and Jimmy told me he wasn't comfortable around the band.

The guys talked about making Lac Blanchet their home base. In September, they put in an offer to buy the cabin. When the owner turned them down, they sweetened it. By the first of October, the cabin was theirs.

A week later, I found out I was pregnant. I didn't get a chance to tell Simon. He and the guys were recording in New York, then they had a string of concerts out west. I holed up in the Montreal flat

I rented with two friends, playing "Winterdust" over and over again, and wondering what I should do.

Simon called at the beginning of December, saying they'd returned to Lac Blanchet. I asked him to meet me at a café in Sainte-Félice.

He blanched when I took off my short coat. "Why didn't you tell me?" he asked.

"I didn't want you to worry."

"Worry?" He reached for my hand. "This is great. I'm going to be a dad!"

I handed in my notice at the *Star* on the same day the entertainment editor told me he'd finally got approval to bring me into his department. For a moment or two, the significance of what I was turning down hit me: this was my dream job. But I squared my shoulders, and reminded myself that I now had another focus. I packed up my belongings, and moved to Lac Blanchet.

Snow had fallen early that year, and the Laurentian countryside was Christmas card-pretty with snow on the fir trees, roofs and fences. The guys bought a snowmobile to navigate the long lane in from the highway where we now parked our vehicles. It meant no one got stuck at the cabin, but it also meant only two of us could get away at any given time. I only left Lac Blanchet a handful of times that winter, mostly for doctors' appointments in Montreal.

Cal, Mike and Jimmy all took off before Christmas. Cal stayed with his kids in New York well into January. His wife had started divorce proceedings, and he had appointments with lawyers. Mike spent six weeks with friends in Barbados. And Jimmy went to San Diego to be with Raul.

Simon and I spent Christmas by ourselves. I decided to get into the festive spirit by planning a traditional Christmas dinner. Simon scuttled that idea when he saw me writing up my grocery list. "I don't want my lady wearing herself out over a hot stove," he said.

He ordered the Chef's Christmas Feast from Bon Appétit in Sainte-Félice, which turned out to be an excellent idea. I'd never cooked a Christmas dinner, so the turkey would have been dry and the vegetables overcooked.

I decorated the cabin with fir boughs, and Simon cut down a spruce tree that we festooned with strings of popcorn and tiny lights. Bon Appétit made its delivery by snowmobile on Christmas afternoon, and what a feast it was! Winter vegetable soup and brioche, followed by roast turkey stuffed with sage, baked ham, a sweet potato casserole and hazelnut Brussels sprouts. I dug into it with gusto. I was eating for two, after all.

Simon just picked at his food. He left the table while I was tucking into my sticky toffee pudding, and headed downstairs. I'd almost finished cleaning up the kitchen when he returned.

"Writing a song?" I asked.

He just grunted, and stretched out in front of the fireplace.

***

The winter wonderland at Lac Blanchet lost its charm as the weeks went by. And not a lot of music was getting made. Even in February when all four guys were at the cabin, they seldom made it down to the studio until late afternoon. Many days they didn't go down at all.

Cal and Mike started to take the snowmobile for runs on the chain of lakes that ran from Lac Blanchet all the way to Sainte-Félice. Simon never went with them. He couldn't swim, and he kept his distance from the lake, summer and winter. "They're zonked out of their minds," he said as we watched the snowmobile zoom across the ice one afternoon.

I was surprised because I hadn't seen Cal and Mike smoking up that day. That's when Simon told me they were doing harder drugs. It freaked me out.

"You're going to get yourselves killed," I told them when they returned. They laughed at me. Cal, who liked to boast that he'd spent summers on his uncle's farm as a kid, called me a city girl.

A few days later, the winter sun was sinking below the horizon, and Cal and Mike still hadn't returned from a spin on the lakes. I was worried, and Simon was too. He kept pacing in front of the fireplace, stopping only to peer out the window. "They may have run out of gas," he said.

"Or gone through the ice," I whispered.

A few minutes later, we saw Mike trudging across the frozen lake. Simon ran outside without his jacket.

"Call an ambulance, Katie," he shouted as he helped Mike inside. "Cal's hurt. Snowmobile slammed into a rock on the next lake."

I called the operator, who connected me to emergency assistance. Then I got some blankets and a thermos of tea for Simon and Mike to take to Cal.

It was dark when two snowmobiles, one pulling a rescue sled, turned into our drive. I told the paramedics that the accident had taken place on the next lake, and I watched their lights as they crossed the ice. I hoped they'd be able to find our guys.

They returned 30 minutes later, Simon and Mike riding behind the paramedics, Cal strapped to the sled. I slipped on a poncho, and went outside. Cal seemed to be in a lot of pain. "He's broken an arm and a couple of ribs," a paramedic told me in French.

"Will he be OK?" I asked.

"He should be."

Simon and Mike rode to the highway with the paramedics, and followed the ambulance to the hospital in Simon's Mustang. I stayed at the cabin. Feeling restless, I decided to take a good look around. In a bookcase in the living room, I found an envelope of white powder, which I flushed down the toilet. Then I went down to the basement studio, which I'd only caught glimpses of when I'd brought coffee to the guys. I hadn't been told to keep out of there, but I knew I wasn't welcome.

The walls of the room were paneled with pine, and orange shag carpet covered the floor. An upright piano stood against one wall, its closed lid holding an array of dirty ash trays. A mixing board and a giant tape recorder were against another wall. A yellow drum kit, amplifiers, four microphones on stands, two fallen over on the floor, and several guitars were in the center of the space. A film of dust covered everything.

A wall of records in stacked plastic milk crates separated the studio from a space at the far end of the room with a corduroy couch, a bed with rumpled sheets, and a coffee table. The table top held a large glass casserole dish dusted with white powder, two razor blades and a couple of rolled-up dollar bills. This was clearly where the action was taking place.

Money was strewn around everywhere. And plenty of it. Lots of American $100 bills.

Sick at heart, I returned to the main floor. The drugs had silenced Night Shift's music.

I didn't expect Simon and Mike to return that night, but they paid two snowmobilers to drive them up the lane to Lac Blanchet.

"You almost got killed today," I said to Mike, when he walked in with Simon. "You can't run a snowmobile when you're high."

Mike gave me a big grin. "Relax. I won't be going out for a while. I've got no one to ride with now, do I?"

***

The baby was due in mid-April. I worried that I wouldn't be able to get to the hospital if the snow melted and our lane was a morass of mud. So, at the end of March, I returned to the flat in Montreal, and slept on the living room couch because my room had been rented. Simon left for New York.

He flew to Montreal the day after Alicia was born. "Cute kid," he said, running a finger down her cheek. But as soon as he'd signed the Declaration of Birth form, he headed off to Lac Blanchet.

He'd given me money for a hotel, and Alicia and I remained in the city for two weeks. We had doctors' appointments, and friends from the newspaper visited us at the hotel. I didn't go to Sudbury to see my family. When I'd told my parents I was expecting a baby, they said I'd disgraced them. And I guess I had. They were immigrants from Europe, religious, and they had a lot of pride.

It would have been great if Simon had been with us in Montreal, but nothing could dampen my joy that April. The axis of my world had shifted the moment I saw my daughter. With her button nose, her 10 tiny fingers and her 10 sweet toes, the blue-eyed mite was absolutely perfect. Holding her in my arms, I finally knew the meaning of happiness.

Alicia and I took a bus to Sainte-Félice in early May. Simon picked us up in town, and we arrived at Lac Blanchet just before the black flies.

***

Things had changed that summer. Jimmy hadn't returned from his trip to San Diego in March. Cal and Mike had different girls at the cabin every weekend. No one went down to the studio anymore. And no one bothered hiding the drugs from me.

Everyone was on edge. When Alicia cried, and babies do cry, the sound grated on the guys' nerves. Especially on Simon's. "Shut that kid up, won't you?" he'd shout at me.

When I got up to feed her during the night, he complained that I was disturbing his sleep. "That kid gets more love than me," he said more than once.

When he was up, he seldom looked at our daughter, never picked her up. He rolled his eyes when I spoke baby talk to her. One day he tossed a stack of freshly laundered baby clothes off a couch and onto the floor. "You've turned this place into a goddamn nursery," he said.

"She's your baby, too," I shot back.

"I wish you'd never had her," he said, and stalked out of the room.

I cradled our child and wept, somehow convincing myself that Simon was jittery because of Lenny Rossi. He'd never had anything good to say about the band's manager, and now he was claiming that Lenny was stealing their money. He said so again when he came back into the room.

24

When I suggested he talk to their lawyer, Simon told me they were letting Lenny go. And that he'd called a halt to touring.

"Don't you have contracts for those concerts in September?" I asked.

He shrugged. "Jimmy's gone. We don't have a drummer."

"Jimmy doesn't like winters in Canada, but—"

"What don't you understand?" Anger burned in Simon's eyes. "Jimmy's gone. We don't have a drummer so we don't have a band."

"Can't you get another drummer?" There had to be dozens of talented people who'd want to play with Night Shift.

"Shut the fuck up!" And he whacked me across the face.

The pain was so intense that it stunned me for a few moments. Then I stumbled away from Simon, tightening my arms around Alicia.

He apologized later, told me he needed more sleep. He seemed really sorry, but things went downhill fast after that. The guys were blowing through their money. Cases of champagne, shipments of oysters and mussels and caviar, meals delivered from the best restaurants in the Laurentians. All kinds of girls. And lots of white powder. They partied long into the night, and the noise they made frequently awoke Alicia.

When I was alone with Simon, we argued. I begged him to stop doing drugs until I realized he and his friends were too far into their habit to quit cold turkey.

I tried to get him help. I tried really hard. "I found a clinic in Montreal where they treat addiction as an illness," I told him. "They can help you manage it."

He sneered at me. "I'm not an addict. Everyone I know does drugs. Everyone but you."

I took him by the shoulders. "Everyone does not do drugs, Simon. You're throwing away everything you worked so hard for: the band, your wonderful music...you're throwing away your life."

His face hardened as he pulled my hands off him. And I realized that nothing I could say or do would make a difference. Only Simon could help Simon.

The nights—the days, too—grew wilder. Mike was high when he crashed into a tree racing his Corvette down the lane. He escaped with only bruises, but I told him he was lucky to be alive. He just laughed, and got Simon to drive him to Montreal to buy a new car.

The next day, I threatened to leave. Simon told me to go ahead. "But my kid stays with me," he said. "I'm her father. I can give her everything she needs. And more."

He was right; he could give Alicia a lot more than I could. But I didn't trust him with her. It would be so easy for him to hurt her when he was stoned.

The next afternoon, I heard Alicia screaming in the bedroom where she and Simon were napping. When I ran in, I found him tossing her into the air and catching her. She was terrified. He threw her higher and higher. She screamed louder, her little head thrown back, but he kept tossing her into the air. I rushed over and grabbed her.

"You're such a spoilsport, Katie," he said, collapsing onto the bed. "I was havin' fun with my kid."

His kid, who he'd never wanted. He'd told me so often enough.

After that, I made certain Alicia was always within my sight. When Simon wanted to move her crib into Jimmy's empty room, I wouldn't let him.

I quietly opened a bank account in Sainte-Félice with the $400 I'd saved when I was working at the *Star*. And I started going to the bank twice a week to deposit small sums: bills that Simon left on the dresser in our room, change I found in his pockets, and money left over from his grocery allowance. I tried to make my trips to town when he was sleeping, knowing he'd be annoyed if I wasn't around to hand him a coffee or a beer.

One morning, I discovered my Chevy wasn't in its usual spot beside the cabin. "Must've been stolen," Simon said when I asked him about it. He wouldn't meet my eyes.

I realized he was lying. He'd got someone to take the car away so I couldn't leave. I was furious, and I was frightened. "We'd better report it to the police," I said, calling his bluff.

"No, no police," he shouted. "We don't want to call attention to ourselves. And you don't need a car, Katie. I'll drive you wherever you want."

I went into the bedroom, closed the door, and wept. Without a car, my daughter and I were prisoners at Lac Blanchet.

Very early the next morning, I crept down to the studio and gathered up all the cash that was lying around. Then I tiptoed back to the bedroom, and swiped Simon's keys off the dresser. My only plan was to get in the Mustang and keep driving.

Alicia whimpered when I put her into her carry cot. She broke into loud, hungry cries as we left the cabin, and all the way out to the car. I laid the carry cot on the back seat, and I was quietly closing the door when Simon ran out of the cabin, naked as a blue jay. "Where the hell do you think you're going?" he yelled.

"Into town for groceries."

He took the carry cot out of the back seat. "The kid stays here."

I pulled the carry cot away from him. "I didn't want her to wake you if she cried."

"Get back in the cabin," he said, and we all went inside.

I returned the cash to the basement while he was in the shower. When he was dressed, I had him drive me into town for groceries.

After that, he slept with his keys under the mattress on his side of the bed.

***

By mid-July, Simon and Alicia and I were on our own at Lac Blanchet. Cal had taken his kids on holiday, and Mike was visiting his family in New Jersey. Without Cal and Mike and their girls, the cabin was a lot quieter, almost peaceful. Simon had started coming to bed earlier, and he was up earlier. He was taking more notice of Alicia, too. But that terrified me.

I had steaks on the barbecue one evening when I saw, to my dismay, that he had laid out a line of white powder on the dining room table.

I sat down beside him. "Our steaks will be ready in five minutes. Could you please not do this?"

He looked daggers at me. "Bugger off."

"What about dinner?"

"Fuck dinner."

He rolled up a dollar bill, and snorted the coke. Then he put an LP on the stereo, and stretched out on a couch.

I ate dinner alone, listening to Grace Slick belting out "Somebody to Love."

Simon came out to the porch as I was giving Alicia her evening bottle. "The kid gets all your attention," he said, lounging against the doorframe. "Wish we could go back to last summer, babe. Just you and me."

Wrapping my arms tightly around my baby, I looked up at him. His face was shiny with sweat. The pupils of his eyes were dilated.

It was late when he finally came to bed. I was putting Alicia back down in her crib when he opened the bedroom door. "Might have known," he said. "Can't you get it into your head that three's a crowd? We're moving this crib tomorrow."

***

The next day was a scorcher, one of those days when it's a big effort just to walk across a room. It was close to noon when Simon came out on the porch where I was giving Alicia her lunch. "My two lovely ladies," he said, nuzzling my neck.

I wondered why he was in such a good mood, but a look at his eyes told me he was high.

"It's too hot to do much today," I said, my mind clicking away. "We should spend the afternoon down at the lake."

"Whatever you like." Simon was definitely tripping.

I put Alicia in her crib for her nap, pleased to see her eyes close quickly in the afternoon heat. She was asleep when I left the room.

"Kid OK?" Simon asked when I joined him on the porch.

"She'll sleep for a couple of hours." I took his arm, and we went down to the water. He was wearing sunglasses, but I sensed his surprise when I took a fat joint out of my beach bag. A joint I'd made especially for him.

"Join me?" I said.

He gave me a lazy grin. "Now, that's my girl."

"It'll be better out on the water." I waved the book of matches at him as I sashayed over to the canoe at the dock.

He followed me like a drugged-out dog.

"Katie, you know how I am about water," he said when he was at the water's edge.

"We'll be on the water, not in it. We'll keep close to shore where the water's shallow."

I helped him into the tippy canoe. When he was settled at the bow, I passed him the joint and the matches. He lit up, took a deep drag and closed his eyes.

"I've started a new song," he said when he exhaled.

"That's marvelous."

"But it's not easy getting my thoughts together these days. Probably because it's so fuckin' hot."

The joint fell out of his hand and into the water. His head drooped, his chin touching his chest. A snore escaped his lips.

I looked around. No one was in sight as I steered the canoe toward the middle of the lake.

I eased myself into a standing position, and dove overboard. Then I reached up with both arms, grabbed a gunwale and flipped over the light canoe.

28

Simon thrashed in the water. Reaching out for me, he grabbed my wrist. He had a strong grip, but it weakened as he panicked, and I was able to wriggle free. I dove deeper into the water, moving away from him.

I kept swimming, pushing the canoe with me. Glancing back, I saw his pale face above the water, his mouth open, his eyes wide with terror. Then he sank like a stone.

I swam to shore, thinking what a pity it was that things had turned out this way. Simon wasn't a bad man. It was his addiction that made him act in destructive ways. And stopped the music.

He was dragging Alicia and me down with him, so I did the only thing I could. I made sure he went down first.

IN HIS ELEMENT

Merrilee Robson

Merrilee Robson's first novel, *Murder is Uncooperative*, is set in a Vancouver housing co-op. Her short stories have appeared in *Ellery Queen Mystery Magazine*, *The People's Friend*, *Mystery Weekly*, *Over My Dead Body*, *Mysteryrat's Maze* podcast, and a number of anthologies.

She is a former director of Crime Writers of Canada and active in Sisters in Crime, the Short Mystery Fiction Society, and the Historical Novel Society. She lives in Vancouver with her husband and the cats.

I didn't see him in the twilight gloom.

I was keeping my eyes down, watching where I was going in the slippery snow. Here, near the water, the snow wasn't too deep yet but I knew it was piling up in other areas.

The wind off the river was blowing right through my coat and making my bad hip ache. The sky had that orange glow that told me much more snow was on its way.

It was Salome's bark that alerted me. But it was more of a welcoming bark than a warning, as if she didn't see him as a threat.

A light dusting of snow covered the shoulders of the figure on the bench. He must have been sitting there for awhile. Just the thought of doing that on such a cold night made me shiver even more.

I tightened my hand on the spaniel's leash, not sure what to expect as the man slowly stood and shuffled toward me.

"I think I might be lost," he said. "Can you help me?"

I gave a quick glance around. I had seen a security guard when I'd first set off on my walk, but now the area seemed deserted. I had moved away from the busier part of this historic fishing village, where brightly colored lights celebrated the season and throngs of people strolled along the boardwalk, even at this time of year.

Earlier I'd seen lots of people stopping for fish and chips at the pier, buying crabs to take home for dinner, or browsing the shops for Christmas presents.

But now on a late December evening, in this area where a museum recreated life as it had been in the early years of the last century, the wood-frame buildings were closed and dark. The village was silent except for the splash of the water and the sigh of the icy wind.

I managed a smile. Tourists often needed directions; no need to worry.

"Sure," I said, "where do you want to go?"

"I want to go home."

His voice was quavering, and I realized he was shivering with the cold. He was wearing a thin cotton jacket more suitable for early fall than the dead of winter, and his shoes looked soaked through.

At first I thought he was about my age. It was hard to tell in the dark. But then he lifted one trembling hand, without the benefit of winter gloves, to brush the snow from his hair. The one streetlight briefly illuminated a thin hand, covered with age spots and lots of wrinkles. I decided he must be at least 15 years older than I was, around 80, if not older.

"Of course you do, on a night like this," I said. Probably not a disoriented tourist, then. "It can be a bit confusing around here, can't it?"

It was true. My own condo was just a short walk away, and there were other warm, brightly lit homes in the nearby Steveston village. But here on the boardwalk, with the old buildings casting shadows, they seemed very far away.

"Where do you live?" I asked. Salome was pulling on her leash, anxious to get home and fed. She would be happy to be out of the cold, and so would I.

"Well, that's the problem," he said, his teeth now chattering. "I had all my things, I was arranging them here." He gestured with one hand at the deserted buildings. "And then when I turned around, I couldn't remember…."

I looked down the boardwalk for the security guard I'd seen earlier, or anyone who might take responsibility for this man. This wasn't a distracted tourist. He needed help.

The spot was still deserted.

"Do you have something with your address on it?"

32

He patted his pockets, then shrugged.

"OK, then what's your name?"

"Robert," he answered. He paused and I held my breath, worried that a first name was all I was going to get. Then, "Robert Granville."

"I'm Claire," I said, removing my glove and offering my hand to him. His was icy and his grasp was weak, the hand little more than skin and bones.

Salome whined again. The snow was now sticking to her back and I was sure her feet were even colder than mine.

There was no one else in sight. The snow had driven sensible people indoors.

I sighed. "Look, we're both freezing. I live nearby. Why don't we go to my place, and we'll see if we can get you sorted?"

He nodded, and I thought I saw relief on his face.

I slowed my steps to match his. I had on sturdy winter boots, but he was wearing leather shoes that weren't suitable for this weather. I took his arm after he slipped a time or two, but we soon made it back to my condo.

The place looked cozy. After drying my dog's feet, I switched on the gas fireplace and Salome curled up in front of it. My winter clothes had kept me dry enough, but I thought my next priority should be to attend to my shivering guest.

I would normally feel wary having a strange man in my home, but he was not much taller than me and was a lot thinner.

I couldn't leave him in his wet clothes, even for a few minutes.

I handed him my fleece robe, and gestured to the powder room by the front door. "Put this on," I said, "and give me your clothes to dry."

I bundled everything into the dryer. I was relieved to see that he had handed me his sodden socks, pants, shirt and jacket, but no underwear, so he probably wasn't completely naked under that robe. I hoped so anyway. That would be further than I wanted to go with my Good Samaritan act.

Soon my living room was full of mingled smells: warm dog; drying wool; and lemon-ginger tea with a touch of honey.

I picked up my phone, hoping it would be easy to find a number or address for Robert Granville.

I could see nothing local. But my search brought up a link for an art gallery that caught my attention.

I clicked on the link and my tiny screen filled with swirls of color.

I squinted at my phone. It was hard to tell, but the picture of the man next to the painting looked like my guest.

"Robert, are you an artist?"

He put down his mug and a smile lit his face. "My paintings," he said eagerly. "Did you find them? I had them all arranged and then…they were gone." His smile vanished. "Everything was gone. Do you know where they are?"

I shook my head, and went into the den for my laptop. I needed a bigger screen.

The paintings were stunning. The blues and greens of the coastal waters and the nearby mountains lit up the screen, shining like jewels.

I'm not that familiar with the local art scene, but even I recognized one of the paintings.

It showed a small fishing boat in the trough of a wave. The figures on the boat, clad in bright rain gear, were too tiny to make out their faces, but their posture conveyed the fear they were feeling in those storm-tossed seas.

The wave towering over them was as transparent as green glass.

And at its peak, an orca surged, ready to burst from the wave in a move that was filled with joyful exuberance.

In His Element, the painting was titled. The playfulness of the whale, contrasted with the fearful posture of the men, made it clear that they didn't belong in that wild sea.

The painting was famous.

And the photo of the artist next to the painting was the man in my living room.

I felt a small thrill at this brush with celebrity. But, at the moment, I was more concerned with practical matters. The link to the art gallery gave me a way to find out where Robert belonged.

But, of course, my phone call to the gallery went straight to voice mail.

I did what I should have done when I'd first found him wandering down by the water. I called the police.

But the call wasn't very satisfying.

It was clear that Robert had some form of dementia. If he'd wandered away from a care facility, he should have been reported missing.

But the dispatcher had no information about a missing senior.

And the police were busy with other emergencies.

34

"Does he need medical care?" the dispatcher asked. When I told her an ambulance was not required, she asked, "Do you feel he's a risk to himself, or to you?"

I assured her we were both dry and warm, and that I didn't feel threatened by him.

"We'll have someone there as soon as we can," she said.

I wondered how soon that would be. The radio was describing downed power lines, snapped by the high winds or knocked down by falling snow-laden branches. Motorists, unprepared for the weather, were stranded on the highway and there were reports of numerous accidents.

A glance out the French doors showed the snow piling up in deep drifts on my patio.

I thought we would be waiting a while.

I poured us both some more tea.

I glanced at my computer, which displayed another hit for Robert Granville.

It was a news article about the theft of the very painting I had just looked at. There had been a break-in at the private gallery where the painting had been housed. Only that painting had been stolen.

Some of the public comments at the bottom of the online article mentioned that the robbery appeared suspicious. The gallery had good security, so there was speculation about an inside job. But the police had reported only that an investigation was ongoing.

I sighed. That glorious painting was in the hands of thieves. And one of the art experts that the reporter had interviewed had suggested that the painting might be on its way to a private buyer, possibly overseas.

That painting might never be seen again.

And, judging by the confused and worried look of the man in front of me, he wouldn't be painting many more like it.

I smiled at him in what I hoped was an encouraging way. Then I heard a sound I hadn't even hoped to hear, a voice calling, "Dad....Robert!"

My guest didn't seem to react at all.

"That sounds like someone is looking for you." I moved to look out the French doors at the snowy neighborhood. "Do you know who that is? Your son?" I couldn't keep the relief out of my voice.

But Robert just muttered. "I just want to go home. And I need to find my things. If I could just remember where I put everything..."

I shrugged, then pushed open the patio door as much as I could against the deep snow and called out to the man on the sidewalk.

"Who are you looking for?"

"My dad. Have you seen an old guy wandering around? I'm afraid he might be lost out here."

He sounded more angry than afraid, but I was well aware of the stress of caring for aging loved ones. When he'd confirmed his father's name, I directed him around to the front entrance of the building, where I knew the manager had cleared the snow.

I opened the door for him, eager to hand over the responsibility for Robert Granville.

The man hurried into my apartment, without even pausing to wipe his boots. I tried not to mind the clumps of snow melting all over my carpet, knowing that he must have been frantic about his missing father.

"Dad, what are you doing here? I've been looking for you for hours."

But Robert shrank back in his chair, giving only a frightened moan.

The younger man couldn't hide his frown. "Dad, it's me, Jim. We need to go." He reached out to take his father's arm.

Robert looked frail, but he put all his strength into clinging to the arm of the chair. "No!" was all he said, the word trailing off into a wail.

I looked at the two men. There was no obvious family resemblance between them. The younger man was tall and sturdy, with thick, dark hair slicked back from a broad forehead. Robert's hair was thin and white, but I doubted it had ever been dark and springy like that. The younger man had dark brown eyes under heavy black brows, while Robert's eyes were a washed-out blue.

I hesitated. I should have been happy to have him taken off my hands, but somehow I couldn't shake the idea that I was responsible for Robert's safety.

"He doesn't seem to recognize you," I said, hesitantly.

"I'm his only son. But, of course, he doesn't recognize me." His frown deepened. "He's not right in the head."

I had friends who had cared for relatives with dementia. And I had heard the sadness in their voices when their mother or father or husband no longer recognized them. I had heard frustration, and sometimes resentment in their voices too. But there was something else in this man's voice.

I glanced at Robert's shoes, which I'd stuffed with newspaper and left in front of the fireplace. I walked over to check them.

"These are still wet," I said with some relief, "and his clothes are still in the dryer. Can you wait until they're dry?"

"I need to get going," he said in a loud voice that made Robert shrink further back into his chair.

I put on my best grandma voice. "But it's so cold outside. I'm sure you don't want your father to catch cold. It will be so much better for him if he's not in wet clothes. Surely you can stay a few minutes longer. Can I get you some tea while you wait?"

I didn't wait for an answer but picked up the pot and headed for the kitchen. "This is getting a bit cool," I said over my shoulder. "It will just take a few minutes to boil some more water and make a new pot. I'll get another cup for you."

I was wondering how soon the police would arrive. I didn't like the idea of sending Robert off with an angry man he didn't seem to recognize. But if he was family...

As I switched off the boiling kettle, I heard the younger man say, "Where are the paintings, Dad? What the hell did you do with them?"

I held my breath. Was it possible that Robert had something to do with the stolen painting? I wished I had paid more attention to the article I'd read about the theft. I wasn't sure if Robert owned the painting or if the gallery was selling it on behalf of an art collector.

Robert answered by repeating the question he had asked me. "My paintings? Do you know where they are? I had them all arranged and then when I turned around, they were gone." As I went back to the living room I saw the same worried look on his face.

The son grudgingly accepted the mug of tea. He took a sip, grimaced, then put it down on the coffee table.

"Those clothes must be dry by now," he grumbled. "We should..."

"What's that?" I said suddenly, interrupting him. "Shhh, I can't hear."

"I don't hear anything," the son said loudly. "Now Dad, we need to..."

But Robert had heard it too. He started to get out of the chair. "That's...that's..."

It was a woman's voice this time. Unlike the son, who had sounded angry, this woman was frantic. "Dad, can you hear me? Robert, are you there?"

I rushed to the window. Just for a moment, I thought that Robert's son was going to try to stop me. But he moved back, allowing me to pass.

The snow was even heavier now, but I could see a figure on the sidewalk, shining a flashlight over the old buildings across the street, peering under snow-shrouded bushes, calling Robert's name.

The snow had drifted against the patio doors, making them impossible to open this time. I tried attracting the woman's attention by calling out the window but she didn't seem to hear me. So I grabbed my coat, shoved my feet back into my boots, and hurried out the front door to talk to her.

I was back within minutes with a woman who claimed to be Robert's daughter.

I was glad we had returned so quickly. The young man was trying to shove Robert's feet into his damp shoes, although Robert was resisting.

"Jim, what are you doing? Leave him alone! You're hurting him!"

"Don't tell me what to do, Brenda. You're the one who let him wander off!"

"I needed to go the store, Jim. I needed to get food for our father's dinner. I can't be with him 24 hours a day. It's not like you ever help."

I looked at the two of them. I hadn't signed on to be part of a family argument when it wasn't even my family.

The woman at least looked like Robert. She had the same pale blue eyes, a thin frame, and fine brown hair. And, he seemed to recognize her.

"You're…" His voice trailed off. "Have you come to take me home?"

She smiled at him. "Yes, Dad. Remember, I'm Brenda. We'll go home and have dinner soon. But Dad, did you take the car?"

Robert screwed up his face, as if that would help him remember. "I…I think I needed it. I had all my things."

Brenda sighed. "Dad, you know you're not supposed to drive."

Her brother sneered. "You left the car keys where he could get them? How stupid was that? Of course, he can't remember he's not supposed to drive. He can't even remember what he had for breakfast. And he sure can't remember—" He broke off. "I don't think you're up to looking after him. I think he should come with me." He made another attempt to cram Robert's foot into the wet shoe, although the older man twisted his leg away from him.

"Jim, leave him alone," Brenda said. "He doesn't want to go with you. He doesn't even know who you are. You haven't visited him in months, so don't pretend you care about him.

"And, yes, I know I shouldn't have left the spare keys where he could find them. I made a mistake, OK? But I was just popping out to the store to pick up a few things and I thought I'd walk. I wanted a bit of fresh air. I was gone longer than I intended because of the snow. I didn't think it would be this bad."

Robert was shaking his head. "The painting is gone," he muttered. "He brought it back and I was so glad to see it again. *In His Element*, back."

Brenda stared at her father, then turned to her brother. "Jim," she said, her voice highly pitched, "what's he talking about? Did you have something to do with that painting?"

"Don't be ridiculous, how could I...?"

"Hide it in plain sight," Robert said. "That's what he was saying to that other man. 'Hide it in plain sight'. Then he laughed and laughed."

Brenda's face was ashen. "I don't know exactly what he's saying, Jim, but it sounds like he thinks you had something to do with stealing his painting."

"You know you can't believe anything he says," Jim growled.

"I wanted it back," Robert went on. "I was so glad to see my painting again. He told that man he would leave it there for a while, until it was safe."

Brenda gently touched her father's arm. "What man, Dad?"

Robert pointed at his son. "Him, and the other man. I was glad to have the painting back. But he wouldn't let me keep it. He told the other man he would take it away again. And my other paintings, too. I couldn't let him take them."

Robert frowned at his son, then gave Brenda and me a pleading look. "I wanted them to be safe. I needed to put them somewhere where he wouldn't find them."

Brenda pulled out her phone. "Well, I need to call the police. That painting is worth thousands and if you know anything about it—"

Jim gave up on the shoes. He grabbed his father by the arm and dragged him past us through the still-open front door of my apartment, swinging an arm at his sister and knocking her over as he went past.

I rushed after the pair, my phone in my hand, ready to dial 911.

Robert must have slipped on the damp tiles of the lobby and fallen, because Jim was dragging him by his arms toward the door, cursing as he went.

And that was when the police turned up, finally responding to my earlier call.

It was all a bit of a blur after that.

The young officer helped Robert to his feet and was trying to find out what was going on when Jim punched him and tried to rush out the door. Then there were more officers and talk of assault charges. And, finally, Jim was led away in handcuffs.

Then the police coaxed a garbled tale from Robert about paintings that disappeared and reappeared.

"I think," Brenda said, "that my brother might have been involved in stealing one of my dad's paintings from the art gallery."

The officer's eyes widened when she told him that, and widened even more when she mentioned the price the gallery had been asking for the painting.

"Dad wouldn't have got any money from the sale of that painting," she explained. "He sold it years ago to the man who was selling it. But the gallery thought that sale would drive up the market for his other paintings, the ones he still owns."

She pushed her wispy hair away from her face. "Dad needs more care than I can give him. The gallery thought they could bring his paintings onto the market gradually and make enough money to get him some really good care." She sighed. "My brother didn't agree with that strategy."

Robert interrupted her. "They're my paintings. He wanted them. He kept saying he needed money." He looked at his daughter, confused. "Why did he say I should give my paintings to him? I don't even know him."

Brenda patted his arm. "It's Jim, Dad. It's your son, Jim."

Robert ignored her, muttering, "I needed to keep them safe. He told the other man he would leave them there for a while and come back to get them later. I couldn't let him take them."

Brenda looked at the officer, who seemed completely confused by Robert's rambling.

She smiled at him. "I'm used to talking to Dad, and I know my brother. I think Jim somehow stole that painting from the gallery, then needed to stash it somewhere. I think he thought it would be a good idea to leave it with Dad's other paintings. We had to close his studio when he got too forgetful, so some of them are stored at my place for the moment.

"Dad used to rent a studio near the water here. Maybe he was trying to go back there. He took the car, so maybe he brought the paintings with him. Dad, do you know where you left the car?"

Robert looked bewildered.

"Oh, well," she said. "We can try looking near his old studio. It's near here; that's where I was heading when you came to get me," she said.

The young officer might normally have been happy to report that the missing senior had been found and return to his other duties, but now he seemed to be thrilled that he might be close to solving a major art theft and recovering a missing painting.

I should have been relieved to hand over my responsibility, but I was just as anxious as the officer was to see if we could find the painting.

We bundled up and headed out into the snow.

The cars on the street were all shrouded in white, difficult to tell apart, but one of them responded with a beep when Brenda touched her key fob.

"Did you leave the paintings in the car, Dad?" Brenda asked, rushing across the street and yanking the door open.

The dim interior lighting revealed rectangles of various sizes piled in the back seat.

"My paintings!" Robert cried. "They came back!"

There were some smaller paintings in the trunk. The colors glowed in the light of the officer's flashlight.

But not one of them was *In His Element.*

Brenda bit her lip. "I thought…Well, I think he was trying to go back to his old studio. I'm sure he doesn't have the keys anymore but maybe… It's just down here."

We trailed after her through the deep snow. I slowed down to offer Robert my arm again as he slipped in his inadequate shoes. He was likely getting as wet and cold as he'd been when I found him. But he seemed stronger. He followed his daughter as eagerly as the rest of us.

At first we saw nothing.

The building was dark, the door locked.

"You don't still have a key, do you, Dad?" Brenda asked.

Robert patted his pockets, shaking his head.

Then, the officer, who'd been shining his flashlight around the perimeter of the building, gave a shout.

The light revealed the edge of something square jutting out of the snow piled against the building.

And when the officer reached down and lifted it up, I saw a whale leaping free of a wave, a joyful image.

"Oh, Dad," Brenda said with a sigh, "I hope it's not damaged." She turned to the officer. "I'm sure you have to take it to your station, but I should probably call someone to find out how it should be treated. And I need to find out what's happening with my brother."

Her anxious voice went on, but I was watching Robert.

He stood in the snow, not shivering anymore. And the smile on his face, as he looked at his painting, matched exactly the joyful exuberance of the whale.

WAITING IN THE WINGS

Caro Soles

Caro Soles' novels include mysteries, gay lit, science fiction, erotica, and the occasional bit of dark fantasy. She received the Derrick Murdoch Award from the Crime Writers of Canada, and has been short listed for the Lambda Literary Award, the Aurora Award, and the Stoker Award. 2019 saw the publication of her short story collection Do You Know Me?

Her novel, Marlo's Dance, *is a police procedural set in the world of the pleasure-loving, dual-gendered hermaphrodites of Merculian. In September, her literary novel,* Dancing with Chairs in the Music House, *was released by Inanna Publications. Caro lives in Toronto, loves dachshunds, books, opera and ballet, not necessarily in that order.*

The sun shone on the rope trees of the Pleasure Gardens, releasing the heady scent of their flowers above Marlo Dasha Bogardini's head. He sat complacently eating a cloud cone as he watched the passing crowd, blissfully unaware that his treat was dripping out of the bottom of the cone, and down one side of his work tunic. Nearby, two small children were dancing side by side to the music of the Merculian pipes, played by their doting parents.

"Isn't that the cutest thing, hun!" A bunch of Terran tourists, both male and female, paused to watch. Their harried Merculian guide held a yellow umbrella above his head so he could be easily seen by his much bigger followers.

"They're learning touch dancing," the guide explained. "We Merculians are touch empaths, you know, but still this is a skill that needs a lot of practice."

One of the children made a mistake and the other one kicked him. The dark-haired parent leaped up to give the injured child a hug.

"Look! That one's a female," exclaimed one of the male tourists, apparently having glimpsed the small breasts of the dark-haired parent. "I thought you guys are all flat-chested hermaphrodites."

"We are!" The guide was losing patience. "When we get pregnant, our bodies change. When the child is weened, we regain our figures. Now, shall we go on to the Art Wall?" He waved his umbrella and set off at a good clip toward the main gate.

Marlo watched them go with a smile. It always took a while for tourists to grasp the concept of Merculian sexuality and the use of "he" as their pronoun didn't help. Finally noticing the stain on his tunic, he began to wipe at it with the end of his sash just as his com-dev flashed. Marlo scowled at the device. "It's still my break!" he told it crossly, then answered as usual: "Dasha Bogardini here."

"Yeah, well you better get elsewhere fast!" His boss, Old Livid, rarely left him in peace to finish his breaks from Regulator HQ.

"Where?"

"I'll send you the coordinates. Some big-name stage designer just up and died and his lover is screaming bloody murder to everyone. And I mean everyone! Apparently the dead one is quite young. Just get there fast and handle it."

"But—"

His boss was gone.

Marlo kept dabbing at the long stain on his tunic as he walked to the gates of the Pleasure Gardens, deciding to grab an air-cab since Old Livid said it was urgent. It didn't sound like a job for a senior class A investigator. On the other hand, he had no urgent cases pending.

He stepped onto a lift-disk. As he rose swiftly to the top of the cab-pad, he wondered what "quite young" meant. Merculians usually only died after very long and full lives. Down below, he could see the yellow parasol of the harried tour guide who was trying to explain the Art Wall to his wayward bunch of Terrans. Marlo climbed into the air-cab and gave the coordinates.

Ten minutes later he arrived outside a bright green house in the Rumali district. A crowd of vidsters was hovering about, taking snaps and talking among themselves. The long white airbus with the Regulator crest hovered outside the small garden, which may have alerted them. But why was the after-death team still here? He waded through the crowd of newshounds, ignoring their pleas for a statement. About what? He clapped and the door flashed open almost as if the Keeper had been waiting behind it. Maybe he had, Marlo thought, stepping inside the shadowed hall. He slipped on his ribbon of office with the official seal masking the tiny camera and recorder. From somewhere within came long moaning wails.

"*Chai* Forilan is inconsolable," said the Keeper, dabbing at his eyes. "He won't let them take away the, ah...the body...You must do something!"

"The after-death team is here, then?" Marlo asked gently.

The Keeper nodded, one hand clutching the large gold key of office he wore around his neck. "*Chai* Evalindo's personal healer came as well and then *Chai* Forilan's sibling, *Chai* At'hali. He's still here, contacting...everyone."

The one making all the commotion at HQ, Marlo thought. The At'hali name was a familiar one in Merculian government circles. As he followed the Keeper down the hall toward to the source of the wailing, it occurred to Marlo that he was here more as a diplomat than to do any real investigating.

By this time the wailing had become louder, stopping only for the distraught lover to catch his breath for a renewed effort. Marlo wondered how he would react to losing his beloved so suddenly and unexpectedly. Even the idea brought tears to his eyes. He blinked them away as he entered the large airy sleeping chamber, filled with greenish light from the tinted dome. He recognized Charlo, the post-death specialist and several others waiting patiently against the wall.

Chai Forilan sprawled half naked across the bed, clutching his dead lover in his arms.

"I've come to help, if I can," Marlo said softly during a break in the screeching.

The young Merculian looked up, his face blotchy and red, streaked with tears. "Who are you?" His voice was hoarse.

"Forgive me. I'm *Com* Marlo Dasha Bogardini, Investigator with the Cap City Regulators."

"Oh, thanks be to the gods! Can you find out what happened? Who did this? Please!" His tear-filled blue eyes stared at Marlo in desperation. Even in his misery he was beautiful, his tight gold curls forming a halo around his head. Marlo remembered that he used to be a dancer before accepting a love-jewel.

"If I am to help, I'll have to talk to you," Marlo said, inching closer, "and we can't do it in here."

"I can't leave him!"

"We'll just be next door." He held out his hand.

Forilan sat up and blew his nose on the pillowcase. Then he reached over and adjusted the embroidered collar of his dead lover's sleeping gown, patting it in place. "I'll talk to you."

Everyone drew away from the door as Marlo led the former dancer out of the chamber and into the small room across the hall.

"Can you tell me what happened?"

"I don't know! I fell asleep and when I woke up... I can't live without him!" Forilan burst into raucous tears.

The Keeper rushed in, knelt down beside him and adjusted a silk robe around Forilan's shoulders. "I used to be his dresser before he moved in here," he said to Marlo. "Perhaps you could talk to *Chai* At'hali? Surely you can see that Fori can't help. His older sibling's in the reception room to your right."

Marlo glanced back as he left the room, leaving the Keeper holding the sobbing Forilan in his arms.

Chai At'hali was small and wiry, with blond curls like his sibling, but there the resemblance ended. His eyes were small and piercing, and his chin too long. He examined Marlo closely as they introduced themselves.

"My young sibling has always tended towards the hysterical, *Com.* Don't pay much attention to anything he says." He motioned toward a low chair and sat down himself, leaning forward and crossing his ankles. "The thing you need to know about Evalindo is that there is an inherited illness in his family. Every generation, one or two of them die early from it and there's no known cure. There's nothing mysterious about his death, as I'm sure the medical report will tell you. I just wanted to make sure you knew before causing any more pain to any of us." He stood up suddenly and waited while Marlo hauled himself to his feet more slowly. "Thank you for coming so quickly." He bowed Marlo out the door.

The Regulator blinked in the sunshine, a little disoriented by finding himself outside so quickly. A strange household, he thought. He patted his stomach absently and noticed his sash was coming undone. As he tied it up snugly, he realized the vidsters were taking his picture. Fabulous.

***

Back at HQ, it seemed there had been a little excitement. The entire tech unit had been dispatched to a home in the Hills District when the house wouldn't acknowledge the owner's DNA and refused to open the doors or windows to let him in. It seemed his lover had erased all traces of him from the system after a nasty quarrel.

"I thought that wasn't possible," said Marlo.

"They should toss the lover in detention," said Eldred.

"I think our tech unit should hire him." Oslani grinned. "So what happened with the dead stage designer?"

"A great deal of howling and wailing." Marlo threw his shoulder bag down on the table in the team room. "Could someone run a check to see if there's anything to show a genetic disease in Evalindo's family that kills off one or two every generation?"

"I've heard of that," Eldred said. "It's rare. I'll check into it."

Marlo scratched his head. It should be death by natural causes, but something was niggling at him. If the death was natural, as he had been assured, why call in the Regulators? That meant that Charlo would have to be there, and he would take the body to his subterranean labs, looking for the exact cause of death. Why would anyone want that done if everything was natural?

Marlo padded over to his cozy but disorganized office. He pulled an old pink biscuit out of a half-empty package he found on his bottom shelf and chewed on it thoughtfully as he pulled up all the data he could find on Forilan. Before moving in with Evalindo about a year ago, he had been on the stage as a lowly member of the chorus in Merculian's most prestigious dance company. He had met Evalindo when the designer came to stage some new production and he left when it was over, never to dance again, apparently. Odd.

Delving deeper, he discovered that the Keeper had also been at that theater, but in the costume department and he had also left, presumably to become the Keeper at Evalindo's house. Odd career change, but then he had made some odd career changes in his younger days, too.

"Marlo, I'm waiting for your report." Old Livid appeared beside him, silently, as usual.

How could such a small figure radiate such authority and menace, Marlo wondered, staring at his steely eyed boss.

"This was supposed to be a simple job: show up, be reassuring, leave."

"Exactly what I did, *Com*," Marlo said firmly.

Old Livid reached over and switched the screen to a newsfeed. An image of Marlo standing outside the dead designer's home looking perplexed as he tried to tie his trailing sash flashed into sight. "Then why are you looking like this?"

"I was firm and reassuring inside," Marlo assured him.

Old Livid shook his head. "Write the report, hand it in, and buy a belt!" He stomped out.

"Flying farts," muttered Marlo.

***

Later that day Marlo was in the midst of an ongoing argument with Eldred about the joys of a healthy Merculian lifestyle, which in Marlo's opinion were non-existent, when an incoming call interrupted them.

"Hey, sweet cheeks, have I got some news for you."

"OK, Charlo, don't keep me in suspense."

"Come on down so I can see your lovely face while I tell you."

Marlo sighed. The lascivious Charlo had been talking to him like this for years now. Sometimes it was fun but other times, just annoying. He knew better than to argue. It would be faster to just go.

The Skullery, as Charlo's domain was known at Reg HQ, was in the basement, lit by artificial sunlight and painted bright pink to try to counteract the sterile atmosphere of the place. The room was large and cool, the air constantly refreshed from outside. A humming noise stopped when Marlo walked in.

"What's your big news?" he asked, noting that the body was behind a screen.

Charlo turned toward him, opening his arms. "Come closer, sweet cheeks."

"Enough. Just tell me whatever it is."

Charlo pouted. "You're no fun today." Then he dropped the come-hither pose and motioned to a bank of blinking machines. "As expected, the deceased has Paroxysmal Blood Rubiosi, the inherited disease you were told about. But I don't think that's what killed him."

"Go on."

"I haven't finished all the testing, but so far I've found several substances in his blood that shouldn't be there. One is perfectly benign, one I don't know about yet, and one is illegal. Does that warrant a kiss? A hug, maybe?"

"Hmmm. Is the illegal one recreational?"

"I don't see how, which is why I can't figure out why he was using it. It's Thalanox and too much can kill you. Other than that, he seems to be in good health. Take a look." He swept aside the screen.

Marlo stepped back. "I saw enough of him at the house, thanks."

"Stop!" Old Livid rushed in the door. "The family wants the body back immediately. It should never have come here in the first place. It's a natural death."

"Ah, not exactly." Charlo went on to explain what he had found.

"Nothing definitive then," Liviano said. "Send the body back."

"But boss, my tests aren't finished. And I found Thalanox! That can be fatal."

"Was it?"

"I need more tests."

"If you don't know for sure now, the body goes back. His own healer signed the death registration. Five minutes to get his clothes on and back he goes!" He turned around and marched out.

A high-pitched buzzer pulsed somewhere in the large room.

Charlo rushed over to one of the machines. "Wait!" he shouted. "It's red! Positive for poison!"

***

Old Livid was not happy that they appeared to have a murder case on their hands. "Keep doing whatever it is you wanted to do," he snapped at Marlo, then retired to his office and slammed the door. Immediately the blue privacy light went on.

Marlo called his team together and leaned on the table, gathering his thoughts. "Who called us about this in the first place?" he asked. "Someone wanted us to investigate and I don't think it was anyone in the house."

"Someone could have been there earlier, then left," suggested the newbie.

No one paid any attention.

"It was the neighbor," Oslani said after analyzing some data.

"So we just assumed it was the sibling, *Chai* At'hali," Marlo said. "Another oddity. Eldred, go and talk to him. Find out why he called us in. Oslani, do a deep scoop into background on the deceased and the lover. You, kid, check into the finances of the household. Don't make waves," he added. "Ferdalyn, you're a big dance fan. What do you know about this designer?"

"The fans all adored him!" exclaimed Ferdalyn enthusiastically. "I even met him once, last year when he did the new *In the Forest* production. He was really nice."

"Hmm. Someone didn't think so. Get all you can find on Thalanox. I'll start doing interviews with people who knew the designer."

The place to start, Marlo decided, pulling a belt from behind his office door, was the famous dance theater where Evalindo met his young lover. People there would know them both. There must be something somewhere to explain this tragedy.

He was standing in front of the lift disk, using the shiny metal wall on the lift as a mirror as he patted his sun-streaked hair into place, when he realized it was someone else's face smiling back at him. A familiar face. Sherry-brown eyes, red-gold hair, head tilted to one side.

"*Chai* At'hali Benvolini!" he exclaimed, stepping back. "How did you get past the barrier?"

"Please, just call me Beny. I was coming to see you. Could we perhaps go for a cup of hot chocolate while we talk?"

Marlo nodded and stepped onto the disk beside Beny. He should have expected this, he thought. Beny must be related to Forilan somehow. He was known as a musician but also seemed to have one foot in the shadowy world of back-door diplomacy. He had been helpful to Marlo before, but this time Marlo doubted he was here to help.

When they were seated comfortably on the terrace behind HQ with cups of hot chocolate in front of them, Beny leaned forward confidentially. "I'm sorry I startled you back there, Marlo. As you probably guessed by now, Forilan is my young cousin and he's desolate. I was hoping you could explain why Evalindo's body has not been released to us?"

Marlo took a sip of chocolate. "Can you tell me why the deceased's own family isn't here asking these questions?"

"His parents are both dead, I'm afraid. There was a terrible accident in the outer harbor a few years ago. As far as I know, there are no siblings." Beny spread out his hands and shook his head. "Poor Forilan. His family was absolutely furious when he left the company to live with Evalindo, but now he needs our support."

"But…your spouse is a principal dancer with the company," Marlo said. "Why would Forilan have to leave in order to live with his lover?"

Beny shrugged. "That's just it. He wouldn't. But he said he wanted to devote himself completely to his beloved. Ah, youth."

"Well, I'm afraid our specialist is not quite satisfied, Beny. He has found traces of foreign substances that could be poisonous when taken in large doses."

"And you think Forilan would *poison* him?" exclaimed Beny. His voice was harsh but he softened the effect with a sweet smile.

"I'm not accusing anyone." Marlo stirred his chocolate a little too vigorously. It slopped over his cup and onto the table, staining the lace on Beny's sleeve.

Beny tucked the lace out of sight. "You know, the older he got, the more obsessed Evalindo became in his efforts to outwit his disease. He went to see all sorts of quacks and was up for trying all kinds of supplements and drinks, even some of alien origin. His latest was a Serpian powder, I think. Forilan said he mixed it for him every night before they went to bed. He was so devoted."

Marlo mopped up the chocolate with his handkerchief. "I'm sorry I can't give you any more specific information."

"I know you would if you could, Marlo. I hope you don't think I'm trying to pressure you."

But you are, Marlo thought. A very subtle pressure but pressure nonetheless. He said nothing.

Beny stood up and bowed. "Thanks for talking to me. And if you see Forilan again, please be gentle. He's very fragile."

Marlo watched him walk away. He would have to visit Forilan but not before he had more information about him and the dead lover. And for that, he would have to go to the Merculian National Dance Theater.

***

An hour and a half later, Marlo sat down in a corner of the small salon off the grand entrance lobby to think. All the people he had talked to on the administration side of the theater praised Evalindo to the skies. He was brilliant, original, charismatic and amusing. Everyone loved him.

"Talk to the dancers," the lightning expert told him. "And make sure you talk to Triani."

"What sort of thing are they going to tell me?" Marlo asked.

"What he was really like to work with."

"What about you?"

"He was OK. Demanding, though. Made me rethink some technical things I'd been doing for a while and I liked that. But I tell you, he was careless and a real slave driver with the dancers. There were accidents, one very bad one. I blame him. So do some of the others."

Was Evalindo to blame?

"Certainly not." That was the managing director. "Accidents happen all the time on stage. All the time."

But once Marlo began talking to the dancers, it was a different story.

"Utter nonsense," said Beny's spouse, who was a star of the company. "Yes, accidents happen now and then but that production was dangerous. Not for the principals. He pretty much left us alone. Except for Triani, and they had some terrible rows. Talk to him."

"Everyone says Evalindo was a charming genius."

"He was, but he had another side to him that wasn't so pleasant."

51

Marlo walked down to the small rehearsal hall, following the music. When it stopped, a group of chattering dancers streamed out on their way to lunch. Marlo opened the door and found Triani tossing dance shoes into his bag.

"Holy shit! Look who's here! I see your fashion sense hasn't improved."

"I'm afraid not." Marlo sat down on a chair and took a deep breath. It was always tricky dealing with the sexy, foul-mouthed superstar dancer with the hair-trigger temper.

"You here about Evalindo, right, sweetie? That controlling bastard won't be mourned by many, certainly not me."

"Really? I've been hearing nothing but praise."

Triani laughed. "Oh sure. You're talking to front of house, right? They didn't have to work with him." Triani pulled a chair closer to Marlo, pulled off his sweat-soaked top and sat down. Marlo tried not to look at the smooth, muscled chest, the expanse of golden skin drawing his eyes down to the low-slung purple tights. "He hated me on sight, mostly because from the moment he laid eyes on pretty little Forilan, he wanted him. And he knew I was fucking him."

Marlo nodded. Of course.

"I got tired of the kid pretty fast because he has fluff for brains but Evalindo still hated me."

"Did you know his dresser? He left the company when Forilan did."

"His *dresser*? Holy shit! That's what he's calling himself now?" Triani threw his dark head back and laughed heartily. "What a pile of crap! No one below the rank of principal has a personal dresser in this company. The costume department has fitters who go around checking on everyone to make sure all is well but they're not dressers. In my opinion, he had the hots for Forilan himself but didn't stand a chance once that rat Evalindo arrived."

"I see. How did you deal with him?"

"The rat? I argued with him constantly, about technical things mostly. The others didn't have the nerve. And I was right about most of it. He could dream up amazing theatrical effects but he wasn't a dance expert. I am. As it turned out, some of that stunning machinery really was dangerous."

Triani leaned back, ran a hand under the waistband of his tights and scratched himself absently.

Marlo flushed. "What happened?"

"Someone was nearly killed." Triani sat up again. "Look, sweetie, it's really too technical to go into but to get the general idea, try to imagine a huge wheel at the back of the stage with a bit of water flowing over it and groups of dancers in twos and threes constantly dancing in a flowing motion down one side. Remember the water. It splashed so part of the shitty thing was often slippery. Eventually one of the kids slipped and fell, right from the top. And it was huge. Thanks to that oh-so-wonderful know-it-all asshole, Carondi will never dance again. In fact, he just got released from urgent care a few weeks ago and is finally able to walk normally. And you wonder why I hate the shit?"

"You know this kid?"

"Of course I fucking know him! Carondi was a second soloist, you—" Triani bit his lip. He jumped to his feet and pulled a pink silk top out of his dance bag. "Look, I know him just like I know everyone in the company. Nothing special about him but he didn't deserve that. He was a friend of Forilan's, by the way. I have to go."

"When did this happen?" Marlo called after him.

"Near the end of the run about six months ago." Triani walked away without looking back.

Marlo watched the long shapely legs, the tight buttocks, the provocative, swinging hips. He licked his lips, cross at himself for how the dancer always made him feel.

Carondi. At last, someone with a real grudge against the dead genius. How far would he go to get back at the one who had ended his career? If he was a friend, did he visit Forilan often once he could walk again? Is that how he got close enough to administer poison?

The theater wasn't that far from Regulator HQ and Marlo decided to walk. It would give him more time to think. Halfway back, he stopped at a Snack House. Food always helped his thought processes, he told himself, ordering some *rolinis*. By the time he had called his team together and was standing in front of them back at HQ, he was ready to make an announcement.

"I think we have a suspect. Maybe two. But first, tell me what you've found about the designer." He sat down.

Oslani cleared his throat. "Evalindo came from the River District."

"Really?"

Marlo was astonished. That rough area of the city was a neighborhood tourists were warned to stay out of. It was a haven for misfits, illegal aliens, most of whom were armed, and those who flouted the law at every turn. They lived in a warren of alleys and tiny houses all jumbled together in a maze designed to thwart any Regulators who might try to bring any of them to justice. If Evalindo came from there, he would have no difficulty getting hold of any sort of drug, Merculian or alien.

Oslani grinned, pleased with the effect of his bombshell.

"Let me remind you that not everyone who lives there is an out-and-out villain," said Eldred.

"Point taken. Go on, Oslani."

"Nothing unusual apart from the fact he made his way on his own and quickly became one of the top stage designers in the city, winning several prizes. He uses only his first name for business."

"Any red flags?"

"Not really. A few shady financial dealings but nothing actionable. He owns the house where he died and has a substantial number of credits in his name for one so young. As for Forilan, he came up through the dance system, and was accepted into the top company. He isn't particularly brilliant, but his good looks seem to have helped along the way. No red flags there apart from the odd way he just left the company after all his work to get there."

"Interesting. Here's what I've learned from interviews. Everyone loved Evalindo except the dancers who worked with him. Triani fought with him constantly, and says his work put the dancers at risk and named one who was badly injured in the last production. Carondi something. Check him out. He can never dance again thanks to Evalindo, which gives him a real motive for doing the designer in and makes him our main suspect."

"But how could he do it?"

"He was a friend of Forilan's. We'll have to check how often he visited the house recently."

"I'll do it." The newbie took off in search of image data.

"The big thing I discovered is that in an effort to stave off his illness, Evalindo drank a potion every night, prepared by Forilan. So the lover had opportunity. But why?"

Oslani leaned back in his chair. "The neighbor says they'd been fighting a lot lately. Inside. Outside. All around the house. He says it was about Forilan returning to dancing. Evalindo "forbade" it, the neighbor's words. And he hears and sees a lot. Apparently not enough to do, the old bitch."

"It seems the designer had to control everything, even his lover," Marlo said. "So Forilan is looking like a possible suspect, too."

"What about the Thalanox?" Eldred asked.

"It's used for a lot things, apparently." Ferdalyn brought up a list and projected it on the wall. "Small amounts are used as a preservative, for example. It's used in air-tight wrappings for food, too."

"What do the Serpians use it for?" asked Marlo suddenly.

"Serpians? I don't know. Why?"

"Something someone said. I have to go talk to Charlo."

"Oh, won't he be happy," muttered Eldred.

But Charlo, although delighted to see him, could shed no light on the possible uses of Thalanox in Serpian powders. He suggested talking to a Serpian.

Marlo sighed. The only Serpian he knew well enough to contact out of the blue was Thar-von Del, at the Serpian Embassy. He had only met him a few times, enough to know he was just as formal and standoffish as any other Serpian, male or female, but at least he was used to impulsive, demonstrative Merculians. And he would probably answer his questions without demanding diplomatic immunity or some such. They were a cautious race.

When contacted, Thar-von insisted on Marlo coming to the embassy to talk. He had very little time before the embassy closed for three days for some important Serpian holiday. Marlo arrived at the eastern door as instructed, and found himself in a long gallery. The floor seemed to be composed of patterned black sand, which was constantly agitated into tiny swirls, as if being breathed on by a giant. One wall was made of pebbled green glass, the other a glittering mosaic which could be seen as figures only from farther away. It was all a bit disorienting.

"*Com* Marlo Bogardini." The tall pale-blue male bowed slightly, one hand touching his own shoulder. "Come this way, please. It's a better place to talk."

"Thanks for seeing me." Marlo followed meekly, trying not to kick up too much sand and keeping the appropriate distance away from the Serpian.

"This is one of our meditation rooms but it will do." Thar-von ushered him into a room with unfamiliar star constellations on the walls and a very high ceiling. There was nothing in it but a long bench in the middle, which seemed to be on a swivel, making it hard to climb up on for the short Merculian.

Thar-von sat on the opposite end of the bench and looked at Marlo with his serious navy blue eyes. "This has something to do with "powders," as I understand it."

Marlo nodded. He had to concentrate to keep his balance since his feet barely touched the ground. He pulled the rolled-up data sheet from his shoulder bag and slid it along the bench to the Serpian. "This is the post-death report."

Thar-von studied the sheet and nodded. "I see. So by powder, you meant the form in which the chemical was administered."

Marlo nodded. That seemed pretty obvious to him, but he said nothing.

"This is harmless to us. We take it in various forms as a soothing drink for digestive problems, and mixed another way as a pick-me-up, similar to your wake water but stronger. What it would do to help a Merculian blood disease is beyond me."

"I suspect it did little good, but Evalindo was desperate for a cure and would believe almost anything, I gather." Such as some scam artist from the River District.

Thar-von arranged a row of small violet packages on the bench between them, then added a bottle and a roll of large disk-like pills. "These are some of the forms it comes in: liquid, pellets and granules—what you call powder."

"Where do you get them?"

"The embassy is supplied directly from Serpianus, but there are Serpian traders in the market for our countrymen who are not working here. Also, he may have purchased a counterfeit product from an unscrupulous dealer."

"How could one tell the difference?"

Thar-von collected the packages and handed one to Marlo. "No matter what wrapping it comes in, it should have this holographic stamp on it if it is genuine. It is impossible to replicate."

Probably for tax purposes, Marlo thought, inspecting the stamp. It looked like a maze puzzle to him, but it might just as well be writing in the Serpian alphabet.

"If the drug is synthetic, that might account for the larger-than-usual amount of Thalanox," Thar-von went on. "The chemist was careless."

"Or stupid."

"One does not rule out the other." Thar-von smiled slightly, and got to his feet.

Marlo slid off the bench awkwardly and almost fell. He righted himself quickly, relieved that Thar-von made no move to help him, and followed his guide back through the gallery to the door.

It had been cool in the embassy and Marlo was glad to get back to the warm sunlight. He hurried around the corner, and paused to take off his shoes and shake out the black sand that had been bothering him. It sparkled eerily as it spun to the ground, then turned brown. Odd. But he had no time to think about sand from another planet. He needed to see the packages Evalindo had stored on his medicine shelf. The suspicious death might turn out to be accidental after all.

***

The house of mourning was eerily quiet when Marlo returned to it. He had to wait this time before the Keeper finally appeared to let him in, looking pale but much more calm than before.

"I tried to talk him into sitting outside but nothing will persuade Forilan to leave the sleeping chamber," he said. "Let me tell him you're here." As Marlo watched him go, he realized the Keeper was wearing a long afternoon robe over his sleeping garment. Odd at that time of day, but mourning makes one do odd things.

When motioned into the room, he found Forilan sitting cross-legged in the middle of the bed clutching a pillow. His eyes looked hollow and his golden hair now seemed lifeless. Marlo wondered if he had eaten a thing since waking up with his lover dead at his side.

"Have you found the one who killed him?" Forilan asked, his voice so soft Marlo could barely hear him.

"We will." Marlo sat gingerly on the side of the bed and reached for his hand. Deep sorrow and a sense of hopelessness assaulted him at once. "There, there," he murmured as if to a child. "I just have a few more questions. Is that all right?"

Marlo turned to the Keeper who was hovering in the doorway. "Perhaps you could bring us something to drink and a snack," he suggested.

"He won't eat."

"I will," said Marlo, with an ingratiating smile.

After he left, Marlo patted the cold hand before relinquishing it and digging out the powder Thar-Von had shown him. "Is this what you mixed up for Evalindo every night?"

Forilan glanced at it and nodded.

"Could you show me where they're kept?"

There was no reply. The wan dancer was staring out the window, off in his own world.

"The powders and other pills are in the dressing room." The Keeper was back with a tray with hot chocolate and a sliced protein bun. Not the exciting fare Marlo had been hoping for, but he smiled and took a drink of the chocolate gratefully.

While the Keeper tried to coax Forilan to eat, Marlo got up, hung his ribbon of office over his head and switched on its tiny recording equipment before inspecting the dressing room. At the back of the dressing room were three shelves crammed with packages and pills and lozenges of all sorts. Many were the usual recreational kind found in any Merculian home, but a few were not. On the middle shelf was a supply of the violet packages used for the evening potion. He studied them, and they each had the official stamp in one corner. He frowned. He had been so sure.

He sat down again, and took a slice of bun. Only then did he realize that the Keeper had brought a cup for himself and was now settled in with his employer. Perhaps more of a friend than an employee. Marlo remembered that Triani had laughed to hear that the Keeper had described himself as Forilan's "dresser".

"Is it hard to find the powders?" he asked, helping himself to another slice of bun.

"Fori gets them at the off-world market, don't you?" said the Keeper, laying a hand on Forilan's arm to get his attention.

The youth nodded, and seemed to come back to their world.

"It's nice to be able to help," Marlo said, watching them.

"Well, he doesn't have much time for that sort of thing," Forilan said. "Didn't, I mean." He paused and wiped his eyes. "When I couldn't buy them, Basendi did. He likes to help."

"Of course." Basendi. The Keeper. Marlo poured some honey on what was left of his bun.

"I do what I can. More chocolate, *Com*?"

Marlo turned around suddenly, and let his hand sweep the cup and pitcher off the tray, spilling the thick brown liquid onto the bed. "Oh! I'm so sorry!"

"It's fine. I can fix it." The Keeper jumped up nimbly and in one swift movement pulled the top cover off the bed and bundled everything up in his arms. "I'll be right back, dear," he said, and trotted out the door.

"I'm so clumsy," Marlo said, sitting down again. "*Chai* Forilan, is there some other place where there might be any more medicine?"

Forilan stared at him, apparently trying to focus. "Just here, in the dressing room. Oh, and in Basendi's rooms, I suppose. I couldn't go on without him, you know!"

"There, there. I'm sure he's a great help to you. Where is his room, by the way?"

He had to repeat the question and when he found out, he hurried there, hoping Basendi would take a while to clean up the mess he had made. The Keeper's rooms were crowded with bolts of bright fabric for sewing and several mannikin forms, one looking about the size of Forilan. He must have brought all this from the theater, Marlo thought, heading for Basendi's dressing room. There, at the back, was a row of the violet packets…and these were without the stamp labelling them as genuine. They looked bigger than the ones on Forilan's shelf. He dropped one of the suspicious packages into his pocket.

"You think you can just come in here and disrupt our lives? Forilan has been through enough!"

"I agree." Marlo turned around slowly.

Basendi stood facing him, legs apart, holding a large *faisa* weapon in both hands. "You shouldn't have come back. He was just calming down and now he'll be upset again."

"But you'll take care of him, won't you?"

"Of course I will! I love him. And that's more than that devil Evalindo did. He just wanted to own him. To control him like he was one of his toys. He wouldn't let him go back to dancing!"

"But you would?"

"Of course! That's what real love is." Basendi pushed back his untidy hair, then grasped the weapon again. "Back up, ya *razzer*."

"Are you from the River District, too? Like Evalindo?" Marlo took a small step backward.

"Everyone uses that slang word. Keep moving. Back!"

Marlo took another cautious step. He could still feel some sand in one shoe. It was distracting. "I thought Forilan made the potions for Evalindo. It was you?"

"Shut up your face! Fori had nothing to do with this, nah! Someone had to stop the bastard ruining that poor dear's life! So I switched the packets every night, knowing Fori wouldn't notice. Little by little, the nightly drinks got stronger, until finally, nah, the asshole didn't wake up. Ain't that just snaps! Now, once I get rid of you, ya razzer,…"

Basendi braced himself to fire just as Marlo threw himself under the tightly packed rack of clothes and the door burst open. The room filled with Regulators shouting and scattering noisy fog bombs. Eldred rushed into the dressing room and hauled Marlo out of the room in his strong arms, through the front window and into the sunshine.

Marlo sank to the ground, coughing. "It took you long enough."

"It would have been faster if you'd told us what you were up to," scolded Eldred, handing him a bottle of water. "Luckily, Old Livid noticed your live feed. You should have turned it on sooner."

"Don't be cross. I'll get enough of that from the boss."

Eldred dropped down beside him. "So the Keeper is from the River District, too. That's probably where he got the weapon. It isn't easy to come by anywhere else."

"Got the bad powders there, too, I suppose." Marlo took off his shoe and shook out the last of the alien sand. He felt strangely empty. This wasn't the way he had wanted to solve the case but at least it was over. He wondered what would happen to poor Forilan now.

Eldred pulled him to him to his feet. "Come on. I think I saw a Snack House not far from here. You need some gastronomic therapy."

"I do," said Marlo with a smile. "I really do. But no hot chocolate, please. I've lost my taste for it."

THE BACKPACK

Catherine Astolfo

Catherine Astolfo's short stories and poems have been published in a number of Canadian literary presses and anthologies. She won the Arthur Ellis Award for Best Canadian Crime Short Story in 2012 and 2018.

Catherine is a Derrick Murdoch award winner for service to Crime Writers of Canada and a past President. She's the author of five novels and two novellas, as well as several (as yet) unproduced movie scripts. She's a member of Crime Writers of Canada, The Mesdames of Mayhem and The Deadly Dames Critique Group.

Mary Ellen believes nothing would have happened if she and Terry had not reached a milestone of disappointment in their marriage. She would not have become fascinated with The Boy. She certainly would not have noticed the backpack.

Although she can't identify an exact date for the appearance of the young man, she can pinpoint the moment she realized she and Terry had shifted into a bad place as a couple. Mary Ellen's niece posted online that she received 101 happy birthday messages for her 21st.

Mary Ellen commented, "If she's that old, how old am I?"

Terry tsk'd before he responded in a tone of irritation. "You know she's 40 years younger than you are."

The age joke was a rhetorical question they'd shared for many years. Handed down from her mother's dementia and her horror at being older than she thought. Mary Ellen even added a chuckle to prompt mutual laughter.

They have—had—lots of shared jokes and memories. They used to be able to read each other's minds. They had been able to convey all kinds of opinions and feelings with one look or a phrase.

Nowadays they are not in sync at all. She does one thing; he redoes it. He leaves out his favorite mug for later; she washes it and puts it away.

On weekends they were always together. They hiked numerous trails around the city. At home she and Terry would sit and listen to music for hours on end. Now she can't remember the last time they walked, let alone hiked. Or sat together for longer than a dinner hour.

For a while after the diagnosis, they followed the same habits when Mary Ellen was up to it. She had to give up her dance studio, of course, after 25 years. Happily, her partner bought the business and kept the franchise going. It was an amicable, generous agreement. Mary Ellen still receives large annual bonuses.

It's ironic that she's the one who is now at home and he is working. Terry always bragged that, in terms of finances, he could retire well before 65. He always said he wouldn't hesitate.

"The second I determine The Company no longer needs me, I will retire. I have enough money to live life the way I want so I won't look back, no siree, not for a minute."

Mary Ellen would have worked forever. Danced forever. Or more accurately, she would have watched her young protégées dance.

It's also more than ironic that she is the one who has suffered an illness rather than Terry. He is a big man with voracious appetites for unhealthy things. Despite ingesting copious amounts of alcohol and fatty foods, plus smoking cigars, Terry has no physical problems. The doctor warns him now and then about clogged arteries, diabetes, high blood pressure and so on, but Terry has lots of energy and absolutely no pain. He sloughs off any advice when Mary Ellen encourages him to eat better. He pats his belly and hugs her dismissively whenever she brings up the topic.

"I'm not going to die in perfect shape," he says. "I'm going to be like that woman who said she wants to die shouting 'What a ride!'"

His snoring reaches majestic decibel levels, propelling them into separate bedrooms. Another distance that Mary Ellen doesn't mind. She likes her own space and she's perfectly content to have a whole bed to herself. Terry is extremely happy with the arrangement. Mary Ellen knows how much he likes to snack in bed. He rarely visits her. When he does, the sex is fumbling and awkward but pleasant. Not something she craves.

Mary Ellen would never have given The Boy a glance if not for her own illness. The disease changed her life from one of excitement and drama to one of boredom. Tall and thin with a dancer's physique, her body never failed her until now. Besides being painful, Ramsay Hunt Syndrome is visually nasty. Mary Ellen has realized that she must be vain. Or she is more self-conscious than she imagined. The damage that RHS has wreaked on her face is deeply humiliating to her. Mary Ellen used to like her appearance very much, thank you.

She assumes her disfigured countenance is the trouble between Terry and her. He denies it, of course. Says he knows the disease isn't her fault so why would he hold it against her? However, Mary Ellen herself is repulsed by the nonsymmetrical look of her face. Half-closed eye. Pseudo smirk. A cloth at the ready to wipe away drool. She can't stand to look in the mirror. Why should Terry's reaction be different?

He has The Office, of course. The Company takes up the top floor of a blue-glassed building in the middle of the city. Although he constantly complains about work, Terry loves it. He is gregarious and witty, a great salesman.

If she hadn't loved him so much, she would have described him as a blowhard. Sometimes listening to him tell a story to their friends was excruciating. Terry tended to exaggerate his part in everything. As if nothing in the world could happen without him. But for Mary Ellen, he was the center of her universe from the moment they met. She treated his flaws as tolerable inconsistencies.

Recently she has experienced unexpected bouts of irritation with Terry. She chalks it up to being ill and often in pain. She notices that Terry never includes her in any of his plans or stories. It's always I will retire, I have enough money, I can travel later...never *we*. She hates listening to him ramble on about the people at work. He portrays them as beneath him, stupid and annoying.

Terry always followed a consistent timetable, but lately he has begun to extend his hours. To pass the time, Mary Ellen tries to read but her eyes are often uncooperative. She listens to audio books. Inevitably she gives up because she hates the way the narrators sound. She now watches television almost constantly.

Mary Ellen slowly comes to realize she is spending most of her time living other people's lives. People who hoard. People who need a head-sized pimple removed from their shoulders. Family pitted against family in a battle of halfwits. Perhaps that is why she starts to study the apartment dwellers living around her. They, at least, are real.

Their condominium is one of the original buildings on this side of the city. Over time, other condos have sprung up around them. The new high-rise buildings house stark, miniscule apartments. Hundreds of them crammed into one building. Their window eyes, mostly blank, block Mary Ellen's coveted view of the lake. To glimpse the sun on the water, she now has to pull a chair to one corner of the kitchen. From there, she can peer around the neighboring building and see a small bit of shoreline.

Down below, lots of people come and go along the sidewalk to the driveways and paths that lead in and out of the dwellings. She gets used to some of the walkers' routines.

Her kitchen window used to offer a lake view, but now looks directly into a window next door. There's a new resident in that apartment whose drapes are never drawn. The room is jammed with furnishings, including an inflated mattress covered with a tangled sleeping bag. A desk, a chair, a small sofa, and a bookcase fill the remaining space. Boxes and plastic bins are stacked everywhere, including on the furniture.

A teenager, a boy to Mary Ellen, inhabits the space most of the day. He slumbers all morning. Rises at noon. Sits at his computer all afternoon, except for occasional forays for food or drink. At night, he's gone until well after Mary Ellen goes to bed. But every morning when she eats her breakfast, there he is, sound asleep.

What piques her curiosity is the daily packing of his bright red bag. He unloads small items from one or two of the big boxes in the room and stuffs the backpack to capacity. The next day, there it is, empty. Snuggled up beside his comatose figure. Although she can't see the contents of the packages, Mary Ellen assumes he is a drug dealer. You would have thought he'd choose a bag in a subtler color in which to carry illegal products.

The afternoon (morning for him) when he first looks up and sees her peering at him, she expects him to give her the finger. Or close the curtains if he has any. Instead, he looks across with a huge grin and waves.

The Boy is extremely attractive. He has slightly curly black hair and huge eyes. His face is symmetrical. When he smiles, Mary Ellen can see that his teeth are white. His lips are thick enough to be called kissable. She feels a bit queasy at that last thought, since he looks about 19, and she is old enough to be his grandmother.

She knows that her grin resembles something conjured from a horror movie, but his friendliness is contagious and provokes an involuntary response. Mary Ellen smiles. Tentatively, she follows that up with a wave.

He disappears for a few moments and returns with a cup. He holds it up to her. For a moment, Mary Ellen can't decide what he means but quickly realizes it's a toast. She raises her cup of coffee back to him. He rewards her with another infectious smile.

Without fanfare, The Boy sits at his computer and gets busy. After a while, Mary Ellen begins to feel ridiculous. She gets up from the chair and begins to tidy the apartment.

They are a very neat couple, another quality that makes a good marriage fit. Mary Ellen hired a cleaning service when she worked and during her recovery, but now does everything herself. She has perhaps become a little obsessive-compulsive, but tidying and cleaning keep her occupied. She does the shopping, visits the pharmacy and even fills their pill packs weekly.

Once she has fluffed pillows, picked up a sock, shoved a small load of laundry into the washer, straightened books, dusted a few sunlit shelves, and measured all their paintings to make sure they are straight, she sits in the living room. She picks up her latest novel and tries to read. Only a few pages later, her half-closed eye is streaming with tears. The other refuses to relay the words to her brain.

She puts the book down and flops into the living room chair. Points the remote at the television. Nothing happens. Mary Ellen feels a flush of rage. She almost throws the object at the screen. Right now someone might be waiting for crucial surgery to remove a giant pimple from their butt. She stands up and has a tantrum, right there in the living room. Jumps up and down—though she doesn't really leave the ground very far—and punches her fists in the air. She takes big breaths to steady her equilibrium. The remote survives the ordeal. So does the television.

Mary Ellen gives up. Her heart stops its relentless pounding as she settles back down on her kitchen chair. She takes a cup of water and some cookies to appear purposeful. After all, she tells herself, this is where she would normally sit. It's the only remaining view of the lake she has.

She tries not to glance too often at The Boy. He types constantly, earphones affixed. His work, whatever that is, appears to demand all his concentration. His posture is straight and determined. He doesn't even lean against the back of his chair. He never wavers, not once glancing to the right or left.

Mary Ellen is able to keep one eye on the water. Sunlight dances on the calm lake. A sailboat or two glides past her view. Entranced by a boat bearing bright green and orange sails, she almost misses the moment when The Boy stands up.

He flings off the earphones. In a controlled and organized rush, he fills the rucksack from one of the boxes, his back to the window. Stretches his spine and flexes his fingers when he's done. Fluidly turns to face the window.

Mary Ellen quickly averts her eyes. Stares at the water. For a few seconds, she pretends not to notice his attempts to gain her attention. Then she smiles. Waves back in what she hopes is a surprised manner. As if she didn't know he was there.

He grins and makes a signal that seems to mean they'll have another toast. Mary Ellen lifts her cup of water. He gives what looks like a laugh and shakes his head. He disappears.

When he comes back, he holds a wine glass that looks very full. Mary Ellen is surprised. After a brief hesitation, she remembers that it's quite some time past noon. She trots over to the wine rack. Opens a bottle of red. Pours a healthy amount.

She's afraid he won't have waited for her but he has. He lifts his glass; she lifts hers. They both smile and drink. Mary Ellen takes a small sip. He watches her closely, miming a chuckle again. He wags a finger at her, accompanied by that beautiful smile.

No, no, he's saying, *take a real drink.*

Mary Ellen laughs. The sound startles her, as though she's suddenly strayed from a silent movie into a talky. She takes a big gulp of her wine. Now they both open their mouths in laughter.

He lifts a finger in a wait-a-second gesture. When she nods, he turns to his desk and appears to write. He holds up a large white sheet of paper with letters in black marker.

"Your name?" he has printed.

Mary Ellen returns the wait-a-sec finger. She rushes to the den. Roots through her desk to find paper and a marker. Back at the window she holds up the paper. "Mary Ellen. Yours?"

"Jupiter," he writes back.

At first she thinks he is joking, but he shrugs and writes, "Hippy parents."

Mary Ellen laughs and toasts him. He toasts back.

"Got 2 go. CU tmrw."

She has a bit of trouble deciphering what he means, but doesn't want to let on, so she lifts her glass again and drinks. When she looks back, he's gone. Mary Ellen thinks he means they'll do this again tomorrow. She feels ridiculously excited.

As she makes dinner, and later eats hers alone, Mary Ellen continues to drink wine. She finishes one bottle and starts on another. The food is delicious. She has become an extremely good cook. Terry especially loves her pasta sauce and chicken parmesan. When he turns up to eat, that is.

She cheerfully puts his portion of supper onto a plate and into the refrigerator. Way before nine, she props herself up in bed with an audiobook and the last glass of the second bottle. She's asleep and doesn't hear Terry come home. Mary Ellen also doesn't hear him leave for work. In fact, she's not sure he was ever there.

***

Over lots of coffee, water and greasy food the next morning, Mary Ellen wonders what it would have been like to have a son. Or a grandson. Their pact before marriage was two children. When the doctor told them they were expecting twins, they laughed at how simple the solution had been. One pregnancy! One fell swoop of infant and toddler care. The result, two perfect children all at once.

Eleanor and Teresa did their best to disabuse their parents of the illusion of perfection. They screeched through infancy. Went into teenage mode at the age of two. They inherited all of Mary Ellen and Terry's bad genes. Noses too big. Eyes too small. Hips so wide they tended toward clumsiness. Not coordinated enough to be athletic. A propensity for acne and obesity. Disagreeable, miserable, pessimistic, angry girls morphed into disagreeable, miserable, pessimistic, angry women.

Terry and Mary Ellen could not understand where they had gone wrong. One of many therapists suggested that, as a couple, they were too close to each other for anyone else to feel loved. Ha! If only that therapist could see them now.

Since she has become ugly, Mary Ellen theorizes that her daughters' problems all stem from being abnormally physically unattractive and ungainly. She wishes she could share her current emotions and new awareness with them. Perhaps they would stop blaming their parents for that accident of genes. But they are in faraway spots around the globe and only make a call at Christmas. Some years at least. If they have long-term relationships or offspring, they haven't told their parents.

Instead of twin girls, what if they'd had a son like The Boy? (Mary Ellen cannot say "Jupiter." It's far too ridiculous.) A cheerful drug dealer who mostly stays at home would almost be preferable. He's affable and friendly. Has a great smile and is extremely attractive. She would trade one of him for both of hers.

Mary Ellen shakes her head at the last thought. She must still be drunk. She doesn't even know this young man. He sells drugs, perhaps turns innocents into addicts. Is she losing her mind? Has the

RHS begun to misshape her brain as well? She refuses to sit in her corner spot as if The Boy is at fault for her shameful thoughts.

Instead, she cleans all the places that neither of them can see. Removes all the dust bunnies because they are, Mary Ellen read recently, filled with mites. Picks up lost paper clips and socks and bits of cracker. Seeds from the multigrain bread Terry prefers.

Finally, exhausted, Mary Ellen sits at the kitchen table. Her eyes stray to the corner. The Boy is still bundled in his sleeping bag. She gets up and decides to walk off her funk. It's a beautiful day.

Mary Ellen dons the sun hat she has worn for years. Wide-brimmed, bright blue, it has a neckerchief that can be buttoned up to cover half her face. Little had she known how much she would come to use that attachment. Huge round sunglasses complete the disguise. She feels almost jaunty.

The walkway around the property is fairly crowded. Mary Ellen looks straight ahead, hoping none of the few people they know will recognize her. She rounds the path. Starts the trek home when someone comes up beside her and taps her on the shoulder. At first, with the sun shining in her eyes, Mary Ellen does not recognize the person.

"Mrs. Reid?"

The young woman is tall, with blond hair caught up in a ponytail. Her body is thin but lithe, a dancer's...it suddenly clicks.

"Ember!"

They spontaneously hug. Although contact between students and teachers is now frowned upon, when Mary Ellen was the teacher, she shared many embraces with her students. Ember often needed a hug because her mother had passed away when she was only two.

Mary Ellen grins so widely that the snap on her neckerchief pops open. She has to dab away some spittle. She ducks her head in embarrassment and stops smiling.

Ember breathes a deep sigh.

"Oh, Mrs. Reid. I'm so sorry!"

Ember was one of Mary Ellen's favorite students. Talented, determined, passionate, gregarious, even-tempered, the girl is everything Eleanor and Teresa are not. She is now about 17 and hasn't changed a bit.

They link arms. Ember leads her to an empty bench.

"Tell me what's happened."

Mary Ellen feels as though their roles have reversed. She is the child who has lost something enormous. Ember is the comforting adult.

"I have an illness called RHS, which, as you can see, has made quite a mess of my face."

Mary Ellen fastens the neckerchief clasp again, hiding once more.

"Truly, though, I am fine."

"I have missed you," Ember says. "Have you missed me?"

"Of course I've missed you, my dear. Did you make the ballet company? The one you hoped for?"

Her protégée won a scholarship to the National Ballet School late in her elementary school years. For a long time, Ember continued to visit Mary Ellen's studio to say hello. It has been quite a while since they have seen each other. Her heart is so full and the girl so accepting that she forgets about the twisted landscape of her face. She begins to chat without restraint.

They talk about Ember's success, her traditional and steady path to a career in professional ballet. Mary Ellen catches up on the students with whom Ember has kept in touch. They speak of Terry (though Mary Ellen keeps that positive) and lament the state of the world.

Suddenly a loud ping alerts the young woman to the time.

"Oh crap, I was supposed to be at my cousin's place an hour ago," she says, but she doesn't sound apologetic. "I don't care," she confirms. "I am thrilled I got to see you. Do you live around here, Mrs. Reid?"

"Yes, we live right there." Mary Ellen points.

"Huh! My cousin just moved into the building next door. Do you think we could meet again soon?"

"I'd love that," Mary Ellen says sincerely, surprised and deeply pleased by Ember's suggestion.

They exchange cell phone numbers. As the girl dances off—literally pirouetting and whirling down the path—she promises to message and set a date.

***

Mary Ellen makes a creative dinner, cheered by her visit with her former student. Thirty minutes after he would normally arrive home, Terry sends a text.

"Sorry you were asleep last night. I'll be home around 8 PM. Hope you can wait up!"

She thinks there is a critical tone to his message, and feels that flash of anger again. She has to breathe deeply to avoid losing her temper.

"What an asshole," she mutters aloud.

Not very carefully, Mary Ellen throws the casserole into a dish and shoves it into the refrigerator. She chops up some cheese, tosses some crackers on a plate and pours a generous glass of wine. She sits in her kitchen corner.

When she sees them, the wine slips too quickly down her throat. She has a brief coughing fit. The inflatable bed in the boy's room stands upright. The sofa has been pushed back. Boxes are piled a little higher. There is now a large enough space for two people to dance.

The dancing is spectacular. Their synchronicity takes Mary Ellen's breath away. They use precise, crisp movements to accommodate the small area, but these only enhance the performance. They are an exquisite pair, both tall and slim. Muscular in all the right places. Dips, twirls, toe-bending moves in a concise choreographed vision. Mary Ellen thinks the dance could not be any better if they were on a proper stage. It is perfect. They are perfect.

She wipes drool from her open mouth. Tears flow down her face. Her emotions emerge in a confusion of joy and grief. When they stop to hold a heartrending motion, freeze it just for her, smiling broadly at her, Mary Ellen openly cries. These are not fake stage smiles. Ember and Jupiter look overjoyed by the coincidence. Her former student, her Boy.

Parents who choose odd names must give birth to creative geniuses. Eleanor and Teresa are such old-fashioned monikers. Perhaps that is the problem with their daughters. When she focuses again on the two dancers, Mary Ellen realizes that beauty, stunning, heart-stopping, captivating beauty, is the real difference. She puts her hand on the glass as though she could touch them. They do the same.

The Boy turns away after a moment and writes something. "You like?" he asks.

Mary Ellen scribbles her quick reply. "I LOVE!!!"

They both look pleased. The Boy disappears for a moment and returns with two wine glasses. He points to his glass, grins, then points to Ember's and shakes his head, no. Mary Ellen understands the gesture to mean *No alcohol for a minor*. As if he is a strictly law-abiding citizen. Simultaneously, they all salute one another.

Ember takes a moment to write, "You were my best teacher."

Mary Ellen cries again, but this time there is no confusion. Her tears are pure joy. She almost forgets that The Boy is a drug dealer.

***

After that day, Mary Ellen's life changes completely. She spends a couple of afternoons a week watching them dance in the apartment next door. She picnics with them in the garden gazebo of her building. At her request, they call her Mary Ellen. She learns that Ember has recently lost her father, too, and now lives with her aunt, Jupiter's mother. The poor girl is not very happy about the arrangement. However, not only is The Boy's mother's place close to the ballet theater but her aunt is also a dancer.

"I keep telling Ember she can stay with me," Jupiter says. "My mother can be a pain in the ass."

"And sleep where?" Ember asks. "In the bathtub?"

The Boy learned to dance from his mother, who is an excellent teacher, single mom, and a judgmental taskmaster.

Their conversations become increasingly personal and intimate. The garden where they meet is deserted in the middle of the week. The Boy sits beside her. Ember busily sets out the luncheon that Mary Ellen has packed in her picnic basket.

Mary Ellen chooses a moment to finally ask the question that has dominated her mind.

"Jupiter"—she can barely get his name out, but her smirk is permanent so he won't be able to tell that she thinks it's a ridiculous name—"how can you be a drug dealer? You seem like such a lovely person."

The Boy frowns, appears confused. He and Ember exchange glances.

"The backpack?" Mary Ellen prompts.

A frisson of understanding passes over his face. He laughs. Throws his arms around her shoulders.

"I'm a pharmaceutical student," he says, hugging her. The gesture seems to say, *How could you think that of me, you silly goose?*

"Or I should say I *was*. Studied for two years after high school to be a doctor in pharmacy."

"Then he developed his own formulas," Ember says proudly. "Now he makes a mint from his vitamin business."

"I still take the courses online," The Boy assures Mary Ellen. "I do want to be a pharmacist eventually so I can develop my vitamins into a global—and legal—product."

"So currently you are doing something illegal." Mary Ellen wants clarification, not judgement.

"Technically, yes. But the vitamins are good for people. I have thousands of customers around the world."

"He gives back to the community, too," Ember says. "Every day he takes vitamins to homeless people in different areas."

The Boy nods in a humble acknowledgement. "I've developed something entirely new that acts like a food supplement. Provides the minerals and vitamins in a unique way to keep someone healthy even if they don't have a great diet."

"Or access to good food," Ember adds. "These homeless people can't afford the healthy stuff."

"I'm very passionate about my products," The Boy says.

Those sky-blue eyes of his are serious.

"I really want to cure world hunger. I believe this new supplement could do that. Literally save millions of people from starvation. Right now, I sell high-end vitamins to the rich so that eventually I can give safe food replacements to the poor for free."

"You really make a lot of money?" Mary Ellen is astounded.

The Boy remains humbly quiet so Ember fills the silence. "He owns his condo and pays his tuition and mine, on top of putting money away to someday save the world."

Ember's eyes reflect her name: gray with sparks of fire that are now alit with a true believer's fervor. Mary Ellen isn't surprised that her former student is a devotee. She's ambitious and determined. Even if she didn't believe in her cousin's products, she would squash any misgivings to have her tuition paid by him.

As for Mary Ellen, she is a follower of sorts, too. She harbors deep suspicions regarding food supplements and replacements, having been the victim of a few quacks who passed themselves off as being superior to medical doctors. But she likes The Boy and genuinely loves Ember. Mary Ellen is willing to suspend her disbelief in order to be in their sphere. Or at least pretend to suspend it.

The Boy appears to be anxious for approval. He lowers his chin and his smile disappears. "You should see my apartment, Mary Ellen. The only rooms I can live in are my bedroom, the kitchen and the bathroom. The rest of the space is designated as my lab."

"Every day, Jupiter visits the homeless. Not just in the city, but all around."

Ember waves as though referring to the entire world. The Boy nods, continuing the humble posture.

"That's why you see me filling my backpack every day," he says. "For my newest composition, I use all natural ingredients."

Mary Ellen makes sure her tone is contrite. She still considers the vitamins or food supplements or whatever to be illicit. Untested against national or international standards. However, she will not risk losing him. He has renewed her connection to Ember and for that she will always be grateful.

"I should have known you weren't a drug dealer," she says.

He seems to believe her.

***

The days of summer pass quickly. Filled with laughter, dance, wine toasts and dreams. Eventually, she shares the truth about her life. The lack of a relationship with Eleanor, Teresa, and now with Terry. They tell her more about absent fathers and mothers who expect too much or who are neglectful. Relationships that end suddenly and can no longer be fixed. Mary Ellen tells them about RHS and the emotions that accompany disfigurement and disability.

Mary Ellen feels closer to these two young people than she ever did to her own children. She doesn't share Ember and The Boy with Terry. She doesn't want him to barge into their threesome. She senses that he will try to take over. Or they will hate him. Neither result is something she wants to chance.

Mary Ellen no longer admonishes Terry for his late nights or early mornings. In fact, she is attentive to him. Listens to his stories the way she used to. Full of admiration and love. He doesn't seem to notice that he is no longer her center.

***

In the fall, Ember returns to her dance company. Her visits are restricted to the weekends. This change causes some anxiety for Mary Ellen because Terry might be home during the only occasions when she can see the girl. Luckily it's a warm, dry autumn and Terry is able to golf quite often. Mary Ellen still has her Saturdays with the young cousins. She decides not to think about what she will do when winter comes.

To fill the gaps in her week, Mary Ellen watches television. She begins to scrutinize the 24-four hour news channels that have gained popularity. She becomes addicted to the adrenalin-fueled chaos and drama. Their constant panicked bleats about city life paint a bleak picture, filled with death.

She watches The Boy sleep, wake, and fill his backpack on a daily basis. They salute one another with coffee or wine. Mary Ellen realizes she has lost some interest in him. Without Ember doubling the beauty of his space, without the joy of their exquisite dancing, he appears halved. Boring. A chemical nerd who follows a fixed routine is not exactly stimulating. Perhaps this is how Terry feels about her now. A once beautiful ballet dancer and savvy business owner cut in half by a cruel disease.

73

Mary Ellen is surprised and thrilled when she hears a knock on the door one afternoon and opens it to see Ember standing there. The girl is a mess in the way that only truly lovely people can be. Still gorgeous, despite hair springing wildly around her face.

Her huge gray eyes spill tears down her cheeks, in what resembles a sob scene in an artsy film.

"What's wrong, Ember? Oh my darling, come in and tell me."

They stumble into the living room. Sit close together on the sofa. Ember continues to cry. Mary Ellen fetches a box of tissues and waits patiently.

"He's not a pharmacist." The girl can finally speak, although each word sounds like a hiccup.

"Jupiter?"

Ember nods. "He must be a drug dealer."

Mary Ellen realizes that she's not surprised. The Boy's story about vitamins and food supplements simply does not ring true.

"How do you know?"

"Have you been paying attention to the news?"

At first Mary Ellen thinks Ember must have guessed at her addiction, but quickly realizes it's an actual question.

"Some," she answers vaguely.

"Well, I have. Especially the newspapers. I scroll online looking for reviews and shows. Recently, I've noticed that homeless people are dying at a growing rate."

Mary Ellen doesn't read newspapers. There has been no television coverage on this topic. She nods to keep Ember talking.

"A lot of them were Jupiter's customers."

When Mary Ellen appears to be confused, Ember's tone becomes impatient. "The ones who got his new food supplement." Between breaths, she hammers the point home to Mary Ellen. "Some of those old folks have died. One after another. Recently."

"Oh. I see. You...you've met them? You recognized their names?"

"Yes. I went with him sometimes to distribute the pills. I got to know some of them. I cannot be entangled in anything illegal. I'm going to be a professional dancer and—"

Pounding on the door makes Ember jump. Mary Ellen isn't fazed. This can only be one person.

She leads the distraught Boy into the apartment. In the hallway, he shrugs off his heavy backpack, still full. Mary Ellen tucks it tidily into the closet. He heads straight for the living room to sit beside his cousin.

He bursts into tears. Mary Ellen finds it interesting that Ember doesn't touch him.

"When I went to the park, there were cops everywhere," he says between sobs. "I asked someone what was going on. They said two of my customers died. And that a whole bunch of others around the region have died."

"Homeless people, especially elderly ones, die all the time," Mary Ellen says quietly.

"You don't understand. They were all my customers."

"I will ask you once more, Jupiter. Are you dealing drugs?"

He turns his beautiful eyes toward her. Despite the tears, his face is breathtaking.

"No, Mary Ellen. I swear to you. I am not."

He looks at Ember. "I am not a drug dealer."

"Then why are all your customers dying?" his cousin asks.

The Boy's face crumples. He appears to be devastated. "You know how I use only natural ingredients?"

Mary Ellen and Ember both nod.

"Well, I was experimenting with some plants that assist in making the heart pump a little better. A lot of my clients have terrible diets, have been on or are still on illegal drugs, or alcohol, and I thought I could make them healthier by..."

He takes a long, shuddering breath. The tears flow steadily. His words are stilted yet formal, as if he has rehearsed this explanation.

"In my new formula, I've been using a touch of the plant, foxglove, from which the usual heart medications are derived. Digitalis, you know? I thought I had the dosage right."

"But clearly you did not," Ember snarls. "How could you be so arrogant? How could you involve me in something so risky? Don't you know what this could do to my reputation?"

"I just want to help people."

Once again The Boy looks to be truly sorry. But Mary Ellen sees something in his eyes that does not quite convince her.

Perhaps Ember sees it too. She leaps from the sofa. He tries to catch her hand, and she flings it away.

"I can't be part of this shit. I can't be taking money from someone who kills people in the name of a science experiment. I have my career and I must be unblemished."

She strides toward the hallway.

"How will you pay for your precious ballet then?" he hollers after her.

Ember stops. Turns around. Both she and Mary Ellen see the transformation in The Boy's face. Arrogant. Callous. Confident they are under his control.

Mary Ellen takes a deep breath. Suddenly, she understands how deceitful beauty can be. How it can cover the evil intent that courses through a villain's veins. A ruined face like hers could never hide disappointment or displeasure. In fact, it hides only joy.

"I'll find a way," Ember says to her cousin, her voice quiet and determined. "I will not be a part of your life any longer."

Mary Ellen is certain her protégée will accomplish her goals on her own. So is Jupiter. He stands and rushes after her.

"Ember, please. Don't. I mostly gave it to the old homeless ones. They would have died anyway. And some of them are doing just fine. I can adjust the formula. Pharmaceuticals are the future. I will be famous once I perfect this product. A few lives lost in order to save hundreds of thousands..."

He speaks the greed of so many before him. Mary Ellen is wounded by the banality of his words. Until this moment she had delighted in his uniqueness. His beauty, intelligence and ambition. Now she sees that he is just like all the rest. Ordinary.

Ember, too, reveals her self-centered focus as she stomps toward the door. No thought for her cousin, or for her former teacher, or even those poor old homeless people who died for a flawed cause. She cares only about how their deaths might affect her career.

Mary Ellen follows them into the hallway, where they continue to argue. Ember shakes Jupiter off. Slams the door behind her. As he reaches for the door, The Boy turns to face Mary Ellen, a sad smile on his face. Those kissable lips pout. The symmetry of his perfect features and the blue of his eyes almost draw her back into his pool of deception.

"I'm disappointed in your lack of faith in me, Mary Ellen. One day I might have discovered a drug to prevent RHS, or to return that hideous face to normal."

He drags his finger lightly down her cheek.

"Now I have to go dismantle my lab. But I'll be back in business soon. Please give my regrets to Terry."

"Terry?"

The Boy opens the door and pauses. He abandons any pretense of civility.

"Of course. You don't think I'd waste my time with a wretched old woman like you, do you? I like to keep tabs on my salespeople."

"What do you mean?"

"All those extra hours poor old Terry has put in. He's been selling my products through his company. He might even have slipped some of that new formula in with the old. That could be very bad for him."

He holds the door with his hip and looks straight at her.

"You won't say anything to anyone, right, Mary Ellen? You don't want to implicate your poor hubby. Or your brilliant protégée."

She makes him wait a few beats before answering. "I don't even know what you're talking about," she finally says.

***

Over the next few days, Mary Ellen watches as The Boy transforms his apartment. He removes all the bins and boxes. Changes his bedroom into an actual sleeping space. She sees him only when he's getting ready for bed.

At those times, he makes certain she is watching. He still toasts her occasionally. When she has a glass of wine, she lifts it in his direction but the smile and the salute mean different things now. Everything has a different meaning now.

His red backpack is still hidden in her front closet. In his panic, the Boy seems to have forgotten about it. Mary Ellen sees the bag when she reaches for her shoes. It's unzipped and open, filled with tiny vials. Their bright yellow lids wink out at her.

She stares at it for a long moment then zips it up again. Mary Ellen dons her shoes for a walk to the market. She has looked up more delicious recipes to cook for dinner.

That night, Terry is more gregarious than usual. He tells outrageous stories of the people at work. They drink a lot of wine with dinner. She even invites him to her bed. When he toddles off to his room, she sighs with relief. Pours a final glass and sits at the kitchen window.

The Boy walks into view, a glass of wine in hand, as if they have arranged to meet. He lifts his glass toward her. They both drink. He raises his wait-a-second finger and disappears. He returns with a piece of paper.

"Every last bit of evidence gone."

Ceremoniously he tears the paper into shreds. His smile is wide and infectious. From a distance, he looks innocent. Likeable. Even lovable.

Mary Ellen picks up the message she has already prepared.

"Except for your backpack. Come get it."

The Boy shows immediate understanding, then alarm. He really is a very smart boy who has made one big mistake. When he comes to the door, Mary Ellen shoves the bag at him. Closes and locks the door. She wonders if he will notice that it's lighter than it was before. She watches from the kitchen until he enters his bedroom. Sees him stuff the backpack under his bed.

***

The next morning, Terry is very quiet. Mary Ellen wonders if wine is a cure for snoring. She glances at the clock while she makes coffee and realizes he is late. Perhaps he'll return to his former schedule. She's not certain that pleases her.

She decides to take him a cup. When she enters his room, she knows immediately that the silence is unnatural. Mary Ellen places the coffee on his bedside table and looks down at him. His eyes are wide open, his mouth slack. His complexion a stark white. She places her fingers on his neck, but there is no answering pulse.

Mary Ellen pats him on the head.

"You were a mediocre husband, Terry," she says, "until you got into bed with the devil."

She picks up the coffee cup. Dumps the liquid into the sink. Places the cup in the dishwasher. Returning to Terry's bedroom, Mary Ellen places several bright yellow-capped vials on his bedside table. She puts a few in his bathroom. Then she calls 911.

Suddenly her apartment is swarmed by people. So many that Mary Ellen feels irrelevant. She sits on the sofa like a stranger at someone else's party.

A police officer speaks to her kindly. "Is there anyone we can call for you?"

"Oh. Yes, of course. Our daughters."

Mary Ellen digs up her address book from the magazine rack. "Will you do that for me?"

"We certainly can do that for you, if you want."

Mary Ellen is sure that the officer's soft, patient voice will be far better in Teresa and Eleanor's ears than her own would. She might not be able to disguise her relief.

Another officer, this one more professional than empathetic, speaks to her next.

"Have you noticed any recent changes in your husband's health? Has he started any different medications?"

Mary Ellen is quiet for a moment. "No. Terry's very energetic. The doctor warns him now and then about his heart, but Terry always says he's going to go out shouting 'What a ride!'"

Although dying in his sleep before reaching 65 is not likely what he had in mind, Mary Ellen thinks. She does hope he enjoyed their romp last night.

The medical person is silent. Perhaps a little puzzled by her answer.

Mary Ellen thinks of something else. "Well, there is one change. He's been taking some kind of vitamin that he got from The Boy next door."

She looks up at the medical examiner, who asks for more details. Takes notes. A police officer brandishes a vial from Terry's bedroom.

"Are these the new vitamins?"

"Yes."

The medic nods and turns away once she has told him all she knows. Soon the apartment is very still. Everyone has left. Even Terry.

Mary Ellen speaks with her daughters on the phone. They'll arrive in a few days to help plan their father's funeral. They are sad, caring and sweet. Perhaps, Mary Ellen thinks, she will build a relationship with Eleanor and Teresa after all. One based on inner rather than outer beauty.

***

The coroner calls her the next morning. He explains that Terry's cause of death was myocardial infarction—a heart attack—but they are exploring the connection between his death and the vitamins he was taking. She tells the medical examiner that she would be shocked if the supplements were unhealthy. The supplier is such a nice Boy.

That night, she pours herself some wine. Sits at her kitchen perch. She just happens to be there when a SWAT team rushes into The Boy's room. In no time, they find the backpack under his bed. He really is forgetful. Or too proud to dispose of the final evidence of his brilliance.

Even if he mentions Ember or Terry, she and the girl have already agreed to support each other. Her former teacher can afford to cover her tuition. The two women know nothing about pharmaceuticals or sales.

Before they lead him away, The Boy turns to look at her one last time. His face betrays disappointment, but also a touch of respect.

Mary Ellen raises her glass in a final salute.

Ω

NAPOLEON'S NOSE

Joan O'Callaghan

Joan O'Callaghan graduated from the University of Western Ontario with an Honours B.A. in English Language and Literature. She then attended York University where she earned an M.A. in English Literature, and then a B.Ed. from the University of Toronto.

She is the author of three books, and her short stories have been published in several anthologies. Her short story, "Runaway," took third prize in the national Bony Pete short story contest and was published in World Enough and Crime *(2014). Her Flash Fiction story, "Torch Song for Two Voices" won first prize in Polar Expressions national short story and poetry competition, and was subsequently published in* That Golden Summer *(Polar Expressions Publishing, 2014).*

Karen Whitney thought he was the ugliest creature she'd ever laid eyes on. Through the mud and the burrs she could see that his coat was black and white—a tuxedo, she thought. Snaggle-toothed, with long whiskers and a bedraggled tail that swept the ground. One ear had clearly come out the worse in a fight and now drooped with bits missing. She felt sorry for the cat, which huddled under a forsythia bush in her garden seeking shelter from the driving rain. She hung her wet slicker to dry, then took two shallow bowls and put a little milk into one and salmon from a can in the other. She placed both bowls on the back porch, hoping the cat would find them.

Her husband Brock, said little during dinner. Afterwards he hurried out, saying he had to be back at the hospital where he worked as a radiologist.

Karen loaded the dinner dishes into the dishwasher, then checked the back porch. She smiled to see that the salmon was gone, and the milk as well.

The next day, Saturday, dawned bright and sunny. Karen didn't see the cat anywhere, but once again she put food out on the back porch.

Later, as she weeded her garden, she felt herself scrutinized. She pushed back her straw hat, wiped the sweat from her eyes and looked up. A pair of amber eyes, shining like two beacons from the dark interior of the forsythia bush, peered at her. Slowly, she straightened up and held out a hand. The cat turned and, with a flick of his tail, was gone.

"What did you do today?" Brock asked as he sat down to dinner.

She knew her husband would not approve of the cat, so she did not mention it. Instead, she smiled and said, "I got my hair done and weeded the tulip beds. How was your day?"

He merely grunted, got up from the table and poured himself a vodka tonic.

The next morning, Karen went grocery shopping. On impulse, she stopped in a nearby pet store and bought cat food, treats, and a comfy cushion, hoping she could persuade the cat, which she'd already named Napoleon, to take up residence on the back porch.

Every day for the next three weeks, Karen put cat food and milk on the back porch. Every day, the food was eaten and some of the milk was gone. One morning, she awoke earlier than usual. Peeking out the kitchen window, she saw the cat asleep on the cushion. She tiptoed to the door and opened it as softly as she could. The cat immediately leaped up and off the porch, disappearing into the bushes. Karen was disappointed, but put out food and milk, and scattered a few of the cat treats she'd bought. The cat did not return that day or the next. The food, milk and treats remained untouched.

After three days, the cat food once again disappeared. Karen was elated. The next morning she crept into the kitchen and looked out the window. Napoleon was asleep on the cushion.

She watched the cat awaken, open his amber eyes and stretch languidly, first one foreleg, then the other, lazily unsheathing his claws. He turned his head and, with his pointed pink tongue, licked his whiskers, his back, and then his white paws. Watching him, Karen revised her earlier opinion. He was, she decided, a rather handsome fellow. His coat was shinier. He had filled out a bit and wasn't so scrawny. His floppy ear with its ragged edge gave him a rakish appearance.

When she went out to weed her garden, she took a few cat treats with her. Napoleon once again watched her from the safety of the forsythia bush. She turned very slowly to face him. He retreated slightly but did not run away. Slowly she put her hand into the pocket of her jacket and withdrew some of the treats, dropping one on the ground in front of her. The cat's whiskers twitched. He lowered his belly almost to the ground and crept toward her. Karen kept perfectly still. The cat came as close to her as he dared, and snatched the treat. She dropped another. He approached again and took it.

The following morning, Karen reminded her husband that she was scheduled for her annual mammogram that afternoon.

He said, "I'll see that Sam gets a copy of the report." Sam Bernstein was their family physician. It was unusual for a husband to read his wife's mammogram, Karen knew, but in a small town like Oakwood Falls, where Brock was the only radiologist, there was no other option.

At the hospital, she changed into a cotton gown and waited for the technician to call her. Finally, it was her turn. Karen did as she was told, moving this way and that, holding her breath when instructed to. The technician disappeared from the small room, leaving Karen alone. After a few minutes she returned. "Your husband has ordered an ultrasound."

Karen paled. "Why?"

"Just routine," the technician reassured her. "He wants to check something."

Worried, Karen followed her to another room where she lay on a table. The technician spread gel on her left breast, turned on the machine, and gently moved the probe back and forth. After a while, she told Karen she could go.

When Brock arrived home, she asked him about the ultrasound. He poured himself a vodka tonic before answering. "Just a fibroadenoma. Nothing to worry about. Nothing at all. What's for dinner?"

The rainy days of spring in Oakwood Falls gave way to the warm sunny days of summer. Karen spent more time outside in her backyard. Her flowers bloomed, the lush grass remained soft and green, the mature trees provided welcome shade and every manner of bird visited the feeder. Once or twice, she spotted Napoleon stalking the birds, but the metal pole prevented him from climbing. He had to be content with crouching in the grass, his tail swishing back and forth, whiskers twitching.

Karen's light brown hair acquired attractive blonde streaks from exposure to the sun, and her skin took on a golden tone. During the long, hot summer days, she sat in the back yard under a tree, a glass of iced tea beside her, a bestselling novel in her hand and cat treats in her lap. Napoleon no longer feared her, but he was wary. He'd eye the treats hungrily, waiting for her to toss them to the ground.

Karen noticed that her husband had lost weight. His clothes hung on him. His handsome face was thin and haggard. He was pale and lines had appeared on his forehead and down the sides of his mouth. She asked if something was troubling him but he said no, he was just working too hard. He was spending more and more time away from home. Often, she was asleep when he came in.

One afternoon, while Karen sat reading in the backyard, the doorbell rang. She set her book aside and strode through the house to the front door. A tall man stood there.

"Is Dr. Whitney at home?"

Karen was unable to place the slight accent. She shook her head.

"Please tell him that Sergei came by to see him." He turned abruptly and left.

The man was well-muscled. The light blue golf shirt and tan cargo pants complemented his fair, longish hair and deep blue eyes. He did not look back, but climbed into a black car with tinted windows and drove off.

When Brock came home, she handed him a vodka tonic. "Who is Sergei?"

Brock's hand jerked, splashing his drink onto his shirt and pants. His face turned white. "Why do you want to know?" he rasped.

"A man came this afternoon. He said to say that Sergei came to see you."

"Nobody." Brock fetched a cloth from the kitchen and wiped his clothes. "A patient, that's all. If he comes again, don't speak to him."

Karen wondered why her husband had such a strong reaction.

A few days after Sergei's visit, as she sat in the backyard, Napoleon jumped into her lap. She held her breath not daring to move, lest she scare him away. He stretched his long lean body across her lap and extended his white front paws, claws sheathed. Carefully, she held a cat treat in front of him. He sniffed tentatively at her hand, then opened his mouth and delicately took the little biscuit. But when she tried to feed him a second, he jumped down and disappeared into the forsythia bush.

The next day it rained and Karen stayed inside. Napoleon slept on his cushion on the back porch and ate the food she put out for him. Much to her surprise, Brock came home at noon as she was heating some soup. She was flustered because she had not prepared lunch for him.

He waved away her apology. "That's OK. You didn't know I'd be home. I can grab a bite in the food court at the hospital. Sit down. There's something I want to talk to you about." He sat at the kitchen table and patted the seat next to him. Wondering what was coming, Karen sat down.

Brock put a document on the table. He smiled. "I've been thinking that we should get a different life insurance policy, one that gives us better coverage. Every day, I see people who've been injured or who are ill. Many of them didn't expect this to happen and wonder how they'll be able to make ends meet. I don't want either of us to find ourselves in that position.

"I've done a lot of research. This policy will give us excellent coverage, much better than the one we have now. I've already signed. I just need you to sign it."

"Won't this cost a lot more?" Karen asked.

Brock shrugged. "The premiums will be higher, but the coverage is better. We'll have peace of mind."

Karen picked up the document and began reading it.

"Trust me, everything's in order." He took the document out of her hand and flipped to the last page. "Just sign here. I have to be back for a meeting."

Karen nodded and, taking the pen he offered, signed where he indicated.

"I'll be late getting home tonight," Brock said, shrugging his shoulders into his raincoat. "Lots of accidents because of the weather."

By morning the rain had stopped and the sun shone in a blue, cloudless sky. When Karen slipped into her chair, Napoleon jumped into her lap. She dug into the pocket of her capris and held out a treat for him. While he nibbled it, she stroked his head and was rewarded by a rumbling from the depths of his chest. He was purring.

The next morning as Karen put out food and milk for Napoleon, he trotted out from behind a box and rubbed against her legs, purring loudly. Then he lapped daintily from the dish of milk.

When she was comfortably ensconced under her oak tree, he hopped into her lap and hunkered down there, his triangular face turned toward her, his lambent amber eyes gazing up into her own. She stroked his soft fur.

She fed Napoleon a treat. "I worry about Brock. He's lost weight and doesn't look well. He's drinking more than he should.

But if I say anything, he just replies that he's a doctor and knows better than me. He works too hard. He's hardly ever home." Her voice trailed off.

It was as if the cat's presence had somehow turned on a tap allowing her internal thoughts to flow freely. Napoleon listened to it all and she felt that he understood her as nobody ever had.

As she talked and talked, the cat snuggled against her and placed a paw on her left breast. His claws remained sheathed, but he gently stroked her over and over in the same spot. She laughed and scratched his ears, reaching over him for a treat and feeding it to him.

Day after day, Karen and Napoleon sat together in the yard. She told the cat about meeting Brock when he was an intern and she was a university student, how handsome he'd been with his black hair and brown eyes, how she'd fallen in love. She talked about their marriage and its long, empty silences. She described her favorite books to him, retelling the parts she liked best.

And the cat listened, every now and again flicking the end of his tail in response to his name, or butting his head against her hand to tell her he wanted his head rubbed. And always, his paw rested on her left breast, moving slowly back and forth.

One evening as Karen carved the chicken she'd roasted for dinner, she cut out a few small pieces for Napoleon. So engrossed was she that she didn't see Brock come into the kitchen. She looked up as just he reached the door to the back porch.

"I need some fresh air," he said. And then there was a roar. "Get that mangy beast out of here."

Karen rushed to the door in time to see Napoleon fleeing into the bushes.

"We should enclose the porch. Next thing you know we'll have skunks and raccoons nesting here."

Karen had never defied her husband before, but the sight of Napoleon running terrified from Brock's wrath was too much for her.

"That's my cat and he's not going anywhere. Don't you ever frighten him again!"

Brock put his drink down. "Your cat? Since when do you have a cat?"

"Yes." She lifted her chin. "He's my cat."

Brock opened his mouth as if to speak. Then, to her surprise, he merely shrugged, picked up his drink, and went over to the cabinet that served as a bar in the living room, and topped up his glass. "Just keep that animal out of the house and away from me."

He took a sip of his drink. "The new surgeon and his lady friend have invited us to come over for a drink Saturday night. His name's Tom Barton."

As usual, Karen put out food and milk for Napoleon, but when she looked the next morning, none of it had been touched. She took some cat treats out on the porch and called softly, "Napoleon, here kitty—" No black-and-white cat with a torn ear responded to her call. Silently, she put Brock's breakfast on the table.

"What's the matter?" he asked.

"The cat's gone. You scared him away."

If Brock noticed her accusatory tone, he gave no indication. "No big loss," he said. "It's a stray. Probably full of fleas." He picked up his keys from the table in the front hall. "Have a nice day."

Karen moped around the house all morning, wondering what had become of Napoleon. In the afternoon, she picked up her book, poured herself a glass of iced tea, and grabbed a handful of cat treats. She settled herself in her chair and opened the book, but was unable to concentrate. She called, "Napoleon, come. Look what I have for you." It was faint, but she heard it. "Napoleon," she called again, shaking the treats in her hand. Louder this time. *Miaow.* There was a rush of air as Napoleon emerged from the forsythia bush and leaped into her lap.

"Napoleon," Karen was laughing and crying at the same time. "I thought I'd lost you. You mustn't mind Brock. I would never let him hurt you." She laid her cheek against his head. She studied the cat. "Where have you been?" she scolded, plucking a burr from his back with one hand.

When the cat had determined that there were no more treats to be had, he curled up in his customary position and began prodding Karen's left breast with his paw.

It seemed to Karen that he was pawing her breast with greater urgency than usual. "Whatever is the matter, Napoleon?"

Of course, the cat made no reply, only continued his rhythmic kneading.

Karen hummed to herself as she prepared dinner.

"You're in a better mood," said Brock.

She didn't answer.

***

The next afternoon she was in her chair under the tree, Napoleon in her lap.

"Mrs. Whitney."

87

Napoleon jumped down and disappeared into the forsythia bush. Karen looked up to see Sergei striding purposefully toward her. He was dressed in a black T-shirt that emphasized his fine physique and lightly tanned skin, as well as black pants, and black wrap-around sunglasses.

"Mrs. Whitney," he repeated. "How are you?"

"My husband isn't home."

"I know that."

Karen leaned back in her chair, thinking. Cautiously, she said, "Brock's at the hospital. Aren't you a patient?"

Sergei chuckled. "Is that what he told you?"

She nodded, watching him.

"We've had some dealings. You are well, then?"

"Certainly. Why wouldn't I be?"

A strange look passed over Sergei's face. To Karen he almost looked guilty.

She noticed fine drops of sweat beading on his forehead. "It's hot out here. Would you like some iced tea? I have a pitcher in the refrigerator." She jumped up.

He laid a hand on her forearm. "Please do not stress yourself. I'll fetch a chair while you pour the iced tea."

Karen felt an unexpected *frisson* in her arm where he'd touched her. She bent her head, hoping he wouldn't notice her reaction. When she came out of the house with the pitcher and a glass, Sergei was surveying the backyard. He nodded approvingly. "It's beautiful. I can see why you enjoy spending time here."

"Is there a message for my husband? Last time you came, you left a message for him."

"Yes. And I know you delivered it. No, Karen—may I call you Karen? I came to see you."

"Me? Why?"

He shrugged and smiled. "Is this your cat?"

Karen turned to see Napoleon peering at them from the forsythia bush. The cat stepped forward and hopped into Sergei's lap.

"My goodness! It was weeks before I could get him to sit in my lap."

Sergei stroked Napoleon and tickled him under the chin. The cat arched his neck and purred. "I see you've been in a brawl," he said, fingering the torn ear gently. To Karen, he said, "I always had a cat at home."

"Where's home?"

"St. Petersburg. Russia, not Florida."

So the accent was Russian, Karen thought. "I'd love to see St. Petersburg." She nodded toward Napoleon. "He's a stray. I found him in a rainstorm hiding in the bushes. I began feeding him and now we're good friends."

"Is he as good friends with Dr. Whitney?"

Her face fell. "No. My husband doesn't like him."

"I do not think Dr. Whitney likes very many things," Sergei said softly.

Napoleon jumped lightly from Sergei into Karen's lap. He brushed against her and began once again to paw her left breast.

Sergei watched, frowning slightly. "Smart cat. What is his name?"

"I call him Napoleon."

Sergei laughed. "A good name. It suits him. Do you know why he does that?"

She shook her head. "No. He always goes for the same spot. Did any of your cats do that?"

"No, but I know of a cat that did."

"What does it mean?"

He set the empty glass on the table. "Karen, please take care of yourself." He stood up, leaned over and kissed her lightly on the cheek. Then he was gone.

Karen touched her cheek where he'd kissed her, puzzled yet enjoying a rush of warmth she hadn't experienced for many years. She shook herself. You're a married woman, she told herself.

***

The next morning as she was clearing away the breakfast dishes, the doorbell rang. She dried her hands and opened the door. Sergei stood there, holding a large bag. She stared at him, rooted to the spot.

"May I come in?"

She nodded, speechless.

"Perhaps there is coffee?"

"Of course," she said. "In the kitchen."

He stirred cream and sugar into the mug she handed him, then placed the bag on the table. "I brought you a little gift." He pulled a book out of the bag. *St. Petersburg in Pictures* was the title.

"This is wonderful – thank you so much." Karen leafed through the book, admiring the color photographs. "I'll enjoy this."

"I didn't forget Emperor Napoleon." He turned the bag upside down. Out rolled a furry toy mouse that squeaked when Sergei squeezed it, and a package of cat treats.

"I must go now," he said. "But before I do, I want you to have this." He handed her a piece of paper. "My cell phone number." He placed his hands on her shoulders and looked into her eyes. "You may need it. Never hesitate to call me." He kissed the top of her head.

She loved the sensation of his hands on her shoulders, and the faint scent of sweat and musky aftershave. For the first time in years, she felt vibrant and alive.

He lifted her chin and kissed her lightly on the lips. "Goodbye."

Karen had difficulty sleeping that night. Her thoughts alternated between reliving the sensation of Sergei's touch, and wondering why he'd been so insistent she have his cell phone number.

***

Saturday evening was warm enough that they could sit outside on the deck. Tom Barton was witty and entertaining, and Karen enjoyed herself more than she'd expected.

A few hours later, Tom's friend, Maria, excused herself. "I have to walk Toby, my dog."

"What kind of dog?" Karen asked.

"He's a mutt, but very cute. He was found running around in the streets. Once we had him cleaned up and treated, I adopted him. I'm a veterinary-technician."

"Sounds like my cat," said Karen.

"Do you know that cats have very sensitive noses? They can actually smell disease."

"I didn't know that."

"I'll send you an article about it. Give me your e-mail address. There are trials going on now with cancer patients," Maria said and turned to the two men. "What do the doctors say about this?"

Brock sniffed. "Hocus-Pocus. Like the ancients who thought they could predict the future by studying the entrails of birds."

Tom shrugged. "Who knows? Maybe there's something to it."

"We should go," Brock said, handing Karen her wrap.

On Monday morning after Brock had left for the hospital, Karen received a scanned copy of the article from Maria. Dogs and cats, she read, were being used as disease detectives, able to sniff out illness when ordinary diagnostic tools had failed.

She gasped. There was a photo of a ginger cat, its paw resting on a woman's breast. A biopsy revealed a tumor, right where the cat had placed its paw. Karen sat back in her chair. Was she ill? Is that what Napoleon was trying to tell her with his constant stroking? But her husband had told her she was fine. A fibroadenoma, he'd said.

She picked up the telephone and called the imaging center. She was told to speak to her family doctor. With trembling fingers, she dialed the number for Dr. Bernstein's office, and told the receptionist what she wanted. The woman promised to scan the report and send it to her. But after a couple of hours, she phoned back.

"I'm sorry, Mrs. Whitney. I can't locate your mammogram report. I don't think we ever received it. I called the hospital and asked them to resend it but they don't have the report, only the original images and they're useless without a radiologist's analysis."

Karen sought to quell her rising panic. What had happened to her mammogram report? She hung up the phone and sat for a few minutes to calm herself. Then she let herself into Brock's study and turned on his computer. Password-protected. She tried everything she could think of—names, places, birth dates, anniversaries. She came up empty. There was no way to access his files.

Maybe there was a way. She remembered the scrap of paper with Sergei's phone number on it.

When he answered, she asked if he knew how to access password-protected files.

"Give me two hours and I'll be there," he promised.

Karen peered out the window, willing him to arrive. As soon as the black car with the tinted windows pulled up to the curb, she ran to the door. "Thank heavens, you're here."

He put an arm around her and led her to a chair in the living room.

She told him about the cat, the article Maria had sent, the missing mammogram report, how Brock had assured her there was nothing wrong.

Sergei studied her without smiling.

And then, suddenly, it was all crystal clear. Karen jumped to her feet and glared at him. "You knew, didn't you? That's what you meant when you said you knew a cat that acted like Napoleon. You didn't tell me." She added coldly, "Maybe you should just leave."

"Karen, I'm going to get you some brandy. Then we'll look at this computer. At least let me explain." He picked up a bottle of *Courvoisier* from the nearby cabinet and poured a small amount into a glass.

She took the drink would not look at him.

He sat down opposite her and began to speak. "How much do you know about your husband's gambling?"

"Gambling?"

"It's why he's out so much, especially at night. I work for my uncle, Nikolai Anasenko. You have heard of him?"

Karen's eyes widened. Nikolai Anasenko ran gambling establishments around the country. "Brock owes money to Nikolai Anasenko?"

"He owes my uncle a great deal of money. That was the reason for my first visit here, to collect from him. A few weeks ago, Dr. Whitney came to see Nikolai and asked him to be patient a little longer. His wife was ill with cancer, he said, and on her death, he'd collect on a large insurance policy that would cover the debt."

Karen covered her face with her hands. "You knew this when you came the second time?"

"I did. But it was only after I met you and realized you did not know about the cancer, that I began to get a clearer picture. Especially when I saw Napoleon patting your breast. Your husband did not want you to get treatment because he could not collect the money if you survived."

As Karen listened, a slow-burning anger began to replace the sorrow and fear.

"Please let me help you," Sergei said softly, crossing the room. He cupped Karen's face in his hands.

"I don't know what to do first." Karen's mouth tightened. "He was going to let me die so he could collect the money. He won't get away with this. That I can promise you."

Sergei laughed. "That's the spirit! First, let's see what he has on the computer. If the mammogram report is there, it will save valuable time when you see a doctor. That will be the next step." He took her hand.

"The computer's in his study. This way."

"Leave your husband to me," he said as he followed her into the study. "I learned a few tricks when I was in *PVO Strany*."

"*PVO—*?"

"Soviet Air Defence Forces. Now, no more questions." He sat down at the computer and within a few minutes, had accessed Brock's files. He did a search using Karen's name and up came a series of documents. He then narrowed the search by date and there was the report. He stood and Karen slid into the chair.

Her eyes latched onto the words "suspicious," "tumor" and "left breast." She forced herself to keep reading but nothing else registered. She printed a copy of the report, then closed the file.

92

Sergei typed *Citizens Insurance Company* into the search bar. The document they found confirmed that Brock had taken out a $1 million life insurance policy on her. When Karen looked to see the amount of the policy she had on his life, there was none. She printed a copy of that as well.

She turned to Sergei. "What do I do now?"

He gazed at her, then took her in his arms. With one hand, he cradled her head against his chest. "You must promise to do exactly as I say."

"And what might that be?" Brock stood in the doorway. He stepped into the room. "Does Uncle Nikolai know about your extra-curricular activities, Sergei?" He grasped Karen's wrist. "Just what do the two of you think you're doing in here?"

Karen brought up her free hand and slapped her husband across the face hard. "You bastard," she hissed. "You would've let me die."

The momentary distraction was all Sergei needed. He cannonballed across the room, headbutting Brock in the stomach. Brock went down in a heap, pulling Karen with him.

"Let go of her." In one swift movement, Sergei had a foot on Brock's arm. "Or I'll break your arm." He nodded to Karen. "Get up and stand behind me."

Brock laughed. "Do you really think I'd let her go? With everything she knows?" He tightened his grip on Karen. "She stays with me. You, on the other hand, are going to leave now. Out of respect for your uncle, I'll give you 15 minutes before I call the police and tell them I surprised an intruder threatening my wife."

"A good story, Dr. Whitney. Too bad you won't be able to tell it to anyone." He reached into his shirt, the outline of a shoulder holster now visible, and withdrew an OTs-38 Stechkin revolver. "When the police get around to checking on why you haven't been to the hospital, they will find your body and assume the intruder escaped. Now. No more bluffing. Let her go."

Brock released Karen's wrist. She stumbled to her feet.

Sergei flicked off the safety and pointed the revolver at Brock. "I prefer not to use this, but if it becomes necessary…" He shrugged. "Get up slowly. Keep your hands where I can see them." With a practised movement of his wrist, he slid his other hand into his pocket and pulled out a length of wire, tossing it to Karen. "Tie his hands behind his back."

Karen did as she was told, making sure to pull the wire tight so that Brock gasped with pain. Then she stood back, arms folded across her chest.

"The good doctor and I are going for a ride." Sergei prodded Brock with the gun. "Pack an overnight bag and wait for me. I may be a while."

The hours ticked by slowly. Karen straightened up Brock's study, removing all signs of a struggle. She packed her case, as Sergei had told her, and sat down to wait.

It was nearly midnight when Karen heard a car door slam. Cautiously, she opened the front door to admit Sergei. "Where's Brock?"

"He's been taken care of. Have you packed a bag? I've made arrangements for you at a private clinic in New Hampshire. The doctor is a friend of Nikolai's. We leave now."

"My case is in the front hall along with a bag of Napoleon's things. I don't want to leave him. In his own way, he saved my life. He comes with me."

The Russian laughed. "Let's find him."

Napoleon was asleep on the back porch.

"There's something I have to do first," Karen said. As Sergei watched, she ran outside and, pulling the wedding ring from her left hand, flung it far into the bushes. "Now we can go."

They drove for several hours, stopping once for coffee, and arrived at the secluded clinic as the sun was coming up. Karen and Napoleon were settled into the room that had been prepared for her.

Later that day, Karen was seen by Dr. Federoff, who confirmed the presence of a suspicious tumor in her left breast. She would undergo a lumpectomy the next morning. In the meantime, she explored the grounds of the clinic. A library, cinema, walking paths, and fine dining were among the amenities for patients to enjoy.

The next day, following the lumpectomy, Karen was seated on the terrace outside her room, enjoying the sunshine, Napoleon in her lap, when Sergei arrived. She smiled. "Dr. Federoff tells me the tumor is small. The prognosis was excellent."

He handed her a coffee and a newspaper. "I told you Brock had been taken care of. You can read about it."

It was the *Oakwood Falls Gazette*. The front page headline blared at her.

Oakwood Falls Radiologist Dies Under
Mysterious Circumstances.
The body of Oakwood Falls radiologist, Dr.
Brock Whitney, was discovered by Oakwood Falls
Hospital staff when they arrived for work this

94

morning. Whitney was stretched out on one of the hospital's two Linear Accelerators, used for administering radiation to cancer patients. The results of an autopsy have not yet been released, but a staff member said, "He was fried." Hospital administrators have refused to comment, but they did acknowledge that the accelerator was running and the radiation turned to the highest frequency when the body was found.

Karen handed the newspaper back to Sergei. "Occupational hazard for a radiologist."

Sergei reached over to fondle Napoleon's ears. "Especially one who can't pay his debts."

Author's note: Many thanks to Dr. Andrea Eisen, Sunnybrook Hospital, for her input and assistance.

There is a significant body of research to show that cats and dogs both are capable of smelling disease in humans. Researchers speculate that this is likely due to changes in body chemistry that can be detected by the animals' heightened sense of smell.

THE ROCKING R

John M. Floyd

John M. Floyd's short fiction has appeared in Alfred Hitchcock's Mystery Magazine, Ellery Queen's Mystery Magazine, The Strand Magazine, Mississippi Noir, Mystery Weekly, The Saturday Evening Post, *and other publications. He is the author of nine books, including* Rainbow's End, Midnight, Clockwork, Deception, *and* Fifty Mysteries.

A former Air Force captain and IBM systems engineer, John is also an Edgar Award nominee, a four-time Derringer Award winner, a three-time Pushcart Prize nominee, and the 2018 recipient of the Edward D. Hoch Memorial Golden Derringer Award for lifetime achievement in short mystery fiction. John and his wife Carolyn live in Mississippi.

"Feels like it did years ago, out here," Frank Roland said. "Even looks the same."

It was indeed a fine spring morning, the sky blue and cloudless, the wind pleasantly cool, the pecan trees glowing green with a brand-new coat of leaves. Frank and his wife Betsy were on the front porch of their home just south of town, rocking away in a pair of chairs Frank's father had made long ago in the little woodworking shop behind the house. The old shed was still there, minus the tools, and now served mostly as a playhouse for grandchildren.

Betsy turned to him and smiled. "Don't you wish we looked the same?"

"You do," he said. "Pretty as ever."

"Even with all my hair gone?"

He waved a hand in dismissal. "It'll grow back."

"We'll see." She was still smiling, and seemed to be studying the trees in the distance. Both of them knew there was little chance this latest round of chemo would be her last. But at least the recent scans showed an improvement, and for now that was cause for hope. Hope had been something in short supply around here. "For now, I'm content to sit here in the sun."

"We're on the porch, not in the sun."

"In my mind I'm in the sun. Warm and happy. Maybe on the beach, like on our honeymoon."

"Ha! You *are* in a reminiscing mood, ain't you?"

She was about to reply when her cell phone buzzed in her apron pocket.

"So much for the old days," Frank said.

Betsy looked at the screen. "It's the sheriff," she said, and held the phone to her ear. "Mornin', Billy. What's up?"

Frank watched her face change. After a moment she said, "Hold on a second." She pressed the speakerphone button. "Say that again."

Sheriff Bill Preston's deep voice, sounding tinny on the speaker, said, "Merchants Bank was robbed earlier this morning, around 9:30. Two suspects, no gunfire, nobody hurt. Only lead we have is that one of the tellers saw the vehicle they used to get away in."

"What'd it look like?"

"Blue Ford pickup, kinda like Frank's, except it had a white top. Went east down Main, but they coulda gone either way after that, so don't know which direction they're headed." He paused to take a breath. "That's why I'm calling. You and Frank sittin' on the porch?"

Small towns, Frank thought. Everybody knew everything about everybody.

"We been out here most of the morning," Betsy said. "What do you need?"

"Need to ask you something. Highway 14's still washed out, and that leaves only two ways out of town. North or south. I'm fixin' to alert the Highway Patrol, and I wanted to know if you might've seen a truck like that go past your place in the past hour or so."

Betsy frowned. "Ford pickup, blue body, white top?"

"Right. Fifteen years old or more."

"No," she said. "That *is* a lot like ours. I woulda noticed it."

"Ask Frank, too."

"I'm here, Billy," Frank said. "You're on speaker. I didn't see 'em, either." The call itself wasn't surprising. Betsy and the sheriff had gone to school together, and were still good friends. What was surprising was the time—it was now almost 11 a.m. "If all this happened at 9:30, why'd you wait so long to start looking for these guys?"

The sheriff blew a sigh into the phone. "It's that damn new bank manager, Griffin. He was so worried about finding out how much money was taken and so forth, it took him forever to get around to calling me."

"How much *did* they take?" Frank asked.

"About $60,000, according to Griffin."

Frank was quiet for a moment, the only sound the rhythmic *squeak* of the rockers on the floorboards of the porch. Beside him, Betsy frowned at the blue horizon as if watching for storm clouds.

"What do you know about the robbers, Billy?" she asked.

"Not much. Both were about average height and wore full masks and gloves, so we don't know if they were men, women, white, black, brown, or what. One strange thing: neither said a word. Not a single word, the whole time. Just pointed and motioned."

"They sound local, then."

"That's what I was thinking," the sheriff said. "Afraid somebody might recognize their voices. But witnesses also told me they moved real smooth and careful. No rushing around, no false moves. That sounds more like professionals, to me."

"Me, too," Frank said.

Nobody spoke for a moment, apparently lost in thought.

Finally Sheriff Preston said, "Gotta go, folks. You say you're pretty sure that blue-and-white truck didn't pass your house?"

"Pretty sure," Betsy said. "I do remember going inside to the bathroom once, and when I came back Frank was dozing, so I'm not 100 percent certain."

"OK, Bets. If y'all didn't see 'em, they musta gone north." He paused. "How you feelin', lately?"

"I'm better, Billy. In remission, they hope, but it's a little early to be sure. I have to go back in next month, and they'll do more tests. For now, I'm fine."

"Stay that way. Good memories, right?"

She smiled again. "Great memories."

A silence passed. At last the sheriff said, "Y'all are OK otherwise?"

"Otherwise?"

"Well...I know this has been expensive, your treatments and all. What I mean is, are you two doing OK...moneywise?"

"We're fine, Billy. And you're a sweetheart for asking."

"I am a sweetheart, for sure," he said, sounding relieved. "Look, I better get goin'. Thanks again, to you both."

Betsy disconnected and sat still for a minute, staring thoughtfully at nothing in particular. Then she turned to look at the ancient solid-blue pickup in their driveway. Frank followed her gaze. It had been a good one, that truck, hauling them for many years to town and back, and also down to the Coast now and then, as well as to visit relatives in Alabama. Their old hound dog, Bonaparte, lay dozing in the shade between its front tires.

"I agree with Billy," Betsy said at last. "That Joe Griffin is a jerk." She turned to face her husband. "You know, I've always liked mystery stories, read all the Sherlock Holmes years ago, watched all the *CSI* shows on TV and whatnot—but I wouldn't have Billy Preston's job if you paid me."

"I think they actually do pay him," Frank said.

She chuckled. "But he's old, like us. He shouldn't have to be worrying about all this."

"What should he be worrying about?"

"I don't know," she said. "Maybe his golf swing, or his tomato plants, or the fishing holes with the biggest catfish, or the best time of year for Disney World."

Frank grinned. "You still want to go there, don't you?"

"Sure I do. Why not? Who knows how much time we have left?" She fixed their truck with a thoughtful stare. "We wouldn't have to fly—our trusty pickup could make the trip."

"I don't know about that. Old Blue's not getting any younger. And neither are we."

"You keep saying that," she said.

"Well, it's true."

They were both quiet for a moment.

"Them two robbers," Betsy said finally. "You know how Billy said they moved slow and careful? That might not mean they were professionals. It might just mean they were old."

Frank laughed. "Makes sense, don't it?"

"Old don't mean dead, right? Old folks could rob a bank, if they wanted to."

"Don't see why not," he said.

Another silence. Somewhere to the north, toward town, a crow cawed.

"In the case of the truck," Betsy said, "maybe it's time we upgraded." She paused as if in deep thought. "How about a Dodge Ram?"

"I ain't sure Bonaparte would like that." At the sound of his name, the dog raised his head, looked at them from his spot under the pickup, and thumped his tail.

"Boney doesn't get a vote."

After another pause Frank said, "What exactly would we do there, Bets?"

"Where? Disney World?"

"Yeah. I mean, I can't see you on Splash Mountain, or talking to Mickey and Goofy."

"We could see EPCOT. I've heard it's fun."

"I've heard it stands for Every Person Comes Out Tired."

She hooted a laugh, and rocked a little harder. "I know you, Frank Roland. You just don't want to leave the farm."

He held up a finger. "The farm. That's another thing that bothers me. We got two hundred acres here, once raised cattle and horses, had a corral there beside the barn. What do you have to do to be called a rancher instead of a farmer?"

Both of them gave that some thought. Out on the road beyond their lawn, an old Cadillac rattled its way toward town, pulling a cloud of yellow dust behind it. Hiram Larson, probably headed for the post office.

"To be a proper ranch," Betsy said, "it needs to have a name. You know, like Southfork or Lone Pine or Twelvemile or Big Sky. I heard of a ranch once called The Rolling C. How's that for a cool name?" She looked at her husband and brightened. "We could be the Rolling R. The Rolling Rolands."

"Or the Rocking Rolands," he said, patting the arm of his chair. "To be accurate."

Betsy nodded, grinning. "Our brand could be a capital R with a rocker underneath."

"The name's probably already taken, and the brand too."

"Then we'll pick something else," she said. "Since we sold the cows, we don't have anything to brand anyway."

"Look out, Bonaparte!" Frank called.

Now both of them were laughing.

The moment passed, and they went back to rocking and staring at the land spread out before them in shades of green and brown. But she was right, Frank thought. It really was time to do something different. Time seemed more precious now than ever.

"Tell you what," he said. "I'll start shopping for a new truck, and you make the vacation plans."

"And neither of us will criticize the other," she said.

"Agreed."

The breeze grew warmer, the sun climbed toward noon, a fluffy white cloud shaped like a butterfly appeared and floated west to east. The dog woke to snap at a bee, and drifted again into sleep. Frank loaded a pipe, lit it with a kitchen match and puffed away, while Betsy went back to studying the truck parked in the driveway.

After several minutes of scrutiny, she frowned and pointed to a small white patch in the still-wet coat of blue paint, just above the driver's side window.

"You missed a spot," she said.

MEDICINE

Vanessa Westermann

Vanessa Westermann's debut mystery, An Excuse For Murder, *was published in 2019 by The Wild Rose Press. Vanessa is a former Arthur Ellis Awards judge, and has spoken on the evolution of women's crime writing at the Toronto Chapter of Sisters in Crime. She holds an M.A. in English Literature, as well as a Bachelor of Education, and has taught creative writing. Her blog, "Vanessa's Picks", features literary reviews and author interviews. She is a member of both Crime Writers of Canada and The International Thriller Writers.*

Vanessa is currently plotting her next (fictitious) murder, while drinking copious amounts of tea.

She lifted the scalpel. The delicate nature of the task at hand had her hesitating. Not fear.

"Cut!" The word exploded through the room.

Her fingers tensed on the blade once, then she let it drop to the table with a clatter of metal on metal. She could feel her pulse throbbing in her throat as her heart rate picked up. "What now?"

The director strode toward her. "There should be a tremor. A *tremor!*"

The other actors shifted uneasily, but she held her ground. "A surgeon's hands don't tremble."

"Yours do now." That snap in his tone, it was a sign they all recognized. His patience was wearing thin.

I am Dr. Grace Steele. She repeated the mantra to herself, as she always did when she needed courage. She straightened her spine, squared her shoulders and faced him head-on. "Grace wouldn't operate if her hands were shaking."

"When was the last time you updated your résumé?"

The question blindsided her. "I don't—"

"Correct me if I'm wrong, but the last time I checked, your profession was actor." Strong, clear diction. His voice carried well, echoed. "Not writer. Or maybe I missed your medical degree?"

All those spotlights trained on her, burning with heat. Her cheeks flushed. She raised her chin. "Without *me*, Grace wouldn't exist."

"Sweetheart, she just wouldn't have your smile."

The flash of fury had her gritting her teeth. There was a time when he wouldn't have spoken to her like this, but those days were long gone. She'd never deluded herself into thinking her beauty would last. There were some who did, but she knew better. Eternal youth was nothing more than an expensive fantasy. But they were using her age as an excuse to turn Grace into a trope, to weaken her, and that was unforgiveable.

Trapped on the small screen, memorizing medical jargon, she had devoted the better part of her life to this role. She knew the character inside and out. The woman's confidence was her own. Grace's nervous habits were hers. Some might have said the writers had stolen from her heart and soul, but she had given it willingly to Grace, to bring her to life. A sacrifice she would gladly make to the end of her days.

But the clock was ticking on her career. And it was all thanks to him.

The director moved around the operating table. "You are being paid to perform, not to think. I expect you to do your job. Follow the script." He pointed a warning finger at her. "Word for word."

From behind her came a murmur of agreement. She didn't need to turn around to know who it was from. Pretty, fresh-faced Caitlyn. Young, willing and eager, as always. But not very bright.

He hushed the young woman with a glance. So there was still trouble in paradise. Good.

She raised the scalpel. Light skittered dangerously off the blade. He wanted a performance? She'd give him one.

"And, action!"

Despite the ache in her fingers, she moved with precision, with control. As Grace would.

"Cut!" Again, the director stopped the cameras. His face was white now with fury and disbelief. "It seems you're determined to ruin the shot."

"I'm not sure what you want me to do." Pain twisted in her stomach. Her mouth was dry. She'd give him one last chance. He could still back down.

"Stop improvising or I'll remove you from this scene entirely."

There was gray at his temples, deeper creases around his mouth. But, for him, it made no difference. "Improvising? I haven't changed any lines."

"Don't pull the innocent act on me. You're subverting them," he hissed, "and I won't have it."

All eyes were on her, but they didn't linger the way they used to. They judged. Assessed.

An unnatural silence had fallen over the set. They were all wondering how long it would be before she backed down. The director wiped a hand over his mouth, and seemed to weigh his options. "Walk with me." He placed a hand on the nape of her neck. To others, it might have looked comforting. Supportive, even.

Appearances were misleading. She knew that well. Beneath her carefully maintained complexion was scar tissue. Hard and knotted.

She was going to be replaced.

Far enough away from the other actors, the director stopped and turned to her. "Why do you insist on making things difficult?"

As if she was a child throwing a tantrum. "You're destroying her, Chris."

"No." He smiled. "I'm killing her."

"Let her show strength." She would beg if she had to. "Give her that."

"You're forgetting two very important phrases: viewer ratings and suffering sells. And Grace will suffer." His voice was gentle as a caress, but his words left their mark, seared her skin. "She will break. And the ratings will skyrocket."

"It's thanks to me that you got those viewers in the first place."

His lips curved in a wry smile. "Show the writers a little appreciation."

"They gave me the lines, but I gave Grace life." Suddenly dizzy, the room tilted beneath her feet. She reached out a hand for the wall. The symptoms were Grace's, but they were one and the same person. Her own high blood pressure was proof of that. "I'm not—"

Her vision darkened at the edges. She took a deep breath, tried again. "I don't feel well." It was a confession, and she hated confiding in him, of all people.

"I'm tired of this. I gave you your career," he snarled. "And what is given—" His breath was warm on her face. "—can be taken away."

By now, the threat was familiar. A reminder that he was God, and she was nothing more than a washed-up starlet.

If only he knew that today, the power was coursing through her veins, potent as any drug. She dragged in a breath, tried to clear her mind. She needed to focus. They were working with her script now. "I'm well aware of that, Chris. But this show still revolves around me."

"For now."

How many episodes did she have left? She scanned every script for signs, searching for them in the dialogue, the action, the parentheticals. Grace was taking more frequent breaks between patients. This season, she had to refer back to patient records, though her memory had always been sharp. Two episodes ago, in scene three, she experienced confusion. Last episode, it was dizziness. The symptoms were occurring more frequently.

It was Caitlyn who would replace her, she was sure of it.

He sighed. "Take five, Julie. Then finish the scene."

When he'd cast her, he'd told her she looked like Julie Andrews. The nickname was just another cue for the role she should play. Shifting from Dr. Grace Steele to Julie. Luckily, she'd always been good at playing the ingénue.

She gave him a bright smile. No one else would notice how brittle it was. Always be gracious about the role you are offered, that's what they'd told them in the early days. "Thank you." This time, she truly was grateful. She needed to rest. Her biggest performance was about to begin. "I'll sit for just a moment."

Drained, she sank into a chair to watch the set. Instead of picking up her book as she sometimes did between takes, she looked around. Forgotten now, sitting there on the sidelines, she had the observer's role.

Just look at them, she thought with a twist of bitterness. So young. So alive. Alight with energy. How many reports of the argument were already spreading through social media?

She no longer belonged here.

One more deep breath. She composed herself and stood. She would do what was asked of her. It was a small price to pay.

Rejoining the others, she announced in a voice that was firm and clear, "I'm ready."

This time, the scene went smoothly. When the episode aired, no one watching from home would spot the moment her heart broke.

***

It was one of those days when nothing seemed to go right. The cast had worked together long enough to know one another's habits. Everyone had survival techniques that helped to get through the endless hours of filming.

So she knew where to find Caitlyn. The pot of coffee was fresh, the cups lined up in a neat row.

She put a hand on the young woman's arm. "Oh, Caitlyn, you should know by now, he takes his coffee sweeter than that."

Startled, Caitlyn returned the smile. "I always seem to get it wrong."

One cream, two sugars. Even the extras soon learned how the director drank his coffee. It was never a request, always an order.

"Here, let me." She took the cup from Caitlyn. Turned back to the counter. Just the right distance away.

It only took a second to slip the pill into the coffee. The slightly acidic liquid and the heat would quickly dissolve the coating.

He wanted her to suffer?

She might no longer get the love interests, but she could still make a man weak in the knees. Ingestion of cyanide would do that. Along with abdominal pain, headache, shortness of breath. Coma. And certain death. Cyanide was known to have a dramatic and immediate effect on the heart. That was what made it so perfect.

Caitlyn might say the actress playing Dr. Grace Steele had put something in the director's coffee before he died. But they'd never believe Caitlyn, when they found the remaining pills in her purse. They'd assume murder was the result of another lovers' tiff.

"A spoonful of sugar..." She hummed the tune under her breath as she added another heaping teaspoon to the coffee. Gave it a stir.

I am Dr. Grace Steele. The words filled her with strength. Calm washed over her. The aches, the pains, faded. She was no longer weary, no longer drained.

One dose, that was all it took.

She felt better already.

Ω

CHANGE OF HEART

Laura Kuhlmann

Laura Kuhlmann is a cancer researcher and writer from Romania, living and working in Toronto. She graduated from Heidelberg University, Germany, with a doctorate in biology, researching the chemistry of cancer cells.

Laura's story, "Gone at First Sight," was included in the Toronto Writers' Co-Op anthology, Voices 2018. *Her fiction has appeared in several anthologies, including* Barely Casting a Shadow *(2018) and* Voices *(2019 and 2020). She was featured at the 2020 Emerging Writer Reading Series, sponsored by the Toronto Arts Council. Laura's stories often feature immigrants. She is a member of Sisters in Crime International and is editing her first novel.*

The sound of the tray crashing on the living room's floor hit our garden party like lightning on a cloudless summer night. Through the glass door I saw Roćio on her knees, in front of the mangled apple pie she had baked for José's retirement party. We all dropped our plates and hurried inside. Roćio's face was flushed and she was breathing heavily. She pressed her hands over her heart.

"*Dios mios*," she whispered as I knelt beside her. "My heart…is beating out of my chest." She reached a shaking hand to me and grasped the strap of my dress as if she was trying to pull herself up.

José thundered down the staircase and emerged in the living room, his shirt untucked and half unbuttoned. He took Roćio in his arms.

"*Che passo, mi amor.*"

I couldn't follow their exchange, I was busy briefing the 911 operator. Woman in her 60s, suffering from arrhythmia, fell in her living room. No, she didn't hit her head. Shortness of breath and palpitations. Coherent but scared. We laid her down on the floor. Grenadier Pond Lane, just west of Toronto's High Park. Please hurry.

"Where's your purse?" José asked Roćio, as he cradled her head in his lap.

Roćio tried to lift her head, moaned and pressed her hand to her breast again. "Oh...it's like...a bird flapping its wings."

"Her purse," José said. "Where's her purse?"

I glanced at the couch, then the counter. I ran outside and checked the table, the chairs, the shadows. I realized how dim José's porch lights were.

I rushed back inside the living room, smelling of baked sugar and cinnamon. "I can't find it. What do you need?"

"Her blood thinners." He caressed her temples.

"José, we're not giving her drugs until the ambulance gets here."

"I'm so dizzy," Roćio said.

Everyone stared at us in silence.

"By the lake," Roćio whispered. "I left my purse on the bench."

Her breathing was labored.

José looked at me with glossy eyes. "Please, Alex, could you get it?"

"José, we shouldn't treat her ourselves," I repeated.

"Please!" His voice cracked and tears escaped from his eyes.

I grabbed my phone and ran out. I went around the grill, brushed by the birdfeeder and took the steps descending toward the pond.

The choir of cicadas and crickets rose as I plunged into the darkness. Tall maple and oak trees bordered the descending path. I turned on my phone's flashlight and continued down the steps until I reached the little bench facing the pond.

The air in the clearing at the foot of the stairs was heavy with the smell of hot sap and rotting algae. The sound of a siren broke through the deafening cry of cicadas. Blue light pulsed above me, on top of the hill.

I ran my flashlight over the bench and on the ground beneath it—no purse. A lipstick and a folding mirror lay in the scorched grass. Branches cracked in the thicket behind me and to my left.

What the hell?

I turned and trained my light on the trees lining the edge of the pond. Until tonight I had never noticed how badly José's back yard needed a trim. How close together the trees were. How

110

impenetrable their shadows. Branches snapped farther away from my weak light, farther up the hill. Was someone running? Why?

A pause, then a thump. Did someone jump the fence to the neighbor's side? Adrenaline made my fingertips tingle. A mixture of dread and excitement washed over me.

I let the light shine on the ground and found Roćio's phone, lying at the root of a tall maple tree. I stepped into the grove, swiping my flashlight from left to right. It fell on a bright blue dress. A tanned arm, hugging a log.

Bright blue—I'd seen that dress tonight. I advanced to the figure on the ground. Bile rose in my throat.

Maria, Roćio's friend from Mexico City. I had only seen her a couple of times before. A short, plump little woman. Often smiling, sometimes lost in thought. Her dress was stained, her bun in disarray, her black hair looked wet. I stepped closer. Her temple was dented. A stone lay on the ground not far away, wet and shiny. More bile rose in my throat.

Don't you dare vomit on a crime scene!

First, I needed to check whether she was still alive. I knelt beside her. No pulse. Her pupils were blown, unreactive.

I hurried back up the hill and ran into Nicole at the top of the stairs.

"What took you so long? The paramedics want us to bring her medication."

Nicole looked down at my hands, holding only my phone. "Where's the purse?"

She hooked up her tight maroon skirt and took one step down. I blocked her descent.

"Let's go inside," I urged her. My brain was going through the drill—nobody gets close to the body. I should have called 911, but I was too worried about Roćio and needed my flashlight to go up the hill.

Nicole pushed a strand of bleached hair, damp with perspiration, out of her eyes. She scowled at me and deep lines cut into her tanned skin.

"Did you not hear me? We need to find her medicine."

"The bathroom cabinet," I said as I nudged her back to the house.

She walked hesitantly ahead of me, her body half-turned toward the stairs.

A male and a female paramedic hovered over Roćio, getting ready to lift her on the gurney. José was wringing his hands at the far corner of the room. His son Miguel stepped from behind the wall and held him by his shoulders. I scanned the people in the room: did anyone look like he or she might have taken a sprint through a thicket?

Nicole's husband's hands were dirty, but he had been flipping burgers. Was that soot from the barbecue, or dirt from scrambling up a hill? Tony, José's graduate student, had a tear on the sleeve of his shirt. Had it been there before? He wasn't with us on the back porch when Roćio fell. Neither was Miguel. That's right, Miguel had gone down to the basement to bring up a bag of coal. When had I last seen him? What about Nicole? She had gone inside the house to take a phone call before all hell broke loose. How long had she been away?

Roćio turned her head to me and let out a long moan which I realized was meant to be a string of words.

Dear lord, I thought, *she's having a stroke.*

Everyone except the paramedics turned their heads toward me. Had I said that out loud?

"Did you find her purse?" José cried.

"Well…" I said.

The paramedics strapped Roćio to the gurney.

"I'm going to look for it," Nicole said. She turned on her heels, aiming for the open door.

I grabbed her by the arm and held her in place.

She stared at me. "Let go, Alexa!"

She tried to step away again, but I held tight.

"No one's going down to the lake," I said.

"Roćio needs…" Nicole objected.

"There's a body down there."

The paramedics lifted their heads to stare at me. There was shock and surprise in everyone's eyes. Then they looked around, trying to determine who was missing.

"Where's Maria?" Tony asked.

The same operator as before asked, "911, what is your emergency?"

***

Detective Goncharov was wearing a Kevlar vest that looked too big on his thin chest. His blue checkered shirt was wet under the armpits. I was impressed by his determination to follow the rules, even if it meant melting away in 90% humidity at a secured crime scene.

He glanced at my nails again. I looked at the charred meat trapped behind the nail beds.

"Hamburger," I told him. "I'm a messy eater."

"Mind if we take a sample?" More a statement than a question.

A crime scene technician panted to the top of the stairs and paused beside the birdfeeder.

"Are you sure you never touched the body, Miss Fischer?" Goncharov asked me.

"Only to check for a pulse."

"Even though you thought you saw brain matter?"

"I thought it was standard procedure."

He frowned at my comment.

"Watching a lot of CSI, Miss Fischer?" Goncharov asked.

"Excuse me?"

The sliding door to the living room opened and closed behind me.

"That where you learned about standard procedures?" Goncharov asked.

Seeds crunched under heavy footsteps. I turned to see a tall man with dark brown hair streaked with silver approaching us. My mouth opened in surprise.

"Detective Ashby," the crime scene technician said.

Goncharov glanced at Ashby's Kevlar-less torso, frowned, then flipped through his notes again.

"This very observant young lady was the one to find the body," Goncharov told Ashby. "She's knowledgeable about police procedures too."

Detective Ashby smiled. "She bloody well should be. She used to be a cop."

Goncharov's eyes snapped back to me. "Thought you said you were a scientist." He flipped through his notes. "Research associate? Working in the same department as Dr. Fernandez?"

"I am a research associate. But I don't work with José. We collaborate sometimes."

"How does a cop become a scientist?" Goncharov asked.

"I was a scientist first. Joined the force for a couple of years. Then returned to the lab."

Goncharov wiped the sweat from his face.

Just lose the Kevlar, dude, I thought.

"How do you know her?" Goncharov asked Ashby.

"Worked with Alexa before she retired."

"Which division?" Goncharov asked me.

"Not here," I replied. "The U.S." If he wanted more, he could ask Ashby.

Goncharov frowned, looking confused.

"So let me see if I got this right, Miss Fischer. You're a born-again scientist who used to be a cop in the U.S., currently working in Toronto, who prefers going by her middle name?"

"You got that right." I gave him a cold smile.

Goncharov scribbled. "Anything else I should know?"

No. Anything else you need to bust my balls about? "Yeah, you wanted to collect what's under my nails," I said.

"Do it now," Ashby said. "Mr. Fernandez wants to see his wife, and he asked if Alexa can drive him to the hospital."

"Why can't he drive?" Goncharov asked as the technician scraped under my nails.

"He's pretty shaken up. I'd rather he didn't," Ashby said.

"Let the son drive him then."

"The son's got a DUI."

I suspected Ashby wanted me to be his ears at the hospital.

"You're free to go, Miss Fischer," Goncharov said as the technician gave him a thumbs-up. "We'll call you if we need any information."

"Good night, detectives."

I turned on my heels and beelined for the living room door.

"Why's Miss Sherlock using her middle name?" Goncharov asked. "She undercover or something?"

I didn't falter, didn't slow down, despite the fact that my heart was beating out of my chest. Why was my past always catching up with me?

"Leave her alone, Pavel," Ashby said in a low voice. "She was a good cop."

I thought it was the hot air clogging my windpipe, making it hard to breathe. It wasn't until I felt my hands shaking that I realized I was fighting another panic attack.

***

José rocked back and forth on the chair in the waiting room. His eyes followed every passing EMT and nurse. Miguel, who had changed into a silk shirt, squeezed his father's hand. Tony sat next to me, his nose and mouth hidden behind his hands. Although Tony's mom worked at Toronto Western Hospital, I still didn't understand why he needed to wait with us. He was just a PhD student.

"What happened to your shirt?" I pointed at his sleeve.

He studied the hole in his sleeve, as if surprised to see it. "Got caught in the door handle."

What door handle? I wondered.

A tall, olive-skinned man wearing dark-blue scrubs walked toward José.

"Mr. Fernandez?" he said. "My name is Oscar Sanchez. I'm the resident on call."

Dr. Sanchez clasped José's hand in his, then guided both José and Miguel to a corridor that curved behind the main elevators. Beside me, Tony bounced his leg. His nervousness was making me antsy. Five minutes passed.

"I need to use the bathroom," Tony said.

I couldn't take it anymore. As soon as Tony disappeared, I left to find José and the doctor.

Miguel's sobs from around the corner startled me. A circular mirror reflected the three men in the corridor to my right, seated in front of another set of elevators. Their shapes were distorted by the convex mirror.

"What do you mean it's spread to her bones?" Miguel asked.

I took in a deep breath and held it.

"*Mi hijo…*" José's voice cracked. "Roćio didn't want our last months together to be…"

"How long have you known?" Miguel's voice was choked by tears.

"Son, Roćio needed to make her peace with God first."

"I didn't ask that! I asked how long you've known."

José's shoulders shook silently. Miguel embraced his dad.

I couldn't remain in the shadows like a thief. I continued down the corridor, feigning surprise at finding them there.

"Is Roćio OK?" I asked.

Miguel looked at me, his face wet with tears. The pain in his eyes broke my heart. He turned to face the doctor, oblivious to the snot coming out of his nose. "Can we see her?" he asked.

"It'll have to be brief. We don't usually allow visitors in the ICU." Dr. Sanchez touched José's shoulder, squeezed it. He waited as José hugged his son.

The implication was clear. Roćio's chances were not good.

I handed José his car keys. Miguel touched the golden cross on his chest, and his lips moved in silent prayer as the elevator doors closed. I bit my lips to chase the tears away. Miguel reminded me so much of Roćio, although he wasn't her biological son. They both liked to wear elegant clothing and jewelry, always well turned out and distinguished.

Will I ever see Roćio again? I wondered. *What happened to her?* I knew about the arrhythmia; she had complained about the fistful of medicine she needed to take for her heart. To prevent clots or a stroke, to lower her blood pressure. But I had no inkling that she had cancer. I couldn't help but wonder if her stroke was linked to

Maria's death. Foul play or accident? As I pondered the list of potential suspects, my own pain dissipated.

Work had always been my medicine. Until it also became my disease.

I walked back to the ER reception desk. Tony showed up 15 minutes later, all flustered.

"This place is a maze. Where is everyone?"

"José and Miguel will spend the night here."

I fished a couple of TTC tokens from my wallet. Our footsteps echoed on the empty street as we walked north toward Bathurst subway station. I glanced at Tony's hands, which were twitching.

He caught my gaze and paused. "Do you think it was Rocío's medicine?" he asked. "Maybe she didn't take enough or…"

"Or?"

He was too antsy for my already amped-up nerves.

"Or maybe she took something else?"

"Took what?" I asked.

Tony stared up the empty street.

I leaned closer to him. "Tony, took what?"

"I don't…didn't…" He sighed. "I went to use the upstairs bathroom. The door was open."

Sweat glistened on his brow.

"Rocío dropped a pill down the sink when I walked in," he continued. "She looked flustered."

The night air felt suddenly chilly. "Tony, the doctor needs to know." I said.

Had Rocío taken something that interfered with her medication?

He raised his hands defensively. "No, no. She didn't swallow anything. It couldn't have been that. Right?"

***

Ryan met me on Thursday after work at the coffee shop at Bloor and Ellis Park Road. I watched him push his wet hair off his forehead as he jogged across the street.

"Detective Ashby," I tsk'd as he sat across from me at the low table. "Jaywalking?"

"You sound like my mother." He leaned over the coffee I had placed on his side of the table. "I see you're still buying me coffee although we're no longer on a first-name basis?"

I smiled. "I thought your partner liked to keep things formal."

He shook his head and took a sip. "Mmm." Another sip. "Goncharov's a little green, but he's a good copper."

"Think he may be stiffer than rigor mortis."

Ryan laughed. Took another sip. "It'll take more than coffee to get me to talk about the case."

"What makes you think I'm here about the case?" My cheeks tingled. I should be better at lying than this. I was in deep cover for a few months, for crying out loud.

He lowered the half-empty cup onto the saucer. "I'll share mine, if you share yours."

I tilted my head, puzzled. "I already told you everything I heard at the hospital."

His smile was gone. "How's Roćio?" Ryan asked.

I shook my head. "Still in a coma. Not looking good." Was that all he wanted?

"What do you know about her and Maria?"

"I met Maria at the barbeque José organized on Victoria Day. Roćio seemed to be fond of her."

"Did Roćio mention how the two of them met?"

"She was vague about that, but they seemed to grow very close, very fast. I think Roćio said they had mutual family back in Mexico City."

"How well do you know José and his wife?"

"We have dinner once a month. José and I collaborate. Not too close, but not distant." Definitely not close enough to know about the cancer.

"Do they seem like a loving family?"

"José adores Roćio and so does Miguel. Miguel's mom, José's late wife, died when Miguel was only three. Roćio raised Miguel as her own son. José jokes that she spoils him rotten." I smiled.

"They didn't have children together?"

"No. Roćio once said she wished they had adopted when they were younger. She said she wanted to give children a chance to grow in a loving family. That they shouldn't be punished by society for whatever sins their parents committed." My voice shook.

"What's your take on Maria?"

"She seemed nice. She was enrolled in a master's program at York University. I thought that was unusual, given she's in her 40s. She told us she used to work as a nurse in Mexico." I retrieved the memory of our first barbeque—her sweet smile every time she was asked a question. "Seemed like she was trying to rebuild her life in Canada. Always carried big handbags with flower patterns or hummingbirds."

A smile flickered on Ryan's face. "Maria ever talk about her family in Mexico?"

"No. Are you having trouble locating the family?"

"She was an orphan. Was raised in an orphanage, never married."

That gave me pause. Roćio had mentioned they had shared relatives back home, hadn't she? If Maria was an orphan, that seemed to be a stretch.

"Everything else checked out," Ryan said. "She graduated this spring, Master's in neurobiology." He sighed.

"What?"

Ryan scrolled through his phone, then handed it to me. It showed a photo of a table, covered by a red-and-blue tablecloth. A wooden sculpture stood in the left corner. A small green hummingbird necklace hung from it. Next to the sculpture sat a glass pipe. In the center of the table was a pile of heavy-looking books, their covers green and brown or decorated with painted leaves. The one on top was titled *Herbal Antibiotics: Natural Remedies*. To its right was a small bronze bowl.

"Flip left," Ryan instructed.

The next picture was a close-up of the bowl. In it were several small Ziploc bags, containing flaky crystals the color of brown sugar.

I looked up at Ryan. Now I knew what he wanted from me. "Is this from Maria's apartment?"

Ryan picked up his pocket notebook and opened it to a dog-eared page. "Have you ever heard of...Ah, screw it. You read this."

He handed me his notebook.

I peered at his writing. 5-methoxy-N-dimethyl Tryptamine. My brain shortened it on reflex to 5-MeO-DMT. "The Toad?" I chuckled. "You wrote the name wrong, by the way."

Ryan plucked the notebook from my hands. "So you know about it?"

"It's a psychedelic."

He rotated his hand, signaling me to go on. Had my comment on his spelling error annoyed him?

"It's derived from the venom glands of the Sonoran Desert toad. Probably the most potent psychotropic out there. Super-intense high, short-lasting though. Not the choice of merchandise for the dealers I chased."

"Why not?"

"It's more niche. More the realm of psychonauts."

"Psychonauts?" he asked. "You mean people who get high so they can talk to God and shit?"

I winced at his simplistic definition, but chose not to correct him.

"Never heard of it being abused," I said. "Hell, when I joined the force it wasn't even on the banned list. They added it in 2011. It's not really on the official radar." Ryan's phone screen dimmed. "So Maria smoked pot and had 5-MeO-DMT in her apartment?"

"And shrooms. And MDMA." Also known as Ecstasy.

I mouthed a silent *wow*. "How much?"

"More than what I'd call a personal stash."

I remembered Roćio's silk dresses, elegant in an old-fashioned way. The upper-middle-class banker, married to a biochemistry professor, the mother of an introverted step-son studying literature in Vancouver. Would Roćio befriend a drug dealer? Was Maria even a dealer?

"Landlady says Maria was quiet," Ryan said. "Never late on rent. Paid cash." He stared into my eyes.

I knew what he was implying. "Definitely puts a new spin to the story." My brain buzzed, as it rearranged the puzzle pieces Ryan had thrown at me.

"Goncharov's checking to see if Maria worked for any local players," Ryan said. "She rented north of Carlton. He canvased Allan Gardens, but so far nobody recognizes her."

I had briefly lived near Sherbourne and Shutter, not far from Allan Gardens—a rough neighborhood where people minded their own business. Maybe no one recognized Maria, or maybe nobody wanted to talk.

"I don't know," I said. "MDMA. Magic mushrooms. Pot. The Toad." I thought of Maria's books. "None of those are addictive. They're not the drugs you see being abused by your local junkie. And excepting MDMA, they're all derived from natural sources."

"You think she hoarded 200 speed capsules for herself?" Ryan grinned as he took another sip of coffee.

"You think because she's Mexican she must be a drug dealer?"

His lips pulled back as if I'd scolded him. "If she wasn't a dealer then what was she?"

"A guide," I replied. Ryan frowned. I spat out another idea. "A healer." José's words came back to me: *Roćio needed to make her peace with God.* "Metastatic cancer is a game changer. A road ender. Roćio may have looked for a spiritual guide. Some of them offer psychedelic trips." Trips that take you closer to God. "I wouldn't abandon the idea that someone at the party offed her."

"That's what I'm checking." Ryan pointed at his wet hair. "Took a deep dive in a dumpster for that."

"Why on earth would you do that?"

"Asked your buddy, Tony, to part with the shirt he was wearing Saturday night. He said he threw it away because it had a hole in it." Ryan shook his head and downed the rest of the coffee. "I don't know if these kids are criminally lazy or criminally stupid."

"You know what worries me?" I asked. "If Maria was Roćio's spiritual guide, I fear she may have given her something that worsened her arrhythmia."

"Like what?"

"You mentioned MDMA." Ecstasy.

Ryan raised an eyebrow. He looked skeptical.

"So you think Roćio's stroke was not an accident?" he asked.

"Well, no. But her heart was weak. If she tried simulants…"

"Speaking of sickness, what are you doing about yours?"

I leaned back in my chair. "Excuse me?"

"You want to investigate so badly, it's not even funny."

Heat rose in my face. "I'm just curious."

"What happened to that FBI job your fiancé mentioned?"

"I'm not going back to law enforcement." My heart drummed against my ribs. I remembered Roćio's last words to me: birds in her chest. "I love research."

"Sure you do. But listen to an old copper—don't ignore your feelings."

I crossed my arms over my chest. "What feelings?"

"Regret."

I scoffed "Regret over my old job?"

"Guilt." He passed a hand in front of his face. "You've put up this wall, tried to shut down your feelings."

"I feel plenty," I said in monotone voice.

"Could've fooled me."

"Alright, old man," I said and grabbed the cup in front of him. "Is there anything else you'd like to tell me?"

He dug under one of his nails. "Don't know why I'm telling you this. Maria's visa expired. Found the receipts from an immigration lawyer. She was applying for PR. Express entry."

Permanent residence? "How? You had to deal with this for your fiancé. Eligibility's a bitch." Maria's lack of a job offer in Canada or former work history would not have helped her case.

"Don't know, her lawyer's out of the country until next week. But regarding the receipt we found, we traced the credit card to Roćio."

I was totally confused now.

José's name flashed on my phone's screen. I picked up. José managed to say my name before his voice disintegrated in an avalanche of sobs. His pain travelled from my ears to my chest, where it embedded itself between my lungs.

"I'm so sorry, José," was all I managed to say.

Across the table, Ryan lowered his head.

***

Nicole sealed the cardboard box labelled *shoes* before returning to the kitchen. Yesterday, one week after her death, José had finally been able to put his wife to rest. Now Nicole and I were helping him pack Roćio's things. Nicole walked to the stove to stir the pot of stew.

"Can I help?" I asked.

She pointed to the backyard, where José sat on a chair. "Check on him, please."

I stepped outside. José was watching the animals converging on his birdfeeder. A squirrel slid down the feeder, gripped it with its front paws while its hind legs dangled above the ground. It fell onto the gray stone bellow, then jumped up and chased away a chipmunk whose cheeks were bursting with seeds.

"Animals are so greedy," José said in a low voice.

"So are humans," I said.

"Humans are animals." José exhaled loudly. "That Detective Goncharov."

I wondered what the detective had done to annoy José enough to pull him out of his grief.

"The other detective seemed more..." I searched my brain for the right word, "humane."

"Until he starts asking about Roćio's will. He said she had made an appointment with an estate lawyer." José shook his head. "The *humane* detective is investigating Roćio's death as a potential homicide."

I knew Ryan was investigating the possibility that Roćio's demise was due to an accidental poisoning. But homicide?

"He thinks Maria's murder and Roćio's stroke are not a coincidence," José said.

Another dagger implanted itself in my breastbone. Had I seeded that idea in Ryan's head last week? It had been one of my hypotheses. I bit my lip. Damn it, how many more times would I get myself involved in an investigation where I didn't belong? Curiosity had always been my biggest flaw.

And now poor José might have to pay the price for my curiosity.

The familiar pulse thrummed in my fingers. My palms were warm and clammy. I closed my fist, focused on my breathing. No, I was not in Seattle anymore. I was not leaning over my dying colleague. That was in the past.

The sun, burning my skin, chased the memory of that damp night away.

"They stormed in here with a warrant." José's eyes narrowed. He was breathing heavily. "Checked our medicine cabinet, our bedroom, everything. They think I poisoned her."

"I'm sure they're just covering every angle, to be safe."

What about Roćio's will, though? I wondered. *Stop it, Alexa! You've caused enough harm already.*

"At least I laid her to rest." José's gaze landed on the blooming snapdragon. "I'll bring her flowers tomorrow. She planted so many flowers, thinking they'd bring hummingbirds to our garden. We got bees instead." He laughed and covered his eyes with his palm.

"Do me a favor," he asked. "Could you bring the bottle of tequila from the living room table? And two glasses?"

I walked into the empty living room. Where was Nicole?

"And the bottle of sangrita in the fridge," José called through the open door.

I carried the tequila and the red bottle of chaser in one hand, and two tall shot glasses in the other.

José opened the tequila bottle, poured both of us a shot. The clear liquid gurgled like a stream flowing through pebbles.

I took one sip of the smooth liquor, and chased it down with the sweet-sour sangrita.

José glanced at me. "Good?"

I nodded.

He downed his glass, and poured himself another one. "Hear her sing," he said as the liquor burbled into his glass. "That's a marble." He pointed at the tip of the bottle. "They rarely make the bottles like that nowadays." He sipped quietly.

A clear droplet fell from under the screwed lid and landed with a quiet splash in the liquid below. It must've been trapped in that marble José mentioned.

José waited for the tiny ripples in the tequila to die out before speaking again. "I'm flying home on Monday."

"José," I straightened in my seat, "maybe it's best to wait. The police…"

"What are they going to do? Arrest me? For what? Visiting Roćio's family?"

"The detectives might find your traveling suspicious."

He downed his glass again. "Let them think what they want. I never hurt Roćio. I loved her. Everybody loved her. Roćio was a saint."

José poured himself a third glass. I resisted the urge to pry it out of his hands.

"Could you come by the house when I'm away?" He looked at the flowers in bloom. "To water her plants? She loved those plants."

Out of the blue, he hunched over and started to cry. Loud sobs that shook his shoulders.

I reached across the table to clasp his shoulder.

"She loved the plants," he whispered through sobs. "And I don't know how to take care of them."

"I'll keep the plants alive," I said.

Through sobs, José instructed me to go to Roćio's home office on the second floor. He told me to grab the spare key in her desk drawer.

The subtle scent of lily of the valley enveloped me as I stepped over the threshold of her office. Roćio's perfume. I knew why José didn't want to set foot in the room. I could hear the AC humming in the hallway as I retrieved the key from the drawer. Then the AC stopped. In the silence I became aware of a scraping sound coming from the bedroom.

A rustle of paper, a discreet clap, like that of a box lid being lowered, then more scraping. I tiptoed to the bedroom and pushed the door open with my fingers.

Nicole was lying on her stomach, pulling a green box from under Roćio's and José's bed. She knelt and passed her hand over the embroidery on the lid: a green hummingbird.

The AC hummed back to life. Nicole turned to find me squinting at her from the bedroom door.

She pushed a strand of hair from her forehead with a hand covered in dust bunnies. Was that fear in her eyes?

"We didn't clean under the bed, it's filthy down there." Nicole looked at the box in her hand. "Roćio wanted me to have this."

"Mind if we ask José?"

"Go ahead." She pointed at the key in my hand. "Mind if we ask José about that too?"

Nicole pushed her aged body off the floor and passed by me into the hallway. "If you're done enjoying the afternoon sun, you could give me a hand," she said.

The breath I released was almost a growl.

I stumped down the stairs. Through the living room glass door, I saw Miguel sitting in my chair, next to José, doing a shot from my glass. He must've entered the patio through the side door. He carried a small, elegant duffle bag with him. I wondered when he had arrived and where he was going. My thoughts were interrupted when Nicole pushed a broom into my hand.

***

Nicole's scowl was even deeper when Ryan knocked on her door that night with me in tow.

"Ms. Richardson," he said, flashing his badge, "mind if I ask you a few more questions?"

Nicole led us to a rickety table at the back of her yard, past a small pool where her teenaged kids splashed their father.

"Ms. Richardson, I understand you removed a box belonging to Ms. Fernandez from her bedroom this afternoon?"

Nicole threw me a withering look. "Why is she here?"

"Because I want her to be," Ryan replied. "A green box, with a hummingbird on the lid?"

"I don't have to give you people anything. Roćio left it to me."

Ryan had the most intimidating "don't bullshit me" smile I had ever seen on a cop. Nicole's scowl vanished, and was replaced by worry. She got up, brought the box from the house and dropped it on the table in front of Ryan. The outer material looked like velvet.

Inside Ryan found snapshots of Nicole and Roćio. Tucked underneath them, a folded Post-it with a few names on it. Including Maria's. The writing was small and cramped.

Ryan flattened the paper and laid it in front of Nicole. She fidgeted.

"Doesn't look like Ms. Fernandez's writing," Ryan said.

"OK, I gave her a list of guides I trusted."

"Guides for what?"

"Spiritual guides, for psychedelic trips." Nicole glanced at her kids over our heads. Her neck shrank and she leaned forward. "My husband doesn't know I'm a psychonaut."

Ryan stared Nicole down. "So you introduced Roćio to Maria."

"Yes."

"You told me they had mutual family back in Mexico City."

"That's what they told me. I thought it was funny. What were the chances they'd meet all the way up here?"

"So why did Rocío want a spiritual guide?" Ryan asked

To make her peace with God, I thought. José must've known.

"Rocío found out in March that her breast cancer had spread to her bones. The doctor gave her six months. She refused therapy, knowing it was hopeless, but wanted something for the pain. I told her about my trips."

"Was Maria your guide?" Ryan asked.

Nicole nodded. "Maria's a professional. She guided me when I tried The Toad. She knows how to talk to people, ease their fears. Many people are afraid of what they'll see, of letting go of the 'objective' world." She scoffed.

"When did Rocío and Maria meet?" Ryan asked.

"At the beginning of May. I'm not a liar."

"No, just withholding information from the police." Ryan smiled, and without missing a beat continued. "Did Rocío take a trip with Maria?"

"I don't know. Rocío was afraid to let go. Maria had offered to guide her through a psilocybin trip."

Magic mushrooms.

"What did Rocío tell you?" Ryan asked.

"Maria always tests a subject beforehand, to see how they handle a trance. It helps her decide on a dose." Nicole paused, leaned back in her chair as she stared at the green box on the table. The look on her face, her choice of present tense, made me think she had forgotten that Maria was no longer alive. Sadness softened her scowl.

"How did Maria test her subjects?" I asked. Ryan stiffened beside me but didn't interject.

"Either Ecstasy or breathing."

"Breathing?" I asked.

"Holotropic breathing." Her gaze drifted from me to Ryan. We must have both looked utterly lost. "They're breathing exercises." Nicole expanded her chest and moved her hand up and down in front of her sternum. "You breathe in deeply and rapidly, each time exhaling as strongly as you can. They're used by experienced meditators as well. The breathing feels strange at first, but after a few minutes your body takes over. You fall into a rhythm."

I was worried about something else. "Did Roćio talk about taking Ecstasy to prepare for her trip?" I asked.

Nicole shook her head. "No way. She talked to her doctor. He told her it could trigger her arrhythmia." She paused again. "But she did say she was going to give the breathing exercises a try."

There goes our theory that Maria's stash triggered Roćio's stroke. Magic mushrooms wouldn't have interfered with her condition.

"Why did you take the box, Nicole?" Ryan asked.

"Roćio didn't want José to know she was planning a trip." Nicole choked as she fought back tears. "And I didn't want people to think my best friend was a druggie. I know how people judge. That's why I never told my husband or my friends I'm a psychonaut. It's not something people on our street condone."

On the ride back, I asked Ryan, "Did you find MDMA in Roćio's blood?"

"We didn't find anything in Roćio's blood." He looked at the green box on my lap. "You can return it to José after we process it." He squeezed the steering wheel. "Tonight was a waste of time."

I wasn't so sure.

***

Two days later, I was still perusing the internet, trying to find information on holotropic breathing. Testimonials swore that it was a miracle cure for depression, that it improved oxygenation and fought infections. The oxygenation part was what bothered me. I searched for fatality reports. I found one: a man suffering from an aneurysm. Holotropic breathing was practically hyperventilation. More oxygen dissolved in the blood, which altered the blood's pH, making it more basic. It was the reason people often got dizzy after doing these exercises.

Then I finally found it: a case report confirming that changing carbon dioxide and oxygen levels in the blood can alter the heart's rhythm. I slouched in my chair as I dialed Ryan and explained my hypothesis.

"You can't find anything in Roćio's blood, because it's not there anymore. It was too much oxygen. The breathing exercises triggered her arrhythmia. The effects can be delayed by a few hours." Roćio probably thought holotropic breathing was safe. I certainly would have thought so. "That's why she was flushed when Tony walked in on her in the bathroom. Her death was probably an accident."

"Still doesn't tell us who killed Maria," Ryan replied. "Or why."

***

I thanked José's neighbor for letting me jump the fence into José's backyard. I wanted to check out Ryan's new hypothesis: that Maria's murderer was an outsider. An angry psychonaut? An angry dealer who saw Maria as competition?

The neighbor had just returned from his cruise and was aghast that a murderer had used his backyard to escape. The fence separating his lawn from José's was low, easy to jump. As was the ornamental fence dividing the front lawns of both properties. The neighborhood was built on trust. Easy to exploit by a malicious entity.

The medical examiner had agreed that the holotropic breathing exercises could have caused Roćio's arrhythmia, which in turn caused her stroke. In the absence of any proof of foul play, Roćio's cause of death was ruled as "natural." She must have been updating her will in the wake of her diagnosis, I thought.

Still, before dropping me off at José's house, Goncharov had asked if I remembered Roćio mentioning a friend who needed help with her visa. He didn't refer specifically to Maria's PR application, but he didn't need to. I too thought it strange that Roćio had footed the bill for Maria's immigration lawyer.

What did I know, though? I sat on the steps I had gone down the night Maria was killed. I turned on my phone and checked my e-mail. My fiancé had sent me a link to a job he thought might interest me. His employer, the DEA, was hiring. I archived the message. Those days were behind me.

I passed my hand over the velvet lid of the green box. I wanted to put it back before José returned from Mexico.

Also, I had to water the plants. I rose and turned too quickly, lost my balance and fell forward. The box flew from my hand, landing on an upper step with a *thud*.

You clumsy fool! I thought.

I brushed the dirt off the velvet as I climbed the stairs. I was digging the key from the pocket of my shorts when I heard a strange rattle inside the box. I shook it, heard it again. Key in my right hand, I lifted the lid. And found what I had believed to be the bottom of the box tilted upward, at a slight angle.

Carefully, I pulled the fake bottom out of the box. Below it lay an old sepia photograph. A young Roćio, her cheeks smooth, her hair covered by a light-colored scarf. In her arms was a baby, probably a newborn, swaddled in white cloth wearing a small necklace in the shape of a hummingbird. I remembered the necklace on the sculpture in Maria's room. My brain scrambled for a logical explanation—Roćio didn't have children. Or did she?

I flipped the photo over. In large flowery calligraphy, someone had written in black ink: *Mi corazón siempre te pertenecerá, mi Colibri*. Below, a date: *28 de marzo, 1973*.

I slammed the lid back onto the box, grabbed my phone and translated the sentence. "*My heart will always belong to you, my Hummingbird*." My head spun. 1973. Roćio would have been what, 19? The baby in her arms would be 42 now. Maria's age.

I recalled Roćio's words: "*I wish I had adopted. All those children, wondering why their parents never took them home. We shouldn't punish the children for the mistakes of their parents.*"

Could the hummingbird in the photo be the same one I saw in the photo in Maria's room? Was Maria Roćio's daughter? Was that how they'd found each other? Why Roćio was sponsoring Maria's residency application? Why Roćio was changing her will?

I unlocked the side door to José's house, and dialed Ryan's number. The house was silent, and too warm. José was in Mexico. Miguel had returned to his internship in Vancouver. Nobody had been in the house in a week.

Ryan's phone rang as I ran down the stairs. I heard a click at the other end.

"Ryan, thank God! I think Maria may have been Roćio's daughter. I just found a picture..."

"...voice mail box is full," a female voice told me. "Please hang up..."

I disconnected and yelled at the phone, "The fuck, clean your fucking voice mail..."

I threw the box onto the low glass table and stared at the bookshelf next to it. The tequila bottle José and I had drunk from stood half-empty on the top shelf.

I tried Goncharov's number. It rang, just as a droplet fell from the marble lid of the bottle into the clear tequila below.

The hair stood up on the back on my neck.

Someone drank from it recently.

Someone was in the house. Someone heard me trying to tell Ryan that Roćio had a daughter.

I sprinted for the sliding door to the backyard, the door closest to me.

A body slammed into me from behind as I cracked the door open. I cried out. My phone flew out of my hand. An arm snaked around my neck, and I instinctively lowered my chin. Tried to push the arm up, protect my windpipe. The tip of my right sneaker found the crack in the door, pushed it to the left. The pressure on my neck loosened, and a hand grabbed me by the hair and pushed me back hard. I landed on my back. My head hit the floor. I looked up.

Miguel!

He lurched toward me. I kicked hard, aiming for his face, and he fell back against the door. I scrambled to my feet and ran for the stairs. Up the stairs.

He grabbed my ankle and pulled me back. I fell sideways, cried out when my hip and ribs hit the edge of the steps. I kicked again, freed my ankle, lost a shoe.

I sprinted up the steps on shaky legs. When I got to the entrance, I lifted the tiny wooden table and swung it with all the force I could muster. It hit Miguel in the cheek. He fell. Moaned, but remained still on the floor. I rushed for the front door, fumbled with the lock, broke free.

As I ran up the driveway, I saw Goncharov's car. I waved my hands. Never thought I'd ever be so happy to see him.

***

"You look great," Goncharov said as he handed me a bag of ice and a towel.

Was Goncharov able to joke? He wiped the sweat from his brow; of course, he was wearing his Kevlar.

I leaned back on the lawn chair, in José's backyard, and placed the ice on my throbbing cheek. I already had an icepack on the back of my head. I had told the EMT to take care of Miguel first.

I was lucky Goncharov had stopped to grab a coffee nearby after dropping me off at José's home. He had rushed back as soon as he heard the scuffle over the phone.

"Kid must've found out he had a stepsister," Goncharov said. "Freaked out when mommy tried to split the will."

"Or the affection," I said. "Is he talking?"

"He will."

"Stupid. There was plenty to go around."

"Greed," Goncharov said. "Powerful feeling." He looked at me. "Nice job, Miss Former Cop. Guess you still have it in you."

His phone rang, and he walked into the house.

Did I still have it in me? I wondered.

I opened my phone with one hand and searched for the e-mail about the DEA job. I could apply. Just for the heck of it. Don't have to take the job if I don't want to.

A low buzz drew my attention. A green hummingbird hovered over Roćio's flowers, dipped its beak into the nectar. Then another showed up. And then two more.

The bird that had been beating in Roćio's chest throughout the last months of her life. Not her arrhythmia. Maria. Her *Colibri*.

I dropped the icepack in my lap and wept, as the shimmer of hummingbirds drank from Roćio's flowers.

Ω

MERCY

Rosemary Aubert

Rosemary Aubert is the author of the acclaimed Ellis Portal mystery series. Rosemary's research for crime fiction includes a 25 year career as a professional in the Canadian criminal justice system. She has also published romance novels, poetry collections and a book of short stories.

Rosemary has lectured across Canada and in the United States and has taught writing for private organizations, as well as being an instructor in the School of Continuing Studies at the University of Toronto and at Loyalist College. She is a two-time winner of the Arthur Ellis Award for crime fiction.

Because of the virus, hospital security would only let me stand on my toes and put my hand on the windowpane for the few minutes they brought her to the window.

Every time I saw her hair I started to cry, but I had to be strong and control my tears.

At first she seemed the same. Then one day it all changed, and she let me see how desperate she was.

Mercy had always been the best-dressed, best-groomed person in my circle. She went to the hairdresser every Thursday for all of the 12 years I knew her. But now, even through the window, I could see that not only had Mercy's hair gone a long time without being cut, it was now greasy and plastered to her head.

The skin of her face looked gray. I couldn't tell whether that was because I was seeing it through the smudged glass of the facility window or because, as I suspected, her face had not been washed in a long time.

I remembered the long afternoons we had spent trying out each other's Estée Lauder, Chanel, and L'Oréal. Mercy was 20 years older than I was. We'd met at a downtown department store where, for a short time, we had part-time jobs. When we left the jobs, and over the course of 10 years or so, we became good friends, spending countless hours doing what had once been called "girl things": shopping, movies, book groups (mysteries and romances), and exercise classes.

As the years went by, I didn't notice we were getting older, that I was moving from adulthood to middle age, that Mercy was becoming an old woman. I was shocked when her family took her away and put her in what I called "a facility".

That was several years ago. In the beginning, I could visit her whenever I wanted, so I came a few afternoons every week. At first I didn't realize that she seemed to find it hard to concentrate on our conversations. Sometimes she asked me a question that I had just answered. Sometimes she referred to a pleasure that we had shared—a short trip out of town, a shopping expedition at a new and elegant plaza—as if we had just done these things when, in reality, we had done them years before.

The epidemic that was raging in the city made it much more difficult to be mobile or to spend time with anyone in care. Eventually, I was refused entry at the front door of the facility and told that not only was I being kept away at the request of Mercy's grandchildren, I was also being barred because I was non-medical personnel.

Still I went, even though I could do nothing but stand outside Mercy's window and wait for the rare moments when she became visible behind the dusky glass.

I think she knew I was out there most of the time.

Once in a while, she didn't show up. I waited an hour or two with no luck.

But the following day, she would be there before I was and I could tell that, despite the restrictions on our encounters, she was happy to see me and hopeful I would continue to visit, which I most certainly intended to do.

***

We were fine getting on like this for a good three weeks.

But, on the first day of the fourth week, she wasn't at the window at the usual time. Thinking she might have overslept or that medical personnel had detained her, I settled in for a wait.

After an hour, she came to the window, standing so close that her face almost touched the glass.

Before she could even acknowledge she had seen me, she was pulled roughly away. A look of terror suffused her face before she was yanked out of view.

The next day she was back at the window, with her usual welcoming expression on her face. We shared a few moments with our hands up against the glass. Then she stepped back. When she got closer again, she was holding up a small, wrinkled piece of paper. On it were written two words: "Free me."

Before I could react with shock, she was gone. And I knew I would never see her at the window again.

***

I replayed this scene in my mind for hours, and realized there were only two ways to free Mercy. The first was to break through the facility's security and somehow carry her out of there. This was, of course, impossible. Through some sort of subterfuge, I might make my way past the armed hospital guards, the provincial police and the city cops, all of whom were standing vigilant at the entrance. But getting past them carrying a patient was an idea too ridiculous to contemplate.

So I was left with only one other option. I don't know why I didn't hesitate to consider this desperate alternative, but I didn't.

It would require the same trickery to get past the security forces.

Free me.

At first this seemed impossible. Security was as tight at the back of the hospital as it was anywhere else. I walked around the outside of the building, looking for an opening that could be breached. Just as I was about to give up, a huge garbage truck arrived and began to scoop up piles of toxic refuse.

Rubber gloves, masks, gowns, face shields...

So, wearing a double mask, gloves, plastic shoe covers, and a full-length robe, I entered through a rear doorway. Nobody stopped me.

I made my way along the ground floor. Every room contained at least two beds and every bed held an elderly patient who was strapped down with a ventilator covering his or her face.

The sound of assisted breathing filled the air as though each bed, each patient, were an instrument playing in a morbid orchestra.

It seemed to take me forever to find Mercy, and when I did, she was lying still, her eyes closed, her lungs desperately sucking in the fetid air of her room. Or so it seemed. In fact, she was breathing the fake fresh air of the machine.

133

Her face was too covered up for me to discern any expression on it, and she was so still that I held my own breath to be sure I was hearing hers.

On the bed beside her lay the rumpled note: *Free me.*

I stared at her face. It was as though all the years of our friendship folded into one moment, and in that moment, I knew that I had to do the one thing that she would have wanted me to do.

I leaned down and kissed her forehead. She did not stir.

I heard voices in the hall outside the room. I was prepared to pretend I was a nurse, but the voices faded and it wasn't necessary to do anything but follow the wires leading from the ventilator to the power bar on the floor.

I yanked the plug.

I was afraid the machine might have an emergency power supply. I waited, holding my breath.

At first, nothing happened.

Then everything went silent. Mercy's breathing stopped.

I made my way to the elevator. When I arrived at the first floor, I headed for a side door and tore off my disguise. I threw it into a toxic waste bin before security could spot me.

Of course, they were not nearly as concerned about someone getting away from the hospital as they had been about someone getting in.

Then I went home to wait for the inevitable. How long, I wondered would it take before I developed a sore throat, a cough and a fever, and had difficulty drawing my breath….

SOMETIMES MIRACLES HAPPEN

Steve Shrott

Steve Shrott is an internationally published award-winning writer. His credits include Sherlock Holmes Mystery Magazine, Mystery Weekly, *and* Black Cat Mystery Magazine. *Steve's story "The House" appears in Flame Tree Press's crime anthology.*

His humorous tale, "Good Times", was inducted into The National Museum of Dentistry. Steve has also had two humorous mystery novels published: Audition for Death *and* Dead Men Don't Get Married.

Martin shuffled into Benito's Bar, his face white as a bone, his breathing labored. He sat down at a back table, and leaned against the chair as if waiting for the last rites.

A few moments later, Carl, a stocky man wearing a Fedora joined him.

"Hey, Marty, how's it hanging?"

Martin propped himself up in his chair. "Not good."

Carl examined Martin's emaciated figure as if it were a turkey carcass hanging in a poultry plant. "You got that right, bud."

The waitress took their drink orders. A few moments later, she brought Carl a beer and Martin a glass of water.

Carl chugged down most of his drink, then wiped his mouth with his hand. Martin sipped his water as if it were a rare delicacy.

"When you first told me you were sick, I thought you meant a cold or flu. I didn't get that it was something much worse."

Sweat trickled down Martin's forehead. He took out his handkerchief and wiped it away.

"I remember you in your heyday, Marty. Always full of vigor. You never sat down at the tables, you were always moving. One minute you were playing craps, the next you were betting on the nags."

"Things have deteriorated."

Carl finished his beer, then slapped the bottle on the table. "Did you bring the money?"

Martin's shaky hand reached into his pocket and pulled out a brown envelope. "There's 25 grand here. The rest when you have it."

Carl grabbed the envelope and stuffed it into his pocket as if it were a small animal that was trying to escape.

"Don't you want to count it?"

"I trust you. Besides, I think you know what would happen if you tried to screw me. Right?"

Martin stared into Carl's cold green eyes and nodded. He stood up, his body shivering and headed toward the door.

He stopped for a moment, then turned back to Carl. "Remember, it's gotta be a perfect match."

Carl rolled his eyes. "I'm a professional for Christ's sake. I'll contact you in two days."

Martin stumbled out of the bar and collapsed into the waiting cab.

The cabbie tried to engage him in conversation about the weather, and how politicians were all scammers, but Martin didn't have the strength to speak. His thoughts were all about how strange it was that he had someone like Carl in his life. After all he, Martin, was a bank manager, and Carl, well, he was something else entirely.

He had first met him while gambling at Caesar's Palace in Atlantic City. Martin had lost 80 grand and was in a deep funk. He had made a terrible mistake and "borrowed" the money from the bank. He worried he'd go to jail if he didn't replace it before the big bosses found out.

Martin had been drinking that day at the casino, which explained why he told all this to the man sitting beside him. That man was Carl. He offered to lend Martin the funds at a high interest rate.

A week later, Martin discovered what he should have known at the outset, that Carl was a mobster. And, more important, he learned that not paying him back on time could result in losing a finger, a toe, or even his life.

Martin somehow scraped the money together, and gave it to Carl before he lost any appendages or ended up with a toe tag. When he started getting sicker, he knew there was only one person to call.

When the cab arrived at the tall glass-and-brick building, he paid the driver, then ambled up the cement pathway, stopping every few moments to marshal his strength. He entered the medical center and headed down what seemed to him to be a never-ending hallway.

Nurse Appleby with her humorless smile took Martin directly to the doctor's office.

There he waited, along with his depressing thoughts. A few moments later, Dr. Hastings, a white-haired physician, entered the room. After the pleasantries, he had Martin lie down, shirtless, on the examining table. "How are you feeling?"

Martin shook his head.

Hastings probed and prodded him. Then he told Martin to get dressed and sit down while he took a seat behind a big oak desk.

"I have one question for you, Martin. Why the hell did you stop dialysis?"

Martin inhaled a long deep breath. "I just couldn't hack it anymore, Doc. The cramps, constant itching, nausea. It was all too much." He shook his head as if he were trying to shake the disease out of his body.

Hastings took a moment to reply. Then he stood up and stepped toward Martin. "I don't believe in authoritative medicine where the physician demands the patient do this or that. But my strongest feeling is that you need to get back on dialysis pronto. Look at yourself. You're a shell of what you were. You only have one kidney now and it's not working well."

"What if I could get another kidney?"

The doctor's eyes snapped open as if he had touched a live power line. "Get a kidney? Martin, there's a huge shortage of donors right now, and you're way down on the list."

Martin looked up at him, a weak smile forming on his lips. "Sometimes miracles happen, Doc."

Hastings grimaced, shook his head. "You can't live in a dream world hoping that some miracle will occur and you'll get a transplant by Tuesday. I'd suggest you make the right decision before it's too late."

Martin left the office, not surprised by the doctor's comments, and headed home, where he had a long nap.

When he awoke, he felt refreshed and more optimistic than he'd been in a while. He told himself it was all going to work out.

***

Three days later, Martin still hadn't heard from Carl. He called him, enraged. "What the hell's going on? You said two days."

"Sorry, bud, these things take time. Having trouble finding what we need."

"My life's in the balance, jerk."

There was a pause on the line, then Carl spoke slowly, carefully articulating each word. "Jerk? Did you just call me a jerk?"

"Yeah, I did. You told me you'd have it in two days. And now its three days, jerk."

"You know, I've taken people out for saying less."

"I don't care. Just get me my damn kidney."

"Fine, you'll have it tomorrow. I'll come to your place. Have the rest of the cash."

Martin blew out air as he hung up, looking forward to the next day.

The following morning, Martin awoke with chills and a stabbing pain in his chest and back. He struggled to get out of bed. And when he did, he fell to the ground, and blacked out.

When he awoke hours later, he was drained. He tried to get off the floor, but he didn't have the energy.

He heard a knock at the door and struggled again to rise. He couldn't, so he crawled along the floor. Panting, he reached up to the knob and pulled the door open.

Carl stood there like a king, staring down at his lowly servant. He held a red plastic container in his hand. "What are you doing on the ground?"

"I fell."

Carl didn't react. "Where's the rest of the cash?"

Martin struggled to get the words out. "Is it a...a...match?"

"Yeah, yeah, it's a match."

"Can...I see it?"

Exasperated, Carl snapped open the container. Martin saw the kidney, and silently thanked God. He pointed to the envelope on his desk. Carl grabbed the money, then sat the container onto the floor, slid it over to Martin, who clutched it with the steely grip of a drowning man being thrown a life preserver.

"See you later, jerk." Carl slammed the door.

Martin held the container for a moment. Then he carefully placed it onto the ground and called 911. "I...need...help."

Then he collapsed

***

"How are you feeling?" Dr. Hastings asked as Martin awoke. "You're in the hospital."

138

"The hospital?" In his hazy state, Martin couldn't comprehend what the doctor was saying. He looked around the small room and at the bed he was on.

"Yes. Remember you called the ambulance to bring you here?"

Martin now saw all the tubes connected to his body and the catheter in his arm from the IV drip. "Yeah, kinda."

"Bad news, your heart has been compromised by the toxicity of…"

Martin waved his hands around wildly. "Did you put in the kidney?"

The doctor's face turned solemn. Then he slowly shook his head. "No."

Martin's eyes opened wide. "Why the hell not? It's a match, right?"

The doctor took a deep breath. "Yes, it's a match."

Martin breathed a sigh of relief. "Doc, I know how you feel about me buying a kidney. But screw the morals. You said yourself, I was doomed without it. Put it in...please, please."

The doctor swallowed hard and looked Martin in the eye. "I'm afraid there's an issue."

"What? You said it was a match."

"Turn on your side."

As Martin forced himself to move, the doctor grabbed a mirror from the table. He held it up so Martin could see his own back.

Martin's brow crinkled. "What are all those scars, Doc? I don't remember getting them."

"The thing is, that kidney in the container is a match because," he paused and took a deep breath, "it's yours."

Martin barely heard him as he fell into his final sleep.

Ω

THE BRIDGE CASE

Susan Bowman

Susan Bowman enjoys writing, baking and playing with her five grandkids. Living in the Midlands in England means she has good access to theatres, the opera and ballet. She used to work in a medical laboratory and later trained as a counsellor so she could volunteer at drop-in centers and for refuges.

Susan earned a degree in creative writing, philosophy and psychology later in life. She has just finished editing her first novel.

Transcript of a statement by Susan Brown. 31st March, 2020.
Those present: DC Joanne Edwards; DS David Smith; Mrs. Susan Brown.

DS. SMITH: Please tell us what you remember about the events of 26th March.

S. BROWN: It's very hard to know where to begin.

DS. SMITH: Begin at the beginning.

S. BROWN: That's easy for you to say, but I'm not sure where the beginning is.

Sheila has been acting strangely recently. She gets things confused—we laugh and say it's an age thing. What do they call it? "Senior moments."

Well, Sheila has been getting a lot of those—oh dear, *did* get a lot of those. She went ballistic recently when I put smoked salmon on the sandwiches.

Anyway, by the time I got there an almighty row was going on. I've no idea how long they had been rowing, but they had got themselves really worked up. Vanessa was screaming at Sheila. She said, "You dried up, miserable cow! No wonder he's not interested in you. You've become scrawny and scruffy." And Sheila said, "You're about as attractive as …" I couldn't believe my ears.

Vanessa and Sheila had been best mates since…well, since school. They were very close. They did lots of stuff together, even went on holidays. So then, just as I walked into the room, Sheila yelled, "If you weren't such a tart and laid it on a plate for him, he wouldn't have looked twice at you." She didn't even notice me come into the room. She was shouting all sorts of malicious stuff at Vanessa. She said, "You walk around with your tits hanging out and your skirts much too high."

Oh, yes, and then she said, "You think nothing of stealing somebody else's husband just because you couldn't keep yours happy."

Well, it was obvious Sheila had gone too far. Vanessa was furious. She picked something up from the sideboard and flung it full force at Sheila. Oh my God, the next thing I remember, we—me, Vanessa and Barb—were standing over Sheila and she was bleeding. It was like time stood still; slow-motion, like…you know when people say their lives flashed before them? Well, it was like that.

Barb said, "Jeez, Sue, call for an ambulance. Hurry!"

***

I read the statement for the second time and felt pretty sure we had a case. Vanessa Jones had acted with malice; she had thrown a large, heavy object at someone she was having a flaming row with. Yes, she was provoked, but that's no defense. She intended to harm the victim.

I'd been with the Crown prosecution service for eight years, and I'd been called in on this case. There seemed to be little evidence for a murder charge. It looked like involuntary manslaughter, but I half-expected the coroner to report it as an accident. Still, I only had a copy of the one statement, and I needed to get my hands on the others. And I needed time to do some background research. I would receive some information from the police department. They were keen to get a conviction on their record sheet, that much was obvious by the speed with which they'd contacted us.

I had been invited to witness an interview with Vanessa Jones, the woman at the center of the investigation. Despite her claims of close friendship, she had caused the death of Sheila Brace, or so it seemed.

Vanessa sat in a holding cell. The plain brickwork and cold starkness of the place, the toilet in the corner, and the cold plastic cover on the bench made it feel desolate. She sat still, hadn't moved once in the three hours she'd been there, her head hung low, shoulders slumped, her body language suggesting defeat. Had she realized how much trouble she was in, and did her demeanor implicate her guilt? Or, was she grieving for the loss of a dear friend? The police were holding her for questioning. There'd been no charges yet. She wasn't under arrest and, as always, the police were aware of how long they could hold her without laying charges.

I'd worked with DC Joanne Edwards before, and she extended her hand when I entered the viewing room. DCI Rick Hart, who I knew by sight, smiled and offered me a seat. On the video linkup, we watched as DS Dave Smith introduced himself to Vanessa and her brief, Jon Hilton. I had not worked with Hilton previously.

After reminding Vanessa why she was there, Smith started the tape and quickly got to the point.

"When you threw the ashtray at Mrs. Sheila Brace, did you intend her harm?"

"No, of course I didn't. I love—loved Sheila. She was my best friend, and I didn't throw it at her. I threw it at the bloody wall."

Vanessa Jones appeared to be shocked at the suggestion. She dabbed at her heavily made-up eyes with a tissue and, although she was upset, she pulled herself together quickly. "I didn't hit her with that ashtray."

"You threw the ashtray at the wall?"

The detective scanned the notes in his hand, glanced toward the camera in the corner, then at DC Edwards, and gave an almost imperceptible shrug as if questioning this new information. "So, can you tell me what happened next, Ms. Jones?" he asked.

"I thought you knew. It wasn't that bloody ashtray that got her, it was the mirror on the wall behind her. It was smashed by the ashtray and glass flew everywhere. That's why we didn't know what was wrong with Sheila until we went to help her. But, oh my God, I didn't mean to kill her, you can't think…"

"And what happened next?" the sergeant interrupted.

"Well, as I remember it, nothing really, except it went very quiet and Sheila stopped shouting, and kind of looked startled. Her eyes got really big—wide open as if she was in shock. She stood very still and the color drained from her face. Nobody moved, it was like time stopped. Then she sort of slumped in her seat and fell sideways onto the floor."

"Then what happened, Ms. Jones?"

"I heard someone say, "What the hell?"…and "What happened, is she alright?" and Barbara said, "Bloody hell, Vanessa, what did you do...?'' Then she screamed at Sue to phone for an ambulance. I think Barb was a bit hysterical. She kept walking up and down and repeating, "Oh my God, oh my God.'' We went around the table to where Sheila was lying, and then, oh dear..." Vanessa sobbed quietly into her sodden tissue. "...then we saw the blood."

"Did you realize straightaway what had happened, with the mirror and all?"

"Well, yes, glass was everywhere and a big wedge of it was sticking out of Sheila's back."

DC Edwards offered Vanessa a clean tissue from the box on the table. Vanessa blew loudly into it, sniffed and casually said, "I'm quite used to blood because I was a nurse before I retired but, you know, this was my very dear friend."

Vanessa seemed to drift off in her own thoughts. She jumped when Detective Smith spoke again.

"What exactly did you do to help your friend, Ms. Jones?"

"I saw this huge piece of glass sticking out of her, so I removed it and applied pressure to the wound. I stayed like that until the ambulance came, but it was too late. I could see she was slipping away."

Vanessa lost control then and cried openly until, finally cried out, she took a few shuddering breaths, reached for the tissues and dabbed at her face, which was now red and swollen.

DC Edwards filled a glass with water from a pitcher and handed it to Vanessa, who grasped it tightly and sipped from it. The two detectives looked at each other and DC Edwards gave a nod.

The other detective straightened his shoulders and continued. "What were you and Sheila arguing about that got you both so worked up?"

"She was calling me all sorts of names, being very rude and I was trying to defend myself."

"Yes, I get that, but what started it all, Ms. Jones?"

"She called me a tart and accused me of being easy. She said I paraded my body to attract men. Sheila has always been jealous of me. I was the prettier one when we were young, and boys liked me. Sheila was shy and quiet, and she didn't have many boyfriends. Mind you she did alright with Simon. He's... very nice."

The officers looked at each other again, and DS Smith asked, "Did Sheila accuse you of sleeping with her husband?"

"Yes, she did," replied Vanessa, "among other things."

"And were you sleeping with her husband?" asked DS Smith.

Vanessa appeared surprised by the direct question. "I don't think I want to answer that question," she said, looking at her brief for approval.

Jon Hilton nodded, leaned in toward the tape machine and said, "My client has no further comment."

Dave Smith grinned sideways toward the two-way mirror and told Vanessa Jones, "That's OK, Miss. I don't really think you need to."

A myriad of thoughts crossed my mind as I listened to Vanessa's statement. On one hand, she appeared terribly upset about the loss of her lifelong pal, yet she was calm and unflustered during questioning. This lady was difficult to read. I didn't know what to make of her and was looking forward to the coroner's report. Vanessa Jones was allowed to leave, but instructed to remain close by in case further questions arose.

***

The next morning, I was mulling over the possibilities, catching up with answering e-mails and jotting down a grocery list when Dave Smith called.

"Hi, Dave. What's happening?" I asked.

"Nothing much, Maria. Thought you might be interested. We're about to interview a Mrs. Barbara Trent. She's the third witness in the Bridge case."

I certainly was interested, and I told Dave I wouldn't miss it.

"Hopefully we'll get a fuller picture from this woman," he said.

I thanked him and hung up. Dave Smith and DCI Nick Hart hoped this witness would fill in the blanks as to what had taken place at Barbara Trent's house on the afternoon of 26th March. Both Dave and Nick were in the interview room when I got there.

I was alone in the viewing room. Barbara was facing the mirror and I could see her well. She was a mousy woman. Her hair was salt and pepper, she wore a gray corduroy skirt and her voluminous cardigan was also gray. She had neglected her appearance for a long time and it showed. But I did notice her beautiful blue eyes, bright and clear, almost too lovely for a woman otherwise so dowdy and of a "certain age," which I guessed to be between 55 and 60.

She was nervous, clearly unused to being in a police station. She shuffled in her seat uncomfortably and constantly wrung her hands. When asked to give her name and address, she cleared her throat and spoke in a timid voice. DS Smith clicked the tape into life and began.

"Could you tell us why you and three other women were gathered in your dining room on the 26th, Ms. Trent?"

"Yes, yes of course. We were about to play bridge," she answered.

"And was this a regular arrangement?"

"Yes it was. We played bridge roughly twice a month, but we took it in turns to host."

"I see, and it was your turn on the 26th?"

"That's right. We meet, chat, have a spot of lunch, and then play cards, although these days we seem to spend more time chatting and less playing cards. Sheila was finding it difficult to concentrate lately. She seemed vacant, perhaps unwell? We'd often only play one rubber."

"Do you remember, Ms. Trent, what Vanessa and Sheila were arguing about? Did you hear all of the argument?"

"I'm afraid I did. Sheila was accusing Vanessa of sleeping with her husband, Simon. We had got used to Sheila's rantings lately, and we expected the row to fizzle out. We all knew that Vanessa liked the men, but it was outrageous to accuse her of being involved with Simon. She was denying it, of course, but the row escalated quickly and became a horrible slanging match."

Barbara leaned in to the table as she almost whispered, "And then, out of nowhere, Vanessa reached for the heavy ashtray that I kept on the sideboard and she threw it with such force I thought it might kill Sheila if it hit her."

"She was very angry then?"

"Oh, yes. I don't think I've ever seen her so angry, but so was Sheila. She said, "I know it's true, Vanessa, he told me everything." And that's when she called Vanessa a trollop and said that she ought to act her age and leave other peoples' husbands alone."

"Do you believe that she was trying to hit the victim with the ashtray?"

"I really couldn't say...I can't imagine...I just don't know."

"And later, when you discovered what had happened, did you think that Ms. Jones was trying to save Sheila before the ambulance arrived? Did it seem to you that she was doing the right thing by her?"

"Well, oh, I see what you mean. I thought so. She was a nurse, after all, and so you'd expect that she'd know what to do, and they were very close. They did everything together, loved each other, but I have wondered since...why didn't she try to resuscitate Sheila? Then again, it was all very sudden and unexpected. Vanessa just sat there with Sheila's head on her lap, rocking to and fro. She was sobbing, I remember, not making a sound but big fat tears fell from her face onto Sheila's. And when the paramedics arrived, they had to pull her away so that they could see to Sheila."

It seemed that DS Smith and I were thinking along the same lines. Surely a nurse, and she had only retired some seven years ago, would know that one shouldn't remove anything from a wound until the patient is delivered to hospital, as the wound would likely bleed out. What I needed to think about was this: did Vanessa act appropriately? Had she really tried to save Vanessa and, if she hadn't, what did that suggest? Surely a trained medic would know not to remove the fragment of glass from the wound, but even if she had forgotten, why did she not practice CPR on Sheila?

She didn't even put her friend into the recovery position, check her airway or cover her as she waited for the ambulance. Also, if Vanessa had really tried to stop the bleeding, she would have turned Sheila onto her front in order to apply enough pressure to the wound. She would surely have called for towels or cloths to stop the bleeding.

Oversight or malice? I wondered.

I woke early the next morning. The sun was bright, and it cast beautiful patterns of light around the bedroom as the rays bounced off a crystal vase on the windowsill. I was thinking about getting out of bed when my phone rang. It was DS Dave Smith.

"Good morning, Maria. Hope I didn't disturb you," he said.

"No, not at all. I was just about to make coffee."

"I have news for you. The coroner just called, and he's ordered a post mortem. Oh, and I spoke to Simon Brace yesterday. He's a smarmy git, obviously thinks the case has nothing to do with him. I don't think he even knew what the women were arguing about, clearly not grieving—told me the marriage was long dead."

"OK, but did you ask him about the affair?"

"Asked him outright, got a straight answer. He told me they'd been at it for years, casual like. He said he'd no intention of leaving his wife. Just enjoying a bit on the side. And, get this, Sheila had been suspicious and tackled him about it just last weekend. He, of course, denied it.

"So, there you are, Maria, but it doesn't really help us a lot with the case. It all hangs on the coroner really, and the post mortem results. Should hear something in a couple of days, and then we can decide which way to jump."

"OK, thanks for letting me know."

"No probs. I'll leave you to get your coffee. I'll let you know when the coroner's done."

I was surprised about the post mortem request. It was pretty obvious to us all what had killed the victim, but I guessed the coroner needed to know exactly how the glass had caused her death. Perhaps, like Dave and me, he wondered if Vanessa could have saved her, and whether removing the glass had actually caused her demise.

It was raining heavily on Monday morning as I ran from the car to the front door of the station and almost collided with Joanne Edwards. The tall, dark-haired detective constable informed me that Dave had received a call from the coroner at the crack of dawn telling him the report was complete, and that the PM had thrown up some surprises. Shaking our coats and brollies free from rain water, we stepped into the lift.

"The DS called this morning and asked me to meet him at the coroner's office. He's gone back to question Simon Brace, Sheila's husband," she told me.

"I'm intrigued, Jo, tell…"

"Let's wait for the boss, but you can read the report yourself while we do," she said.

That's exactly what I did as I waited for Dave to return. Joanne had not exaggerated—the PM did indeed prove interesting.

About an hour later, DS Smith greeted me with a warm hug as he joined me in his office. He seemed cheerful as he sat down at his desk, called through for some coffee and looked at me.

"Well?" he asked. "Bit of a turn up. Puts a different spin on things, eh?"

"I have to say it took me by surprise," I replied.

We were referring to the report from the pathologist, which stated that Sheila Brace had died from "blood loss following the incision of a glass shard of about seven inches in length into the renal artery causing shock and loss of kidney function." The surprise element was that the victim was suffering from a malignant brain tumor, which was, according to the report, terminal and metastasized to several areas of the body. Sheila Brace had but a short time to live.

Dave had naturally requested an interview with Simon, Sheila's widower, to gauge whether he was aware of her condition. It appeared that he was not, and, according to Dave, he exhibited some vestige of humanity and sorrow at the news. Indeed, he collapsed in shock and was taken by ambulance to the hospital complaining of chest pains. It seemed that Sheila had not told her husband about her illness and, although genuinely saddened by the revelation, we would never know if the knowledge might have changed his relationship with his wife.

"I want to get Vanessa Jones back in. Let's find out what she knew," Dave said. "I've got a funny feeling that she won't be surprised at the news."

DS Smith sent a car to collect Vanessa Jones, and she was in the interview room within the hour. She waived the right to counsel and the interview began.

"For the purpose of the tape, those present are DC Edwards and DS Smith, Ms. Vanessa Jones, and Miss Maria Cosenza for the Crown."

The detective leaned across the table, looked straight into Vanessa's eyes and asked, "Were you aware, Vanessa, that Sheila was dying from Glioblastoma Multiform, a malignant tumor in the brain?"

Vanessa remained composed as she replied, "Of course I knew, Sergeant. I was her best friend, practically her only friend in the whole world. I was the one who took her to the hospital the day she learned her diagnosis. I was the one who was with her when she was told that she had weeks to live, and I was the one who helped her to keep her condition secret, especially from Simon."

"Why did she want to keep her illness from people?"

"She thought they would try to make her have treatment, and she knew treatment was futile. She was dying and she wanted, she needed to die with dignity. The only thing she was worried about was the pain. As her tumor grew, the cancer spread. She had it throughout her body. She did a great job of keeping her secret. People noticed that she sometimes acted strangely, but they put it down to her age. "Let them think I have Alzheimer's, Van," she said, "but don't let them fuss.""

"And so we kept her secret, and she made me promise to help her at the end, with me being a nurse."

"But the end came sooner than either of you expected," said Joanne.

"Yes, it did, and it was a blessing. Dying from blood loss is very peaceful, euphoric even; there was no pain, no fear, just a beautiful calm."

"Did Sheila say anything to you, Vanessa, before she died?"

"Yes, she did. She said 'Thank you.'"

***

The coroner called for an inquest because, although the post mortem showed that Sheila died from shock due to blood loss and trauma to her body, he was not confident enough to hang his hat on a cause of death any more than the police or the CPS were. A date was set for the inquest, and those concerned got on with other cases while waiting to give evidence.

I was still troubled by Vanessa's story. Given the fact that she had practically confessed to allowing—even aiding—Sheila to bleed to death, I still wasn't convinced of her motive. On the surface, her action appeared to be a kind gesture to let her friend slip away peacefully. Yet, the law was there to ensure that people do not act as God, and that was the mainstay of my evidence to the judge. Even so, Vanessa could not have anticipated the exceptional sequence of events that had led to Sheila's death. Was she in some way responsible?

Sheila Brace's body was released by the coroner for burial, and the family set a date. The funeral was a quiet affair, close family, few friends and Vanessa seemed genuinely distraught, while Simon did a sterling job of comforting her.

If only he had comforted his wife that much, I thought.

I watched from the edge of the churchyard before accepting that there was little reason for my remaining suspicions of Vanessa and Simon.

***

A few weeks later, I received an e-mail from the coroner to inform me that the inquest had thoroughly investigated the Bridge Case. The transcript of the hearing was attached, and I opened it eagerly.

The post mortem report showed that the injury to Sheila's body was the reason she had died, and that her cancer had nothing to do with it. Thus, the evidence of the three female witnesses was paramount in ascertaining how the victim had received said injury. Vanessa had faced a few probing questions concerning her relationship with Sheila and Simon Brace, who she described as "very close friends."

The judge was interested in Sheila's medical condition too. Although he referred to it as "a terrible situation," he asserted that it was not relevant to the case. Supported by the evidence of the other witnesses, Vanessa's explanation of how she had thrown the ashtray at the wall was accepted.

In summing up, the judge expressed his sympathy to the family. He added that he would have been satisfied with a verdict of accidental death; however, on reflection, he said, "The act of throwing the heavy object was not an accident. It was a considered action." The entire courtroom held its breath as he continued. "But the ashtray did not kill the victim. It was, as we now know, a shard of broken glass that did the damage, and I do not believe anyone could have anticipated what happened."

The judge returned a verdict of death by misadventure. There was nothing more for me to do but officially withdraw from the case and the investigation was closed.

***

It was a couple of months later, while sharing a nice bottle of house red with Dave Smith, that I noticed them. They sat in a booth in a quiet corner of the bar, and Simon had his hand a fair way up Vanessa's thigh. He was whispering sweet nothings into her ear as she giggled seductively. I wanted to puke. I was overwhelmed by anger and a sense that I had been part of the injustice, which now saw Vanessa smooching in the corner of a bar with the husband of her late "very dear friend."

"You know what?" Dave said. "We have to write this one off, Maria. You were never going to get a prosecution out of this case. For whatever reason, Vanessa Jones allowed her friend to die. You need to remember the outcome for Sheila Brace—a peaceful and pain-free death."

Dave was right, of course, and it was that thought that helped me sleep at night.

Ω

A PILL A DAY KEEPS THE BLUES AWAY

Elizabeth Hosang

Elizabeth Hosang is a computer engineer by day and author by night. Her short stories have appeared in over a dozen anthologies, including all three editions of The Whole She-Bang, *published by Toronto Sisters in Crime. One of her two contributions to* The Whole She-Bang 3 *was a finalist for the 2017 Arthur Ellis award for Crime Writing. She has been published in* The Killer Wore Cranberry 3 *and* Moon Shot: Murder and Mayhem on the Edge of Space *for Untreed Reads, as well as contributing a story to* Alice Unbound: Beyond Wonderland *for Exile Editions.*

A loud thump jerked Andrea out of a restless sleep. She tossed aside her comforter and dashed down the stairs two at a time. Flicking on the light, she saw her mother, Jean, sprawled face-down on the floor. Her crutches lay on either side of her, and the kitchen table was shoved to one side.

"What happened?" Andrea asked, crouching down.

"There was someone at the back door," Jean said as she rolled over and pushed herself into a sitting position on the edge of the sunken family room. The twisted sheets on the hide-a-bed bore witness to a restless night.

"Let me help you," Andrea said, putting her hands behind her mother's shoulders to prop her up.

Jean pushed her daughter's hands away. "I can do it myself," she said curtly.

Andrea sat back and curled her hands into fists to keep from reaching out. "Are you hurt?"

"No more so than I was when I went to bed," Jean insisted.

Andrea examined the bandage covering the stump below her mother's right knee for bloodstains. "Did you land on your leg?"

"No," Jean said, but she raised her hand to her forehead where a long purple mark was swelling, wincing as she touched it.

"You aren't supposed to get out of bed without help," Andrea said, going to the refrigerator for an ice pack. She grabbed a clean dish towel from a drawer and wrapped it around the cold plastic pack. "Here," she said, thrusting it in front of her mother's face.

"I told you, there was someone at the patio door. I didn't have time to call for backup."

"I'm not backup, Mom," Andrea said, frustration making her voice crack and bringing tears to her eyes. "And you aren't on duty, you're on sick leave. It's only been three weeks since the amputation. You can't hop up out of bed every time a raccoon goes digging through the garbage cans."

"It wasn't a raccoon," Jean insisted. "I've been a police officer for 20 years. I lost my foot, not my mind."

"I didn't say you were crazy," Andrea snapped, stomping across the kitchen. She clenched her fists again, counted to ten, and relaxed her hands before returning to sit on the floor next to her mother. "I know this is hard. But you're still in pain, you're on new medications, and you're sleeping on a 10-year-old hide-a-bed where you can feel every wire. You said yourself you've been having wild dreams. If you'd answered a call and someone in your condition said she'd heard a suspicious noise, what would you tell her?"

Jean looked away and pressed the towel against her forehead, her lips clamped tightly. "I'd say she'd probably imagined it. But I'd still check the yard."

"I'll check the yard tomorrow, I promise," Andrea said. "Unless you want me to go out there right now in my pajamas with nothing but a flashlight?"

Her mother didn't say anything, but closed her eyes and leaned into the towel.

"Let me help you back into bed. I'll check the backyard tomorrow, I promise."

***

The next morning Andrea opened the front door to a large man in nursing scrubs, wearing an identification badge from the home care agency and a smile that was almost as big as he was. "Good morning, Steve," Andrea said as she ushered him into the house. He'd told her during his first visit that he had been a semi-pro offensive lineman before changing careers, and she believed him.

The top of her head only came to his shoulder, and his arm was bigger around than her thigh.

"Good morning," Steve replied as he slipped his shoes off and rubbed gel sanitizer onto his hands. "How's she doing?"

"She can hear you," Jean called from the family room.

"She fell out of bed last night," Andrea said. She took a cardboard box from the hall closet and followed him into the family room, where her mother was stretched out on the hide-a-bed. Andrea set the box on the kitchen table and pulled out a pocket knife to cut away the tape sealing the box. Opening it, she pulled out the inventory sheet from the medical supply company that itemized this week's delivery of bandages, medical tape and other items.

"I didn't fall," Jean said. "I got up to investigate a possible intruder."

"She heard a noise," Andrea said, resisting the urge to say "alleged".

"Well, I'm sure that he ran away as soon as he realized whose house this was," Steve said. He took the box from Andrea and pulled out rubber gloves, a plastic tray, and a bottle of saline.

Jean made a "harrumph" noise, but she uncrossed her arms and sat up to give him better access as he set about cleaning the incision and changing the dressing on her stump.

Andrea took advantage of the nurse's presence to slip upstairs and brush her teeth. It had been six weeks since the suspect in a string of robberies had rushed up from his mother's basement wielding a shotgun. Detective Robert Jansen, Jean's partner, had been close enough to grab for the gun and redirect it from her chest, but the blast had caught her right foot and shin. The damage to the bones and ligaments had been too severe to repair, or even fuse. Jean was pragmatic enough to accept that amputation and a prosthetic were her best option for walking again, at least in theory. In practice, it was hard. She was every inch a cop: fierce, independent, and stubborn. Andrea could count on one hand the number of times she'd seen her mother ask for help. Now she needed a wheelchair or crutches to get around the house. Andrea was struggling to find the right balance between offering assistance when it was needed, and not making her mother feel helpless.

After brushing her teeth, Andrea went to her childhood bedroom to change clothes and make her bed. Jean couldn't get up the stairs, but she would still expect her daughter to maintain the standards she'd been raised with. At some point she sat down, and a wave of exhaustion hit her. She only came out of her reverie when she heard Steve laugh. With a sigh she pulled her hair back into a ponytail and headed downstairs.

"Everything OK?" she asked. Steve was standing at the kitchen table, sorting through the box of medical supplies.

"No problem," he replied. "Just checking out what Gary ordered."

"If you can't find what you're looking for, it might be in one of the other boxes." Andrea went into the dining room and came back with two small cardboard boxes with the same labels as the one on the table. She set them down and flipped them open, pulling out the inventory sheets. "Do we really need a little box of supplies every week? Wouldn't it be easier to send one large box?"

"It depends on what your mother needs," Steve replied. "How long have you been home from the hospital?"

"Four weeks," Jean said. She adjusted the pillow under her right knee, carefully positioning the stump so it was not resting on the mattress.

"Four weeks, four boxes," Steve muttered. "Well, I can at least sort them out for you." He pulled packages out of the newest box, sorting them into piles: sterile dressings, medical tape, saline bottles, scissors in sterile packaging. Andrea opened the box closest to her and sorted the contents into the same piles.

"How is Gary?" Jean asked. "All the agency said was that he was unavailable. Is he sick?"

"What's the matter?" Steve asked. "Tired of me already?"

"Not at all," Andrea said, placing a thick stack of dressings on the table. "We were just surprised by the change. With the post-COVID-19 protocols, we thought the agency was trying to send the same nurse all the time. Gary's been coming since Mom came home from the hospital."

"That's the goal," Steve replied. "Unfortunately, Gary was in a car crash. He's still in the hospital, so we've had to divide his patients among the rest of the staff." He pulled a brown plastic bottle with a white label out of the box he was working on.

"What's that?" Andrea asked.

"Vitamin D," Steve replied, turning the bottle over in his gloved hands. He shook it and they heard the rattle of pills.

Andrea lifted a piece of paper off the table. "There aren't any vitamins listed on the inventory sheet."

"The medical supply company doesn't deliver vitamins," Steve said.

"Let me see that," Jean said. She reached for her crutches. "And give me a pair of gloves."

"Don't get up," Andrea said, as Steve held out a sealed package of silicon gloves like the ones he was wearing. Andrea sighed as her mother rose from the hide-a-bed and maneuvered herself onto one of the kitchen chairs.

Jean pulled on the gloves and took the bottle from Steve. "It's a standard commercial brand of vitamins, but there's no safety seal around the bottle." She screwed off the cap and looked inside, then shook several pale green pills into her hand. Steve and Andrea leaned closer. The pills in Jean's hand had the number "80" stamped into them.

"OxyContin," Jean said.

***

Twenty minutes later, Robert, Jean's partner, arrived and joined them at the kitchen table, where he examined the pill bottle.

"Any chance the doctor ordered these?" Robert asked, as he poured some of the pills into his gloved hand.

"No way," Steve said. "Doctors don't write prescriptions for vitamins, and the medical supply company doesn't deliver prescription drugs."

Robert tipped the pills back into the bottle and peered into it. "There's maybe four hundred pills, from the looks of it." He screwed the lid back on and placed the bottle in a bag marked Evidence. "Are there any bottles in the other boxes?"

"No," Andrea said, "but they were already opened."

"Opened by my previous nurse, Gary," Jean said. She pulled one of the boxes closer to her and pointed to it. "That's my name and address on the label, so it wasn't delivered here by mistake. But see that small green circle in the bottom left corner? It looks like it was applied after the label was printed. It's on the label of two of the other boxes as well, but not on the first box I received."

"You didn't order these?" Robert asked Steve.

"No, I just started coming this week. Gary was originally assigned to Jean." The big nurse was frowning at the table, where the boxes and their contents were spread. "It did seem odd that Jean was getting a delivery every week. Normally we only order supplies when we start running out. There are enough bandages here to supply a small army."

"Why no green dot on the first box?" Robert asked, pulling it toward him.

"Because it arrived before Gary did," Jean said. She looked to Steve for confirmation, but it was Andrea who replied.

"The first box arrived two days after the surgery, while Mom was still in the hospital. I had just arrived home after visiting her, and I didn't know what to do with it."

"The company doesn't assign nurses to patients until they get word from the hospital that the patient is at home," Steve said. "But the supplies are ordered once the surgery is complete. They want to be sure that the home nurse has everything needed."

"You don't bring the bandages and gloves with you from house to house?" Robert asked.

"No way. We'd have to drive around in a van," Steve explained. "Every patient needs different supplies. Jean needs bandages so I can change her dressing. Cancer patients don't need bandages, but they do need supplies to clean their injection ports. Plus there's the possibility of cross-contamination. We didn't take supplies from house to house before COVID-19. We sure don't do it now."

"So the boxes with the dots only started showing up after Gary was assigned to Jean," Robert said. He pulled out a notebook and started writing. "How well do you know Gary?" he asked Steve.

"Well enough to say hello, but he's just a co-worker. I've never heard any complaints about him."

"He seemed nice enough. Pleasant to talk to, competent at his job. He was good with Mom," Andrea said, then winced.

"I'm not a dementia patient. I don't need to be managed," Jean snapped.

"Sorry, I didn't mean to say that you were. He was just gentle with your injury."

Robert cleared his throat. "So you think someone at the medical supply company is using home deliveries to distribute oxy?"

"Not to the users, but to the pushers," Jean said. "That's too large a shipment to be for just one person. Usually."

"How many home health-care companies are there in the city?" Robert asked.

"Twenty-two," Jean replied. "We counted while we were waiting for you."

"But only one or two companies that distribute medical supplies."

"Just the one," Steve confirmed. "I hope you don't think our company is behind this. Most of the people I work with are professionals."

"Don't worry, Steve," Andrea said. "Mom knows you're too smart to have pulled out the pills in front of her."

"Gary's in hospital?" Robert asked.

"As far as we know, but they won't release details over the phone," Jean said.

"Of course not," Robert said. "You didn't try calling them, did you?" Jean said nothing, but Andrea gave a brief nod. Robert sighed. "OK, partner. I'll see if I can interview the suspect, and let you know what he says."

Andrea escorted the two men to the front door, following them onto the porch and closing the door behind her. After getting Steve's promise not to discuss the drugs with anyone, she waved him goodbye while Robert made a few more notes.

"How is she?" he asked at last.

"She's still Detective Romero. Take no prisoners, show no weakness, don't take no for an answer." She let out a long breath, and her shoulders sagged. "She's counting the days until she can get fitted for a prosthetic and start chasing bad guys again. She's terrified of being moved to an administrative job. She keeps talking about that Olympic sprinter, saying at least he could run like a normal person before he became a criminal. She's even talking about getting a holster built into her prosthetic so she can carry without an ankle holster!"

Robert laughed. "That's actually not a bad idea."

"I think she's still in denial. She keeps talking about all the things she will do when she gets back to normal, but she won't be going back. She has to go forward, to find a different kind of normal, and it's going to take time to get there. Last night, she leaped out of bed because she thought she heard someone at the patio door, trying to break in! That's how she got the bruise on her forehead."

Robert stuck his hands in his pockets and sighed. "I think you're right about her being in denial. She needs to grieve, but it's going to take a while."

"It doesn't help that she managed to have a crime delivered to her doorstep," Andrea grumbled.

Robert laughed again. "Hang in there, kid. I'll drop by in a few days to visit. I can talk shop, run a few cases by her, so she doesn't feel left out."

"Thanks." Andrea smiled weakly, then braced herself before going back inside."

***

That evening Andrea retreated to her bedroom and took a deep breath. Jean had talked investigation strategies all afternoon, calling Robert every half hour with a new suggestion, and e-mailing him constantly. She'd even printed off documents that she wouldn't let her daughter see, citing police confidentiality, before calling

Robert back for more consultations. Andrea wasn't sure if her mother was being helpful or just annoying her partner, but it was the most animated she'd seen her since the shooting. Andrea collapsed onto her bed, hoping her mother would sleep through the night after all of the day's excitement.

A piercing whistle jerked Andrea awake. She was halfway down the stairs before she realized where she was going. A clang and a man's loud cry of pain sent her leaping down the rest of the steps.

"Mom!" Andrea flipped on the light to see her mother leaning on the wall beside the patio doors, one crutch held like a baseball bat, while she eyed the body on the floor. A breeze coming through the open patio door stirred the venetian blinds. The safety bar that braced the sliding door lay on the floor, and the kitchen table had been shoved four feet away from the door.

"How did he get in?" Andrea demanded. "I checked that door myself before I went to bed."

"I moved it," Jean said proudly. "I removed the bar and moved the table over so I'd have room to work." The body on the floor moaned and started to roll over, clutching the back of his head. Jean flipped her crutch around, then jabbed the rounded bottom end between his shoulder blades. "I said don't move," she growled, pressing on the crutch until he put his hands back down. "I knew he'd be back. That was far too much oxy for him to just let it go." Her phone chimed, but Jean just nodded at her daughter. "Get that for me?"

"It's Robert," Andrea said as she picked up the phone. "Hello?"

"What's keeping him?" Jean demanded.

"Andrea? I just got a text message from your mother saying someone was at the door."

"Yep, she's got him pinned," Andrea said. "You can send in the backup."

***

An hour later uniformed police officers finally hauled the intruder away in handcuffs, and the paramedics packed up their kit after clearing him for a possible concussion.

"So he was the supplier?" Andrea asked.

"Yep. Alberto Petrov," Robert said. "His cousin works for the medical supply company. Turns out they didn't find out about Gary's accident until this week's shipment had been sent. The drug unit has been watching him, but they didn't have anything concrete until tonight."

"Don't you just have him for breaking and entering?" Growing up with a cop mother, Andrea knew a thing or two about evidence.

"Nope, caught him red-handed," her mother crowed. She pointed to the medical supply box on the kitchen counter. "He went straight for the box, cut it open, and pulled out the vitamin bottle."

"I thought Robert took the pills and the supply boxes with him," Andrea said. She looked at the kitchen counter, where there were five cardboard boxes of different shapes and sizes bearing the logo of a popular online store. Only one box was open, its sides covered with brown craft paper hiding the logo, and a large white label on its side. "And where did all these boxes come from?"

Jean's self-satisfied smirk edged into outright smugness. "I put them on the counter as decoys. I also threw in your vitamin D bottle and topped it up with Smarties so it was full. It's a different brand, but in the dark it was close enough. Then I replaced the shipping label with a mock-up of the one from the medical supply company, and threw in some bandages. The box was the right size and shape, and had the right label. It's gonna be pretty hard to explain why he cut open a sealed box of medical supplies and took a bottle of vitamins instead of just stealing all the boxes, unless he was looking for something specific."

"You did all this after I went to bed?" Andrea wanted to know.

"Well, I printed the fake shipping label this afternoon. But I set up all the boxes tonight. And I confirmed with Robert that there was a mobile unit in the area."

"Congratulations, Mom, you solved a crime while on medical leave," Andrea said. "You truly are a super cop. Now if you don't mind, I'm going back to bed. And you owe me a new bottle of vitamins."

Ω

SLEEP, PERCHANCE TO DIE

Blair Keetch

Blair Keetch's short story "A Contrapuntal Duet" was the 2019 Winner for emerging crime writers and was included in the most recent Mesdames of Mayhem anthology, In the Key of Thirteen. *Recently, his short story "Deadly Cargo" was included in the mystery anthology* Heartbreaks & Half-Truths. *Blair is thrilled to again be part of the Carrick Publishing family with his latest story "Sleep, Perchance to Die" included in* A Grave Diagnosis.

Blair is an avid traveler and his favorite places include France, Argentina, Vietnam & Korea. As a result, he can order wine in multiple languages.

Death had no place intruding on that fine February morning.

It was a leap year and the 29th day of the month. And in keeping with the out of ordinary, the weather was unseasonably mild with blue and sunny skies more typical of spring, which was another two months away.

I'd cracked the window to allow some fresh air in, and so I could sing along with Tom Petty.

I parked my SUV and glanced over at Molly, who shivered slightly.

"You cold?"

She looked back at me, her dark eyes immense. Did I detect a glimmer of fear in them? Hard to tell. Mornings are not Molly's strong suit.

"Don't worry." I gave her a reassuring smile. "Everything will be OK."

***

It wasn't OK.

That much was clear from the expression on Dr. Lani's face when she entered the examination room. Usually, some small talk, even mild flirting (to my mind at least), but today she was brisk and businesslike.

"This isn't going to be easy." Dr. Lani was dressed in full battle mode—lab coat and clipboard. Her armor when presenting bad news, I thought. "I wasn't expecting this. But X-rays don't lie." She held up a folder but didn't show me the contents.

Molly had suffered a couple of fainting spells in the past month, but the initial opinion was that they were due to dehydration or a stomach bug.

My mouth was suddenly dry. "Are you sure?"

She looked to be as distraught as I was. "Unfortunately, yes."

"I don't understand," I stammered. I looked helplessly at Molly.

Dr. Lani placed all the X-rays onto a display screen and switched on the light.

I looked at the illuminated slides, but to me they were mostly indecipherable. I glanced at Molly, but she studiously ignored everyone in the room.

"See this?" Dr. Lani pointed at a white spot. "A tumor."

"Could it be benign?" I was clutching at straws.

A reluctant shake of her head. "I've seen this type before. Very aggressive. Plus, her blood work is crazy. Enzymes off the chart."

Unashamed, I let my eyes mist up. "Sorry, I wasn't expecting this."

"Don't be," the doctor said. "She's a wonderful girl."

***

I waited until we were in the parking lot before I lost it. Wracking sobs, tears streamed down my face, and snot ran out of my nose. "I'm sorry, Molly," I gasped. "I promise to be strong."

She looked at me with concern, her luminous eyes radiating nothing but love. I opened the passenger door. "Come on, get in."

She hesitated for a moment, and I realized how low her energy had become. How long had I ignored the signs? She jumped in and settled herself into the seat. I decided not to open the window. I didn't want to risk her getting a cold or anything that would reduce our precious time together.

The music came back on too loud and too uncomfortable. The parking lot was filling up with people dropping off their dogs for grooming or daycare. Life continued in cheerful routines while I felt hollowed out.

***

My initial plan had been to treat myself to a hearty breakfast of steak and eggs, but I'd lost my appetite. So a walk along the boardwalk, followed by a romp at the off-leash park seemed like a good alternative. I was heading south toward the beach when my phone rang.

I switched to hands free, but before I could speak, a raspy male voice demanded, "Do you know what day today is?"

I didn't recognize the voice, but I answered nonetheless. "Tuesday?"

"Correct, but not good enough."

"Leap Year Day."

"And what else?"

My sadness threatened to overwhelm me, and I was tempted to hang up. "I don't know. Something foolish like Blueberry Pie Day, or something more worthwhile, maybe Child Soldier Day."

"It's Rare Disease Day," the voice informed me. "Last day of February every year."

I bit back my exasperation. "How can I help you?"

After what seemed like a long pause, he said, "I need your help. Someone is trying to kill me."

His matter-of-fact tone caught me off guard. "Ah, that leads to dozens upon dozens of questions. I'm free Thursday morning onwards."

A pause followed by violent coughing. "No, no," he sputtered. "Time is of the essence. I need to see you today. In the next hour or two."

I looked at Molly, thinking of my pledge of a long stroll along the boardwalk. But her trusting eyes reflected only forgiveness.

"Fine," I said. "Give me the address."

***

His residence was on a less-traveled section of the Bridle Path, a part of town filled with ritzy mansions. The location held an advantage for me. I was able to stop briefly at nearby Edwards Garden, a large park near the swanky neighborhood.

A large *No Dogs Allowed* sign was prominently displayed by the park entrance, but it was February and there were hardly any visitors, and wasn't Molly entitled to some dying wishes?

After a 10-minute romp in the park, I drove to the Bridle Path, through the open private gates and parked in front of a two-level mansion in an Italian villa style. Likely stunning in Tuscany, but here in wintry Toronto, its temperate beauty looked forlorn.

The neighborhood was posh and exclusive. Drake or some other celebrity might be your neighbor, although most of these homes were owned by wealthy dentists and cosmetic surgeons.

As I climbed out of my car, the double oak doors on the portico swung open to reveal a gaunt figure, dressed in an expensive navy suit and rumpled, baggy white shirt with no tie.

"You made good time, thank you," said the man with the raspy voice. "My mornings are good, but by mid-afternoon the grayness closes in. Earlier and earlier."

He noticed Molly shifting in the front seat and offered her a ghoulish smile. "A dog. How wonderful. The name?"

"Molly." I opened the front car door and Molly needed no incentive to jump out.

He gave her a small bow. "Molly," he said. "I'm Loudon Partridge. Please come in."

We followed him into the house. I mulled over his name. It sounded vaguely familiar, but I came up with no clear connections.

The mid-morning sun poured in through large windows that reached up to the second floor. A marble spiral staircase led us upward.

"Let's go to the library," he whispered. "You can meet the help."

Stepping into the room, I realized that Loudon didn't have help, he had a team. Close to a dozen people milled about, all dressed casually but diverse in their ages and appearances.

One figure, a pert redhead, likely in her early 30s, pulled away from the gathering and approached me, her hand extended. "You must be The Detective." She mimed air quotes. "I'm Andie, The Lawyer. I'll introduce you to everyone in a bit, but in a nutshell, there's The Banker, The Executive Assistant, The Publicist, The Chef, and The Driver, just to name a few. Professor Plum has stepped away for a moment." She gave an ironic smile.

I stared at the ensemble, trying to guess who was who, but she spoke again. "His medical team is having a working coffee break."

"Medical team?" I repeated.

"Do you know what SFI is?" Loudon cut in.

I looked at Molly as if she could answer. "Unfortunately, not," I admitted.

"Don't worry," he said with a sneer. "Neither do most of my doctors." He waved a hand listlessly. "SFI. Sporadic Fatal Insomnia."

"In all fairness, its symptoms mirror a lot of other diseases, and it's very uncommon." A petite woman joined us. "I'm part of the maligned medical team. Phyllis."

I recalled Loudon's comment about Rare Disease Day. "And Loudon has SFI?"

Phyllis nodded. "Yes, and it's infinitesimally rare."

I noticed she had not offered a formal title when introducing herself. That, along with her casual clothes and demeanor, made me wonder. "Are you a doctor?"

She shrugged. "In my homeland of Guatemala, but here I am the lead nursing coordinator."

Loudon had started to rock back and forth in an agitated manner. "It's coming, it's coming," he moaned.

"Fatal Insomnia?" I asked.

"Exceedingly rare," Phyllis repeated. "Maybe a dozen cases each year. Usually hereditary and known as Familial Fatal Insomnia, but there are a few exceptions with no discernable origins classified as Sporadic Fatal Insomnia."

"Thanks to some damned ancestors I've never met, I'm screwed because of some prion deformity. Totally screwed." With a trembling hand, Loudon yanked open a curtain and flinched at the bright sunlight. With his pale skin and drawn features, he was like a vampire—more Nosferatu than Tom Cruise.

Phyllis gently pulled me to one side. "He has good days and bad days. But the bad days now outnumber the good."

"How long…" I started to ask.

"The prognosis for SFI is grim. Typically, 12 to 18 months after initial diagnosis." She answered my next question before I could ask it. "And it's always fatal. No known treatment."

"The initial diagnosis was made in October of the year before last," Andie interjected.

I did the math. Almost 16 months had passed.

"Yes, at first he did far better than expected. But recently, his deterioration has been rapid and typically, once that occurs, the disease accelerates very quickly."

"I know you can't predict exactly," I murmured.

"Six months at the absolute most," Phyllis said. "Even then I'd be surprised."

I winced at her prognosis, and glanced at Loudon to see his reaction. Her voice was at a normal volume, but her words didn't seem to register with him. Instead, he was pointing across the room.

"Get out," he commanded.

I looked to where he was pointing, perplexed. Molly stood on alert, her fur bristling.

"What do you see?" Phyllis asked calmly, while Andie's eyes nervously searched the room.

"That man, that soldier. In the crimson jacket," Loudon exclaimed. "He brought a musket in here!"

Phyllis patted him reassuringly on the arm. "Don't worry. Andie will ask him to leave."

Andie nodded. She went to the patio doors and gestured for someone to step outside. Phyllis turned to me. "Unfortunately, his hallucinations will only worsen. More vivid, more violent."

I looked back at Loudon. He was standing straighter and his features were more relaxed.

"Glad you could see me this afternoon," he said, as if the previous minutes had been erased from his memory. "And glad you brought along the beautiful Molly." It was as if he'd known Molly forever. "I still have my blue-sky moments," he explained.

I seized the opportunity. "Why did you want to see me? I'm not a doctor."

"No, you're a detective," he agreed. "But I don't understand."

"Don't understand?" I carefully repeated.

"Why someone would bother trying to kill me," he said mournfully, "when everyone knows I'll be dead soon."

***

"So, really, what's the point?" Loudon asked.

We'd moved into the conservatory, complete with piano and antique music stand, though they seemed like expensive props.

"It calms him," Phyllis told me. "Music that is. Wine or whiskey makes him drowsy, but never enough to sleep. Medical marijuana makes him irritable."

"Sounds like you've tried everything," I said.

"It doesn't hurt. There's no prescribed treatment except to make the patient as comfortable as possible."

"Hey, I'm still here," Loudon growled, but he was smiling. "So, what you think?"

I ignored his challenging tone and chose my words carefully. "I'm not interested in your disease, I'm interested in finding out who is trying to kill you. And why."

Molly stood and stretched in her downward dog position, and we all watched.

"Twice," he muttered angrily. "Someone has tried to kill me twice."

I looked questioningly at Phyllis. "There have been two incidents," she admitted.

"Incidents?" Loudon growled. "You mean, attempts."

Phyllis continued. "There was a night in January. The snowstorm just after New Year's Day. Mr. Partridge wandered outside and got trapped in a snowbank. Along the road which is usually deserted at that time of night, but an Uber driver had gotten lost and saw him floundering in the snow."

"Almost died," Loudon informed me solemnly.

"Hypothermia had set in," Phyllis agreed. "He wouldn't have survived the night."

I decided to wait till later to ask for a copy of the police report. "And the second time?"

Phyllis gestured toward the other wing of the house. "The indoor pool," she said. "Same thing. He somehow got inside, fell into the water and was flailing about when Lance found him."

"Lance?"

"Damn poor swimmer," Loudon said. "He nearly killed me trying to rescue me. Luckily, The Cook heard the commotion and pulled us both out."

"His driver," Phyllis explained. "Lance had moved a couple of cars to the rear garage and heard some shouting. Went to investigate and found Mr. Partridge half drowned. The Cook also heard the commotion. Luckily, Lance and Sage and The Cook were able to pull him out."

"And who is Sage?"

Phyllis looked surprised. "His daughter."

***

Molly and I became objects of curiosity wherever we went, and the glances thrown our way by members of the household were no longer covert, but rather open and frank.

To my surprise, the youngest of the group approached us. Wearing a black turtleneck under a gray sports jacket, he exuded a mannered air with a 70s vibe. Perhaps he wished to channel a young Steve McQueen.

Molly gave an uncharacteristic growl, and I realized he wasn't as young as I'd thought. He appeared to be in his early 30s, although his face was weathered more than it should have been at that age.

"Lance." He extended his hand. "The Driver."

The individual members of Loudon's team each identified with the role he had assigned to them, and made a habit of announcing themselves with a capital The, as in The Cook, The Lawyer, The Driver. It felt like being on the set of a 70s disaster film filled with semi-celebrities.

"Driver," Loudon sputtered. "Should also be The Gigolo."

Lance had grace enough to look embarrassed, but I sensed an underlying irritation in his countenance.

"Loudon," he said gently, "it was one of your hallucinations."

"I know what I saw. I saw you carrying Sage, naked, your fancy boots clicking down the hallway, taking her to your room to do God only knows what."

I glanced down at his feet and, sure enough, Lance was wearing dark brown Blundstones.

He turned to Phyllis for support. "He's been hallucinating a lot more lately and, for whatever reason, he won't let go of the fantasies involving me."

"Part of his deterioration," she said with a nod. "He's also seen Sgt. Pepper's Band playing in the driveway, and Nazi paratroopers landing in the backyard."

"Ha!" Loudon exclaimed. "I knew they were hallucinations. It wasn't the Beatles, but that damned imitation band with the three brothers."

"I think he means the Bee Gees," whispered Lance, and we all smiled.

***

"It's going to get worse. A lot worse." Dr. Hall stood beside me as we gazed out the window of the upper landing as Loudon paced back and forth below, oblivious to the snow piled up on the terrace. One of Loudon's medical experts, Hall looked more like The Accountant.

"And there's no mistaking the illness?"

"Not at all," he said. "I admit it took some time to arrive at our diagnosis. Mr. Partridge didn't have a family history. And Sporadic Fatal Insomnia is exceptionally uncommon. But we did an MRI, prion tests, the full spectrum, so once we suspected the cause, everything fell into place."

Loudon abruptly stopped pacing, and stared at some unseen object. It reminded me of Molly when she glimpsed a squirrel. Then he took another step forward, without apparent rhyme or reason.

"And he won't sleep at all?"

"Can't sleep," the doctor corrected. "Have you ever had a sleepless night?" His question was hypothetical. "How do you feel the next day?" Again, no pause for an answer. "Well, imagine that magnified by six months in a row. The effects are devastating."

"Lack of concentration, inability to focus, loss of appetite," I said.

Dr. Hall nodded. "Eventually full-blown dementia."

"Next steps?"

He gave a helpless shrug. "I'm a genetic specialist, not his primary physician. But there are no experts in SFI—it's that unusual. What I expect is more aberrant behavior, more incoherence."

"About his claim that someone is trying to kill him?"

Large wet snowflakes plastered Loudon with a white frosting. Dr. Hall gazed out the window before replying. "His visions run the full gamut from the routine to the extraordinary." He turned back to me. "The larger question is: Why would anyone want to kill him if he will be dead within a year—and probably far sooner?"

That wasn't a question for his medical team. It was for me to solve.

Everyone looked up, startled by a sudden stamping of feet.

Loudon had entered and was energetically pounding his feet, his hair and shoulders encrusted with snow, giving him the appearance of a wild-eyed madman.

"Please let me die in spring," he muttered to himself.

"Don't worry, Pops," a voice chimed behind me. "You're going to live forever."

A slender yet voluptuous girl, with pale unwavering eyes and black hair. Sage was dressed simply but stylishly. Dark brown suede pants and a white silk blouse, with its top buttons defiantly left undone. English country chic mixed with an unnerving sensuality.

She sauntered over and kissed her father on the forehead before brushing the snow off his shoulders. While her clothes implied a young woman in her mid-20s, a closer look revealed she was more likely in her late teens.

She gazed at me with frank, assessing eyes. "You must be the private dick that father hired." She took my hand in hers, more of a caress than a handshake. "I'm Sage. His pride and joy."

The phrase "private dick" was meant to shock, but I paid no heed. I looked directly into Sage's eyes, pointedly ignoring her alluring body.

Her gaze faltered, and I realized she was a mixture of bravado, immaturity and insecurity. Men focused on her beauty, but paid scant attention to her personality. Her body was more mature than her actual age, and she wasn't sure how to use it, whether as a weapon or as a bribe.

I wasted no time rattling her cage. "Unfortunately, your father won't live forever. Maybe not even four months."

Her eyes widened at my bluntness. "My, aren't you direct? No wonder Papa likes you so much." She pouted. "If you play your cards right, maybe he'll show his gratitude by including you in his will. As the others in this motely group are no doubt hoping."

Behind me, there was a sharp intake of breath, likely from The Lawyer.

"Maybe he'll leave something to your dog, as well," Sage mocked.

Ever alert to when people were talking about her, Molly's tail thumped on the floor.

"What do you make of your father's belief that someone is trying to kill him?"

"If that's what he believes, it must be true."

"He thinks you were being carried down the hallway, barely clothed and against your will."

She laughed. "Lance. Handsome, isn't he? But I don't think he's really that strong. Plus isn't he a little old for me?" She intertwined arms with her father. "That's just one of his funny dreams, isn't it, Daddy?"

Loudon shook off his daughter's arm, irritated. "For once, I'm hungry," he said. "Let's eat."

I hoped to talk to Sage for a few more minutes, but she ushered her father toward the dining room. The word sashayed might be out of fashion, but it was an apt description of her walk.

As I watched them go, elderly father and teenaged daughter, Phyllis came up beside me.

"I was a little blunt," I said apologetically, "saying he had only a few months to live."

"Not far off the mark," she said. "No one knows for sure, but I think he's on the cusp of the final stage."

"And what does that mean exactly?"

"More insomnia."

"Meaning more confusion?"

"Yes. And heart palpitations, severe headaches, more hallucinations. Possible suspended hypnagogia, tachycardia and dysarthria." In answer to my enquiring look, "Sorry, rapid heart rate, difficulty verbalizing including slurred speech." Her face softened. "Hypnagogia is the state just before you fall sleep. Eventually dementia will set is and death will soon follow."

I'm not a hypochondriac, but I started to feel the distant drum of a headache. "Shall we move to the dining hall?" I asked.

***

The day had been full of surprises.

I would have liked to have gathered everyone in the drawing room so I could play out my Agatha Christie fantasy, but instead everyone assembled for a late lunch, including Partridge's medical team.

The group gathered around a massive table, helping themselves to a vast array of dishes, while Molly wandered around in hopes of secret treats, given or dropped.

No matter how exhausting it might have been to care for Loudon, his staff certainly ate well.

As if in a parody of "The Last Supper," Loudon Partridge was flanked by his entourage of doctors, advisors, and assistants.

A large muscular man on his right gently fed Loudon some soup.

Phyllis followed my gaze. "Vincent, his PSW. Personal Support Worker," she explained.

"And the others?"

"I'll go from left to right," she said. "Beside Vincent is Dr. F...don't know his full last name, but he's a micro neuro-linguist something, something. Probably writing a paper on Loudon. Next is Aiden, his personal trainer, though Loudon hasn't done a proper workout in three months. At the end, another specialist. Loudon is a bit of a celebrity in the world of rare diseases."

"Not sure if I'd want to be that type of celebrity," I commented.

"On his other side, you know Andie, his personal lawyer. He also has a few other lawyers who aren't here today, specializing in corporate and litigation. Next is his driver."

"Lance," I offered. "Not a chauffeur."

"Loudon felt chauffeur sounded too elitist. Besides, Lance isn't a uniform and cap kind of driver."

I looked at her curiously, but her eyes were flat.

"Next Loudon's daughter, Sage."

"Bit of a handful," I suggested.

"It's a shame she's so spoiled," Phyllis remarked. "She might even be likeable. Too young to handle the wrong kind of attention."

"And Sage's mother?"

"Sarah?" Phyllis hesitated. "You'd need to ask her lawyer or even Loudon himself, though I'm not sure whether he remembers her. She was killed 10 years ago in a car crash."

***

A flash of red hair caught my eye. Andie perused the bookshelves lining the library walls. The books were displayed more to impress than to be read, I thought.

I glanced at the titles. All respected authors. Hemingway. Faulkner. Fitzgerald. Nothing past the last century as far as I could see.

I ran my hands down the spines. "First editions?"

"It's like Loudon has had two lives. One before his diagnosis of SFI, and the other after." Andie pulled a copy of *The Moonstone* off the shelf. "This alone is probably worth several thousand dollars." She glanced around the room, which held thousands of books. "I'll let you do the math on the value of this inventory. But whether any of these have been read, that is anyone's guess."

"Speaking of his wealth," I said, "how did he become so rich?"

Andie looked at me skeptically. "You have no idea who Loudon is?"

"He just contacted me this morning. I haven't had a chance to research him."

Andie studied the nearest shelf. "Despite his stuffy sounding name, Loudon Partridge grew up in a modest suburb. Began his career as a bank teller, found he possessed a flair for finance. Ever heard of Partridge Holdings?"

I thought for a second. "I think I've seen the logo in my retirement portfolio. So he's a rich financier."

Andie shook her head. "A millionaire is rich. Loudon is in the stratosphere. Not quite at the level of Gates or Buffet, but he was getting pretty close when all this happened."

I thought of the daughter's comments. "Any idea who would benefit from his death? Assuming he might be right, and someone is trying to kill him."

"And why not wait another six months and let nature take its course?" she said.

The nine hundred-million-dollar question, I thought. "Who inherits his estate? The daughter, I presume?"

"It's confidential, but Loudon said I could share a rough overview with you." Andie hesitated. "Sage is the primary beneficiary. Apart from some charitable donations."

"Significant charities?" I asked.

"Nothing extraordinary. Loudon believes in giving while he is still alive, and has been very generous with his money. A community center, couple of scholarships, a library and even a hospital wing have been named after him."

"Sage made a sarcastic comment earlier about incentives?"

"Yes, it's in his will, and he's very up-front about it," Andie said. "All of his team—medical or otherwise—will receive a very healthy 'bonus' if Loudon survives more than 18 months after his initial diagnosis."

"How much of a bonus?"

"It varies from caregiver to team member," she paused. "But most will receive something in the mid to high six figure range."

I let that sink in. Loudon's initial diagnosis had been made in October of the year before last. It was now February. "So we're almost at the 16 month mark."

"Yup."

I did a rough calculation. "In eight more weeks, Loudon's team will become very wealthy."

Andie nodded.

Together, we joined the others in the dining room.

***

Sage stood up from the table, sauntered over to her father's personal assistant and leaned in. She whispered into his ear, pretending not to notice Lance's glare from the other side of the table.

Was it my imagination or did Vincent flinch when she touched him? She wrapped her arms around his neck and caressed his pectoral muscles. He was absurdly fit, his clearly defined muscles shifting under his white T-shirt when she touched him.

Vincent's eyes locked onto mine. With slow, deliberate movements, he cut up small pieces of meat and, with surprising tenderness, fed them to Loudon.

"In your opinion, which member of his team most wants to see Loudon dead?" I asked Andie.

"Anyone who is rich has enemies," a baritone voice spoke behind me. A slender man in a tailored navy suit and silk bow tie approached us. He was dressed in a similar fashion to Loudon, but was nevertheless quite different in appearance, with his crisp shirt, expensive haircut and well-manicured hands. His lean body had a tense fitness that put me in mind of a long distance runner.

"Douglas Parker." He introduced himself with a firm handshake.

"You're The Finance Manager," I said, hazarding a guess.

"Hardly." He laughed. "Loudon is the financial genius. I'm probably best described as his Financial Firewall."

175

He explained further. "Loudon is the driving force behind Partridge Holdings. And the face of the firm. But I handle all the major correspondence, all the meetings with key partners."

"And do you also handle incoming complaints?"

Douglas shrugged good-naturedly. "As I said, you don't become this rich without stepping on a few toes. Or making occasional mistakes. And some financial planners were quick to blame Loudon for their losses, instead of admitting to their own poor judgement."

"Mistakes? Did anyone lose enough to want Loudon dead?"

He shook his head dismissively. "I doubt it. People blame their financial planners when they lose money, not some high-level fund manager." He made a miniscule adjustment to his cuffs. "You never know, it's possible. But remember, one man's major loss is minor to another. If I'd lost $5,000 when I was 25, I would have been devastated. Last month, I lost $30,000, but it didn't bother me. I now view it as an opportunity."

I wouldn't be that cavalier over a financial loss, but I pressed on. "No idea who would want Loudon to die sooner rather than later?"

Douglas smiled tightly. "I think everyone is waiting for the beginning of April with bated breath and crossed fingers."

"April Fool's Day?"

"Yes, that's when the new codicil in the will goes into effect." Douglas smiled grimly. "I think everyone would secretly like to hold a party, but they know it would seem a bit uncouth."

"Including yourself?"

His eyes narrowed, but he didn't take the bait. "I'm currently recognized in his will, but I'm not going to lie. An additional half million would be icing on the cake."

"Some cake," I said drily.

Doug glanced around the room and surveyed Loudon's entourage. "For some in this room, the inheritance and additional bonus would be a life changer. This group has a vested interest in making sure Loudon doesn't choke on a ham sandwich, let alone be killed in the middle of the night."

Sage was saying goodbye to Vincent. He was visibly uncomfortable as she whispered in his ear.

Douglas watched the scene unfolding before us. "A little too Lolita for my tastes." Another flash of his smile. "And I think she's got poor Lance wrapped around her little finger."

Sage looked over at Lance who, in return, trembled like a grateful puppy.

"Do you think Sage resents her father's generosity?"

"Upon Loudon's death, she will become a billionaire. I don't think the potential loss of $10 million bothers her."

***

I found myself drawn once again to the library, where I resumed my inspection of Loudon's collection of First Editions. I was raptly studying Agatha Christie's *And Then There Were None* when Vincent approached me.

"Do you know the original title?" he asked.

"Regretfully, both alternate titles."

Vincent glared at me, but chose not to debate the matter of the offending titles. Instead, he pulled down another book from the shelves. "Perhaps this is a better sample of her work." It was *Murder on the Orient Express*.

"Our current situation feels like a reverse mirror image to Christie's plot. Instead of having a motive to kill Loudon, our people all have a motive to keep him alive."

"Let nature take its course," he agreed. "As long as it's after the first of April."

"Live and let live," I said.

"As long as Loudon has quality of life."

I thought of Molly, and the discussion I'd had with the vet earlier that morning. It now seemed worlds away.

"If Loudon took a bad turn on the last day of March, they'd be performing CPR for 24 hours to keep him alive until morning."

"How long have you been a PSW?"

"Seven years."

"Are family members always so appreciative?"

Vincent's eyes flickered toward Sage. "I enjoy my job. And a fleeting moment of pleasure wouldn't be worth it in the long run, to risk my entire career over a pretty girl." His eyes locked with mine. "Plus, I don't think my husband would appreciate it."

"He's a lucky man." I said.

"You have no idea."

***

"Well, who is it?" Loudon's belligerent voice broke the calm of the library.

I hurried to his side. "I only arrived here a few hours ago." I sat beside him in the chair Vincent had vacated. "I don't even know for certain whether someone is trying to harm you."

He looked around the room, wild-eyed, his hands trembling violently.

My first impulse was to plead with him to get some rest, but I realized it would be futile and needlessly cruel to press that point. "Tell me about your hallucinations," I said. "How often do you experience them?"

I wasn't sure whether he heard me, but to my surprise, he calmly answered. "When I suffer hallucinations, I hear music. Frequently classical, and I'm really not that much of a fan. When I saw Lance carrying my daughter down the hallway…"

I interrupted. "What music was playing?"

Loudon frowned for a moment. "That group with a dead singer." We all looked perplexed. "The Lip."

"The Tragically Hip." Phyllis made the connection.

"Yes, damn good music," Loudon said.

Phyllis's eyes widened, and I looked at her inquiringly.

"I heard music that night as well. "Bobcaygeon." One of the doctors was playing it too loudly, but it stopped after a few minutes."

"Not exactly a hallucination," I said.

Before I could continue, Lance interrupted. "Mr. Partridge wishes you to spend the night." His tone suggested that my refusal would not be appreciated.

I looked at Loudon. "You don't employ a butler?"

Lance looked aggrieved. "I'm half butler, half driver."

"Loudon believes having a butler is pretentious," Phyllis said.

"Yet working the staff to exhaustion is acceptable," Lance complained.

"It comes with the territory," Phyllis agreed.

"How long have you been in Mr. Partridge's employ?" I asked.

"Six years."

A wave of weariness overcame me, and I realized what a simple pleasure sleep could be. "Please show me to my room."

I expected Lance, in his capacity as half butler, to lead me to my room. Instead, Andie appeared.

"I heard you're staying overnight," she said. "Please follow me. I'm in the same wing."

She led Molly and me along thickly carpeted corridors, and I couldn't think of anything to say without sounding blatantly flirtatious.

She stopped in front of a heavy wooden door. Nodding at Molly, she said, "I wish that someone would love me unconditionally."

Sometimes a detective's best technique is to say nothing at all, so I remained mute.

178

"Someone like Molly," she added, "who provides love and devotion, asking nothing in return. If only I could be so lucky."

Suddenly, the pain of that morning's news came flooding back, and my eyes involuntarily misted.

Andie touched me gently on the cheek. "Don't worry, Loudon's plight has that effect on people."

She knelt by Molly and kissed her head. I wasn't as lucky. She stood and gave me a friendly nod before leaving me by the bedroom door.

The bedroom was huge. It made me think of my old high school gymnasium, but was far more comfortable. The ceiling was at least 12 feet high. Antique carpets covered the floor, and the bed was large enough for a family of five.

The room was divided by a large sofa that created a viewing area for a mammoth TV that was hung over the fireplace. On the other side, a small kitchenette rivaled the size of those found in most downtown condos. The coffee table was laden with a cheese platter, a selection of olives and cured meats, and bottle of wine. The *ensuite* boasted a walk-in shower complete with a separate polished granite tub.

Molly peered inside the bathroom with interest. "Add a couple of ducks and you'll be fine," I told her.

I studied the photographs that lined the walls near the sofa. A collection of tasteful black-and-white prints. One of Loudon, a cigarette held rakishly between his lips as he stood at the wheel of a sailboat.

Another showed him dressed in a tuxedo with a strikingly good-looking woman by his side. Again, a cigarette held in one hand. The woman was clearly Sage's mother—the same pale eyes and alluring body, but with a gentle expression on her face.

I was surprised to see that Loudon was a former smoker.

I stretched out on the bed, planning to take a quick nap before dinner. As I drifted off, a seed of an idea nibbled at my consciousness.

A loud whimpering woke me. I was completely disoriented until I saw Molly on the carpet with her legs thrashing and her eyes white. Foaming spittle covered her mouth.

"Molly!" I slid off the bed and joined her on the floor. "Not yet, girl, not yet."

After a minute, her breathing settled, and her limbs stopped jerking. Her eyes closed, and I stroked her head until her breathing became low and steady. My own heart continued to race long after I returned to bed.

***

I found Loudon sitting with Phyllis in the main kitchen. Together they watched the cook and his assistant prepare dinner.

The kitchen had the appearance of a TV set for a cooking competition. To complete the effect, it had a viewing bench for people to observe and perhaps even act as judges.

"This is one of the few things Loudon can focus on—people cooking. Only in person, mind you, and not on TV," Phyllis said.

I looked at Loudon, his face shining with sweat, but his eyes focused straight ahead.

"Can I ask you a question, Loudon?" I said.

He watched as the cook finished prepping a leg of lamb before giving a slow nod of his head.

"When did you stop smoking?"

"Ten years ago. After Sarah died." His eyes met mine. "She always said that it would kill me. When we lost her, I realized I had to stay healthy, for Sage."

His attention turned once again to the cook, and I knew that was all I would get from him.

"Phyllis," I said, "I have a favor to ask."

***

Dinner was a more elaborate version of lunch. An even larger variety of food, decadent platters of meat, fish and chicken. Nothing was simple—no vegetables were offered without a coating of cheese or wrapped in bacon.

"Death by cholesterol," I whispered to Andie.

She rewarded me with a smile. "Loudon said he never trusted anyone who didn't enjoy a good steak, although I think Sage is actually a vegan."

Molly strolled past us on her mooch-patrol.

I had a witty rejoinder, but it was drowned out by an unexpected argument on the other side of Loudon.

Vincent's voice rose over the gentle murmuring of the other diners. "That's ridiculous—I'm not going to give Loudon cigarettes."

Phyllis replied in a calm, measured tone. "I'm just saying let him smoke. It's what he wants."

"You know how he wanders about. He's a walking fire hazard."

Phyllis was adamant. "What's wrong with giving him some moments of happiness in his final days?"

Loudon cut his Yorkshire pudding into squares, apparently oblivious while the two argued.

Suddenly aware that everyone was listening, Phyllis and Vincent fell quiet. Everyone resumed eating in silence.

***

A dark room, the middle of the night.

Loudon's breathing was harsh and uneven, yet I knew he was awake. He muttered to himself and I understood only the occasional words.

I was seated in a chair pushed back into a corner with Molly sleeping at my feet, her breathing measured and deep.

In vain, I tried not to look at my phone too frequently, but too much time had passed. I was about to give up on my idea when the door creaked open.

"Loudon?" a voice asked.

Unintelligible mumbling in response.

The door opened, allowing enough light in to confirm my own diagnosis.

"Would you like a smoke?" the voice asked.

"Don't think I should," Loudon's voice slurred back.

"C'mon, I know you want to."

There was a rustling in the dark, like the crumpling of newspaper. I saw the bright red tip of a lit cigarette, then heard a hiss as it was extinguished into something. Hard enough to send a few sparks into the air.

Then no sound for 20 seconds. I saw a red glow and smelled something burning.

Molly had awakened and stood beside me, her fur standing on end, but she knew enough to follow my cue and remain silent.

A lighter flared to life and Lance puffed on a cigarette, then placed it between Loudon's inert fingers. A pillow on the sofa smoldered with increased intensity and tendrils of smoke filled the air.

"A bad habit," I said. "It will stunt your growth."

Lance spun around, his face contorted into a scowl.

He looked for a weapon, but when Vincent turned on the light, Lance was momentarily blinded.

You might have expected our noble Molly to attack. But you would be wrong. She is far too gentle to engage in violence.

Vincent, on the other hand, suffered no such qualms. He strode toward Lance brandishing a small fire extinguisher.

Lance looked at the blocked doorway, then leaped through the exit leading to the patio. He vanished into the winter darkness.

***

The smell of eggs and bacon filled the air, causing Molly to pace relentlessly in anticipation. Phyllis and I sat the at the kitchen island, our plates at the ready in front of us.

"Why Lance?" she asked.

"I'm not a doctor," I said, "but it struck me as odd that all of Loudon's hallucinations contained fantastic elements except those involving Lance. His memories of Lance were mostly accurate, even regarding his clothing, right down to his shoes. Everything but the music."

"Which was separate and not actually part of the hallucination," Phyllis nodded. "But Loudon said Lance was carrying his daughter half-naked down the hallway. Was she drugged?"

I thought back to Sage's expression when she learned that Lance had escaped out into the snowy dawn. "I think she was more than willing. In fact, I think she instigated the romance with Lance, not out of love, but a desire to see how far she could manipulate him."

"But why kill Loudon now?" Phyllis shook her head. "Lance would come into a half a million dollars if he just waited."

"Not so fast," I said. "By my loose calculations, the bonus payout to the whole team would amount to roughly $10 million. But if there was no payout, that money would pad Sage's inheritance. My bet is that she made a deal to cut him in on the surplus. She would have tweaked his vanity, telling him he deserved more than the others in the team."

"But what was Sage's motive?"

"Greed and anger." I paused. "She resented his parental control. She saw herself as a woman, and balked at her dependence on Loudon.

"As for Lance, he had bigger plans. We know that Sage and he were lovers, but Sage thought of it as a fling, while Lance thought it was something more. When I searched his room, I found an engagement ring."

Her eyes widened. "If Loudon had died before the deadline, Lance could marry Sage and become part of an extremely wealthy couple."

"I think Sage was starting to cool, so from Lance's point of view, the sooner a wedding could be held the better. And doing it before the incentives for the others kicked in would be his way of giving everyone the finger."

My steak and eggs had just arrived when Vincent tapped me on the shoulder. "He wants to see you."

***

I found Loudon in bed, garbed in a resplendent dressing gown, deep covers pulled halfway up his chest. Andie sat beside his bed and gently dabbed his face with a damp facecloth.

Vincent whispered to me. "He's gotten much worse in the past few hours."

Loudon's eyes suddenly opened. "She was always more than we could handle. Sarah never knew how to deal with her."

Andie gently pulled me to one side. "Loudon changed his will first thing this morning. Obviously, Lance was removed, and the incentives were actually increased, and an additional name was added."

"And Sage?"

"She will now get an allowance each year, and inherit the bulk of the estate on turning 40."

"Will that be enough to keep Sage in line?" I wondered aloud.

"Time will tell, but I doubt it."

Loudon eyes fluttered again. "One more favor," he said. His lips moved, but I couldn't hear so I leaned over him. "Leave Molly with me. For a little while."

I was blindsided by the request. I looked down at Molly and her eyes looked at me with understanding. I didn't trust myself to speak. To my surprise, Molly leaped onto the bed, offering a glimpse of the puppy she'd been years ago.

Loudon closed his eyes and smiled. He drew a long rattling breath. Molly groaned in unison.

I watched them for a minute before heading outside to wander through the statues in the wintry gardens.

CROSSMATCH

Madona Skaff

*Madona Skaff has published several science fiction and mystery short stories, including the 2014 Arthur Ellis Award finalist "First Impressions" (*The Whole She Bang 2*). More recently, "Backbone" appears in the anthology,* Nothing Without Us. *"The Soul Behind the Face", appears in* In the Key of 13.

She is the author of the Naya Investigates series. The first, Journey of a Thousand Steps *(Renaissance Press), is the story of a young woman recently disabled by MS who turns sleuth to find her missing friend. In the sequel,* Death by Association, *the intrepid sleuth tackles a triple murder.*

Sergeant Biggs couldn't understand why he had been assigned some newly promoted detective who looked about 19 years old. His staff sergeant corrected him, saying she was 29.

Biggs gave him a look that said, *Are you trying to tell me how to do my job?* But his staff sergeant countered with a look that said, *Nice try.*

Time for a new approach.

"I told you that I don't want to be treated like I'm sick."

The staff sergeant softened his voice. "But you are sick. And you need to take it easy."

"I am."

"You call working 20-hour days, seven days a week taking it easy?" He took off his glasses and rubbed his eyes. He sighed heavily, replaced his glasses and stared at Biggs.

"I don't see any reason to change my work habits after all these years," Biggs said.

"You agreed to at least relax when you're at dialysis, not to send out e-mails and call other departments." In answer to Bigg's questioning look, he added, "People tell me things."

"Do you expect me to lie around doing nothing? Crime won't wait."

"You're not fighting it alone. Delegate!"

Biggs opened his mouth to argue.

"End of discussion!" the staff sergeant said. He turned his chair around to study his computer screen.

Dismissed, Biggs left the office.

Trudging back to the squad room, he spotted her. Sergeant Catherine Fisher. She was still standing beside his desk, holding a cardboard box. When she'd arrived, her eyes bright, full of anticipation, and introduced herself as his new partner, he hadn't said a word. Just marched right into the staff sergeant's office. How could he accept working with her, or with anyone? As much as he liked to believe otherwise, he wasn't the same man he'd been a few years ago. He was frequently tired. He got the work done but at a much slower pace. Did he really want a partner to witness that?

"So," she said, her voice soft but determined, picking up the conversation as though he'd never abandoned her, "where should I sit?"

He noticed, glumly, a desk next to his own that hadn't been there the previous night. On it was a desk lamp, a computer and a landline phone. All waiting for their new occupant, which obviously was her.

He slumped into his chair trying not to grit his teeth and nodded in its direction. "Guess right there."

She carefully unpacked a large coffee mug, then pulled out notebooks, pens, pencils and a few books, one that looked like the latest edition of the *Criminal Code of Canada*. Also, some sort of fern. She slid the empty box under her desk and swiveled her chair around to face him.

"Anything interesting that you're working on?" she asked. Her voice and smile were professional.

"Not much these days. I do have a lead that probably won't go anywhere. No point in both of us wasting time. Why don't you get settled in?"

He saw her eyes widen as she looked at her desk. Guess she was settled in. Better give her something to keep her out of—what was left of—his hair.

"How about you take a look at some cold cases? I usually pull one out when things are quiet."

"Sure, that sounds great. Where—" She broke off when she realized that he had grabbed his jacket and was already halfway to the door.

"Damn," she muttered. When she'd arrived and Biggs had rudely escaped into the staff sergeant's office, the other detectives had greeted her warmly with, 'Don't mind him,' and 'Welcome to the team.' She could ask one of them for help, but everyone was busy, either on the phone or with people at their desks.

Time to earn her detective pay and find the files herself. With no filing cabinets in the small squad room, she searched Biggs' desk. There were only a few folders on it. One was a recent armed robbery at a grocery store. In fact, it had occurred that morning. That was probably where he was now. She tried not to be annoyed, consoling herself with the fact that, in a big city, there would be other robberies.

She rummaged through his drawers. Nothing of use. The bottom drawer contained a lot of the usual desk stuff such as memo pads, a ball of elastic bands and large tie wraps that occasionally doubled as handcuffs. As she started to close the drawer, something gray peeked out through the menagerie. She pulled out a file folder. Biggs had probably forgotten all about it under all the stuff. Aha! This must be the cold case he mentioned. It was dated 20 years earlier.

Smiling with pride she took the folder to her desk. After only a few minutes in her new job she'd completed her first assignment. Found a cold case. She opened the folder and was thrilled to discover that it was a murder.

***

Biggs spent the morning collecting information and evidence at the grocery store. He couldn't understand why people bought a surveillance camera, then didn't bother to repair it.

Instead of returning to the station, he navigated the heavy noontime traffic and pulled into the driveway of a middle class bungalow. He went up to the front door and knocked.

A slim woman in her 70s with salt-and-pepper hair opened the door.

"Eddy!" she reached out to hug him.

"Hi, Mom," he said. He was always impressed by the strength of her stranglehold embrace. Nothing frail about her.

"Come in. I was just heating up some lunch. Did you eat yet?" Not waiting for an answer, she went ahead to the kitchen.

He shut the door, slipped off his shoes and followed.

She took a large bowl from the fridge. "Hope you don't mind leftovers. I made Irish stew yesterday." She ladled stew into the pot on the stove. "Would you like something to drink?"

"Just water, please."

She joined him at the table, handing him a glass.

"I love when you drop by unexpectedly." She paused then added, "Is something wrong?"

"No, I was at a crime scene not far from here and thought I'd stop by." He didn't want to admit that he was childishly avoiding his new sidekick.

"Close to *this* neighborhood?" she asked, her forehead creasing, "Anything I should worry about?"

"No, sorry, I didn't mean to worry you. It's several miles— OK it's on the other side of town." During an interrogation, he could tell a suspect any story, any lie, and they'd believe him. He was an accomplished liar, except when it came to his mother. He wasn't even sure why he was trying to make up a story.

"Eddy, you don't need an excuse to visit," she said as though she'd read his mind. She gave him a quick peck on the forehead as she got up to serve the stew. Casually she asked, "How is dialysis going?"

"It's fine." He paused. "But it's starting to mess with my schedule. Maybe it's time to retire."

"That's a bit drastic. Besides, we still have few a few more relatives to check."

"I keep telling you that you're wasting your time looking for a match."

"You know, I've been doing our family tree," she began.

"Mom," he warned, knowing where this was going.

"Using my DNA, I've found a lot of relatives we never knew we had. If we compare yours to…"

"Mom, no!" He paused to rub his forehead. "I'm sorry, I didn't mean to snap. I know you keep hoping we'll find a suitable kidney donor. I don't want to put my DNA online. I'm a cop, I know what shady operations some of these places can be. OK?"

She gave him a tiny smile of defeat.

After lunch, he gave her a kiss and a hug, then left. As she cleared the dishes from the table, she held up his empty water glass and smiled. She carefully set it down. Then she picked up the cell phone, checked the contact list and hit dial.

"Forensics Lab," a man answered.

"Hello, Mr. Forrester. This is Vera Biggs, Eddy's mom."

"Mrs. Biggs, how are you doing?"

"To be honest, not very well." She paused. "I have a favor to ask of you."

***

Arriving in the squad room the next morning, Biggs found Fisher already tapping away on the computer. She hadn't deserved to be treated like a plague on his life. As the senior officer, it made sense that he should teach her the ropes.

She looked up and greeted him with a smile.

"Fisher," he began.

She swiveled her chair to completely face him.

"I have a couple of witnesses to interview. Interested in coming along?"

"Of course, sir," she said, standing up.

"Whoa! I have a few things to do first," he said.

She gave an embarrassed laugh and sat down again.

"Don't worry," he said, "I won't leave without you."

He checked his e-mail and phone messages.

"Fisher, did Forrester call from the lab with any results?" he asked.

She shook her head.

"He says I'm too impatient," Biggs said with a laugh.

"When did you give him the samples?" she asked.

"The end of last week. I was really hoping for something from trace. Hair, fibers, something. Twenty-three home break-ins and not one clue." He shook his head. "Guess it's back to old-fashioned police work."

"Meaning talking to a lot of people," Fisher said, giving him a grin.

"Exactly." He grinned back at her. Maybe teaching her the ropes wouldn't be as painful as he'd thought. "Let's go."

"Yes, sir. I'm right behind you."

***

Over the next few weeks, they broke the string of burglaries, thanks to Fisher. She'd found the common thread among the victims: they all went to the same chiropractor's office. The receptionist passed on the addresses of the more affluent clients to her shady boyfriend. Biggs recognized that Fisher had a natural instinct that couldn't be taught, and she was better than many detectives who had been on the job for years. With a few more years' experience she'd have the best record for closing cases at the station. Maybe even the city. Though he still had to fight occasional fatigue, his mood improved. He knew it was due in part to his new partner. Fisher made him see things from a new perspective.

***

Fisher couldn't believe that she'd been a detective for just over a month. And her initial disappointment at missing that first robbery had been soon forgotten as crime in the city took a major upswing. She'd learned so much from Biggs. How to ask witnesses the right questions. She'd also learned invaluable interrogation techniques. What to ask, when to talk, when to be silent, and most important, how to listen. And she'd had a lot of practice with crimes ranging from simple muggings, all the way up to bank robberies.

The increased criminal activity also meant she hadn't had time to look at the cold case. Biggs kept assuring her that eventually there'd be a lull and she'd have the time to work on her murder case. She loved how he always referred to it as *her* murder case. It made her that more determined to solve it and make Biggs proud of her.

She pulled out the folder from her bottom drawer and spread the crime scene photos on her desk. The victim lay on his back not far from the apartment door, as though he'd opened it and was shot without warning, and had no time to turn and run. Neighbors had claimed they never heard anything, but the officer on the case suspected that they just didn't want to get involved. Nothing had been stolen.

The case had gone cold almost as soon as the body had been discovered. With her fingers crossed, Fisher checked the evidence inventory. She released a breath she hadn't realized she was holding. Evidence from the scene was still there. Since Forensic technology had improved exponentially in recent years, there was a good chance it would bring something to light.

Twenty minutes later, Fisher had the evidence box at her desk. Biggs had left her a note, apologizing for leaving without her, but said he didn't want to intrude as she solved the cold case. She laughed because he'd underlined the word solved. Carefully, she broke the seal on the evidence box and opened it. The victim's clothing and shoes had been bagged and sealed. That meant any evidence would still be pristine. She took the whole box down to Forensics.

***

On the way back upstairs, she met Biggs in the elevator.

"You look happy," he said.

"I just took the cold case evidence down to Forensics. I hope they'll find something."

"I'm sure they will. And it's a good thing you didn't bother coming with me."

"No useful information?"

190

"A cashier remembered that one of the two suspects was short. Which matched all the other descriptions we already have."

They left the elevator and headed for the squad room. "They should have just called in the information," Fisher said.

"Hey, it's the only way I'd get fresh air and exercise!" Biggs said with a laugh.

Fisher sat down at her desk.

Biggs sorted through several papers and file folders, before putting them into his briefcase. "Do you need anything before I head off to the hospital?" he asked her.

"Anything important I should watch out for?"

"I'm still waiting for the DNA results from the grocery robberies."

"The robberies have really escalated in violence," Fisher said. "I hope we catch those guys before they kill someone."

"Forrester promised to put a rush on it," Biggs said. He slipped on his jacket adding, "I'll be back in about three hours. If you need anything, call my cell."

"I don't want to disturb you."

"See here." He lifted up his briefcase. "I'll be finishing up the burglary report. So call. I don't mind being interrupted. I mean it— *please* interrupt me."

She laughed and watched him leave.

Who would have thought that this was the same man who had snubbed her on her first day on the job, then vanished for the rest of the day? She was relieved that he'd changed his attitude toward her. But it wasn't hard to sympathize with him. Her own dad had been on dialysis for years, waiting in vain for a transplant. He'd been hooked up to a machine three times a week for at least three, sometimes four hours. He was always light-headed afterwards, due to a drop in blood pressure. His feet and legs were always painfully swollen. Yet her dad seemed to live in anticipation of those brief moments when he felt healthy and normal.

She wondered if that's how Biggs felt.

***

A week later, they had a promising lead in the string of grocery store robberies. For whatever reason, one of the men wasn't wearing gloves and had carelessly touched the counter, conveniently leaving behind fingerprints. It won't be long now, Biggs thought as he arrived in the squad room.

"Good morning, Fisher," Biggs said, giving her a smile that should have earned him an Academy Award. What he really wanted to do was curl up in a ball somewhere, and shut out the world for a couple of days. Ah, but then it would be time for his next dialysis. Despite his forced good mood, he actually laughed at the irony of what his life was becoming.

A medical appointment earlier that morning had confirmed what he'd suspected. His kidneys were getting worse. Soon dialysis might not be enough to keep him alive. He left the doctor's office, slapped a smile on his face and came to work. Lying to the world. Wishing he could lie to himself.

"Anything on the prints from the bank robbery?" he asked.

"Not yet."

"OK, while we wait..." His phone rang.

"Good morning, Eddy," his mother said. "Are you busy?"

"Never for you," he said.

"I just wanted to tell you something. Promise not to get mad?"

"I can promise to try," Biggs said. He felt his facade slipping. He re-applied the smile and said, "What is it?"

"I've been watching you get worse the past few months. I know you try to hide it but a mother sees these things. I really think the best chance for a transplant is to find a relative. We can't wait until total failure to move you to the top of the list." She broke off abruptly.

He shook his head, resigned to the direction in which the conversation was going. He didn't have the strength to argue.

"Mom, I know you think you're helping, but I've already told you that I'm not giving my DNA to some company."

"I know that you're not comfortable letting strangers analyze your DNA. That's why I had it tested independently."

"You what?" He broke off when Fisher looked up at him. He gave her a placating motion with his hand. When she returned to work, he lowered his voice and said, "How?"

"I called Forrester, your friend in forensics, and explained everything to him. He analyzed your sample."

"How...?"

"When you were here for lunch last month. I gave him your water glass."

"Damn it, Mom." He broke off again, not trusting himself to say more. "Did you send the results?"

Sounding contrite, she said, "I didn't want to do anything until I spoke to you."

"Don't do anything. I'll be right there." He slid his chair back ignoring the screech and stood up.

"Is anything wrong?" Fisher asked.

He paused at her desk. "Something I need to take care of." He took a step to leave then stopped. "Keep an eye on my inbox for any DNA results on the bank robbery. We can't get a search warrant without them. I won't be long."

He hurried to the elevator. He had to get to his mother's place before she did something he'd regret.

Fisher watched Biggs storm out of the office, as if someone had used a fire extinguisher on his good mood. She hoped he'd be OK, wishing she knew how to help.

She needed to follow up on the results for some pollen not native to the area that had been found at a bank robbery. It was best to do that in person. But first she would check Biggs' e-mail for any results. He hadn't even had the chance to turn on the computer.

At the top of the e-mail queue she found a message from Forrester with the Subject line: YOUR DNA. She glanced at the message and read the first line, which started, "*FYI, I was talking to your mom...*" Obviously a personal message, so she stopped reading. Biggs had been friends with Forrester for years, and she'd noticed that much of their correspondence contained some personal banter.

When Biggs had first tasked her with scanning his incoming e-mail, she'd been uncomfortable. She told him it felt like she was invading his privacy. But he'd insisted that he was an open book. Just the same, she soon became skilled at barely glancing at the message, determining the subject, and forwarding only the attachments to herself.

Back at her computer, she filled in the required forms and submitted the results to the RCMP to be added to the national DNA database.

***

Biggs pulled into his mother's driveway faster than he'd intended and almost rear-ended her car. He calmed himself with long deep breaths. There was no point in getting angry with her for following her maternal instincts.

He kept his voice level and calm as he said, "I could stand here for an hour explaining all the risks of handing over your DNA to a corporation. They'd own your DNA, and they'd be free to do whatever they want with it. They can use it to develop drugs, or treatments and you'd never know, or get credit for it. Not to mention the number of times these companies have been hacked and people's personal information has been stolen."

"But Eddy," she said, "how is that worth anything if you're dead?"

He steeled himself against the sight of her moist eyes. Silently, she went to her computer and deleted the file. She also deleted it from the Trash Folder without being asked.

He wondered if she would understand, if she knew what was really at stake.

***

A few days later, Fisher greeted Biggs with a joyous, "I got a hit on my cold case!"

"That's great news," he said, giving her a congratulatory pat on the shoulder. Then he noticed a disturbingly familiar file folder on her desk. "What's that?" he asked, nodding as casually as he could manage.

"The cold case file. I guess that's the type of file folders they used back then. Kind of a sickly gray tinge to them."

"Where did you get it?" He knew the answer. His heart skipped a beat. Literally. Chest pains started. He had to hide his reaction. Sitting down quickly, he turned on his computer.

"Oh, your desk. Remember that first day you told me to work on a cold case? Well, I found this one. It was buried under a lot of stuff, I guess you forgot about it..." She added quickly, "No, no, I don't mean you forgot about it. I mean, you've probably been working on it when you have time. Uh, that's why you kept it in your desk. I'm sorry, I should have asked, cleared it with you first."

He interrupted her. "It's all right."

But she wasn't convinced that it was all right. She'd seen the look in his eyes. Was it anger because she'd stolen his case?

It never occurred to Fisher that the look in his eyes was fear.

Biggs inhaled, forcing his voice to remain level. "I didn't forget the case. But it's been a while since I've worked it." Good, stick to the truth. It would make the lie easier. "All it needed was a pair of fresh eyes." *Or innocent eyes*, he thought. He cleared his throat, regaining control of his emotions. "So, you got something?"

"Well," she began hesitantly, "I managed to get trace DNA from the victim's clothing."

"It could belong to anyone," he said.

"That's what I thought too, but it was actually found on his collar, near his neck. As if someone checked his pulse, or rested a hand or arm on the vic's shoulder. The lab thinks there are traces of salt consistent with sweat or maybe tears. There weren't any hits in the database. But—and this is what's so exciting—remember when you asked me to keep an eye out for the grocery robbery results? Well, when I ran it, I got a familial match with the cold case."

194

"Really?" That was not what he'd expected her to say. He'd sent the robbery DNA results to the database himself. What was she talking about?

He searched through his incoming e-mail. He had a bad habit of not re-checking messages if they were marked as read. There were so many each day. Only now did he realize that he hadn't given a thought to the fact that Fisher was also reading them. He found the e-mail with the results that he'd sent. He continued scanning. He found it. Subject line: YOUR DNA

As he read the e-mail, he felt a vein start to throb in his temple. Forrester was giving him the heads up about his mother's request. He felt bad going behind Biggs' back which is why he'd e-mailed him separately. And, of course, the very efficient Fisher had put them into the system. Damn! If she'd only read the message, she would have realized what it was and wouldn't have...

Now, his DNA was in the system. Too late to explain the mistake considering there was a familial match to a murder. Questions would be asked. Answers would be found. Twenty years of hiding would be wasted.

He stood, staring at his computer screen. He closed his e-mail and tried to keep his voice casual. But to his own ears, his voice sounded strange. "I have an appointment. At the doctor's. Won't be long. Good work." And he headed out of the squad room, down the stairs and out to the parking lot. Once he got into his car, he punched in a rarely used phone number.

"I just wanted to check in on you," Biggs said, "to make sure that everything's OK."

"I'm fine," a man replied. "I was actually thinking about you. I heard your health is declining. Wondering if I could..."

Biggs cut him off. "I just want you to know that your DNA was found at the scene."

"I thought you said there wasn't any evidence linking me to Corbet."

"We don't need as large a sample today. I'd hidden the file, but it was found. Doesn't matter how. You need to stay low."

"I knew I was taking a risk coming back."

"Coming back? You're here?" Biggs shouted.

"Flew in a last week. I've been hiding out in a small motel outside of town. Testing the waters before I contacted you."

"Testing shark-infested waters by jumping in carrying a side of beef?" Biggs hit his steering wheel with the heel of his hand. "Are you crazy? What if someone recognizes you?"

"Don't worry, I look quite different now. I've lost a lot of weight, got in shape. Grew a beard." He paused. "I know you put a lot on the line helping me get out of town. Now, it's my turn to save your life."

"My life isn't at risk." Biggs forced the words out through clenched teeth.

"Yeah, that's why your kidney function has dropped to critical levels."

"How...?"

"I've turned into a computer expert. Did you know that everything's online these days? Including your medical records."

Biggs took several deep breaths. "We better meet."

***

Fisher drummed a rhythmless beat on her desk as she watched Biggs leave. She thought that they'd grown closer since she'd been here. Not drinking buddies or anything so mundane, but she felt that she'd got to know him better. Able to recognize his moods. When he was feeling well. When he lied about feeling fine. The man was a horrible liar, which she'd thought was cute. Until now.

The anger in his eyes was obvious when he'd seen the file folder. It was understandable. She'd taken a cold case from his desk without permission, an action she would always regret. And even worse was the fact that she'd managed to find a lead in only a few weeks, which he'd failed to do after years. His ego had been bruised. Maybe even crushed. Hell, she'd be furious if he'd done the same to her.

When she'd told him that she got a familial match between her murder case and the bank robbery, she'd seen genuine confusion in his face. Again, understandable. What were the odds that relatives would show up at two different crime scenes, decades apart?

But she couldn't explain the panic he'd been unable to hide when he checked his e-mail.

Like an automaton, she sat at his desk. Opened his e-mail. Scanned through the messages and found the DNA results for their robbery case. She checked and discovered that he'd sent these to the RCMP to include in the national database. But this wasn't the e-mail that she'd seen. Or the results that she'd submitted.

She searched back through his in-box, frustrated that if he would only organize it once in a while, it would be easier to find things.

Finally!

Subject line: YOUR DNA.

196

This time she read the full message.

She realized that she'd submitted Biggs' own DNA sample results, thinking that they belonged to the unknown suspect. But that accident had revealed that Biggs was related to the suspect in an unsolved murder. That didn't prove that he knew his relative was a killer. Every family had a black sheep or two in it. But his reactions earlier strongly indicated that he probably did know, and had been covering for the killer. She grabbed her jacket and raced down the stairs to the parking lot, knowing he would be long gone.

To her surprise, she found him sitting in his vehicle. She crept up behind the car, hiding in the mirror's blind spot. He was talking on his cell, very animated. Waving and slamming his hands onto the steering wheel. Then, something told her that he was getting ready to drive off. This would be her best chance to find out what was going on. To figure out how he was involved. To bring a killer who had evaded the law for 20 years to justice. Whoever it turned out to be.

She raced to her car, hoping he wouldn't see her. When he screeched out of the parking lot, she was close behind him.

Following at a safe distance, she realized that he was sticking to the speed limit. She guessed he wanted to avoid notice.

After driving for about 45 minutes, he pulled into a motel on the outskirts of town. Parked in front of Room F. Biggs knocked, and was let in.

Fisher parked her car behind his, blocking him in, in case he tried to run. She couldn't believe she was treating him like a criminal.

Going up to the door, she hesitated. He'd been her mentor, someone she'd come to admire and respect. Should she kick the door in? It appeared to be flimsy enough, so she might get away with only a strained muscle. Maybe she should keep an eye on the door, and call in the Tactical Squad to take Biggs down. She probably should try to get a look inside, just to make sure that Biggs was with the suspect. Or...

She knocked on the door.

A man in his 30s, well-built with neatly cut black hair and a trimmed beard, opened the door. He gave her a smile and said, "Hi, can I help you?"

From behind him, Biggs came into view, saucer-wide eyes staring at her.

"Fisher?" he said, incredulously. "What the hell are you doing here?" Then, blanking his expression and squaring his shoulders, he ordered, "Get in here!"

His commanding voice propelled her forward. As he shut the door, she realized her mistake. She was trapped. With no backup. No one knew where she was.

"You know her?" the man asked Biggs.

"Yeah," he said shaking his head with what she thought was regret. "She's my partner."

She felt a touch of pride that he'd called her his partner. But the regret on his face terrified her.

"She's a cop?" the man said. There could be no doubting the fear in his voice or on his face.

"It's OK, I'll handle this," Biggs told him, waving him to sit down on the bed. "Fisher, what the hell are you doing here?"

"I was worried about you," she blurted out. That wasn't how she'd planned to start. Then words continued to fall out of her mouth, without any conscious control. "You were acting strange. At first I thought you were upset that I took your case and had come close to solving it. I checked through your e-mail and realized that you're related to the murder suspect."

"Sit down," Biggs said.

She hesitated, not wanting to move farther into the room. With the curtains drawn, her only chance was to stay near the door. Make a break for it. Or at least, make enough noise and hope someone heard her.

"Please, have a seat," Biggs said. His voice was calm.

Once again, she obeyed without thought.

"Have you been hiding a murderer for 20 years?" she asked, impressed that her voice was steady, despite her pounding heart.

"I didn't kill anyone," the man said.

"Let me start from the beginning," Biggs said. "This is my cousin, Derrick, who was barely 16 at the time. It's the old story of getting involved with the wrong friends. They were much older than him, and heavy into dealing drugs. Working for Frank Corbet."

"The victim," Fisher said. "So, Corbet tried to force him to sell drugs and your cousin killed him?"

"No," Biggs said. "For whatever reason, maybe because of his age, Corbet didn't want him involved. Told him to study hard and make something of himself."

"OK?" Fisher wasn't sure she was keeping up.

"Like Eddy said, I'm not sure why Corbet liked me," Derrick said. "I remember he told me once that I reminded him of himself at that age. His buddies were running drugs. When he had to choose between following his friends or staying at school, which he hated, quick money won out. He told me he'd always regretted that decision."

"So what happened?" Fisher asked, "Did he change his mind and decide you could use the extra money? Did you kill him by accident?"

"No, Rufus killed him," Derrick said. "He was Corbet's right-hand man. But he'd always hated me. I'm not sure why. Maybe because I was friends with his boss. One night, Rufus calls and tells me that Corbet wants to see me that evening. But since I was already in the neighborhood, I decided to go over early. I didn't think he'd mind because I always dropped by unannounced. It turned out Corbet didn't want to see me."

"It didn't take a rocket scientist to realize that Rufus had set Derrick up," Biggs said.

"I think he planned to kill both of us. Make it look like we killed each other. But when Rufus arrived and saw that I was already there, he lost it. Started yelling at me, calling me a snitch because my cousin was a cop. Then he pulled a gun. He was going to shoot me, but..." His voice broke.

After a moment, he continued, his voice hoarse. "But Corbet, being the guy he was, ordered him to put the gun down, stop acting like a fool. When he tried to get between me and the gun, Rufus fired. Then he aimed at me, and I froze thinking I was going to die. But there was a noise in the hall, I think an apartment door opened, and Rufus panicked. Just before he took off. He warned me to keep quiet or he'd kill my entire family."

"Derrick came to me for help," Biggs said.

"So you told him to run?" Fisher asked, disappointed in her partner.

"No, I tried to get him to go to the police. Guaranteed that I'd keep him safe. But without any solid evidence to place Rufus at the scene..."

"He'd never been to the apartment before," Derrick added. "My word against his. And, you don't know Rufus. No one crossed him. Then, or now."

"So why risk coming back?" Fisher asked.

"He's taking a big risk on the slim chance that he's a compatible kidney donor," Biggs said.

"Not slim chance at all," Derrick said. "I've already been tested. We're a match."

"It's too risky. If Rufus finds out you're here..." Biggs said.

"It's not right that I let him get away with murder all these years," Derrick said. "So, we'll go to the hospital. I give you one of my kidneys. Then we go to the police."

"You make it sound so easy," Biggs said. "And while you're waiting to recover, what happens? This all started because it was too risky for you to testify."

"I've already been in a sort of witness protection. Now, I'll just go back to an official one. That's all."

"That probably won't be necessary," Fisher said. When she had the attention of both men, she added, "There's a good chance Rufus's prints might be on the outside of the door."

"An apartment with so many tenants and visitors," Derrick said. "They probably didn't even bother with the outside of the door."

"They did take prints," Fisher said as she stood up. "Mostly smudged and not too useful at the time."

"But now, as long as the prints were stored correctly, we might find something," Biggs said.

"Your cousin wouldn't need to be involved in the investigation," Fisher said. "And if we find Rufus's prints on the door..."

"We'll be able to place him at the scene," Biggs said. "I can't be involved for obvious reasons. Besides, it's your cold case. Finish what you started."

***

Fisher brought two large bouquets of flowers and a box of homemade chocolate chip cookies to the hospital. The surgery had gone well for both men, and they were finally out of ICU.

"I hear that you officially solved your first murder case," Biggs said. "Congrats."

"Thank you," she said, appreciating the pride in his voice.

"Will I have to testify?" Derrick asked.

"No, my official report said that I ran all the prints on the outside of the door and hit on Rufus's. And since your prints aren't in the system, your name never came up. By the way, you have no idea how many criminals lived in that building at the time and how much work it took to sort and clear them all."

"When is the trial?" Derrick asked.

"During the interrogation, I told Rufus that his prints placed him at the scene, and that there are witness statements saying that he was always trying to usurp power from Corbet. It didn't take long for him to confess and accept a plea deal."

"She means there won't be a trial," Biggs told Derrick.

"We're lucky that his prints were on the outside of the door," Derrick said.

"Yes," Fisher said. She glanced at Biggs.

His eyes narrowed as he studied her for a moment. Then, he nodded and gave her a hint of a smile.

Briggs had taught her well, especially conducting an interrogation. She smiled at her mentor.

Ω

DANNY AND ME

Ed Piwowarczyk

Ed Piwowarczyk is a retired journalist, who has worked for the National Post, Toronto Sun *and the* Sault Star. *He has edited Harlequin manuscripts, and is currently a freelance editor. A lifelong fan of crime fiction, he is also a film and trivia buff. His short fiction has been published in Toronto Sisters in Crime and Mesdames of Mayhem anthologies, most recently in* In the Key of 13.

A voice was calling me in the night, startling me awake. I hadn't heard it in a long while, but there was no doubt whose it was.

"Danny!" I sat up in bed and wiped the sleep from my eyes. I peered into the darkness, trying to see him. Of course, I didn't. I'd never actually *seen* Danny, but I *knew* he was there.

"Hi, Joey. You miss me? How long's it been?"

"I dunno," I mumbled, then realized it had been almost two years since I'd heard him or spoken to him. "Why are you here?"

"Same as always," he replied. "You need me."

"No, I don't," I protested. "I'm not a kid anymore. I'm 18 now."

Danny pressed on. "You're worried about Amy and Wes."

Amy was Amelia Harrison, my mother, and Wes was Wesley Jackson, my new stepfather.

"Your mom hasn't always made good choices when it comes to men," Danny continued.

With her shoulder-length blond hair, sparkling blue eyes, slim figure, and effervescent laugh, Mom could have been a movie actress. She also had family money, and lots of it. All of which meant she never lacked attention from men. Unfortunately, they were often the wrong kind of men—at least, according to my grandparents.

They never talked badly of Mom in front of me, but I'd overheard them discussing how she "ran wild" as soon as she left home for university, moving through a succession of failed relationships.

"Layabouts, louts, gigolos, and fortune hunters, the lot of them," Grandpa had grumbled.

"C'mon," Danny said. "What do your grandparents think of Wes?"

"I…I…don't know," I confessed. "I haven't seen much of them lately."

"What do *you* think of him? Has Amy got it right with Wes, or is he another loser?"

"It's too early to say." I paused, looking for the upside. "Mom looks happier, and he seems nice enough."

"What does he do?"

"He's an artist."

"Like Barry?" Danny sounded incredulous. Barry was my mother's first husband and an artist.

Before I could say anything, he went on, "The situation with Barry, it festered too long. If Wes turns out to be like him, we'll have to act quickly. Agreed?"

I didn't reply.

"All right, then," Danny said. "We'll talk soon. Good night."

I fell back on my pillow, shut my eyes and fell into an uneasy sleep, haunted by memories I had no wish to revisit.

***

I've been told my memory is faulty, so what's real and what isn't when it comes to Barry is jumbled in my mind. But this is what I *believe* happened.

My birth signaled the end of my mother's wild days. She never told me or anyone else who my father was, and decided to raise me as a single mom. That was a bold decision for her to make at the age of 27 in 1959. My grandparents' initial shock was replaced by relief—Amy was *finally* growing up—and delight—they had a grandchild to dote over.

They bought her a two-story, four-bedroom brick home and a station wagon. They also gave her a generous living allowance, enough to raise me and never have to hold a job.

Until I was old enough to play with other kids in the neighborhood and attend school, I remember being the center of Amy's life. Then her focus shifted away from me and to the world of art. She wanted to learn more about the business side, and she landed a position as an administrative assistant at Brushstrokes, a downtown gallery.

That's where she met Barry Pike—or Pike-casso, as he jokingly called himself. He was six feet tall, with sandy hair, dark brown eyes and a dimpled chin. He charmed Amy, my grandparents and me with his stories and jokes. Eight months after they met, Amy and Barry were married. I had just turned 15.

Mom helped Barry convert our home's main-floor bedroom into an artist's studio, complete with brushes, paint, thinners, easels, canvases, drop cloths, a divan—and a well-stocked bar.

Barry was confident that he was the next Jackson Pollock or Mark Rothko. Amy's sweet talk and my grandparents' money persuaded the owners of Brushstrokes to stage a one-man show of his works.

I remember it being a fiasco. Newspaper and art magazine critics dismissed the paintings as derivative and uninspiring, and Barry as visionless. Even worse, after a handful of sales on opening night, buyers stayed away. The show closed after two weeks.

As I lay in bed, I could hear him railing against the philistines whose bourgeois tastes in art prevented them from recognizing his genius. My mother and I became the targets of his frustration. She was no longer his darling or his honey; she was a bitch and a shrew. I was a "whiny bastard."

He began to drink heavily, resulting in a domestic reign of terror. Mom was the target of his slaps, punches and kicks, usually when I wasn't around. She did her best to conceal her welts and bruises with long-sleeved shirts and trousers. When Barry sobered up, he was contrite, so my mother stuck with him. She never said anything to my grandparents.

With the turmoil at home, my schoolwork suffered, and I became more anxious and withdrawn. Classmates and the few friends I had thought I was acting "weird" and began avoiding me.

That's when I started hearing Danny. I couldn't see him, but that didn't matter. He told jokes, played games with me, and listened to my worries and fears about Barry. He became my best friend.

And I was the only one who could *hear* him. When anyone else heard me talking to Danny, they assumed I was talking to myself. That's what Mom did; she dismissed Danny as a figment of my imagination. "Lots of kids have imaginary friends," she told me. "You'll outgrow him."

A few days later, Barry told Amy that I was "muttering" to myself. When she said that it was just make-believe, he replied,

"Isn't he a little old for that stuff? Maybe there's something wrong with him."

So Mom took me to see a psychologist. Despite her insistence that I was fine, Mom squirmed as she sat in Dr. Sandra Tanner's office. I kept glancing her way for hints about what to say or do. That didn't escape Dr. Tanner's notice, and she asked Mom to wait in the reception area while we continued our first session.

Dr. Tanner's voice was gentle and soothing, and I found myself opening up about my troubles at school, about often being afraid or on edge, and about Danny.

Then it was my turn to wait outside while Mom sat down with Dr. Tanner. They closed the office door behind them, but I gently nudged it ajar—just a tiny crack—and sat down beside it.

Their voices were very low at first, little more than a murmur. The doctor suggested we might "seek family counseling," to which Mom replied that she'd "take the matter up with my husband."

Then my mother's voice picked up. "Is Joey…all right?"

"His anxiety and social withdrawal are both indications of schizophrenia," Dr. Tanner said.

"Does this imaginary friend mean Joey has a split personality?" my mother asked. "That's what schizophrenia is all about, isn't it?"

"That's a common belief," Dr. Tanner replied. "But you don't see Joey speaking in another voice or claiming to be someone else, do you?"

"No."

"Hallucinations are another indication of schizophrenia," Dr. Tanner said. "And that's what Danny is—an *auditory* hallucination. We don't hear him. Only your son does."

She paused. "I'd like to have a few more sessions with Joey. I believe a combination of therapy and the right medication will help him, but I need to get to know him better. I hope you'll bring him back."

On the drive home, I was afraid of how Barry would react to Dr. Tanner's suggestions of therapy for me and counseling for the family. Especially if he had been drinking.

After dinner that evening, Mom said she had things she needed to discuss with Barry and told me to go to my room. I lay on my bed, hearing the sound of their distant voices but not making out what they were saying. I closed my eyes and drifted off to sleep.

A distant crash and thud woke me. I sat up, heard Mom cry out, and ran for the stairs. I looked down and saw Barry standing over Mom, who was writhing on the floor.

"You bastard!" I cried and started to race toward them, only to trip on a step and roll down the staircase, landing hard next to my mother.

Barry looked down at us, wide-eyed with horror and disbelief. He fell to his knees, whimpering, "Oh, my God! Oh, my God!" He staggered to his feet and stumbled over to the phone. "We need an ambulance. My wife and my son..."

I tuned out the rest of it. He was contrite now, but alcohol would uncork that violence again.

As I listened to the ambulance siren draw closer, I sensed Danny nearby. "We've got to put an end to this," he whispered. "It's gone on too long."

***

A couple of months passed. Mom's bruises had faded, as had mine. Barry was on his best behavior and busy in his studio. But living with Barry had become like living beneath an active volcano—you never knew when it might erupt. Maybe Mom could do it, but I couldn't live in the shadow of Mount Barry. However, I didn't know what to do.

I turned to Danny, to see what he thought. "Maybe if I talked to Mom, she might...might..."

"Leave him? Not a chance," Danny replied. "If she hasn't done it yet, after what she's been through, she won't do it now."

"How about telling my grandparents? They could do something."

"Yeah, but can't you see what would happen? They'd talk to Amy, she'd defend Barry, and even if they had reservations, they'd go along with what their only child wants. They always have."

"What about the police?"

"Something would have to happen before they came. Then they'd want statements, like you see on TV. Would Amy do that? Huh?"

"No," I whispered.

"Face it. No one is gonna help until it's too late."

Fear and frustration were eating away at me. "What can we *do*?"

Danny was silent for a moment before answering. "We have to get *rid* of him."

I paused as the weight of what he was suggesting hit me. "You can't mean..." I gulped. "Kill Barry? But that's wrong!"

"No, it's about survival. It's you or him. If you don't do it, you and Amy will be back in the hospital. Worse, you could end up *dead.*"

I shook my head. "I can't, I can't."

"Yes, you *can*," Danny asserted. "And you will."

In the end, his insistence overcame my qualms.

"How?" I asked. "He's bigger and stronger than me."

If I had been able to see him, I'm sure Danny would have been smiling. "Simple. We serve him a poisoned cocktail."

Danny's plan hinged on Barry's desire for the best in booze and art supplies.

He only downed premium liquor, and his favorite drink was a martini that combined high-end brands of London gin and dry vermouth.

As for art supplies, everything had to be top-quality, even his paint thinners. Barry didn't use hardware store turpentine to clean his brushes or dilute oil paints. He used a colorless, low-odor solvent favored by artists.

Danny's plan was to take a bottle of gin and replace half of it with the solvent, and do the same with a bottle of dry vermouth. All the ingredients— the liquor in the bar and the solvent on a table with paints—were right there in Barry's studio.

All the liquids were colorless, so Danny figured Barry wouldn't notice the difference between the doctored booze bottles and the ones that hadn't been tampered with, unless he saw that the seals had been broken.

"He can mix a martini however he wants, but half of it will be poisonous," Danny said.

"Won't he be able to smell that something's off about the drink?" I asked.

"The gin and vermouth odors aren't that strong, and the solvent's almost odorless," Danny replied. "Their smells would blend in with those of the oils and paints in the studio. All part of Barry's world."

"So when do we do this?"

"Soon. Very soon."

***

Our opportunity came a few days later when Barry, in one of his genial moods, suggested the three of us take a Saturday afternoon drive in the countryside. Much to my mother's disappointment, I begged off, claiming I had a school project due on Monday.

Once they'd left, I hurried to the basement with the gin, vermouth and solvent and prepared two spiked bottles of liquor according to Danny's directions. I marked a small X on the corner of each bottle's label so I could identify the doctored alcohol, and returned the bottles to the studio bar.

When Barry and Mom returned home, he was ready for his predinner cocktails in the studio. So far, so good, and all according to plan. Danny suggested Barry mix his first one or two drinks from undoctored booze so that he wouldn't be wary if something tasted slightly different when he used what we'd prepared.

Then Barry, still in good spirits, did something that Danny and I hadn't figured on. "Amy, care to join me for a martini? And a bit of Sinatra?"

My mother, also in a jovial mood, replied, "Love to, darling. Just give me a minute to freshen up."

I leaned against my bedroom door and closed my eyes. "No, no, no!" I sobbed in frustration. "What do we do now?" I asked Danny.

"Hurry downstairs and make sure he doesn't haul out the spiked bottles just yet," he ordered. "We don't want anything to happen to your mother."

I dashed into the studio just as Barry was about to pull a pair of bottles out of the bar. "Wait!"

He stopped and looked at me quizzically. "Joey?" He smiled. "You finished your project?"

"Almost." I had my eye on the bottles. How could I check the labels?

"What do you say?" Barry continued. "Care for a bit of Ol' Blue Eyes?"

"Who?"

"Why, Frank Sinatra, darling!" My mother breezed into the room carrying a couple of glasses. "Joey, sweetheart, how nice of you to join us." I hadn't seen her this cheerful in a long while. "Barry, get the music going, and I'll get the drinks."

I thought Barry would protest, but he hummed as he headed over to a small stereo console—about half the size of the one in our living room—in a corner of the room. There was an armchair beside it, and a plastic milk crate nearby to store LPs.

As Barry sorted through the LPs, I ran to the bar ahead of Mom. "Let me help!" I scanned the labels, pulled out two unmarked bottles, and put them on a table. "There!"

"Thank you, Joey!" She tousled my hair. "Now, get yourself a Coke."

"That was close," Danny said as I headed for the kitchen.

"You're telling me!"

"You did great back there," Danny said. "Just keep an eye on them, and everything will be fine. The plan will still work."

Then another potential obstacle occurred to me. "What if she goes back in there with him after dinner?" I asked. "What's to prevent both of them from drinking poisoned cocktails?"

Danny was silent for a moment. "You know where she keeps her tranquilizers, right?"

"In the medicine cabinet upstairs."

"Take some, crush them into powder and slip it into her drink. At dinner. She'll call it an early night."

I glanced toward the studio. "They're going to wonder what happened to me."

"Tell them you forgot something upstairs and that you'll be down in a few minutes."

I did as Danny instructed and prepared the tranquilizer powder, using a scrap of notebook paper for a packet.

When I returned to the studio, Mom and Barry were waltzing around the room as Sinatra crooned "Summer Wind." They smiled and giggled as they danced, and they even got me prancing and singing with them when Sinatra launched into "Downtown."

The family bonhomie continued through a pizza-delivery dinner, accompanied with wine. With the delivery box lid raised as Mom doled out the slices, I was able to slip the powder into her glass unnoticed.

I excused myself as Mom and Barry lingered chatting over their last slices of pizza. I hurried into the studio, pulled out the spiked liquor, and left the bottles on a small table near the armchair and the stereo.

"Barry seems so...*different,*" I said to Danny as I climbed the stairs to my room. "Is what we're doing right?"

"He was well-behaved today," Danny said. "So what. Do you really think he's changed?"

I hesitated. "I dunno."

"It's too late to chicken out now," he said. "He's made Amy's life and yours miserable. Now it's his turn."

***

"Whew!" Mom exclaimed. "I'm feeling woozy. Must be from all the excitement today. But it was a wonderful day."

I crouched at the top of the stairs, watching them embrace.

"How about a nightcap?" Barry asked. "Another martini, maybe? More Sinatra? *Songs for Swingin' Lovers!*?" He chuckled. "That's us."

Mom giggled. "I'm afraid I don't feel very *swingin'* at the moment." She paused. "I love that record. I'm tempted, but I'm bushed. I'll take a rain check, though."

"For sure." He kissed her. "Sleep tight."

I scrambled back to my room and opened a schoolbook as Mom came up the stairs. I saw my bedroom door opening. She entered, leaned over me, and gave me a kiss on the forehead. "Don't work too hard, Joey. See you in the morning."

"G'night," I mumbled as she closed the door behind her.

Ten minutes later, I crept down the hall to check on her. As soon as I heard her breathing gently in her sleep, I returned to the top of the stairs. The studio door was open, but from where I was sitting, I couldn't see Barry. The sounds of Sinatra wafted up to where I sat. "Love is Here to Stay"…"I've Got You Under My Skin"…"Anything Goes"…then the music stopped.

I hurried downstairs and poked my head around the studio doorframe. Barry had fallen to the floor near the armchair. His breath came short and fast as he strained to get up, only to collapse beside a puddle of vomit. He coughed as he lifted his head.

Then he saw me, and his eyes pleaded for help. "Joey!" he wheezed as he struggled to his feet, heaving himself up using the armchair. He managed only a step before crumpling to the floor again.

Horrified, I backed slowly away. Barry gasped, threw up and lay still. I was overcome by guilt and shame.

"C'mon, Joey," Danny prompted. "It's no time to stop. Just stick with the plan."

I'm not sure how long I waited before I returned to the studio. I carefully stepped around Barry's body, and removed the poisoned bottles. I dumped the liquid down the kitchen sink and threw the empties into the trash can outside.

Back in the studio, I set out two bottles, three-quarters full, of undoctored gin and vermouth next to some solvent on the bar, which Danny said was pivotal to our plan. "That way, it'll look like an accident," he'd explained. "He was drunk, grabbed the wrong stuff and made a fatal mistake in mixing his cocktail."

I took a deep breath, then marched slowly up the stairs to my mother and Barry's room.

"Mom! Mom! Wake up!" I cried as I shook her shoulder.

"What's wrong?" she said groggily, sitting up in bed. "What is it?"

"It's Barry! Something's happened. Hurry!"

In the studio, she gasped when she saw Barry and put her hand to her mouth. "Oh, my God!" She turned to me, struggling to keep her voice calm. "Joey, quick! Call an ambulance! Call the police!" Then she ran over to his body, fell on it, and began sobbing.

After I'd phoned for help, I returned to the studio and found my mother sitting up beside Barry's body, wiping tears from her cheeks. I approached her slowly, gave her a tentative hug, and stepped back. I couldn't think of anything to say to comfort her.

"It worked!" Danny cried. "We did it!"

My mother motioned me over to her for another hug, but I stood still. My eyes were focused not on my mother or stepfather, but on the liquor and the solvent. She followed my gaze, looked down at Barry, then back up at me. Her eyes widened in horror.

The sounds of sirens approached.

"Oh, Joey!" she whispered. "What have you done?"

***

My mother kept glancing at me as she spoke to the police. Her eyes were filled with sadness and disappointment, but she said nothing about her suspicions of my hand in Barry's death.

The cops checked the liquor and the solvent, and concluded, as Danny and I had planned, that Barry had accidentally mixed and drank a lethal cocktail. The coroner gave the cause of Barry's death as acute pulmonary edema—excessive fluid in the lungs—brought on by a heart attack.

I expected life to return to what it had been pre-Barry, but it didn't. A few weeks after Barry's funeral, Mom and my grandparents huddled with Dr. Tanner in her office. The next thing I knew, I was a "resident" at the Waverly Center, a private psychiatric facility just north of the city.

I'd just turned 16. When Mom asked how long I'd be there, Dr. Tanner said that would depend on how I responded to treatment: a combination of medication and sessions with her.

In the course of those sessions, I slowly came to accept that Barry had been no monster. I had suffered delusions; the reality of the situation at home was the opposite of what I believed or imagined had happened. For example, my mother had fallen the night she'd cracked her ribs; she hadn't been beaten by Barry. And so on.

I've been here at the Waverly Center two years now, and Dr. Tanner thinks I can go home as soon as Mom and Wes have returned from their honeymoon.

That means I can't let anyone know Danny is back. His return would be seen as a setback, and as pleasant as the Waverly has been, I don't want to extend my stay.

***

As I pack to leave for home, I speak to Danny for what I hope will be the last time.

"Barry wasn't a bad guy, after all," I say. "He didn't do those terrible things."

"That's what they've *told* you, but who are you going to believe?" Danny replies. "Them, or your own eyes?"

I hold firm. "We made a mistake with Barry. Leave Wes alone."

"But—"

"One more thing," I continue. "I...I don't think we should talk anymore. For my sake."

Danny is silent for a moment. Then he sighs. "If you say so." He pauses. "But if Wes starts mistreating you and Amy..."

"I know. You'll be there to help."

"Maybe," he says mischievously, "with another cocktail."

TWO CROOKS WALK INTO A STORE

Melodie Campbell

Called the "Queen of Comedy" by the Toronto Sun*, Melodie Campbell has won the Derringer, Arthur Ellis and eight other awards for crime fiction. She has shared a literary short list with Margaret Atwood, and was a Top 50 Amazon best seller, sandwiched between Tom Clancy and Nora Roberts. Melodie teaches fiction writing at Sheridan College, and is a past executive director of Crime Writers of Canada.* The Goddaughter Does Vegas *is her 15th book.*

The crisis had finally come. Betty Glummer looked down at the untouched bowl of tuna fish and cursed her luck again.

A few months ago, when things had started to look dire, Betty had discovered that a can of no-name tuna at the dollar store was cheaper than dog food. At first, Percy had been delighted. This led to her stockpiling the blasted cans, purchased at 49 cents each. But lately, Percy was turning away from his fishy breakfast, nose in the air, tail held high.

Which meant Betty had to eat the bloody tuna herself. And she was getting mighty sick of it.

Still, there remained the problem of what to feed Percy. A few cups of dry dog food remained; she would leave some of that out, all the while knowing that her fussy canine wouldn't touch the stuff unless he was absolutely starving. Betty's gaze followed the small white poodle as he sauntered out of the narrow galley kitchen, oblivious to the catastrophe about to engulf them.

Money had always been tight, even before Betty's diagnosis. She had survived the cancer, but the treatments had taken all of her savings. So many things were not covered by the government, and then there was the care and boarding for Percy while she was in hospital.

Even as her prognosis improved, Betty felt herself slipping into hot water. A few months ago, the dam burst. Her rent went up by a lot. One hundred dollars! Inflation, they said. Improvements to the exterior of the building, they said. How could she be expected to pay $100 more a month? Government pension cheques didn't increase by $100!

At first, Betty had considered killing the people in charge of her building. Really, she had no qualms about it at all. They were heartless thieves, living in their sky-high condos, picking on poor helpless seniors. But that thought quickly vanished. Prison might provide three meals a day, but Betty was pretty sure they didn't allow pets in there. She wasn't about to be separated from Percy.

So Betty was forced to cut out most discretionary spending. She did so with admirable willpower. Percy no longer went to the doggy salon; Betty managed his bathing and grooming herself. Not only that, but she sold what little good stuff she had—silver and things—to a secondhand store. She even canceled her subscription to cable TV. Those cable companies were blood-sucking piranhas. Everybody knew that.

And now it had come to this. The pension cheque wouldn't arrive until next week. Percy was nearly out of food, and she was out of money.

What to do? What to do?

Betty thought about that as she shoveled smelly tuna fish into her mouth with a spoon. It really was time to take action. And even though Betty was on the other side of 75, action was something she was pretty good at.

***

Two hours later, Betty had her plan in place. It was so simple, really. All she needed was an old purse, because why ruin her newer one? The shabby hard leather bag with the brass corners would do very well.

Betty didn't have a gun, but that didn't matter. She'd seen it in a movie once. You only had to *say* you had a gun, and point to the hole in your purse. Stick your hand in the purse, and pretend you might fire a bullet through the hole. Simplicity itself.

She took a kitchen paring knife to the side of the rectangular handbag and carved a quarter-size hole into it. That should do.

Next, she considered her target. A convenience store on a side street would be the best possibility. Somewhere not too busy, and

216

not close to a school. Too many kids haunt those places when they should be in class.

The store would need to be in another neighborhood. Somewhere they didn't know her, of course. She could wear the light brown curly wig she'd bought some time ago, when the cancer first struck. *Don't think of that,* she said to herself. Even now, the memory of chemo filled her with dread.

Back to the plan. It was a big city, so she wasn't worried about being identified after the fact. The wig covered her thinning white hair, and besides, no one paid much attention to old women. They all look alike to younger people.

Betty hummed "Onward Christian Soldiers" as she made final plans.

***

It was the perfect store. Small and narrow with crowded shelves piled high with goods. Best of all, it was empty except for the thin, unsmiling Asian man behind the counter. Betty nodded at him, then went to find a few cans of that brand-name dog food Percy really liked, the one with the cute little Westie on the label. Best to pick the cans up first. She wouldn't want to go out again today.

Just when she was about to plunk the two cans on the counter, someone pushed her out of the way.

Of all the nerve! She was there first. Betty stared at the rude young man, who was no more than a punk. His hair was stringy, his eyes wild. Worse, he had a real gun, which just wasn't fair.

"Empty it!" he yelled at the man behind the counter. "Put the money on the counter!" He waved the gun in the air, and that's when Betty lost it.

"You...you!" This was HER robbery, damn it. "Get in LINE!" she yelled.

"Shut up, you old bag!" he hollered back.

That did it. Old bag, indeed! She'd show him a bag! Betty took a swing with her handbag and smashed him across the side of the head. The boy yelped and leaped back. The wicked brass corners caught his face on the second swing.

Who did he think he was? He was no match for her. Oh, no, a skinny kid from the street was no match for someone who had survived stage-three cancer and years of poverty. Not to mention, decades of life on a farm. What did this soft city punk know about hardscrabble living? Nothing! He probably didn't even know how to swing an axe!

"Yow!" yelled the boy. "You're crazy!"

Crazy, was she? Hah! With an animal howl, Betty swung with all her might. She felt the purse connect with its target. There was a *pop* and a scream. Betty felt herself falling, but she still got in one more swing.

***

The room smelled of freshly laundered sheets. Somewhere a clock tick-tocked.

"Hello sleepyhead," said a pleasant female voice.

Betty opened her eyes. They didn't want to stay open, but she forced herself to fight through the fog.

"Glad to see you're with us."

The middle-aged woman had tidy short dark hair and wore aqua pajamas with pictures of cartoon dogs on them. *Percy!* She had to get back to Percy.

"You've been out for a while. But don't worry. You're going to be OK. It was just a flesh wound, but you fainted and hit your head on a counter going down. In fact, you're a hero."

A hero? She tried to lift her head, but that made her feel even more woozy.

The nice woman had brown eyes that looked right at her. "Do you remember what happened in the convenience store?"

Betty thought for a moment. Then she nodded her head reluctantly. *Poor Percy.* She had really bungled the job. *Now* what would they eat?

"You foiled a robbery! Everyone's talking about it. The police will be in to see you shortly."

Police? Her heart skipped a beat. Betty stared at the woman, then surveyed the room. Those were hospital scrubs she was wearing, not pajamas. This was a hospital ward, that's what it was. She knew all about hospitals. Knew them only too well.

An older woman in a white uniform came through the doorway. "We saved your wig. One of the nurses remembered you. Cancer, wasn't it?" The second nurse looked sympathetic, and reached out to pat her hand. "I've been there too."

This felt surreal. How could they be talking about cancer, when she had been about to rob a store?

"We noticed your purse had a hole in it." The one woman looked to the other, who cleared her throat and nodded slightly. Betty felt her throat constrict. Had they guessed her plan?

The older nurse continued. "So I hope you don't mind, but we took up a little collection in the staff room. There's enough here to buy a few new purses." She handed Betty an envelope. Betty looked into it and gasped. All those $20 bills!

"Don't forget to tell her about the show."

"Oh, yes!" the older nurse said brightly. "Apparently, the fellow you clobbered was wanted by the police. *Breaking News TV* wants to interview you on live television, and they're willing to pay you for it."

"You'll want this for the cameras." The nurse in the doggy scrubs handed her the wig. "Don't do it for less than $1,000. They can afford it. Government pension doesn't go very far these days, we all know that."

The other woman chimed in. "Don't feel bad about taking money for your story. You've beaten cancer, *and* you've survived a gunshot wound. Time to look out for yourself, dearie."

"I will," squeaked Betty. Her heart filled with hope. Percy could have his favorite dog food now, the money from the TV people would cover the rent increase. They would be safe for at least another year, if she was careful.

Betty clutched the chemo wig in her hands. She would save it for the next time they ran out of money.

THE ETERNAL BAKERY OF THE FRACTAL MIND

M.H. Callway

M. H. Callway is the pen name of Madeleine Harris-Callway. Her critically acclaimed debut novel, Windigo Fire, *was a finalist for the 2015 Arthur Ellis Best First Novel Award. It was also a finalist for both the Debut Dagger and Arthur Ellis Unhanged Arthur awards. Margaret Cannon, the crime fiction reviewer of* The Globe and Mail, *called her "a writer to watch".*

In 2013, Madeleine and Donna Carrick co-founded the Mesdames of Mayhem to promote the work of Canadian women crime writers through social media. The writers' collective has continued to grow and thrive to include 23 leading Canadian Mesdames and Monsieurs.

Francis Rome felt his age. He didn't recognize Vancouver at all. Black glass condo buildings had sprouted in every direction. Where were the British-style shingle-and-stucco bungalows he'd loved?

He stopped for a much-needed breather. Valerie had been dead three months now. He'd reclaimed his freedom at last, but his life in Montreal had not bloomed. Instead, he felt cast adrift in a sea of solitude, beset by a legion of silly geriatric ailments that conspired to steal his precious mobility.

If only he and Valerie had had children, life might have been different. The sad shadow had haunted their marriage. It haunted him still.

This morning he'd flown to Vancouver for his 50th class reunion at the university. For something, indeed anything, to do. The opening reception was scheduled for seven o'clock, which gave him barely enough time to walk over to their beloved old apartment building in the West End. Mindful of Vancouver's ever-threatening rain, he grabbed his raincoat before he left his hotel.

When he and Valerie had lived together in that building, the neighborhood had been a surreal mix of druggies, pensioners, sex workers and gays. He smiled, remembering the 24-hour doughnut store where the drag queens hung out after the gay bars closed. And his and Valerie's favorite pub, the cavernous Blue Horizon Hotel where elderly waitresses with biceps like meaty thighs slammed down glasses of watery beer on soiled terry cloth.

Their apartment building was a plain low-rise on Bryson Street, unremarkable except for its flamingo pink stucco. Their one-bedroom flat was on the second floor. That was where he and Valerie had first made love, their passion unlike anything he'd experienced before or since. They'd been happy there, truly happy.

And they'd met dramatically. Valerie was the young nurse in the emergency room where the ambulance took Francis after he fell hiking on Grouse Mountain. So pretty, with her red-gold hair, hazel eyes and heart-shaped face. He couldn't wait to ask her out. Her love had taken him by storm.

How could time be so cruel and change her so much?

Finally, the sign for Bryson Street. He'd dreamed of seeing it again. Everything as before, slightly weathered yet bathed in a golden glow.

He stared. No, it couldn't be! The pink stucco building was gone. In its place stood a hideous condo tower, like Lego by Ikea.

No mistake, the street sign read Bryson. What a stupid waste of time!

A bus blew past him and pulled up a short distance away in front of a bakery with a blue neon sign. Turning, he stumbled a little on the uneven pavement. Impossible! Wasn't that the bakery where he and Valerie used to grab breakfast before he headed off to class?

Sure enough, it was the very same Blue Star Bakery, its familiar sign outlined in blue neon. Inside it had been plain, slightly grotty, but the pastries... His mouth watered.

He pushed open the glass door and went in.

Nothing had changed, from the pastry display cases on the left to the small vinyl-topped table and two steel-legged chairs on the right. He sank down onto the nearest chair. Could this be the same furniture from 50 years ago? Ugly, functional, practically indestructible? Quite possibly.

He stared into the display case: apple pies, iced birthday cakes, date bars, loaves of bread in plastic bags, ice-box cookies dotted with maraschino cherries. Retro and wonderful.

"Can I help you with something?" An older Asian woman wearing a white baker's uniform stood behind the cash. She eyed him with skeptical suspicion.

"Oh, a coffee please. And do you still have your wonderful cinnamon buns?"

"Of course." She pointed to an aluminum tray resting on the top of the display case.

How could he have missed them? His favorite breakfast buns: their bready sides studded with brown cinnamon, a glacier of white icing on top.

He ordered and paid, and a few moments later, she brought everything over to him. The coffee was watery and tepid, but as he bit into the bun, a sensation of such warmth overwhelmed him that his eyes filled with tears. This must be the elusive emotion he'd only experienced in his early days with Valerie. This must be joy.

"Hey, you OK?" The bakery lady appeared next to the table. She had short gray hair and penetrating dark eyes. He placed her somewhere in her 60s.

"Fine, fine," he said. "I used to come here, you know, when I was a student in the 1970s. I ate breakfast here nearly every single day."

"Right, when you were two years old." She was laughing at him.

"A mere babe, how did you guess?" People had never taken him for younger than his chronological age. Lately, he couldn't even fool himself. He threw her a wry smile. "A Hungarian family owned the bakery when I lived here. Their little daughter used to play in the front window. It's hard to believe that now she'd be a middle-aged woman, probably with children of her own."

"Grandchildren, you mean. You mind?" She took the seat opposite him. Her blue plastic name tag read "Emily Wu".

Wu, that name was familiar. He groped through his murky memory but came up empty. Instead he said, "I'm amazed that the Blue Star Bakery has survived all these years. Tell me, did you buy the bakery from the Hungarian family?"

"No, sorry. It has changed hands many times. Now I am its guardian."

Interesting turn of phrase, he thought. "And you've kept everything the same, even the chair I'm sitting on. Why, I haven't tasted a real cinnamon bun like this for years!"

"Sure. Give the customers what they want. Good for business. Everyone loves bakeries. The one business where the product cycle goes up and never comes down."

"You mean an infinitely wide Gaussian distribution," he said testing the depths of her knowledge.

"We talking mathematics now?"

"Are you a mathematician?"

"In a manner of speaking. Are you?"

"I am, I should say I was, an economist."

Emily Wu smiled. "Ah, yes, economics, the dismal science. Elaborate mathematical models full of sound and futility and in the end, proving absolutely nothing. Not like physics at all."

"Are you a physicist?"

She nodded.

Interesting, he thought. So the bakery must be her retirement project. Quite a departure from probing the universe.

Now he remembered. "Mme. Wu, that's who you remind me of! She made a profound impression on me as a child. Very unusual then to be a woman excelling at physics. Tell me, are you and she related?"

Her enigmatic smile reappeared. "You could say that."

"She made a critically important discovery about the nature of the universe. Heavens, what was it?" He chewed down the rest of his bun, wrestling with his recalcitrant memory. "The conservation of parity, that's it!"

"Actually, Dr. Wu proved that parity was not conserved," Emily Wu said. "Before her work, scientists believed that all physical forces were symmetrical, that the world we see in the mirror is identical to—and no less possible—than our real world. Dr. Wu demonstrated that nature does know left from right, that symmetry is not conserved. At least at the quantum level."

"Oh, I see," Francis said, not understanding at all. "That proves what I've always thought. Quantum physics is more mysticism than practical science."

"You think so?" She lifted an eyebrow. "At the quantum level, reality as we experience it, changes. For instance, liquid helium is a superfluid that crawls out of a bottle."

"I had no idea."

"And going further, some physicists believe that our world is only one of an infinity of parallel universes."

"No offence, but doesn't that make my point?"

She let out a sigh. "OK, fine, I get it. Tell me, why did you drop by the bakery this afternoon? Not for a practical demonstration of quantum physics then?"

Now it was his turn to sigh. "Forgive me, I'm feeling a little lost these days. My wife just died."

"Sorry for that."

"She was ill a long time. Eleven years. Alzheimer's."

"Oh, that's tough."

Francis nodded. Initially he'd fought Valerie's devastating diagnosis, but in the end, he'd had no choice but to accept it. He'd taken solace in routine, visiting her every day at the nursing home, hungering for and occasionally being rewarded by a glimmer of recognition, though she steadily got worse, a slow erosion like the dwindling of mountains. He put his life on hold for her, but in time his heart turned into a paving stone over which too many feet had trod.

If only she would die. If only, if only…

And then she did die. Because he did something unforgiveable…

"No kids?" Emily Wu was asking.

"No, sadly not. What about yourself?"

"One son. Big pain in the butt. How come you don't have kids?"

He hesitated, almost giving in to the cleansing impulse to confide in a stranger about the invasive fertility tests, the horror of Valerie's late miscarriage, their lost daughter. They'd even named the baby Diana.

Instead he said, "It wasn't meant to be."

"You look sad, old gentleman," Emily Wu said.

"Do I? I'm feeling the passage of time, I suppose. Some days I feel as insubstantial as a ghost, slipping through other people's lives. As though I no longer belong in this world." He forced a smile. "Sorry, I'm being a self-pitying old bore."

"No problem. You've come to the right place. My job is to make you happy."

"Thank you, you have," he said.

Outside, a fine rain was falling through the light of the streetlamp. He glanced at his watch. Seven o'clock already? He was missing the university reception. But, sitting here, enfolded by the warmth of the bakery, he realized he didn't mind missing the reception at all.

"Right." Emily Wu slapped her hands on the table. "It's getting late." She stepped over to the front door, locked it and flipped the plastic sign from *Open* to *Closed*. "Time to go. The portal is opening."

"The portal? What are you talking about?"

"You're asking me?" She pulled a silver fountain pen and a piece of blue notepaper from her pocket. Carefully she wrote on the paper and handed it to him. "You will need this."

Under the stamped outline of a dark blue star, she had written out a complex mathematical formula.

"Keep it safe," she said. "This is important."

He shoved the paper into his coat pocket. "Very well, thank you. I really should go now. It's getting late."

"No problem, if you leave now. Come on, hurry up!" She took his arm and steered him through the strip curtain separating the bakery from the kitchen.

He took in the large convection ovens, the rolling metal racks loaded with empty baking trays, the absence of staff. "Where is everybody?" he asked.

"Gone home. This way." She pointed to the blue fire door directly ahead, the only way out. "Go out through there."

"And where do I end up? The back alley?"

"Your guess is as good as mine. Good luck, old gentleman."

She pushed down on the door's metal handle and shoved him through the opening.

***

Black, all he could see was black. He reached out—felt only a void. Something warm and wet ran down his face.

Rain, he realized. The rain that started before he left the bakery.

A brick wall rose up in front of him, the asphalt beneath his feet glistened with wet. He smelled an acrid, sulfurous odor then saw that he was standing next to an overflowing dumpster full of garbage.

Of course, he'd landed in the alley behind the Blue Star Bakery. He'd lost his night vision for a moment. No wonder he'd become disoriented.

He turned to look behind him. The blue exit door had no handle, so he couldn't get back into the bakery that way. Smart lady, that Emily Wu! She'd wanted to get rid of him quickly so she could lock up for the night.

He laughed, shook his head. Why she'd almost had him believing her wild tales about quantum physics, portals and parallel universes. But their conversation had been far more entertaining than the platitudes that would have been exchanged with his fellow graduates at the university reception.

Streetlights beckoned from the end of the alley that gave onto Bryson Street. He turned up his coat collar against the rain and

226

headed toward them. It certainly wouldn't be Vancouver without rain, he thought. He remembered its penetrating chill from his student days, but tonight's rain felt warm. In fact, rather pleasant, although the humid air pressed on his lungs.

He reached the end of the alley. Time for a final goodbye, he thought, and turned to look at the Ikea-Lego tower where his low-rise had once stood.

The tower was gone. In its place stood his old low-rise building. Not painted pink, but dark gray.

How could he have made such a mistake? His heart beat faster. Confusion, losing one's way, those were the signs that had heralded Valerie's dementia.

Now it's my turn to lose my mind! he thought. *Punishment for what I did to her. The gods are laughing!*

Through the rain, he heard an eerie whistling. Followed by a rush of wind as though a flock of birds had gathered overhead.

He looked up. A drone! Light flared out of it, blinding him. A robotic voice hailed him. What was it saying? He cowered like a pinned insect, deafened by the noise.

A large black car glided toward him. Two figures got out: a tall man wearing a long coat and brimmed hat and a short, stocky person in black body armor.

The short one ran at him, wielding a long silver rod. "What are you doing out here?" shouted a harsh female voice. "It's curfew! Answer me!"

He tried to shield his eyes from the glaring searchlight. "I don't understand. Are you the police?"

"Stay where you are! Don't move!" the woman cried. "Detective, come look at his face. It's wrong."

"There's nothing wrong with me!"

A tornado of light spurted from her silver weapon and the world vanished.

***

"Mr. Rome, wake up, please," a man's voice said.

Francis was overwhelmed by an odor of damp mingled with dust. He tried to sit up. His head swam.

"Easy now." Strong hands eased Francis to a sitting position. "Are you all right?"

The man talking to him was young and fashionably dressed in a loose-fitting tan suit, spotless white shirt and blue silk tie patterned with gold stars.

Francis braced his hands on his knees, trying to take in his surroundings. He was sitting on a padded leather bench in front of a strange desk, composed of a single sheet of glass resting on four ornate metal legs. Dragons or gargoyles, he couldn't be sure. Its surface was empty except for a green-shaded brass lamp and three small objects beside it.

"Where am I?" he asked.

"The police station. I am Detective Adrian Chuen."

The police! They'd tracked him down. They knew he'd killed Valerie, they were going to arrest him. A lawyer, he needed a lawyer. He groped for his cell phone and found it was gone.

"Where's my coat?"

"Over there." Chuen gestured toward the smooth wall behind the desk.

Francis spotted his beige raincoat hanging on a hook next to a long camel-hair overcoat and brown fedora. Water from the coats had dripped over the bare concrete floor.

Detective Chuen was the tall man he'd seen on Bryson Street. He mustn't talk, the less he said the better, but he had to know where he stood. "That flash—I lost consciousness. What happened?"

"Constable Moore neutralized you. You should thank your lucky stars she didn't use lethal force. I reined her in just in time."

"Lethal force? Are you mad? Look at me, I'm 73 years old. She attacked me with that…that stun gun thing of hers for no reason at all."

"You were out after curfew, lurking in an alleyway, acting suspiciously. Breaking curfew, as you know, is a capital offence."

"Capital offence? What the hell are you on about? What is this, a prank? If this is a joke, it's a bad one!"

"No joke." Chuen took the brown leather chair on the opposite side of the glass desk. "Look, we're short of time. I need answers from you."

Even in the dim light cast by the brass lamp, the detective's high cheekbones and intense dark eyes looked familiar. *Emily Wu!* Could Detective Chuen be Emily Wu's son? No, that would be impossible, unless…He rubbed his face. Think, think!

Of course! He'd fallen into one of those live adventure games popular with young people. The Blue Star Bakery was its front. That's how players entered the game—through the back kitchen. He remembered how empty it was: no staff, not even a whiff of baked goods.

And who was the erudite Emily Wu? A scripted and skilled actor, her role to vet paying participants before ushering them into the game. By mischance, he must have uttered the admission password and she'd propelled him into this nonsense.

He must get out of it. But how to convince Chuen that he wasn't playing along?

"Look here, there's been a mistake, a misunderstanding," he said. "I visited the Blue Star Bakery out of nostalgia. To eat one of their wonderful cinnamon buns again. I never paid to be in this game."

"Game? You think this is a game?" Chuen's black eyes bored into him. "You know as well as I do that the Blue Star Bakery closes at 4 p.m., long before curfew. Now answer my questions." He held up a gold wristwatch. "What is this strange piece of jewelry?"

"That's my watch."

"And what does a 'watch' do?"

Francis resisted the urge to snap at the detective. The only watches young people recognized were those digital devices that linked them to the internet. "It tells time, that's all it does. Old-fashioned, but then so am I."

"Interesting." Chuen put down the watch and picked up the small black object beside it. "And this thing?"

"That's my phone." Obviously, Chuen and Moore had searched him while he was passed out. He felt a surge of anger, followed by a prickle of fear.

"It doesn't connect to the Authority's wireless service." Chuen fingered the phone's screen. "In fact, it's dead."

"The battery must need recharging. It's an old phone, a Samsung S4."

"Samsung? Never heard of that brand."

Francis watched the detective search through the last object, his worn black wallet. He pulled out a plastic card.

"Driver's license? Unusual format." Chuen looked at Francis then back at the card. "This photo is supposed to be you?"

"Who else would it be?"

Chuen shrugged his well-tailored shoulders. "Fine, we'll say it's you."

Something must be wrong with his face! He remembered Moore's horrified reaction. What if…what if he'd had a stroke?

He seized the edge of Chuen's desk and hauled himself to his feet. He caught a glimpse of his reflection in the glass. Saw the bandage on his forehead.

"What's happened? What did you do to me?"

"You cut yourself when you fell. Sit down, please, or Moore will intervene. You don't want that." Chuen eyed him until he complied.

Threats now? This was getting ridiculous. "Look, if I have to pay to get out of this game, tell me how much and we'll settle up."

"Are you trying to bribe a police officer?"

"Of course not!"

"Good, because bribery is a capital offence."

Madness! Francis slumped on the bench. The bare, windowless room felt cold. How many more hours of this would he have to endure before he could escape?

He clenched and unclenched his hands. Why, he'd sue the bastards! They'd knocked him unconscious. Maybe younger players enjoyed the illicit violence, but surely no one in his right mind would risk it with someone his age.

He shivered. What if...what if this wasn't a game after all, but a trap? An elaborate ruse by the police to twist a confession out of him.

But here in Vancouver, thousands of miles away from Montreal? And why would the police bother? Valerie had been ill for 11 years, a drain on him, her caregivers, even, heaven forbid, the taxpayers. No family or friends. A quick cremation, all evidence gone.

He watched Chuen pull a metallic, book-sized object from the breast pocket of his jacket. Balancing it against the desk lamp, the detective tapped it open to reveal a screen. Orange light shot out from it, projecting a virtual keyboard onto the surface of the desk.

Must be a state-of-the-art tablet, Francis thought.

Chuen typed on the virtual keyboard in silence, pausing once in a while to study his screen. Finally, he leaned back.

"There's no record of a Francis Rome in the Authority's Drivers Data Base," he said. "Nor do you show up in the Banking or Medical data bases."

"Are you looking in Quebec or British Columbia? I live in Montreal. You do know that it's in Quebec, don't you?"

Chuen arched an eyebrow. "No need to get sarcastic. I did get a hit in the Authority's Archives. Apparently, you've been dead for 30 years."

"What!"

"And you're a murderer."

"That...that's insane!" Francis managed. "Who am I supposed to have murdered?"

"Your wife, Valerie Spring. Brutally, I might add."

They knew, the police knew. "That's impossible. My wife died in a nursing home last month. She had advanced Alzheimer's."

"Well, either you or the archives are lying. And the Authority never lies." Chuen's fingers flew over his eerie keyboard. "You bludgeoned your wife to death with a hammer, then blew your head off with a shotgun. If, indeed, that was you, and not a convenient victim who took your place. We'll soon know. Moore took a sample of your blood for DNA analysis."

"That's assault!"

"Worried? You should be."

"I've never been violent in my life. I'd never hurt Valerie that way."

"You were convinced she was cheating on you. To the point of paranoia, according to your daughter."

"I don't have a daughter. Valerie and I never had children."

"Well, no doubt Diana Spring would prefer that to be true. She's our Commander here at the Vancouver Police Authority."

"That's not possible." Francis couldn't breathe, his heart was beating like that of a frantic bird. What if Emily Wu had told him the truth? What if he *had* crossed over into a parallel universe?

"Please, look in my right-side coat pocket," he said. "There's a paper you need to see."

Before Chuen could respond, a golden thread of light cut through the wall, tracing the shape of a door. The wall melted away to reveal a dark opening. Moore stepped through it into the room.

Her straight black hair was slicked back from a bony forehead, her small green eyes were alive with hostility. She still wore her body armor, the long silver rod she'd used on him strapped to her thick waist.

"For you, Detective." She held up a thin tube. "DNA results. Gift from me to you." She tossed it to Chuen.

He caught the tube deftly. With care, he passed it through the orange light streaming from his tablet.

"It's him," Moore said, bristling. "He's Francis Rome. The Authority's DNA data base never lies."

"We need to make sure." Chuen studied his screen. "Diana's been watching us from the moment you requested the DNA results. We both know she has a special interest in this case. And why."

Francis sat up. Diana Spring, his daughter!

Moore chewed her lower lip. "She's coming down, right?"

"Yes," Chuen said. "So why don't you take a closer look at Mr. Rome while there's still time?"

"Why? What's going to happen?" Francis asked.

"He's an excellent example of advanced telomerosis," Chuen went on.

Moore leaned in for a closer look. "Well, he sure is an ugly mother."

"First time for you, right?" Chuen allowed himself a smile.

"So what if it is? Holy shit! He must be, like, 30 years over the barrier. Praise the Survival Law!" Moore thumped a fist over her heart.

"Telomerosis? Survival Law? What the hell are you talking about?" Francis was sweating despite the damp air.

"Telomeres lie at the end of your chromosomes," Chuen said. "They wear down as your cells divide. That's why humans age. Moore's never seen anyone over 50 before."

"Why is that?" Francis asked, although he didn't want to know the answer. He watched Chuen set the DNA tube down on the desk.

"His DNA checks out. He's Francis Rome," Chuen said.

"That's impossible!" Francis said. "I can't be alive and dead at the same time."

"That's the weird part. The dead guy's DNA is a match, too." Chuen toyed with the tube. "Obviously you planted your DNA on your fall guy. Clever, but then our forensic tests weren't as well-developed 30 years ago. Tell me, how did you manage to evade the Survival Law all this time?"

"Because I wasn't here!" Francis said. "Please, for God's sake, listen to me! Look at the note in my coat pocket."

"Come on, Francis." Chuen looked tired. "It's over. Be a man about it." An intense green light shot out from his tablet. "Diana's on her way down. She's going to do him herself."

Diana, his own daughter, planned to kill him. Francis could scarcely breathe. "Please, the note."

"Shut up about that fucking note!" Moore paced the room, running her hands through her hair. "Shut up or I'll do you myself!"

"No harm in looking while we wait." Chuen went over to the coats on the back wall. Francis watched the detective search through his raincoat and pull out Emily Wu's note.

"So what does his stupid note say?" Moore wanted to know.

Chuen shrugged and tucked it into his pants pocket. "Heads up, the Commander's here."

Light traced out the doorway in the concrete wall. A tall young woman in a navy blue suit strode into the room. Red-gold hair, hazel eyes, the same heart-shaped face...

"Valerie!" Her name escaped Francis like a final breath.

"What did you say?" Not Valerie's voice, much deeper. "How dare you speak my mother's name!"

She studied him, her eyes intent. "The Authority's aging software doesn't do you justice," she said at last. "You look a hell of a lot worse in reality. Where have you been hiding out? Who helped you? I need their names."

"I can make him tell, Commander," Moore put in. "Let me at him. I'd be honored."

"Give me your weapon." Diana stretched out her hand for it, her eyes never leaving Francis's face.

"But, sir…"

"That's an order."

Moore hesitated for a moment, but complied.

Diana, his own daughter, was going to kill him!

"Please, don't do this." Even to himself, he sounded pathetic.

"What mercy did you show Mom?" The weapon crackled in her grip.

"Please…I'm not your father!"

"A liar to the end." She aimed the weapon at his heart.

The universe was having its revenge. He'd killed Valerie. He deserved to die. His eyes filled with tears.

"Crying? Bit late for that," she said. "Any last words?"

"Nothing," Francis whispered.

"Commander, wait!" Chuen sounded alarmed. "We need to check one more thing."

"And what's that?" Diana's voice was hard with fury.

"May we speak privately?" Chuen said to her unyielding back. "Please, sir, my duty is to protect you."

"Moore, get out," Diana said.

Looking far from happy, Moore heaved herself up and left through the doorway. Chuen waited until the three of them were alone. "Francis Rome may be a Protected Person," he said.

"That's not possible," Diana said, the weapon rigid in her hand.

"Diana, think about it. He's stayed hidden for nearly a lifetime. He must be connected. To a powerful person in the Authority."

Diana swore, and slowly lowered the weapon. "Why didn't you check this out?"

"I would have, but only you, as Commander, have access to the Dark Web Authority."

"Give me your tablet." She dropped Moore's weapon on the desk and held out her hand.

Chuen picked up his tablet, keyed quickly on the screen and handed it to her.

She pressed her index finger down on the screen. "Retinal scan."

A thin strand of green light burst out of the tablet like a laser. It pierced her eye. She screamed, clutched her face,

Chuen leaped for the silver rod. Seized it and fired.

A torrent of blue light hit her in the chest. She crashed onto the desk. And slid off its slippery surface onto the floor. She landed on her side, eyes open, staring at nothing.

"You killed her!" Francis was in agony. "You killed my child!"

"She's not your child. At least not in this world. Get dressed." Chuen tore Francis's raincoat off its hook and threw it at him. He grabbed his own coat and fedora.

But Francis threw himself down beside Diana and fumbled for her wrist. "I can't feel her pulse."

"I set the rod to stun. She's fine." Chuen adjusted Moore's weapon with a click. He didn't as much as glance down at them.

"We have to make sure she's alive," Francis insisted.

"Come with me now if you want to live." Chuen set his fedora on his head. "Don't get sentimental. She tried to kill you."

Francis dragged himself to his feet. He watched Chuen scoop up his watch, phone and wallet. Numbly, he pulled on his coat. "What's this?" he asked, noticing a large brown stain on it.

"Blood, from when you fell." Chuen said. "We need to get back to the Blue Star Bakery. Move!" With his free hand, he shoved Francis through the dark doorway.

Francis felt a tingle of electricity and a burst of air. The next instant, he was standing beside Chuen in a long, featureless corridor. They were alone.

Without relaxing his grip on Francis's arm, Chuen propelled him down the hall toward a blank wall. A tracing of a light outlined another larger doorway. Once again, Francis felt electricity and a burst of air.

They landed outdoors next to a seamless, black building that rose several stories. Rain poured down on them from the night sky. Mist steamed up from the pavement. Except for Chuen's cruiser, parked by the curb a few feet away, the street looked deserted.

A figure emerged from the passenger side of the police car. Moore!

Smoke drifted from a glass tube in her hand. She stumbled against the hood, the rain bouncing off her body armor, plastering her lank hair to her scalp.

"Hey! What you doing with Rome?" she called out.

"Stay out of this, Moore." Chuen headed toward the car, dragging Francis along with him. "He's mine. Commander's orders. He's a Protected Person."

"Like hell." She took a long drag of smoke from her tube. "Show me the Commander's authorization."

They'd drawn level with Moore and the cruiser. Chuen barked a command. The driver and passenger doors slid open.

"He's my kill." Moore straightened up, blocking their way. "I need this one. My kill score is shit. Diana's on my ass. Give me my gun. I said, give me my goddamn gun!"

Chuen crashed the gun down on her skull. Glass splintered on the sidewalk, followed by a howl of frustration.

"Get in." Chuen pushed Francis through the open door and onto the passenger seat.

Moore was on her hands and knees on the wet pavement, searching frantically. Blood trickled from her scalp, mingling with the rain. "That's my crack dose for the month. I'm out of credits."

"I'm looking out for you, partner."

"Fuck you! You're dead!" Moore scrambled up. Pulled a knife from her waistband.

Chuen turned and fired. A blast of blue electricity hurled her against the glass wall of the police building.

She crashed down onto her back. Her eyes blinked once, twice. Through the open passenger door, Francis watched a fist-sized hole in her throat fill with rain.

Chuen leaped into the driver's seat beside him. The car doors closed. Francis heard Chuen give the order to drive. The car shot away from the curb.

"You killed her," Francis said after a few minutes.

"Yes." Chuen stared through the windshield, his dark eyes fixed on the road. He still held Moore's weapon. "Got her in the throat. She never bothered to do up her body armor. Too tight in the neck."

"She was your partner. You could have stunned her, like Diana."

"It was her or me. Only matter of time before she knifed me like she did her last partner."

Tall buildings rose like cliffs on either side of them as they hurtled down empty street after empty street. Francis's heart and mind were filled with Diana. Had Chuen lied about stunning her? Was she dead, too? He felt breathless, torn in two.

"Why are you helping me?" he asked.

"You're already dead in this world," Chuen said. "You won't survive if you stay here. If I can get you back to the Blue Star Bakery in time, with luck, Mother can send you home."

"Then what she told me about the portal and parallel universes is true. The note she wrote out is a code. To tell you that I...I'm from a different world."

"Yes, all true."

"And you are Emily Wu's son."

Chuen nodded.

"But an ordinary bakery acting as a portal! That's insane! Why isn't Emily Wu working out of some top-secret physics lab?"

"That's easy—she was. But her colleagues cheated her out of the Nobel Prize merely because she was a woman. After that, she decided to work alone. To travel through time and to explore our parallel worlds without interference. In her travels, she observed that bakeries tend to stay constant in time and place. And so, she reasoned, hiding her portal in a popular bakery might keep it safe and secret forever. Besides, she's always had a twisted sense of humor."

"But why push *me* through the portal?"

Chuen threw him a glance. "My guess is you two got talking, right? You told her that you were travelling alone and that you have no family."

"So no one would care if I disappeared."

"Exactly. Age is finally catching up with Mother. For some time now, I've been doing the hands-on exploring for her. But I'm only one person and she's desperate to learn more before she dies. She's been sending other people through the portal. She calls them her 'rovers'."

"Lab rats, you mean! What's happened to these other rovers?"

Chuen looked uneasy. "I'm not sure."

"You mean they're dead!" Francis couldn't contain his anger.

"Some, yes, have died, but others have chosen never to return home," Chuen said.

"Surely none of them wanted to stay in this terrible world!"

Chuen sighed. "Well, they don't always land here. In theory, a rover could end up in any one of an infinite number of different worlds. But the number of different worlds we've discovered is a lot fewer than we'd anticipated. Only 12 worlds, so far."

Francis felt hopelessly overwhelmed. "But suppose I'd landed in one of the other 12 worlds. A world where I was still alive. Would I have met myself? Like a doppelganger?"

"Not exactly." Again Chuen looked troubled. "You see, according to Mother's theory, we are all the same person. Different versions of ourselves. But when you rove into another world, where you are still alive, you subsume your other identity. You become that person. You take their place—and replace their consciousness with yours."

"And what happens to the consciousness of the person you replace?" Francis asked.

Chuen shrugged. "Well, it's gone. Forever."

"You mean you obliterate their consciousness with yours. A kind of spiritual murder," Francis said.

"That's one way to look at it," Chuen said. "Enough questions." He told the car to drive faster.

But Francis wasn't finished. "Why did I end up here in this dark world and not another, perhaps much better one?"

"The probability of landing here, in this dark world, is far greater than landing in any other. Most rovers land here first. That's why I stay on. To help them. Besides," Chuen smiled, "I find this place exciting."

"Allow me to disagree," Francis said. "What happened to this world? What went wrong?"

"Global warming," Chuen said. "Feel how hot and humid it is? The Authority is depopulating the earth to save it. Last week, they moved the Barrier Age down to 40 from 50."

"So at 40 you must die."

Chuen nodded. "If you make it that far. Limited health care, food shortages, drug addictions and violence make for short life spans."

"And even misdemeanors are capital crimes," Francis filled in. "But the law doesn't apply to Protected Persons who, I presume, are the bastards running the place."

"Yes, the old guard, the wealthy elite."

"And is the Authority's strategy working?"

"No, it's too late for that."

The police car left the main road and turned onto a side street. Francis recognized his old apartment building across from the alley where the back entrance to the Blue Star Bakery was located.

"What happens if a rover loses Emily Wu's note?" Francis asked.

Chuen shifted in the driver's seat. "I'm only human. I've missed a few." He ordered the car to stop.

As they climbed out, a brilliant bolt of lightning crackled through the sky. Francis heard a strange whistle under the thundering rainstorm. "The drones!" he cried.

"The portal's about to close." Weapon in hand, Chuen hustled him into the darkness of the alley. Francis could barely make out the blue of the bakery's back door. The reek of the overflowing dumpster surged over him.

"Here, take your things." Chuen handed over his watch, phone and wallet. "No, don't put them in your coat, put them in your jacket."

"Why?"

"Don't argue. Do it! Good, now give me your raincoat. I need the blood on it for your DNA."

Francis handed it to him. Chuen tossed the coat into the overflowing dumpster. It landed, half in, half out.

"Now go." The detective urged him toward the door. "Walk straight at the blue door. It will open, the same way the doors do at the police station."

"What about you?"

Chuen shook his head. "I'm staying."

"But you'll die."

"Don't worry about me." Chuen's teeth flashed in a brief smile. "Here in this world I'm Diana's lover."

"You think that will save you?" Francis cried. "Don't throw your life away for me. I don't deserve it. I did kill my wife!"

"What? Back in our home world?"

Francis heard the drones coming closer. Lights strafed Bryson Street beyond the alley.

"Yes, Valerie had Alzheimer's. It was hopeless. One night I slipped her some pills. She wouldn't let anyone else feed her, only me."

"Francis, you must leave now!" Chuen readied his weapon. "I understand why you gave Valerie the pills. You didn't want to see her suffer."

"No! I was being selfish. What I did was unforgiveable."

Light blazed down the alley. A drone hovered overhead.

"Take this." Chuen pressed Emily Wu's blue note into Francis's hand. "GO, NOW!"

Alarms and lasers blazed from every direction. The dumpster glowed red, the garbage around it caught fire. Through the flames, Francis saw Chuen and the drone firing at each other.

He threw himself at the blue door, but it was hard, unyielding. He banged on it. Fire scorched his hands, his clothes, his hair. The heat was horrific...

***

"Francis, can you hear me?" a voice asked.

Francis coughed, tried to speak. He looked up into the face of Adrian Chuen. Only the detective was dressed as a paramedic.

"Breathe deep now. It's oxygen," a woman said beside him.

"No, no, I'm fine." Francis pushed the mask away.

He was sitting on a vinyl chair with stainless steel legs, the chair in the Blue Star Bakery. Iced cakes and plump apple pies beckoned from the display case in front of him, as well as macaroons and truffles in every color of the rainbow. He rubbed his eyes. There on the aluminum tray were his favorite, cinnamon buns.

"What happened?" he asked.

"You gave Mother here quite a scare," said Chuen.

"You sure did!" Emily Wu piped up from her perch behind the cash register. "One minute, we are talking, you are drinking coffee. Next minute, boom! You fall down on the floor. I think maybe you choke on your cinnamon bun, your favorite snack. So I called the ambulance."

Francis tried to stand, but the woman gently restrained him. He caught sight of her for the first time. Red gold hair, hazel eyes, the same heart-shaped face. "Valerie!" he gasped.

"Dad, I'm Diana, your daughter. Don't you know me?"

"Why are you wearing a paramedic's uniform?"

"Because I'm working today. Honestly, you're damn lucky Adrian and I caught Emily's call."

Francis closed his eyes. Be brave, he told himself. He had to ask. "And Valerie...your mother?"

"Mom is going crazy, you taking off like that without telling her. She's waiting for us at the hospital. This is not good, Dad. It's the twins' birthday party tomorrow," Diana said.

"The twins," Francis echoed.

"Your granddaughters, Adrian and my kids?"

Francis thought quickly. "Sorry to make such a fuss. I just wanted a cinnamon bun. Do we really have to go to the hospital?"

"Dad, you know we do," Chuen said. "Standard procedure. We need to make sure you haven't had a stroke."

A short, heavy-set police officer looked in through the bakery's open front door. "How's the old guy doing?"

"He's OK, Officer Moore," Chuen said over his shoulder. "We're about to leave."

"Good to hear. He had me worried. Traffic's cleared for you." Moore threw them a thumbs up.

Francis let Chuen and Diana ease him onto a stretcher and wheel him out to the waiting ambulance. Outside, the rain had stopped. He smiled. The neon sign above the entrance of the Blue Star Bakery was enhanced by a night sky full of stars.

Diana, Chuen and Moore stood talking together by the open door. Francis caught the phrases "second raincoat he's lost this month," "happening more and more lately," and then "geriatric assessment."

Was he the one who had Alzheimer's disease and not Valerie? Was he the one suffering from delusions? Was his lonely life in Montreal nothing but a bad dream?

He started as Emily Wu climbed up into the ambulance and crouched down beside him.

"You drop this in the bakery." She held up a crumpled piece of blue note paper. "You still want it?"

"Yes, thank you." Francis took the precious note from her.

"Good. Nice talking physics with you." She scrambled out of the ambulance just as Diana got in. Francis could have sworn that Emily turned and winked at him.

"What was that all about?" Diana asked him after the ambulance got going.

"Your mother-in-law and I were talking mathematics. Physics versus economics, and which has more practical applications in our world." With relief, he watched his daughter roll her eyes.

"Honestly, the two of you," she said.

"We're clear thanks to Officer Moore," Chuen said from the driver's seat. "Blue lights all the way."

"Surely we don't need the siren and flashing lights," Francis said.

"Traffic lights, Dad," Diana said. "Red, yellow, blue, like you're always teaching the twins. Red means stop, blue means go."

"Of course, blue means go," he said. "Sorry, it's been a long day. I'm glad to be home. Very glad indeed."

Emily Wu had given him a second chance. He hugged the blue note paper to his chest. One day he might throw it away, but he'd keep it safe for now.

Ω

CHRISTMAS ROSE

Jayne Barnard

JE (Jayne) Barnard writes short fiction as well as the popular Maddie Hatter Adventures and The Falls Mysteries. She won the Alberta Book of the Year award, the Dundurn Unhanged Arthur, the Bony Pete, as well as the Saskatchewan Writers Guild Award, and was shortlisted for the Prix Aurora (twice), the UK Debut Dagger, and the Book Publishing in Alberta Award (twice).

Her most recent book is Where the Ice Falls, *a small-town psychological thriller set in the Alberta foothills.* Why the Rock Falls *comes out in November 2020 from Dundurn Press.*

"Poinsettias aren't poisonous," said the voice from the hall, "but mistletoe is."

Fred Peterson repressed a shudder. If he didn't answer, his mother-in-law would invade his bedroom, even though her wheelchair could barely slide through the doorway.

"Been watching nature shows again, Mother Ivy? Any remedies look good for your osteonecrosis?"

"I could make you mistletoe tea, and you wouldn't know until it was too late."

"That's nice." Fred checked himself in the mirror and approved of his appearance. The new green tie with his red shirt made him look festive. Holly Marley had helped him pick out the tie on her lunch hour, but his wife did not need to know that. Rosemary did not believe in office friendships.

"Everybody wants something, Fred," she often said. "Everybody has an angle. Especially in the oil patch."

She would say it tonight about young Charlie Ferguson, determined to convince him Charlie was after his job. Not even Charlie's interview at Petro-Canada last week shook her. But Charlie wouldn't stay an accountant at a tiny oil company for long. He wanted excitement. Change. Mobility. He wasn't married to Rosemary, who was more than enough change for Fred.

Fred's wife was hollering for him from her private bathroom. He caught "and my allergy meds" and went to ask for a repeat of his new orders.

Rosemary was fixing her first earring, a brushed-platinum dangler that Fred didn't remember seeing before. It would show up on the January statement, along with her evening gown and other necessities. Heaven knew what she had spent on spa treatments and haircuts, not to mention undergarments he would never see. Last year's office party had cost him $5,000, not counting Ivy's caregiver's wages, and he hadn't even got a new tie.

She picked up the second earring. "Where did you get that hideous tie?"

"It's holly green."

"It's stupid. You look like those tacky cartoon Christmas ornaments. Like an incompetent loser. Are you angling for early retirement, Fred? Because I warn you: you'll be digging ditches if Ted lets you go."

"Digging your own grave," chimed in her mother from the hallway.

The practical nurse appeared behind Ivy's wheelchair. "I'm sorry, Mrs. Peterson. She got away from me while I was fixing her Ovaltine." She and Ivy disappeared.

"It's holly green," Fred repeated. "Suitable for a Christmas party."

"It's disgusting. Change it for the one I bought. Put my prescription in my evening clutch on the hall table. Start the car so it's warm for me. And hurry up!"

Fred hurried.

His suit jacket hung on his bedroom doorknob. He slipped it on as he passed. The tie could stay. Holly would like to see him wearing it. Rosemary might not notice until they arrived. Too late then. He went to the kitchen, sneaked a tiny smile to the nurse and found the tube that held Rosemary's brand-new emergency syringe.

"Bye, Mother Ivy," he said. "I hope you have a nice evening."

The old lady's wheels whispered as she turned, watching for him to screw up something else. He dropped the tube into Rosemary's handbag and stole a glance at his new tie in the hall mirror. It looked festive. He hid it under his winter coat.

When Rosemary came out, coldly elegant in cream silk and carrying a pair of gray heels that matched her jewelry, Ivy cackled from the kitchen. "Put it in the wrong bag, he did. Ditch-digging's all he's good for."

"Idiot. I said my evening clutch." Rosemary opened a gray cloth envelope that Fred hadn't noticed. Ivy watched from the kitchen, her shoulders shaking in wheezy laughter.

"I'll start the car." Fred stepped out onto the porch, passing under a beribboned cluster of mistletoe and wondering if some could accidentally fall into Ivy's Ovaltine.

It was a dark, silent drive out to the party in the streams of westbound traffic. Rosemary had already expressed her opinion of the date—"the longest night of the year. As if it won't seem twice as long, with HER gloating around"—and the location—"showing off HER exclusive clubhouse behind the gate in Elbow Valley"—and there was nothing else to say. Elizabeth, Ted's fine new wife and former secretary, had decreed the party would be held near her fine new country home instead of at the Palliser Hotel, where Rosemary, Ted's other former secretary, had always held them. Elizabeth had said the snow-drifted view would be "seasonal". Fred had not troubled her with the odds against a white Christmas in Chinook country.

Sure enough, the bare brown golf course surrounded the faux-stone building that had the appearance of a funeral home. Fred handed his keys to the parking valet, his winter coat to the next valet, and he and Rosemary moved past a softly plucking string quartet toward the new Mrs. Maxwell. She greeted them at the foot of a curving staircase, not quite under a huge cluster of mistletoe.

"The Petersons. How nice. We're up on the mezzanine."

"Liz Manders," said Fred. "Nice to see you again. How's married life?"

Without a word, Rosemary dragged Fred upstairs and paused to survey the early arrivals. A dozen people were clustered by the bar, half-hidden by high stands of poinsettias and trembling stalks of lily-bells mixed with twigs full of red berries. Yew berries clung to a cheery arch of evergreen branches over the appetizer buffet. Every table had a centerpiece of holly and candles. The toxic décor would surely thrill Ivy, but at least she wasn't there to poison his coffee. Her rotting hip bones kept her at home except for medical appointments. *His* home, bought for his marriage, the same day that Rosemary had coolly informed him Ivy was moving into his new house too.

Rosemary reared back. "He's here already."

"Who?" Fred tried to decipher faces among the greenery.

"Charlie Ferguson. Pretend you suspect nothing."

Pretense wasn't necessary, but Fred knew better than to mention that. He followed his wife to the bar, nodding greetings to his co-workers. Ted Maxwell was in their midst, telling jokes and passing drinks, patting the women's arms while he glanced down their cleavage. On the edge of the crowd stood Charlie Ferguson, clinking glasses with a tense-looking brunette. Charlie waved Fred over and turned to his date.

"Darling, let me introduce you to Fred and Rosemary. Fred was my first mentor in oil-patch bookkeeping. What he knows about accounting would fill the library at Drumheller Penitentiary. Fred, Rosemary, meet Catherine Neilson."

Fred laughed before he saw Rosemary's face. Then he gulped. Rosemary did not appreciate accounting jokes. Or prison jokes.

"Catherine Neilson," Rosemary repeated. "Surely not the Neilson who worked in accounting for TGB Oil & Gas before it imploded? I hope you found another job despite the nasty rumors about fraud."

Catherine Neilson blanched. Ted Maxwell turned, frowning. Fred raised his eyebrows in mute apology. Charlie looked coldly at Fred and Rosemary.

"Come, Catherine. Let's get a refill."

"Can I get you a glass of wine, Rosemary?" Fred crept away from a spate of instructions concerning possible allergenic contaminants, the appropriate degree of chill for white wine, blotting condensation before he handed her a glass, and not under any circumstances to accept any booze for himself. While he waited miserably in the bar line up, it did not immediately sink through his gloom that the woman with the exposed back in front of him had a familiar friendly face. Only when she gave her order in an elegant British voice did he recognize her. "Holly," he said, with a sudden lifting of spirits. "How nice to see you."

She looked over one bare shoulder, beaming. "Fred. Let me give you a drink."

Fred blushed from the sheer, giddy pleasure of being smiled at by Holly. "N-no. Thank you. I'm d-driving. I'm, uh, getting my wife a glass of wine. White, please," he added to the bartender, while Rosemary's detailed instructions dissolved beneath Holly's warm brown gaze.

She accepted a mug from behind the bar, something cream-topped with red-and-green sprinkles. "You should try one of these. Spice up your life something wonderful. Oh, you're wearing the tie."

"Rosemary doesn't like it. She said I look like a cartoon character."

"Nonsense. It's just the contrast with your shirt. Try it against my dress." She lifted the tie and laid it against her breast. It seemed very shapely, suddenly.

"Uh," he said, staring at the impressive contour.

"The holly green against this deep sage looks great, don't you think?"

"Uh," said Fred again. "Uh, yes. Much better." He took the mug from her hand and gulped half its contents. "Whew. That's really hot."

"Tequila-ginger cocoa. The only cure is to have another." She turned to the bartender, tugging Fred along by his tie. "We'll have two more of these, please. Make his a virgin."

"How appropriate. The virgin sacrifice." Catherine Neilson was standing at his shoulder, eyes glinting over a half-empty mug of something pink. "I hear rosemary used to be burnt at sacrifices. So festive, and on the Solstice, too."

"Now, dear," said Charlie Ferguson, taking her arm. "We said we wouldn't let one nasty comment spoil things. Let's find better company."

Holly looked at Fred. "What was that all about?"

Fred's misery returned. "Rosemary insinuated that Charlie's friend was part of a fraud. Ted was furious."

"I bet. There's nobody more sensitive about fraud than a man who narrowly escaped a prison term for it. He'll be looking sideways at Charlie for the next decade."

"Charlie's leaving us anyway. What about a prison term?"

"Rosemary never mentioned that? Or Ted?" Holly's eyebrows reached halfway to her hairline. "You're fooling, right?"

Fred shook his head.

She shook hers, too. "You really are an innocent, luv. Well then. You remember Rosemary was Ted's secretary when you first came to work for us?"

Fred nodded. "That's how I met her."

"Ted brought her over from Husky when he struck out on his own. Except, after he sold shares in Maxwell Energy to all his friends and relations, he had a falling-out with his brother-in-law over how the money was being spent. He might have gone to jug if Rosemary hadn't stepped in."

"My wife?" Fred took two mugs from the bar and handed one to Holly.

"Cheers." She clinked his mug. "When the securities investigators showed up, Rosemary told them she hadn't understood the accounting procedures for the shares, and had been afraid to ask Ted for clarification. She said she'd gone on muddling things up for a whole year and hoping it would somehow come right in the end. We all assumed she was covering Ted's arse, but the two of them were doing the books between them, so how could we know who did what? And when you took over, you didn't hold her responsible either."

Fred took a long swallow of his spicy cocoa. It heated all the way down, but it was no match for the chill closing in on his chest. He had spent many overtime hours with Rosemary, trying to sort out those mangled accounts. She had blamed the mess on Ted, saying he'd hoped to save money by not hiring accountants until the company was on its feet. Fred would have sworn Rosemary knew nothing, especially about the more unlikely entries. He gulped more cocoa.

"So what happened?"

Holly shrugged. "The brother-in-law dropped charges in exchange for his money back, and the investigators closed their file in return for Ted's promise to get a qualified accountant. That's you. Are you sure Rosemary didn't tell you this?"

No, Rosemary had told him nothing. From his first day on the job she had played the innocent. The sweet, sexy innocent. Blinded by charms not usually focused on short, middle-aged accountants, he hadn't questioned her version of the company's history. Nor had he questioned her un-secretarial freedom to leave work at will and run up expense accounts. Come to think of it, she had been out of the office so much that Liz Manders had been hired as her assistant. Eventually, Liz did all the work and Rosemary appeared only for long lunch meetings with Ted.

Around the same time Ted had started taking Liz to lunch meetings instead, Rosemary asked Fred out for lunch. Soon they were dining out too, but he wasn't sure how they got from restaurants to the altar, only that it was after Ted gave Rosemary that huge severance package. She needed somebody to invest it for her, after all. None of their co-workers—Fred could see that now—would have wanted to tell him his new wife was covering for Ted's misdeeds with the investors' money.

And where was Rosemary, anyway? Saying a quick goodbye to Holly, Fred visited the aperitif table, expecting to find his wife quizzing the servitors about allergenic ingredients. Few things made Rosemary more irate than being seen in public with hives all over her face. But she wasn't there. He collected a plate of curlicue vegetables, bacon-wrapped scallops, and other Rosemary-safe snacks. As he turned away, he bumped a greenery-covered pedestal, upon which rested a silver dome lid.

"What's under there?" he asked the attendant.

"African ground nuts roasted in a honey-ginger glaze. May I serve you?"

The fellow lifted the silver dome and exposed a sterling bowl of what looked, and smelled, like Fred's long-lost favorite snack, Costco honey-roasted peanuts. These would probably appear on the catering invoice priced as though they had been flown from Africa and individually painted with glaze.

Fred's mouth watered. It had been two years since Rosemary imposed her ban on peanuts. Surely one illicit handful wouldn't hurt. He would keep that hand away from Rosemary. He accepted a red-and-green paper cup of peanuts and moved on, listening to snippets of conversation.

"Some joint, huh?"

"Did you see that swimming pool?"

"Three private massage rooms! I bet they're popular with the trophy wives."

"Are they soundproof?"

The massage rooms, he discovered by accident, were off a hallway at one end of the mezzanine, their access mostly blocked by stands filled with poinsettias. He settled near the plants where he could see the entire party area. Liz Maxwell circulated among the tables. Charlie Ferguson was near the appetizers, coaxing his date to eat. Holly smiled up at some chisel-faced geology consultant. But still no Rosemary.

The holiday-esque music trailed away and Fred at last heard his wife's voice, rising softly from beyond the poinsettias. In one of the massage rooms.

"...should be my house, you skunk."

"You're the one who married first. You could have waited another year."

"Don't you make it my fault! You were moving on as soon as the investigation ended. But the statute of limitations isn't over, Ted. Not for your reputation."

"I made sure you were looked after, didn't I? Hell, I still am. I pay your husband twice what he's worth. I'm always passing on perks to you. Or did you think he got you onto that spa cruise simply by phoning up and inquiring?"

"That was you?" Rosemary's voice lost its edge. "That's so sweet, Teddy. I loved that trip. And I miss you. Couldn't we…?"

Fred's blood boiled. His wife was in that room with his boss. Ted had been paying her off through Fred's salary. He gulped another mouthful of gingered-up cocoa. He had a good mind to barge in on them and…and….

Whatever intentions his brain was trying to formulate were cut short when a hand landed on his arm. A hand with short, sensible nails.

"Holly?"

"Luv, what's wrong? You're parked like a hat rack, dripping bacon grease."

"I'll get rid of this plate," he said, moving away from the door, conscious of relief in the retreat. "I know it's the man's job, but would you please get me another drink? A real one this time. I've had a bit of a shock."

By the time Holly found him again, Fred had turned in his congealing plate and been assisted to blot the grease off his slacks. He took the drink and swallowed a big mouthful, gasping as it singed his throat.

"Thanks. I can't tell you how much it helps to see you smile at me."

"Wow, luv, you must really be upset. We'll find a chair and you can tell me all about it." She laid her hand on his arm.

Another hand landed on his other arm, a hand he knew only too well by its French manicure. Across the room, Ted was talking to Liz, whose rigid expression implied she had spotted him leaving the massage area with Rosemary.

"Fred, find our seats," said Rosemary sharply. "They're about to start serving." She towed him away, talking with that through-the-smile fury that grated on him like fingernails down a blackboard. "I see you spilled something already. Honestly, can't I take you anywhere? You should have found our seats already, so we could switch the cards if we don't like our tablemates."

When they were in their chairs at a nearly empty table, she said, "So Ted finally dumped that gold-digging British chippy."

There was only one British woman present: Holly.

"Wha-what do you mean?"

"You're so naive, Fred. At last year's party, the air crackled whenever she walked past him. This year, they won't even stand on the same side of the room. Besides, you don't think that Cockney tart was hitting on you for your good looks, do you? She's hoping you'll let slip some financial dirt on Ted, so she can use it for job security. 'The boss's ex-tart' doesn't look good on a résumé."

She looked away, greeting the next arrivals, leaving Fred to pick his jaw up off the tablecloth. Holly and that oil-company lothario? Never. And who was ex-secretary Rosemary—herself an ex-Ted tart—to sling dirt about an accredited petroleum engineer? Holly liked him. She did.

A white-suited arm slid a salad plate in front of him, but he had lost his appetite.

Charlie and Catherine arrived, sitting down to stare grimly at their greens. They didn't look hungry either. Catherine resisted the efforts of the waiter to remove the dregs of her drink. The glass tipped, sending a pink creamy stream in Rosemary's direction.

"Oops," said Catherine, catching it with her napkin at the last possible second before it reached Rosemary's teensy gray purse. "So careless of me. That was my last strawberry eggnog, too."

"Indeed," said Rosemary, her voice cold enough to frost Fred's cocoa. "You could have made me ill. I'm highly allergic to strawberries." She turned away to grill the waiter on the ingredients of the salad dressing.

Catherine leaned back, smiling, and applied herself to her salad. Charlie, after a nervous glance between her and Rosemary, caught Fred's eye and shrugged. It was over, he seemed to say. Fred smiled back tentatively and picked up his fork.

Charlie, making conversation in the face of Catherine's determined silence, asked Rosemary about her allergies, which led to her familiar complaint about Fred's carelessness with her adrenalin syringes.

"Cold is the worst thing for an EpiPen," she said, coming around for the third time, "and yet I can't count the number of them I've had to replace because they froze in the glove compartment or boiled on the dashboard! I don't take any chances. If they're even the slightest bit off-color, out they go. I have an up-to-date EpiPen in my purse at all times. People without allergies are so careless."

Holly appeared, leaning in between Fred and Rosemary, setting a mug down on the table. She smiled down into Fred's face, which was suddenly scant inches from the shapely contour of green fabric that his tie had adorned earlier. He gulped.

"Luv, you forgot your drink." She stroked his cheek with a sensible fingernail and departed.

Rosemary muttered "Chippy," and poked at her salad, only to be interrupted by the arrival of Mrs. Maxwell the Third.

"Is everything all right so far?" Liz rested a hand on Rosemary's chair. "It's a new venue, and we want to be sure everything is up to standard."

Rosemary tilted her head, treating the hostess to a knowing smile. "I can see why you're nervous, Elizabeth. The last entertainment you organized was a staff bowling night, wasn't it? Such a long way up from beer and bowling to a country club. Of course, it's not a patch on the parties we used to host at the Palliser. Everyone important in the industry came, and I loved organizing them. The decorations, the food, the wine. Ted used to call me 'Christmas Rose'."

Liz smiled back at her. "Christmas Rose? Trust Ted to put a good spin on a common blossom."

Rosemary's mouth opened.

"Hellebore, darling," Liz practically purred. "The Christmas Rose? The plant?"

Catherine muttered, "Should have 'of a' in the middle."

"Hellebore?" Charlie asked quickly. "A Christmas plant?"

"Helleborus niger, to be correct," Liz explained. "The Christmas Rose has black roots and is irritating to the eyes." As Rosemary snarled, she went on sweetly, "Get a bellyful, and you'll be nauseous for days. Closely related to the green hellebore."

Catherine smirked. "And to the stinking hellebore. I didn't realize you were so knowledgeable about plants, Mrs. Maxwell."

"I can recognize the toxic ones." Liz smiled knowingly at her and moved on, leaving fraught silence behind. Rosemary glared at Catherine as the seafood dishes arrived.

Catherine grinned back, signaling the waiter for another pink eggnog.

Ted Maxwell stopped at the next table over, slapping shoulders and joking, as carefree as if he had not been conniving in a massage room with Fred's truthless wife. Maybe that was his usual party behavior and Fred had simply not noticed it last year. He was sure Holly did not sneak away with other people's husbands. Holly was sensible. And she had good taste in cocktails. Fred gulped the last of his drink, and waved the empty mug at a waiter. He was beginning to enjoy the cocoa and ginger and whatever else was in there. He must remember to ask what it was called.

Some time after Ted had squeezed past with barely a "Happy Holidays," Fred noticed that Rosemary's tiny gray purse was no longer on the table. He didn't draw attention to its absence. Let her worry about her own things for a change. No more crawling on the floor for this accountant. He tackled his roast breast of whatever with gusto. The waiter brought another mug of thingy. After a toast with Catherine, whose latest strawberry eggnog had arrived at the same time, he slurped greedily. The spicy drink was going down well on this fine winter evening. He might even have another before the moon disappeared behind the not-too-distant Rockies. He would take a taxi home, with or without Rosemary. And charge it to Ted.

A gust of evening wind whipped in from an opened patio door, ruffling plants, scattering miscellaneous berries, and causing a few spills as people yanked their glasses away from the poisonous projectiles. When things settled, Rosemary was cursing at a brownish splotch on her sleeve.

"Club soda," said Fred in a helpful mood, passing her his napkin. "Gets anything out." He waved his mug for emphasis, splashing more cocoa.

"You're drunk," said Rosemary, but the ice in her voice failed to chill Fred's joie-de-vivre. She licked the napkin and dabbed at her sleeve.

He grinned. "And you're a blackmailer," he said softly, almost in her ear. "Quit worrying. Ted will buy you a new dress."

Rosemary's eyes slivered behind the spiky black eyelashes. "We'll discuss this later. I'm going to clean up." She dabbed at her lips with the crumpled napkin as she pushed back her chair. She stood up, clutching at her throat. Shrieked.

"I've been poisoned!"

All heads turned, Fred's included. He watched Rosemary slump back into her chair, wiping frantically at her lips with the back of her hand.

"Allergy?"

Rosemary nodded. Her mouth hung open, wheezy breath rasping through it.

Fred sobered up in a flash.

"Quick, we've got to clean it off her lips!" He reached for his napkin, but Catherine was quicker, sloshing her pink-splashed napkin with water and swiping the wet linen across Rosemary's mouth. Makeup smeared in its wake. Rosemary grabbed her wrist, staring with horror at the pink stain.

"Strawberry?" she gasped. "You'll kill me."

Forgetting his earlier vow against crawling, Fred dropped to his knees by her chair. "It's OK, Rosemary. Strawberries will only give you hives. There must have been traces of ground nuts on that napkin, but it barely touched your lips. You'll be all right. Just breathe. Nice and slow."

He pressed his fingers against her wrist. Her pulse jumped like a sack of kittens. Her face flushed, an angry red stain climbing from her neckline. Her mouth hung open as she gasped for air.

"Breathe, honey. Breathe," he said, and hollered over his shoulder. "Somebody find her purse. It was on the table."

"It's probably in the massage room." Liz was looking down at Rosemary with an expression of spurious concern. Ted was right behind her, watching with worry on his smarmy face. A hand passed over Fred's shoulder, holding the tiny gray purse, now dirty and smeared with what looked like a footprint.

"It was under a chair," said Charlie.

"Open it. Get out her syringe and slide it out of its tube." Fred felt the thing slap into his palm. He lifted it to check, just as he had been taught. "Oh, God. It's broken. It must have been stepped on."

"Should I call 9-1-1?" Charlie asked, his cell phone already open.

"Can't wait." Fred fumbled his valet parking tag out of his pocket. "There's another in my car. Glove box. Hurry."

Rosemary's eyes bulged. Her face was puffing up like cotton candy. She was drooling, a sure sign that her throat was swelling shut. All Fred could do was slap her hands gently and encourage her to breathe during the eternity of waiting for the spare. At last Charlie returned. He popped the tube and slid the syringe into Fred's hand. Fred lifted it to the light.

"No cracks. No discoloration. OK, here goes." He positioned the pen against Rosemary's thigh. "Honey, I'm going to give you your shot now. One little pinch and it will be all right again."

He pushed, felt her jerk under his hands. He was vaguely conscious of a crowd around them, but all his attention was focused on Rosemary. Her lips hung open. Her eyes pleaded above smeared mascara. Her body struggled. She wasn't getting any air.

"Can someone do rescue breathing?" he shouted.

Someone emerged from the crowd, tilted Rosemary's head back and pinched her nose. How she would hate knowing her carefully arranged hairstyle was coming apart! Charlie had called 911, and was yelling into his phone. Elbow Valley had its own fire station but on busy weekend nights the ambulance was often pulled in to cover Calgary's outskirts. How far away was it right now?

Holly's sensible hands rested on Fred's shoulders. "Back up a bit," she said. "The guys are going to get her onto the floor so they can do proper CPR."

He let her put him into a chair. She stood behind him, her hands holding him in place. Two guys from the Drilling department worked in tandem on his wife, one keeping up a steady compression rhythm, the other trying to force air past her swollen throat. He watched like it was a movie, feeling oddly blank, while sirens grew louder, then stopped. He saw the paramedics come running past the poinsettia banks, their blue jackets flapping and their heavy bags swinging. He flinched at the huge syringe they plunged into Rosemary. If her heart was still beating, that would put it into overdrive. He watched as they cut into the fine skin of her neck and blood spurted onto the cream silk dress, the tube slid into her throat and was connected to the breathing machine. But he had the feeling it was already too late.

They took her out on a stretcher, still attached to the breathing apparatus that performed its mechanical function. Death couldn't happen at a Christmas party.

Charlie and Holly helped Fred to his feet, put him into his car and drove him through the winter night behind the ambulance. They sat with him in the emergency room at Rockyview Hospital, waiting while the doctor on duty confirmed what he already knew. He heard the word "autopsy" and nodded, then signed where he was told.

Charlie and Holly drove him home and took him inside. Charlie paid the elder-sitter and sent her home. The three of them sat at the table drinking tea in silence.

The doorbell rang at midnight. Two police detectives introduced themselves. They were sympathetic but insistent.

"In cases of sudden death, we need to determine the circumstances as quickly as possible," one said, folding away his Major Crimes I.D.

"Don't bother Fred," Holly said, taking charge. "Charlie and I can tell you whatever you need to know."

Charlie nodded solemnly. "I was sitting at the same table as Fred and his wife."

The detective shook his head. "We have to take separate statements from each of you. You can wait in the next room, or go home and we'll come to you later."

"We'll wait here," Holly said.

Fred looked up. Sweet Holly. She would stay up all night if he hinted that he needed her. But he could not, not in front of the detectives.

"No, please," he said. "Go home. Get some sleep. Thank you both. You were wonderful. I'll manage tonight." Tears pooled in his eyes at their caring. Especially Holly's. He pressed her hand, grinning weakly. "Thanks for the gingered cocoa. I never would have tried it but for you."

Holly cried. She flung her arms around him. Fred buried his nose in her hair for the long, warm hug. When he emerged, Charlie was there, his eyes suspiciously pink at the edges, holding out his arms. Fred accepted the two-second, man-style hug in the spirit of its offering.

"We'll call you tomorrow." Holly allowed herself to be led away. "If you need anything, if you don't want to be alone, just phone and I'll come over. Promise?"

"Promise." Fred nodded until the front door closed behind them. He led the police back to the kitchen and drooped into his chair. "What do you need to know?"

The detective took him through the evening's events. Fred answered every question, skirting only Rosemary's visit to the massage room. When he got to the moment of the patio doors banging open, he let his head fall into his hands.

"I wasted precious seconds doubting Rosemary. I thought she was being dramatic. Maybe her EpiPen wasn't broken then. If her purse hadn't fallen off the table, if I'd gone for the spare right away, she might still be alive. If I'd told Charlie to call 911 right away…" He rocked in his chair, pressed his fingers hard into his scalp.

The detectives waited until he raised his head.

"So there's no doubt in your mind that she died from an allergic reaction? No question that she might have been poisoned? There were plenty of toxic plants in the room. Could she have eaten something by accident?"

Fred shook his head. "She was very careful about her food. Allergies, you know." Let the office gossips tell them how many enemies Rosemary had at that party. Let them test every plant in the expensive decorations. Let them look for poisons in her body all they wanted. He knew what anaphylactic shock looked like. He had spent many hours memorizing the symptoms, identifying the point of no return.

"Any other medications in the house besides your wife's allergy pens?"

"Sure. My mother-in-law, Ivy, has a bunch for managing her bone disease. It's very painful." Fred waved a hand toward the hallway. "The nurses that come in every day look after all that."

The investigators glanced sideways at each other, and one made a note. "You know there will be an autopsy, don't you?"

"They said so at the hospital."

"And you've no objection?"

Fred shook his head.

"Last question, Mr. Peterson. Did your wife have a will?"

Fred shook his head again. "She left her life insurance in a trust to look after her crippled mother. Anything left over will eventually come to me."

The officers thanked him for his time, offered their sympathies again, and left him to spend his first night as a widower.

Fred went to his little office in the basement. It was orderly and bland, an accountant's domain. The desk was an ancient wood affair, bought secondhand with his first professional paycheck. The sagging sofa, the file cabinet, even his battered office chair predated Rosemary. The calendar was a gift from a hopeful insurance agent. Nothing in this room had been bought with Ted's hush money or chosen by Rosemary's grasping soul. He put his feet up on the desk and leaned back. He was free.

Free of Rosemary and her unending demands and her uncertain temper.

Free to go for lunch with Holly whenever she invited him.

Soon he'd be liberated from Ivy's poisonous presence, too. How fast could he get her into a nursing home? Preferably one where they'd keep her sedated so she couldn't annoy the other residents.

In fairness, he owed a debt of gratitude to Ted's money. It had kept up the payments on Rosemary's million-dollar life insurance policy even after she'd left the company. It leased the car that alternately froze and boiled her syringes, leaving a few of them invisibly ineffective. And, when the bills arrived for the Maxwell Energy Christmas party, it would pay for the peanuts—the expensive African ground nuts—that freed Fred from Rosemary's grasp forever.

He pulled the party cup of nuts from his jacket pocket and chewed them one by one, savoring their honey-ginger glaze.

AURA

Mary Fraser

Mary Fraser is a high school Drama teacher, mother and occasional writer. She lives in Mississauga with her three children and husband, all of whom know to leave her alone in a dark room when she has a migraine. Her high school students know that the Drama studio is a body spray-free zone and will defend her at all costs. She is the co-author of the considerably less bloody 175 Best Camp Games. *This is her first published work of crime fiction.*

I get killer migraines. They always start with a trigger. Florescent lighting, maybe. Weather, definitely. Smoked meat, dark chocolate, strong perfume, too much caffeine, not enough caffeine, alcohol—although I'm not supposed to know that yet—or, *ding ding*, all-time-winner, my period. They started a few years ago, before everything happened.

Not that my life was sitcom glittery perfect to begin with. I live in a shitty apartment with my brother, Kurt, and only my brother Kurt, because my parents were terrible. They're dead now.

But I was telling you about my migraines.

Sometimes I don't even know the trigger has occurred, and then, *wham!* The aura hits. Other times, I recognize a trigger and wait for it to bring me down. It's like I pass a boy in the hall and *ugh!*—he's wearing too much body spray—so I go into my shit-it's-coming bunker and wait. Wait for the aura to come, thinking of ways to kill the boy. Except sometimes the aura doesn't come, and I'm in a bunker and feeling vicious for no reason.

I miss a lot of school. I have no friends, except for wannabe emo types who think I'm always away because I tried to kill myself, something they are too chicken shit to do. I don't want to die, I just want to be able to think without my brain exploding.

See? I can't even concentrate. I'm trying to tell you about aura, and I end up talking about death.

Close your eyes. Tight. Now dig your knuckles into your eye sockets. Those white lines? Imagine those go like fireworks across everything you see, zigzagging from one side to the other. Like the jet streams of airplanes, or glow-in-the-dark jellyfish in an aquarium. Imagine they're there even when your eyes are open. Imagine everything glows and twitches, and nothing focuses. That's an aura. It precedes the migraine, like a warning.

Now imagine that someone whacks you across the side of the head with a baseball bat. He hits you on the neck and back, and a couple more times on the head for good measure. And everything is hot and noisy and smelly and bright. That's what comes after the aura. Now you've got a full-blown migraine.

Kurt thinks I'm exaggerating. "Lying," he says. My brother is always looking for lies. He catches about half of my big ones. Yesterday, I lied about three big things and a zillion little ones. First, my homework. I didn't have any, but I said I did because I wanted to be alone in my room.

Second, Sophie. Kurt asked why she was talking to me again, and I told him it was about science. Really, she'd made me a glass mason jar, filled with glitter. Purple and green. Like Sophie's hair. "Shake it," she said. "Watching the glitter will help you calm down."

"Glitter gets in everything," I said. She looked like she was going to cry, and I wanted to say I was sorry, but she ran away.

The third thing I lied about was why I was late getting home. Ms. O'Shaughnessy, my English teacher, wanted to talk to me about my paper. That's what I said, but really I just didn't want to go home yet.

Kurt only guessed the lie about Sophie, but that's because he was in the school hallway, watching me change classes. He knows my schedule. He chose it.

Kurt is not my legal guardian. That's my aunt, Kelly, who lives downtown and pays the bills and calls once a month. Kurt is 19, but in grade 12. It's gonna take him an extra year to graduate because he missed a lot of school when everything happened with Mom and Dad. I missed time too, but I stayed on track. Sort of.

Today is Saturday. There's a thunderstorm tonight, and I'm due for my period tomorrow. I have nowhere to go and nobody to see, but even if I did have friends, it would be best to stay home. It's easier that way. If I'm careful, things will be OK.

I will come out of my room when Kurt makes us something to eat, and I'll sit and eat with him. If I stay in my room the whole evening, Kurt will get worried. He says I've got Dad's temper and I need to be careful. I think he's the one who's like Dad, always needing to know where I am and who I'm talking to. But if I say that aloud, he starts to cry, and then he reminds me of Mom.

The whole thing is beyond screwed up, so instead of having real conversations, we take turns telling rude jokes while we do the dishes together after supper. That's our family time. He looks up his jokes online, but I don't tell him that I know. That counts as a little lie.

Otherwise, Kurt is pretty normal, considering. He plays baseball sometimes. Not on a team, now, just with friends. He has a girlfriend, even. Jessica. She doesn't visit here often. She has a nice big house with parents who have never made newspaper headlines, so Kurt goes there to pretend.

He's going there tonight.

"I don't want you talking to her," he tells me. He means Sophie. He's ironing his shirt, and I'm watching him from the couch.

"But you're allowed to talk to Jessica."

Kurt singes his fingers on the iron and unplugs it. "That's because I can make decisions. You can't think straight. You're not allowed to make decisions for yourself."

Kurt's favorite decision is deciding to hide. He used to hide when Dad and Mom went at it, leaving me as a witness, or worse. But the last time I reminded him of his favorite decision, Kurt cried. Then he ignored me, and didn't buy groceries or put money on my bus pass for three weeks. He only started again when I threatened to call Aunt Kelly. Then he went to the store and got my favorite meat lasagna, and that was his idea of apologizing for everything he's ever done.

"Do Jessica's parents know about you?" I ask. He's buttoning up his shirt and looks as handsome as he ever will, which isn't much.

"They watch the news," he says. I know that means yes, they know about us, although half of what they know is wrong. For example, the news never mentioned that Mom was a bitch. It was easier to blame everything on Dad. Tighter storytelling. Ms. O'Shaughnessy says stories have to have an antagonist and a protagonist, but what if everyone's just awful?

He sits on the coffee table, facing me.

"Jessica is going to school in Ottawa," he tells me, using the same voice the paramedics used that night. As if I might break.

"So?" I ask.

"So I'm going with her."

"Fine."

"So are you."

A band tightens around my forehead.

"I already talked to Aunt Kelly. There's a college that I can go to. Electrical. It's a good career. She'll keep sending us money, and apartments are cheaper there, so we can have a nice one."

"With Jessica?" I stand up.

"Her mom wants her to live in residence. You should meet her mother sometime. You know. Prove that we're normal."

I head for my room. There's no door to slam. Kurt took it off its hinges months ago because I kept slamming it and the landlord started asking questions.

I need to break something, but I own nothing breakable. I smashed Mom's music box with Kurt's baseball bat when I found out she'd put Aunt Kelly in charge. Kurt keeps the bat above the kitchen cabinets now, where I can't reach it. I decapitated Kurt's old trophies when he lied to Sophie about me.

Sophie's glass jar sits on my desk, but I won't break that. Me and Sophie were getting too close, he said. So he told her I was dangerous, that I couldn't be trusted, that the psychologist said I was unstable. He lied. I don't have a psychologist. Kurt won't let me have one. He says they wouldn't understand.

I think he might be right, this time. My brain is fucked up enough with the aura and the migraines. I think maybe migraines damage your brain. I read somewhere that you can take special pills, or injections, or something that makes the blood vessels in your brain change shape. But I think if anybody went in there and started tinkering, my whole head would catch fire like bad wiring and burn me up with it. So I haven't told anyone anything. Kurt promised he wouldn't either. I don't see a neurologist. I don't even see a doctor, which means all I have for the migraines is Tylenol, Advil and Gravol. It's all useless, especially with thunder rolling in the distance.

Instead of smashing things, I lie on my bed and dig my fists into my eye sockets.

Ottawa. Jessica. Electrical. Like my head.

"It'll be good for both of us to get out of here," Kurt calls from the other room. "Nobody will know about it there. You can finish high school. I'll even let you choose your own courses."

"You're so fucking generous," I say, loud enough for him to hear. He ignores me.

"We won't have to keep you away from the meddling ones. You can lie to anyone you want to."

"I don't lie."

"Uh-huh."

"Does Jessica know you're bringing me to Ottawa?"

A pause. "Of course." Too slow.

He comes into my room. Sits on the edge of my bed. "She wants to help. She's going into social work. Trauma victims."

I open my eyes so he can see me roll them. "Are you her inspiration?"

"I told her a few things."

"We said we weren't going to talk about it. We don't need any meddlers. That's the whole point."

"She's not like that."

"We said once people start asking questions, they won't stop." I sit up and swing my feet over the edge of the bed.

I must have sat up too quickly. My eyes can't focus. Everything is spinning.

"I'll tell her not to ask you anything." His hand hovers over my back, not touching me. His shirt still smells of body spray from the last time he saw Jessica. Fake man smell, made in a factory. I flinch, and he moves away.

"I don't want to go." Is that my voice? It's so small.

He stands up. "You have to."

He leaves the room.

A jellyfish-shaped cloud swims past my eyes and hovers for a bit in the bottom right corner before slumping down.

It's just dust. Relax. You're fine. But I can feel the skin on my skull tightening.

Kurt is in the bathroom now. I hear the *thumps* as he throws stuff around, slamming drawers. He's so noisy, it sounds like the police are looking for evidence.

I know that sound.

"Have you seen my body spray?" he calls out.

"I threw it out. That shit gives me migraines. I told you."

The rummaging stops.

He comes back into my room. Goes to my desk. To Sophie's glass jar. Picks it up and hurls it on the ground, but the jar is closed. There are no hard edges and the carpet is soft.

Then, I make a mistake.

I laugh.

Kurt bends down to pick up the jar. I'm sure he's going to throw it in my face.

I keep laughing. I can't stop myself. It's perfect. My face will be smashed to shit, and Jessica will know all about him. She'll leave him, and we'll stay here and continue to torture each other.

"You're sick," he shouts, his face inches from mine.

I grab his head between my hands. I want to shove my knuckles into his eye sockets.

He wrenches free and bolts into the kitchenette, and I follow him. He's shouting, but I can't hear him anymore. He's too loud. Everything is too loud.

He's got his baseball bat. Sophie's glass jar is in the air. There's a swing and a crash, and glitter is oozing from a gash in the drywall, where glass shards are sticking out. The bat rattles onto the floor. Is there glitter in my eyes? I can't see. My vision is cloudy and shining.

The glitter smells awful. The water inside the jar has gone rancid. I am off-balance, and I sink onto the tile floor. I know it's coming: the pain, the whack on the back of the head, the migraine.

Kurt is screaming and grabs his jacket. He is leaving. He will tell Jessica everything. They will make plans for me. They will open my brain and set me on fire. So I grab Kurt's bat.

I stand. I swing.

Later, I will say I couldn't see.

A court-appointed neurologist will testify to the severity of my migraines. I will get all the drugs I need. He will say that my auras cause near-blindness, followed by crippling pain that most certainly has an impact on my mental health.

I will allow people to meddle. An MRI will show brain trauma. An X-ray will show bones that have healed without being set by a doctor. I will cry at the right times, and everything will be OK. Because I will lie.

But for the moment, I can tell you, the jet streams and the jellyfish clouds clear from my vision, and I can see the side of Kurt's head perfectly. And I swing.

The whack is beautifully loud. It is the best loud sound I have ever heard. Then there is a liquid gurgle, and everything is quiet.

I should call an ambulance. Kurt's chest is still moving up and down, although his face is a funny purple color. There is a small puddle of blood under his head, mixing with the glitter on the floor in a way that will be impossible to clean. Purple, green and red. Glitter gets in everything.

I can think clearly now. I grab a washcloth from the kitchen drawer, run it under cold water, and ring it out. On the way back to my room, I fold it neatly into thirds. I lay down on my bed, in the room where I own nothing, the washcloth over my eyes, and wait for the pain to come.

$$\Omega$$

THE POISON-PILL CURE

Blake Stirling

"The Poison Pill Cure" is the first story by Hamilton native Blake Stirling. Although he has always been interested in literature and pursuing a career as a writer, he paused his writing as he graduated from high school and began attending university.

A McMaster University alumni, Blake earned two separate B.A. in History and Religion, specializing in the Medieval and Early Modern periods. More recently he has become interested in utilizing his knowledge of history, anthropology and religion to craft intricate and unique stories.

"You're saying that the victim ate a shark?" I gasped, pressing the phone against my ear.

"No, Manveer, just the cartilage," Dr. Coltan replied with a chuckle. "Some crank in the 90s made claims that sharks don't get cancer, and ever since then desperate people have believed that if they pop a pill containing ground shark cartilage, they can ward off death."

"Wait…" I paused to collect my thoughts. "He had cancer?"

"Manveer, did you not find it odd that this man was hairless?"

"One day it is in vogue to grow out a beard as long as my own and then the next weekend they shave it all off. I'd lose my own hair if I paid attention to the fads of young people. Besides, I wouldn't have suspected a boy his age to be so sick."

"Cancer isn't so courteous as to favor only the elderly, though the victim was hardly a boy. At 21, I believe he's the same age as your daughter."

"Argh. Don't remind me of her," I groaned. "Jasmine attends the same school as our Mr. Bowman did, and she's been pestering me for updates all morning. I've contemplated blocking her."

"I'm glad my own progeny left the nest long before texting became a phenomena, and I'm now old enough to feign senility whenever they try to force me into some online club."

I sighed. "Did you call just to discuss the shark angle, or do you have anything else to report?"

"The suspicions the paramedics had were accurate; the blood tests confirm that Bowman passed away due to acute cyanide poisoning. Probably ate something toxic, but we won't know for sure until we perform more tests. It's a shame the poor fellow survived lymphoma only to die while commuting on the subway."

"Yes, a shame," I agreed.

After reporting Dr. Colton's finds to the commissioner, I didn't dawdle at the station. Michael Bowman's residence lay off Finch Avenue, far from his campus and even farther from the station. I wanted to arrive before his roommates flaked off. News that a promising law student had died the previous night had attracted considerable attention, both from the press and on social media. Even before the autopsy had been performed, rumors had spread of a mugging gone awry and a body being shuffled about the city in a subway car. No doubt when details of the victim's battle with cancer got out, interest in the story would reach a fever pitch.

The victim rented a two-story flat with three other students, who had all been informed of his passing early that morning. While stopped at red lights, I reviewed their names and skimmed an article on cyanide poisoning on my smartphone. I hadn't come across a single case throughout my career, and I doubted that many of my colleagues had a close familiarity with the poison. Death by cyanide evokes images from an Agatha Christie novel. Toronto is a modern city and its residents are far more likely to die from an overdose of heroin or painkillers. Cyanide seemed to me to be as archaic as drinking hemlock.

I was received at the door by a tiny girl, with a mop of brown hair and a puffy, tear-streaked face. Judging by the oil stains on her sweater, she was likely enrolled in an art program.

"Hello," she rasped out. "Is this about Mike?"

"Yes, Ms. Heffernan, I assume?" I asked, recalling the name from my notes. "I'm Detective Singh, the lead investigator on Mr. Bowman's death. May I come in?"

"Sure," she replied. "I've been watching television ever since one of your guys arrived at our door. I can't believe Mike is dead; he seemed so invincible!"

266

"Yes, it is a terrible thing," I replied, as I scanned the hallway. A hideous shade of yellow paint smeared the walls and a whiff of cannabis hung in the air. "Are the other tenants still in?"

"I think so," she mumbled. "The officer told us to stay at home, although he didn't say we had to lock ourselves in our rooms, so I've been watching cartoons in the common room. Is that OK?"

"Yes, yes, that's fine, but can you please fetch the others? I would like to address you all together."

"Uh, sure..." she sniffed daintily, and then bellowed out, "Guys, get your asses downstairs, ASAP!"

The sound of feet could be heard on the aging floors, followed by doors opening and closing, and one tenant yelling, "What is it? Is this about Mike?"

"Yes," Ms. Heffernan shouted back, "a detective is here!" Before she had finished her sentence, one of her cohorts galloped down the stairs. In my own college days, we would have called this boy a geek, but nowadays, I suppose, his type is more mainstream. Acne scars dotted his face, and it looked as if he had slept in his shirt. I guessed this had to be Albert Benoît.

Next we were joined by Viraj Din. He was a South Asian student.

"I trust you've all been informed of Mr. Bowman's passing," I said, "and I would like to assure you that we are investigating this matter thoroughly. We've learned that Mr. Bowman passed away due to poisoning."

"What?" Mr. Din snorted. "It wasn't the cancer?"

"Correct," I replied. "We think it may have been cyanide."

"How does someone die from cyanide?" Mr. Benoît asked.

Ms. Heffernan gasped. "Oh, my God! Is cyanide used in making oil paint?"

"I, uh, don't know," I said, "but I'm certain that oil paint wasn't the cause. You can understand that we are treating Mr. Bowman's death as suspicious."

"Wait, am I a suspect?" Mr. Din asked.

"I want to assure you that we are investigating this matter thoroughly, and that we will inspect your residence to ensure you are all safe."

"You want to inspect our rooms, too?" Mr. Din said. "Don't you need a search warrant for that?"

"We'll begin with the common areas," I calmly explained. "Your kitchen, bathrooms and whatever other spaces you all share. As for your individual dorms, I see no reason to invade your privacy. However, we will ask for your permission to search the rooms. Also, we'll need you to come down to the station so we can scan your fingerprints and collect a genetic sample. This way we can determine if anyone has been here who doesn't belong."

"Oh, yes, of course!" Ms. Heffernan nodded. "When do you want this done?"

"Well, one of my officers should arrive any moment now," I said. "He can ferry the three of you to the police station and bring you back within an hour, two at the most."

"And what if I refuse?" Mr. Din asked.

"Then we'll obtain a warrant," I said.

"Ah, don't be stupid, Viraj!" Ms. Heffernan said. Then she addressed me in a kinder tone. "He thinks you're going to arrest him for a few plants he has in his room. He doesn't understand that no one cares anymore."

"Emilia!" He scowled at her.

"We have no interest in your plants, Mr. Din. On the other hand, if any of you have any objections, let me know now so I can make the proper arrangements for a warrant. Time is a factor in these things. Ideally, we would like to wrap up the inspection and prints today. You may want to bring a book or something with you to the station."

"Well, I've got nothing to hide!" Ms. Heffernan said as she charged passed the boys and up the staircase. "I'll be just a moment, Detective Singh. I have to get my phone!"

"I need my phone too!" Mr. Din huffed as he followed.

Mr. Benoît said, "Well, I guess I should get my *Switch*."

"*Switch*?" I asked with a raised brow.

"Yeah, it's like a *Gameboy*."

"Oh," I replied with an enlightened nod. I still had my *Gameboy* from when I was in university tucked away somewhere.

As I waited for the three of them to return, I walked around the main floor. The kitchen was an absolute disaster, as was the bathroom. The stairwell to the basement smelled funky. I got distracted, though, when I stepped into the common room where Ms. Heffernan had been watching television, and found myself entranced by the cartoon beaming out from the box. It was one of those modern shows, where a spaghetti-armed youth is paired with a talking mutant pet. It was very humorous. I made note of its name, so my wife could begin recording it.

My colleagues arrived soon after the credits, and the three students were bundled off to the station. I turned off the television and began my investigation.

Ms. Heffernan had left several tubes of paint lying about, from which I was able to conclude that, despite her assertion to the contrary, oil paints do not contain cyanide.

I instructed the forensic team to bag every food item in the fridge and cupboards. Then I stepped outside for some fresh air and phoned the landlord, Mr. Wang.

He had been told to deliver a set of keys to the station early in the morning and had neglected to do so. So I told him to meet me at the house within the hour. Mr. Wang didn't take it too well when I informed him that we were investigating a poisoning. He became defensive, saying that he couldn't control what those damn students were flushing down the toilet and that, with all the damage these kids do, he was barely scraping by.

I ended the conversation when it became apparent to me that he was driving while on the phone.

A worn Mr. Wang arrived within 40 minutes, for which I was thankful. I wasn't in the mood for a manhunt. I took a full set of keys from him. Though a keychain had been found on Mr. Bowman's body, it had been signed into evidence, so we needed another set of keys.

I had forgotten to ask the students which room was Michael Bowman's, so I conscripted Mr. Wang to direct me to the proper room. Helping me seemed to calm the man's nerves.

I didn't know what to expect when I pushed open Mr. Bowman's door. I had seen his body, sprawled out on the floor of subway carriage wearing a buttoned shirt and jeans with a backpack slung over his shoulder. What struck me as odd at the time was the lack of logos on his clothing. So many young people are all too eager to brand themselves with T-shirts touting their favorite video games or film franchises or computer companies, but this man sported no advertisements on his apparel. So, when I was greeted with a poster displaying Marx, Engels and other champions of the proletariat in his room, I was surprised. Maybe if I had unbuttoned his shirt, I would have uncovered an image of Che Guevara on a T-shirt.

But I was more interested in the contents of his room than in what he had been wearing. In particular, I wanted to find a capsule containing shark cartilage.

Since the tenants shared the bathroom, there was no obvious spot to begin, no cabinet overhanging a sink. Holding a handkerchief, I carefully prodded through his dresser drawers. There must have been three dozen plastic vials packed into a drawer normally used for socks and underwear. Far too many to sift through without compromising them, so I ordered the team to bag them.

We also found the victim's computer on a small workstation in his room. It took an hour for our team of six officers to search the house. We were slowed down by the house's state of disrepair. The second-floor bathroom had been ripped apart, the basement was filled with trash, and the backyard was home to several soiled mattresses that bore evidence of a bedbug infestation. It was arduous working in such an environment.

Yet it was all for nothing. When I was battling traffic on my trip back to the office, I received a call from Dr. Coltan.

"Hey, Manveer, not sure how far along you are with everything, but the lab tells me they've detected cyanide in the aluminum bottle he was carrying."

I cheerfully thanked him for this update, but I groaned at the thought of all the food we had lifted from the tenants' kitchen and subsequently wasted.

Mr. Bowman's roommates were still waiting for their fingerprints to be taken, and I managed to book an interview room. Ms. Heffernan joined me first, happy to discover an outlet where she could charge her phone.

I advised her that our conversation would be recorded. "How long have you known Mr. Bowman?" I asked.

"Since just before the school year began," she chirped. It was November, so they'd known each other for about three months. "He didn't have hair back then, either."

"And what was your relationship with him?"

"We've fooled around a lot," she said, "and we played games, toked, and sometimes he painted with me."

"How would you describe Mr. Bowman's relationship with Mr. Din and Benoît?"

"Viraj sold him some salve, once in a while."

"Salve?" I repeated. I knew, of course, what she meant, but I needed a clarification for the recording.

"You know…" She spoke coyly. "Cannabis."

"Ah, yes, thank you for that Ms. Heffernan."

"To be honest, though, neither Viraj nor Albert seemed close to Mike. We go to York University and he went to University of Toronto. The only reason he and I became close is because we both watched TV in the common room. The other two kept mostly kept to themselves."

"Thank you, Ms. Heffernan," I said. "Now I have to ask, do you know why anyone would try to murder Mr. Bowman?"

"Murder?" she squeaked. "I thought it was an accident."

"I'm afraid we're increasingly convinced that is not the case."

270

"No, of course not," she mumbled. "He was a nice guy. I'm sure you're mistaken. It had to be an accident."

"I hope you're right, Ms. Heffernan," I said. "We found traces of cyanide in the canteen that was in Mr. Bowman's possession. It's a blue aluminum bottle with his university's logo. Are you familiar with it?"

"Yeah, he kept it in the fridge whenever he wasn't using it," she answered.

I thanked Ms. Heffernan for her candor and reminded her to remove her cell phone from the charging station before she returned to the waiting room.

Mr. Din joined me in the interview room next, while Albert Benoît was still being processed.

As Ms. Heffernan passed Mr. Din in the hallway, she cried out, "They think Mike was murdered!"

As a result, Mr. Din was already agitated by the time he was seated across from me.

"Did you sell any drugs to Mr. Bowman?" I asked, cutting to the point.

"Yes, at first I did," Mr. Din replied. "Mike complained about being in pain a lot, what with the cancer and the chemo and all that. He talked about weed as if it were holy herb, like peyote or some crap. He claimed it helped him sleep."

"So, am I to understand that you stopped selling to him at some point?"

"He learned that the smoke bothered Albert, because of his asthma, and then he started making demands of me. That I should throw out my entire crop and we should make the house smoke-free."

"A proposal that you objected to?"

"Yeah," he said, crossing his arms, "What I do in my room is my own business. Albert has air purifiers and other junk in his room, and I don't complain about the noise those things make!"

I wasn't able to draw any more useful information from Viraj Din. He left and reclaimed his seat in the waiting room.

A moment later, I was joined by Mr. Benoît.

I offered my usual spiel about our interview being recorded and motioned for him to take a seat.

"Did you have a previous relationship with Mr. Bowman before this semester began?"

"Yeah, I did," he answered. "We went to the same high school, though I wouldn't say we were friends or anything. We just recognized one another."

"While cohabitating, did your relationship change?" I asked.

"Uh, yeah, we played together, usually with Emilia, too. Not often though, and we didn't see each other that much since he went to a different university."

"Since Mr. Bowman was a University of Toronto student, he'd have to commute by subway to get to class, while you, Mr. Din, and Ms. Heffernan can take a leisurely stroll. Do you know why Mr. Bowman chose a residence so far from his university?"

"I don't know," Mr. Benoît replied. "Probably for the cheaper rent. I know I wouldn't have chosen this place if I didn't have to. When he was looking for a place, he asked me about mine. I've been living there for over a year now and I told him it was shit. So, he mustn't have been able to find a better place."

Mr. Benoît couldn't come up with any reason for Mr. Bowmen's death other than a political squabble gone awry, and so I gave the three of them permission to return home, with the parting advice that they should visit a supermarket on the way.

Then I made a series of phone calls, first to my wife advising her that I would be late for dinner, then to Mr. Bowman's doctor, who confirmed that the young man's lymphoma was receding, and then to the victim's parents to update them on my investigation.

When I was finished, I saw Dr. Coltan sauntering my way with a smile on his face.

"I found something that might interest you, Manveer," he said as he waved an evidence bag in the air. "The shark cartilage was just one of the strange concoctions Mr. Bowman was ingesting."

He slid the evidence bag across my desk. Inside I found a capsule, likely one I had retrieved earlier that day. "Amygdalin?" I asked as I read the label out loud. "What on earth is that?"

"They're cyanide pills," Dr. Coltan replied with a straight face.

"You're pulling my leg!" I said. "Surely no one is foolish enough to think poison can cure cancer!"

"Oh, Manveer, you underestimate how desperation can motivate a person. I won't try to explain the reasoning, as I'd drive myself mad trying to understand their headspace, but from what I can gather this practice originated in Mexico as a cheap alternative for the American expats."

"Are these things legal?" I asked. "Some sort of black-market drug or contraband shipped into the country along with blocks of cocaine?"

"I'm afraid not," Dr. Coltan said. "They produce it by juicing peach seeds and apple cores. If you have enough determination, you can produce your own cyanide tablets by browsing your local grocer."

"This is absurd." I leaned back into my chair. "How have I not heard of this before?"

"Well, I've been browsing the literature, and as far as I can tell this is the first case of someone dying as a result of this treatment. There have been reports of mild cyanide poisoning among adherents, but no fatalities. Unless it's an opioid, people generally follow the instructions printed on the label, which I'm thankful for because less than a teaspoon of the stuff will kill you."

"So…you think he overdosed?"

"It's certainly possible."

I scanned the vial, looking for the word cyanide printed on it. It wasn't there, but my eyes spotted the recommended dosage, which was one tablet per day. "Wait a second," I muttered. "How was cyanide detected inside the victim's canteen if these are pills?"

"It's not uncommon for people to mix their medicine in juice or smoothies."

"But you found those shark bits inside him...were they still in capsule form?"

"Yeah," Dr. Coltan replied, "it's very likely he swallowed that pill with the drink that did him in."

"And how many of these death pills are missing from the bottle?"

"Probably two-thirds," the doctor answered.

"And I assume this bottle was dusted for prints?"

"Of course." Dr. Coltan chuckled. "I had it fast-tracked when I reviewed the catalogue of items retrieved from the victim's home. Mr. Bowman's fingerprints were found on it."

"Hmm," I mumbled as I checked my phone for the time. It was approaching six. "I wonder if any of the tech boys and girls are still in."

"Something isn't sitting right with you?" Dr. Coltan said, reading my thoughts.

"I want to know where this bottle came from, and I also want Forensics to take another look at it," I answered. "I'm not willing to accept the easy explanation just yet."

***

The next morning we held a press conference and announced our preliminary findings. I had done this before so I was comfortable with the process.

When I returned to the office, I received two reports. The first contained the receipts for all of Mr. Bowman's credit and debit purchases, which were cross-listed with the various medicines we recovered from the victim's home.

The cyanide pills were not listed among them. This didn't necessarily strike me as suspicious, as several homeopathic remedies were also absent from the roster. Nevertheless, I tasked some officers to canvas nearby pharmacies around his home and campus, to find out whether Mr. Bowman had purchased this drug locally.

The next report was more interesting. I'd had a team create a digital model of the bottle and an overlay where each fingerprint was located on it. From this we determined that the bottle had only been held loosely by Mr. Bowman, and only once, as if it had been placed in his hand while he slept. Consulting with his doctor, I learned that Mr. Bowman was often in severe pain and required extensive medication to sleep. Someone might have manipulated the victim to grasp the bottle while he was asleep. It was likely that only a handful of people would have been aware of his nighttime vulnerability, and fewer still would have access to his locked room.

Since the kitchen was shared, one of his roommates could have spiked the canister. By her own admission, Ms. Heffernan had been on intimate terms with Mr. Bowman. She could have entered his room without arousing suspicion.

I obtained search warrants for all three tenants' apartments, and had them all brought in again for questioning.

Mr. Din was at home while the search was underway, and we were able to reach Mr. Benoît by phone. He agreed to be picked up.

We couldn't contact Ms. Heffernan, though, and I was forced to send officers to track her down. In the meantime, I sat down with Mr. Din, who was especially uncooperative, since we had raided his pantry and torn through his personal belongings.

"I need to inform you, Mr. Din, that we found four cannabis plants in your room."

"So what?" he huffed. "I'm allowed to have those. The law says anyone can have a maximum of four plants."

"Let me finish, Mr. Din," I said calmly. "We found four cannabis plants, as well as the three that you had stashed behind your neighbor's shed yesterday. Your neighbor, Ms. Wilson, kindly informed my men about them after we searched your home."

"Sounds to me like they might belong to her," he smirked.

"Yes, maybe that is true," I replied with a smile. "I'm more interested in how you would describe Emilia and Mike's relationship."

"Emilia?" Mr. Din said. "You think she did Mike in? I'm a better suspect than she is!"

"Oh?" That got my interest.

Mr. Din was swift to clarify himself. "I don't mean that I did it, but Emilia is as innocent as they come."

"Well, can you describe their relationship for me?"

"They played video games and watched cartoons together. I never heard any arguments through the walls, if that's what you're getting at."

I continued to press Mr. Din for more information, but it seemed futile.

An officer poked his head into the room and asked to speak with me. In the hallway, he advised me that Ms. Heffernan had been secured in another interview room.

I left Mr. Din to cool his heels and jogged down the hall.

Ms. Heffernan was in a wretched state, once more tear-ridden, but far angrier than when I had first met her. "You didn't have to drag me out of my class!" she shouted at me. "Now people are going to think I'm a criminal!"

"I'm sorry, Ms. Heffernan, but it was urgent. I need to know if you have ever purchased a drug called amygdalin."

"Amyg…what?" she said. "What is that?"

"It's an herbal medicine that we believe killed Mr. Bowman."

"I thought you said Mike died from cyanide…"

"Yes," I replied, "these pills contain cyanide."

"Well, that sounds dangerous," she said. "I don't think Mike would have taken something like that."

"Except we found such pills in his room," I said. "Though we don't think Mr. Bowman purchased them. We think they were planted before or after his canteen was poisoned."

"Why would someone would do that?"

"I don't know why." I was becoming irritated with her. "But I know whoever did this had access to his room. Which you did."

"Are you accusing me?" she asked. "Why do you think I would have any more access than Albert or Viraj, or Mr. Wang for that matter?"

"Because you were sleeping with him."

Her eyes cleared as she pondered what I was saying. Then she laughed, "What? You think me and Mike were a couple? Why would you think that?"

"Because you told me that you two fooled around together."

"Yeah, we fooled around together," she giggled, "in *Minecraft*."

"*Minecraft*?" I repeated. "What is that?"

"A videogame, Detective." She smiled. "You know men and women can just be friends, right? Also, I have a boyfriend back in Thunder Bay. If you had asked Din about that, he would have told you."

"So…you've never been in Mr. Bowman's room?" I asked.

"Sure, I have," she answered. "Though I don't think I've been in his room for, like, a week now. But we've all been in there at some point, Albert, Viraj—oh, I guess I just threw them under the bus. Are you going to start accusing them, too?"

Flustered, I retired for lunch, leaving my three suspects in custody as I drove to the nearest fast food joint. As I ate my burger and fries in the car, I tried to reassess the case and the suspects. I hadn't questioned Albert again, though if Mr. Bowman's room was as accessible as Ms. Heffernan claimed, any of them could have planted the poison. Each suspect had the opportunity and means, but no real motive, at least not one known to me.

My cell phone rang. With greasy fingers, I reached for it in my coat pocket. My daughter was calling me again. I had no desire to speak with her at the moment, so I attempted to return the device back to its sheath. But my finger must have touched the wrong place, and I heard a warm low voice. "Hello, *bhapu*, are you there?"

I was not about to hang up on my daughter. "Yes, Jasmine, I'm here. I'm eating at the moment."

"Then I won't take up much of your time. I just want to know why you've been avoiding me."

"I've just been busy, that's all, dear! Mr. Bowman's case has become very stressful. A lot of people are demanding answers."

"The campus is in an uproar. They're saying the cops are arresting students right in the middle of their classes!"

"No one has been arrested."

"Well, you upset a lot of people," she chided. "A lot of us were grieving for Michael, not just because he was a fellow student, but a lot of people admired him."

"Yes, it takes serious mettle to survive cancer."

"Well, yeah, but it's not just that," she said. "Even before we'd heard about the cancer, Michael was famous. Ever since he'd helped some students organize a lawsuit against their landlord. Since then he's done all sorts of student housing activism."

"Really?" I said. "No one I interviewed shared this information with me."

"If you had answered the phone more often, you would have known about it!"

"Yes, dear," I replied. "I've got work to do, so I'm going to hang up now. If you have any free time on the weekend, you should come by and visit your parents."

"I guess I can do that." She sighed. "I'll see you then, OK *bhapu*?"

"Yes, Jasmine. I look forward to it. Bye-bye!"

I hurled my remaining burger and fries through the car window for the gulls to devour and tossed the packaging onto my passenger seat. I had a fourth suspect, one I had not considered. Mr. Wang had a key to the victim's room, and Michael Bowman had history of quarrelling with landlords. Instead of jumping onto the old cliché of a woman scorned, I should have viewed this case as Karl Marx would have, as a material struggle.

I zipped back to the office with renewed confidence and interviewed all three suspects in succession, asking the same question to all three of them, "Do you know what Mr. Bowman thought of your landlord, Tom Wang?"

"Oh, he hated him," Ms. Heffernan answered.

"He's a communist, what do you think?" Mr. Din replied.

"He was planning on suing him," Mr. Benoît announced.

"Why didn't you bring this up earlier?" I asked him in astonishment.

"To be fair, he was going to sue a lot of people," Benoît said.

"Do you know why?"

"For one thing, he thought the house was an illegal rental property," he replied. "That there were too many tenants for a house of its size, and he was also sure that Din's grow-op was aggravating my asthma. Since Mr. Wang was aware of the weed, Mike figured he was liable. He mentioned some other stuff, too, but I'm not a lawyer so it didn't mean much to me."

If Michael Bowman had confronted Mr. Wang with a catalogue of legal complaints, then the man would certainly have a motive for murder. But, unlike my previous suspects who all had opportunities to spike Mr. Bowman's canteen and plant the pills, Mr. Wang didn't live in the house.

"Did Mr. Wang visit your home before Mr. Bowman passed away?

"Yeah," Mr. Benoît muttered. "And I think Mike must have confronted him, because Wang has been working on the house recently. I've probably seen him more in the past week than I did in my first year in the house. He's been working on the bathroom, the one next to Mike's room, for the past few days, replacing pipes and stuff."

After Mr. Benoît's interview, I had a better picture of Michael Bowman. He was a social activist suffering from lymphoma. He'd ramped up his social crusade, going so far as to move into a dilapidated house to become a greater advocate for change.

Then a panicked landlord slipped poison into his drink.

***

I didn't approach Mr. Wang immediately. I spoke to the tech team, who had cracked the victim's computer and phone, and learned that Mr. Bowman had been researching recent landlord/tenant cases. During the weeks before his death, Mr. Bowman had frequently exchanged calls with Mr. Wang.

Armed with this information, I asked a forensic team to take a closer look at the house, where we found mold growing in the walls and vents. We dug into Tony Wang's finances, which were abysmal, and we also learned that his wife was a cancer survivor.

When I confronted Mr. Wang, he cracked. He said that if Mr. Bowman were to sue him, he would have incited tenants from his other properties to do the same. Mr. Wang said he had tried to appease Mike by fixing the place up. But, looking through Mike's room, he recognized the same medicine his wife had taken, and he began to formulate a plan to get rid of him.

Mr. Wang was arrested on a Saturday, the same day that my daughter deigned to dine with her parents. "Admit it, *bhapu*, you would have solved this case earlier if you hadn't been avoiding me!" Jasmine added that she should be credited in the newspapers for helping to solve the crime.

Eager to tuck into my wife's lovely stir-fry, I replied, "Say what you will, but when you regale your friends with the story of your part in the case, don't neglect to mention that I did all the leg work."

THE DROWNING

Rosalind Croucher

Rosalind Croucher is a poet, writer and author of the short story "The Drowning," a mystery in the style of the television show This is Your Life. *The victim of a puzzling crime, Paula Standing takes her mind off her predicament by imagining who may have done it, and why. Never short on people she's wronged, Paula has a great deal to think about.*

I come to in the night, coughing. My eyes are caked with sand. My face is burned raw by the winter night's wind. I smell the ocean. We're not in Young's Cove anymore. Nothing else is like the salty spray of the Atlantic. Some psycho took me on a road trip. Why?

Yup. Fucked city, New Brunswick. I try to move, but I'm pinned. Buried up to my neck in sand. A lot of work for someone. There's sand in my mouth and something is stuck in my ear. Duct taped, maybe? A crab takes an interest, but he can't get it off either. I scream and shake my head. I get clawed for my trouble. Crab doesn't seem to care how scared I am. I can't grasp what's going on.

I yell for help. Nothing. I crane my neck to try see where I am and what's around me. All that gets me is shooting pain in my head. Panic rises in my throat. I can feel a wound on the back of my head. I can smell my own blood. What the fuck is going on?

I scream myself hoarse, but only the seagulls reply. The wind and waves carry my voice away. I start to wonder which of my many screwups has put me here. Who did I piss off enough that they would take the time and effort to dig a hole, bury me in it and wait for the tide to drown me? At least that seems like the plan, if all those mobster movies were right. Is this someone's idea of a joke? Or am I just guilty of Walking While Woman?

No. I don't think so. What random, opportunistic rapist would go to this kind of effort, and why?

I choke out a laugh at that. Well, I did want some time to myself. What with the pandemic and all, maybe I should be thanking this asshole for the forced isolation. But the cold is stinging, and I'm not a fan of cold. I'm almost grateful most of me is in the warm sand.

***

"Hey, gear-up! You know how contagious this thing is." Inspector Knowles stops her partner, already halfway up the driveway.

"Aw c'mon, Mom, do I have to?" Inspector Trapp catches the mask and gloves Knowles tosses and puts them on.

But at the door Trapp can't let it go, "You know these stupid things give us nothing but a false sense of security. They won't stop us from catching COVID."

"I know, but we have to keep working, so I'll take whatever measures I can. Plus it's mandatory protocol. And it makes the public feel safer."

Trapp rings the main floor bell. "At least with what's going on, we know people will be home. That's handy. Less running around for us."

"There's always a bright side with you. Even in a pandemic. The sky must be lovely in your world."

"Sure is." Trapp winks at her. In spite of her concerns about the virus, Knowles makes the call to go in and sit with the husband to comfort and question him. Not just out of empathy, but because, of course, it's always the spouse. Best place to start looking hard.

Trapp puts on his serious face before the husband opens the door. He holds it only slightly ajar, and the reason soon becomes clear, as a small, lively dog tries to nose its way through the opening.

The man sees their badges. He nudges the dog out of the way to allow them to enter.

Both officers take a step back as the door opens wider. "Mr. Standing? Mr. Colin Standing?"

The man nods. He chokes up a little. "Yes. Have you found her?"

They enter the ground floor of a house, which, like most in this neighborhood, has been sectioned into apartments. A separate entrance leads to an upper level apartment.

Keeping six feet apart is difficult enough in this job. Even more so when talking to a grieving husband. Especially with two curious cats and a playful dog sniffing at their trouser legs. The temptation to reach down and pet the animals is offset by the fear of coronavirus.

The officers watch the man crumble like a sandcastle when they tell him his wife's body has been found. His foundations are washed away.

Between touring the apartment and having him identify his wife's body using digital images provided by the morgue, they do manage to coax a few facts from the victim's husband that could prove useful. His wife had few friends. Most of them lived an hour away in Fredericton. Trapp takes down the details of the two she was out with the previous night. But first there's the neighbor, then the victim's boss and his wife to speak to in town before driving all over hell's half acre.

The officers don't see anything out of place at the Standings' apartment. No bloody clothes. No fresh laundry. No staged tidy-up. No mysterious rugs in random places. No smell of bleach. If Colin Standing attacked his wife, he didn't do it here.

When Knowles finishes with her questions, Standing has some of his own. *What's being done?* "Everything we can, sir." *Are there any leads?* "It's too early for that, sir." *When can we have my wife's body for burial?* "It could take up to a week. We'll call you when the autopsy is completed."

Colin Standing appears to be suffering from genuine shock. He leads them to the door.

The two officers leave their cards, and offer their condolences, again.

When they arrive at the upstairs apartment, a tired-looking, stooped man answers the door. He backs away even as he greets the officers with "Hello." In a Spanish accent, Trapp thinks.

Knowles begins by showing her badge, and Trapp follows suit.

"Good afternoon sir," Knowles says.

The man nods, but looks confused.

"I'm Inspector Knowles and this is Inspector Trapp. We're investigating the murder of your downstairs neighbor, Paula Standing. May we ask you a few questions here at the door? We'll keep back in accordance with the distancing."

The man nods again.

Knowles starts with the basics. "First, can we have your full name, please? And how do you spell it?"

With some difficulty the man spells Torres, then Gustavo.

"OK, and how long did you know Mrs. Standing?"

The man shakes his head. He gestures with his hands for Knowles to stop. "My English not good. Talk slow, please."

Very slowly, and with some hand gestures of her own, Knowles asks, "Is there anyone in the house who speaks English?"

The man shakes his head. *No.* The question seems to sadden him. Or maybe he's just tired. Hell, maybe he's got COVID. That's the sort of thing Knowles wants to know.

"Are you all right, sir?"

He nods his head Yes. "Tired. Only tired."

"We won't keep you long. But as I was saying, how long— for how much time—did you know Mrs. Standing? Weeks? Months? Years? Just approximately…"

The man says he's been living above her about three years, but doesn't know her well. Yes, he has heard arguing from the apartment downstairs, sometimes yelling, sometimes slammed doors.

"And is anyone else living here who may have heard or seen something?"

Again the man shakes his head. *No.*

A few more questions about how he and his downstairs neighbor got along, were there any issues with the victim, etc. The officers are ready to go when they hear coughing from within the apartment.

"My daughter," the man says. "Very sick."

Knowles and Trapp take another step back.

"Could we speak with your daughter, sir?" Knowles asks.

"No, too sick. Has not go out at all."

"OK. And how old is your daughter?"

"Seven years."

So, the daughter won't be any help either. Trapp tells the worried father to go straight to emergency if his girl has trouble breathing. They thank the man again.

***

As soon as the detectives reach the station, the captain is on them. "So she did have COVID, then?"

Trapp answers, "Yes, the husband was pretty sure she did, and post-mortem tests confirmed it."

"I wonder if the killer knew that. And whether he could get infected. You saw no signs of protective gear on or near the body?"

"No, just the earpiece, probably meant to torment her. So we know we're looking for a sadist."

***

It doesn't seem as if there's a chance of anyone seeing me. It's been just me and the crabs out here for God knows how long. I'm guessing I'm neck-deep in either a private beach or a very remote one.

Yeah, I'm pretty sure there's a *why* that would suffice to explain this pickle I'm in. I must have done something. But to whom? Of all the people I've alienated, who finally had enough? It plagues me. I'm suddenly, irrationally, suspicious of everyone I know.

I cough, and feel spittle drip down my chin. Can't cover my mouth, of course, with my hands trapped in this sandy grave. Funny how losing the niceties, like covering one's mouth when coughing, should bother me so much.

It's bitterly cold. Or maybe my fever has returned, I'm not sure. The COVID-19 test was positive two weeks ago, but my symptoms never rose to the level of keeping me indoors. I was still able walk the dog, play with our cats.

Tears are a stinging distraction. I push them back and try to think. It's clear that I can't escape, and there's no one around to hear me. I'm growing weaker. Terror is exhausting. I let the rhythmic sound of the waves carry my mind back to happier times. My sister teaching me to swim at a campground pool.

Maybe she did it. She'd certainly have good reason. Is there too much water under the bridge? She has a long memory. And I can be a pain in the ass.

I've been called impossible. I've always maintained that I'm not impossible, just *extremely* difficult. The difference sometimes being so close as to have no statistical significance. But there's always just a sliver of a chance that I might see sense.

Or maybe it was Debra. I certainly pulled some shit on her. Just me being a weirdo. I lash out when I feel rejected. Push people away. Pushed her away. But is being a bad friend enough to drive someone to this?

Ha! Now I think of it, that's nothing compared to the crazy I put Rachel through, and she never gave up on me. Some people make it difficult for you to love them. I think she and I both realized we had that in common. Sometimes the universe seems to give you just what you need. A friend indeed.

But how could a woman carry me and dump me here? If I put it that way, only Colin comes to mind as strong enough. I force my head to turn as far as possible to look around for drag marks, but I see none. But I can't see behind me, so I could be missing them. I try again to turn my aching head. Nothing. Nothing but pain, sand and the menacing ocean.

Then there's Holden. I could see that. Wanting to be rid of me once and for all. The girl who can't move on. Christ, I was obsessed with him. I'm surprised he never got a restraining order against me. But I did impose one on myself, in a way, with my move to New Brunswick. That got me mostly out of his life. But maybe Young's Cove wasn't far enough away for him.

Who else? Who else have I gone psycho on? That brings me back to Colin. But he's not the murdering kind. I don't think. Although many have argued that we all are, if pushed far enough.

We never truly know what we can take and what we can't until we're tested. Do you leave your pets behind in a flood? Innocent souls completely dependent on you? Do you bring them with you, or use their litter/hay/kibble, to spell a giant HELP and wait on your roof to be rescued? Come hell or high water, who are you really? What mettle are you made of? Only the forge will tell.

Maybe it could be my loving husband. He certainly had to take me at my worst.

And what about my ex-boss and ex-friend? He should probably be added to the list. But would he take enough time away from his company to pull this off? Hard for me to imagine. I did leave him in a jam. Part of me regrets it, but I had to get out when Rachel got sick. One friend recovering from a brain tumor, the other threatening to fire me for taking time off to see her? I couldn't cope with it. I really don't have enough friends to bear losing two at once. But I now see my life plan wasn't what it should have been. I should have had a posse. I should have been easier to get along with.

Now here I am. Karma is a bitch.

***

"First of all, I'm very sorry for your loss, Mrs. Merrick." Trapp is leaning in to address the sister. Not too far. But it is a deliberately empathic demeanor. Partly out of real feeling, and partly to encourage her to trust him.

Knowles asks if she can get herself a drink of water, in order to snoop around. When it comes to immediate family, the need to check their environment for clues overrides the need to maintain distance. Even so, they do their best to stay at least six feet apart.

"What can you tell us about your sister?" Trapp asks.

"She's—she could be—a hard pill to take. People seemed to either love her or hate her. Mostly the latter."

"Why do you say that?"

"I'm not sure what it is. She can be wildly insensitive, although never on purpose. At other times, she can be over-sensitive and introverted. People often think she doesn't like them, when chances are she doesn't really notice them. That can irk people."

"And which side did you fall on?"

"I love her, of course. I mean, we've had our differences, but what sisters haven't?"

"For example?"

"It's so difficult to think now. I'm trying hard to remember the good times, you know?" Her voice cracks and she reflexively covers her mouth.

"I get it, but anything you tell us only helps us to understand her better. And that's how we'll catch whoever did this. So what would be a recent disagreement?"

"Oh, I don't know, we had a thing over Dad not going to her wedding. That was a long time ago. And the death of our parents seemed to estrange us even more. We didn't talk to each other for years."

Knowles had returned from her snoop-a-thon in time to say, "Your dad didn't go to her wedding?"

"Yeah, but that's 15 or 16 years ago now. We've reconciled, but at the time there was a real breach between us. I keep picturing how she was found. Who would want to torture her that way?"

"That's really our question for you. Do you know anyone who could have done something like this? Anyone you can think of who might hold a grudge?"

"No one I know of. No one who would do anything like this. I'm sorry. I wish I could tell you more."

After a few more questions, the officers thank her and ask when they can interview the rest of the family. The brother-in-law and niece arrive home before they leave. He says he was out of town, with an airline ticket as proof. The niece says she was at home with her kids.

Knowles and Trapp arrange to speak with the two nephews the following day. The officers head back to their car, where they carefully remove and bag their masks and gloves, then sanitize their hands. Again.

"You catch that?" Trapp asks.

"All the present tenses? Yeah. I don't think she's our girl."

"Agreed, but sometimes family rivalries run deeper than they appear. I say we keep her on the list."

"Of course. We can't rule anyone out yet. Except the brother-in-law, once we check whether he really was on that flight."

***

The voice in my ear shocks me awake. From the soft darkness of sleep to the cold, black of dread. The voice is telling me—what? I hear static. A man coughing? What else? Waves. All I can see is the sunrise and some stuff along the beach. He's well out of sight. Doesn't matter. He may as well be on the moon.

Then, like God, the earpiece speaks. And, just like in the Old Testament, it is terrifying.

"I said, can you hear me?"

The shouted words scare me almost as much as my predicament. I nod vigorously. Then I realize he must also be able to *hear* me. I start talking to the voice in my ear. "What do you want? Who are you?"

I keep praying someone will see me or hear me. On the Atlantic Coast. As the tide comes in. In November. Not likely. My prayers go unanswered. But someone is out there somewhere, watching me.

"Do you know why you are here?" the voice demands.

"No." My voice is raw.

"Think. If you can figure out why you are here, I'll let you out. Easy as that."

Then there's silence. No hum. No static. Is he gone?

I don't know why, but I keep talking out loud. I guess the sound of my voice comforts me. It also helps me think. If I can figure this out, I get to leave, right? Yeah. I don't really hold out much hope of that. I don't think Mr. Voice went to so much trouble burying me, just to dig me back up if I make a good guess. I think that would be more reason to kill me, if anything. He'd be found out. He'd be caught.

But it does give me something to think about besides the rising water. So let's start with the obvious. Do I know this voice? It doesn't sound disguised. Another reason to doubt that he'll let me go. I try to think hard, but with the static it's difficult to identify the voice. It's a man. And maybe there's something stilted about his speech?

***

"So we know the killer was probably a male. It was a blitz attack with a heavy blunt object. Then there's the weight of the body. Difficult to transport, especially for a woman. I mean, without someone noticing." Trapp is thinking out loud.

"But our guy did come prepared. Nothing at the scene. Waiting for the tide to go out to bury her. Successfully covered his tracks. Then there's the remoteness of the beach, the tide washing away any evidence, such as footprints, and the fact that the only evidence we do have, really isn't evidence. The tape and earbud are too cheap and generic. Anyone could have bought them anywhere. And no prints or DNA on them, except for the victim's.

"We know she had to be buried between tides, so between about 10 p.m. on Saturday the 12th, and 7 a.m. on Sunday, when the next tide came in.

"But time of burial and death are almost useless to us. There's such a wide gap between when she could have been buried and when the kid's GoPro drone found her. So far, almost everyone we've talked to could have done it. Except the brother-in-law. Everyone else was at home. Most of the alibis are verified by family members, if you can call that verification. Thanks, COVID-19, for keeping everyone home.

"Even the sister could probably have managed. It would be difficult for a woman to transport her, but if you're determined enough to bury someone on a beach, chances are you're prepared to go to some trouble. We know she was alive when she was buried. Also, the victim could have woken up at any moment. She wasn't drugged, just knocked out. The killer was prepared to risk that. Whoever it was knew that beach."

"Yeah," Knowles says. "That spot's not marked as private property, but it's been completely deserted every time I've been back. The killer knew he wouldn't be seen or heard there. How did he know that? Who knows about this beach? Who actually goes there? I'm going to do a quick check into the property, and have some uniforms knock on doors. See if anyone new was spotted in the neighborhood lately. Maybe someone asking questions about it. See if it's city property or privately owned. I'll get uniforms to go to the closest gas station and convenience stores, too. If that kid hadn't been playing with his new drone, she probably wouldn't have been found for a good long time. Here's hoping the traffic cams near the scene will tell us something more."

"Did you find anything new when you went back to the scene?" Trapp asks.

"No. Just a feeling I had. She was alive and probably awake from the time she was buried. That's the point, right? To make her panicked and terrified about drowning for as long as possible. I mean, what's the one thing this beach is known for? It has one of the slowest tides around. I think our killer chose the location for that reason. Not just for the isolation, but for the length of time it would take for her to die. I'd say she was put there as early as possible on Saturday. Very close to 10 p.m. when the tide went out."

***

It's silent and pitch-black until a car door slams. The driver walks to the back of the car and opens the trunk. He pulls out something heavy. Something that hides his face as he slings it over his shoulder. Then he turns and dumps the something into a waiting shopping buggy, which barely handles the weight, its wheels splaying out beneath it. But it's all right. It doesn't have to go far.

He struggles to get the overloaded cart across the potholed parking lot. When he gets to the stone stairs that descend to the beach, he dumps the bundle out of the cart, and lets it tumble down the steps. He guides the empty buggy carefully down the steps, one at a time, confident that the clunking sound cannot be heard by anyone passing on the highway.

At the bottom of the stairs, he wrestles the bundle back into the buggy and pulls it over the sand to a deep hole, partly filled with water. He stops and rolls a body out of the tarp. Its face flashes momentarily in the unreliable moonlight, under an overcast sky. The man has his back to the water, showing his face only to his unconscious victim.

A few minutes later, at the top of the stairs, he smooths out the buggy tracks in the parking lot. He is not worried about the tracks on the beach below. Those will soon be washed away.

***

When Knowles arrives at the station, Trapp has news to share. "It looks like you were right about the time she was buried, and why."

"What do you mean?"

"Forensics found a trace amount of smelling salts under her nose. The killer wanted her awake. He wanted her to suffer as long as possible. Not just die, but be fully aware of exactly what was coming. Combine that with the earpiece and I get the feeling this was some sort of retribution. Punishment or payback of some sort. At least, that's my guess. What could such an ordinary woman have done to make someone come up with such a vile plan? From all accounts she may have been odd, but she was not an evil genius."

The captain comes over for his update. "Remember, the why only has to make sense to the killer. We could be dealing with someone completely off his rocker."

A junior officer calls them to his desk. "Uh, guys? You're gonna wanna see this." A view of the street near the beach access shows several vehicles pulling up at the nearby traffic light. Then one turns in to the beach parking lot. "That's the Torres car. Registered to a Mrs. Dora Pinella Torres."

"What the f—" Knowles says. "Have we uncovered a neighborhood dispute gone crazy? And why didn't he mention a wife when we interviewed him? He said there was only his sick daughter."

***

In a car in the lot above the beach, a man is screaming into a cell phone. At first he was calm, but now he is shaking. "You knew! You *knew* you were sick and still you come around *my* children. You don't *think* about others!" His rage momentarily gives way to grief. He lowers the phone and sobs, his body heaving. Quieter now, he continues what he came here to say. "My whole family. Infected. My wife, my son, both dead. My daughter so sick she cannot breathe. Because of your carelessness. You drowned them from the inside out. So now you will drown. They saw death coming for them. So will you."

***

There's always a story behind the story. That's what I'm thinking as the waves lick at my frozen, weary face. After waiting a lifetime for the water to reach me, it now seems to be rising quickly. Not much time left.

Who will feed my cats? My little dog? I feel ridiculous. That the thought of my pets is what finally breaks me. Even though I know that Colin will care for them. But feeding them is my job. I'm not OK with leaving them. I don't want to die. I feel, oddly, like I will miss everyone. Especially the pets. At least I can be pretty sure they weren't involved.

***

The slight man washes his hands at the kitchen sink. Twenty seconds. Just to be safe. Through the window, he watches his daughter and son play with a small dog in the yard. Gloves and mask on, but still too close. He smiles as his youngest shyly gives a treat to the dog. How do you sanitize a dog? The answer is you don't. A moment of concern passes over the father's face. We should all be indoors.

He opens the window, calls out a hello and waves. He tells his children to come in for dinner. Later, he tells them to be more careful. To stay indoors unless there is no one else in the yard. But they really wanted to see the dog.

Anyway, the warning has come too late.

***

In the ICU at Douglas Memorial Hospital, two nurses turn over a woman who struggles to breathe. They've found that COVID-19 patients' oxygen levels go up when they lie on their stomachs.

But there is no hope on their faces. And none on the face of the slight man at her bedside.

***

Back at his upstairs apartment, the man stoops more than usual at the kitchen sink, staring at his hands as he washes them again and again. His home is quiet now. No coughing from the bedroom. His home. Once filled with the sounds of cheer and laughter. They are gone now, everyone he has ever loved. First his wife. Then his son. And finally, yesterday, after the police came to visit him, his beloved daughter.

The only sound left is that of his own labored breathing.

His shoulders shake as he weeps silently.

He places a family photo on the table by his chair. His cough is violent now. He sits down to wait for the police. He knows they'll return. But before they arrive, his cough turns into choking. Then to gasping.

He glances at the phone by his arm for just a moment. He realizes there is no one he wants to call. He sits back, kisses the photo, and struggles to breathe.

***

As the salty water reaches my lips, the faint hope that his talking to me means he might be considering releasing me vanishes. I'm resigned. I deserve this. I owe a debt that must be paid. I couldn't live with myself anyway, knowing what I'd done. Still, I begin to cry. Hot tears run down my cheeks and are united with the rising ocean.

It's a beautiful day. And I'm going to miss it.

LOVE THY NEIGHBOR

Lisa de Nikolits

Originally from South Africa, Lisa de Nikolits is a multiple Independent Publisher Book Award winner and the author of nine published novels. The tenth, The Rage Room, *is scheduled for publication in fall 2020. Her most recent novel,* The Occult Persuasion and The Anarchist's Solution *was longlisted for a Sunburst Award for Excellence in Canadian Literature of The Fantastic.*

Previous works include The Hungry Mirror, West of Wawa, A Glittering Chaos, The Witchdoctor's Bones; Between The Cracks She Fell, The Nearly Girl, No Fury Like That, Rotten Peaches, The Occult Persuasion and The Anarchist's Solution *and* The Rage Room.

Yeah, not so much. But kill him? That came later.

"Look at that guy!" I called my partner, Laurie-Anne, into the sunroom where I was designing a website for a pain-in-the buttinsky client. "Talk about Mr. Clench. What's he got up his ass? Gold pebbles?"

She tut-tutted me, and I felt shamed. Then she leaned a hand on my shoulder.

"Please don't tell me we're losing Arthur The Good," she said. "Oh, frack, look! A *For Sale* sign. Sayonara Arthur."

"Sayonara the best neighbor ever," I said.

"Goodbye Grey Goose vodka on tap," Laurie-Anne sighed.

Laurie-Anne was more of a fan of the vodka than I was. Sure, I had a deep fondness for Arthur for doing us all the greatest favor a semi-detached neighbor could—working away from home for the most part, maintaining the property for the most part and being an all-around standup guy in the fleeting moments when he was home.

The vodka gig began when Arthur first started going to the U.S. for work. "Any faves from the duty-free?" he had asked.

Laurie-Anne admitted she was a fan of Grey Goose, which, by golly, cost a pretty penny here.

"Consider it my pleasure," Arthur said with a grin.

At times, both Laurie-Anne and I had mused there might be a side to Arthur we'd never seen. Like what was with all that sanding? The house was tiny. What was he doing in there? Dismembering bodies? Laurie-Anne asked him about it one time and he looked perplexed.

"Sanding? Nope. Listen, long stint in Texas coming up, keep an eye on things, I'll stock the recycling bin with geese when I get back."

He put the gift bottles in our recycling bin. For some reason, he never wanted to hand them over in person.

And now there was a *For Sale* sign on his lawn. Sayonara Arthur The Good. I echoed Laurie-Anne's sentiment. "Frack!"

Enter the new neighbors. A young family, of the buttoned-up variety, pulled into Arthur's driveway and climbed the porch steps.

Standing next to Mr. Clenched Buttocks was a grasshopper of a wife with an infant on her hip and a two-year-old hanging off her hand, thumb in mouth. Mr. Clenched maintained his stance, hand neatly raised, knock three times, pause, repeat.

"We were driving around the neighborhood and saw your sign just go up. I'm Roy, this is my wife, Carla. I know we don't have an appointment and the house isn't listed, but it's just what we're looking for. The school nearby, the lake, the park. Please, buddy, let us in for five minutes, just five minutes, I swear!"

And we watched Arthur the Good let him and his family in. We shouldn't have been too surprised that Arthur was heading south. He'd met a bona fide beauty queen in the great state of Texas and was heading down into the sunshine to marry her.

"Kids?" Laurie-Anne said to me. "Our walls are paper-thin. These houses are like 200 years old."

"And tiny. Listen," I was confident, "there are four of them. They can't fit in a two-bedroom house. We don't have anything to worry about. They won't buy."

Of course, life being what it is, they bought the house, and we lost Arthur the Good and his gifts of Grey Goose bottles in our recycling bin. Arthur's mysterious sanding noises were replaced by a yappy pug in diapers and a baby that wailed all night, neither of which were as half as bad as the incessant piano racket.

Because Mrs. Grasshopper fancied herself to be some sort of Chopin, big-time. OMG, take it from me, if she'd wailed and the pug had played the piano and the baby yapped, we'd have been better off.

Never mind that Mrs. Chopin played six to eight hours a day. Never mind that the piano needed a good tuning service. Laurie-Anne, a classical guitarist, couldn't fathom how Mrs. Chopin failed to notice the most basic of basics—tune the damn piano.

One day, her nerves frayed, Laurie-Anne ventured over to ask if they could move the piano to the furthermost outer wall. The piano turned out to be an electric one, which led Laurie-Anne to wonder about the tuning issues, but she was more perturbed to see that the piano was already backed onto the furthermost wall.

She explained that our houses, admittedly old and admittedly small, carried sound to the point where we said *gesundheit* when someone sneezed.

Therefore, she asked, would it be possible for the sound to be lowered, even slightly?

She was met with blank stares, and she returned unsettled, saying it was the oddest encounter ever.

"They both just stood there and stared at me. Even the toddler stared at me. I swear the baby stared at me and so did the yappy pug. I explained how I practice playing for 45 minutes and I try not to play too loudly, and if I'm disturbing them, I'll move to the basement to play. They didn't reply at all, to any of it. It was like meeting the twins from *The Shining* only times two, and with an old dog in diapers."

Laurie-Anne wasn't used to not getting along with people. Everybody liked her and she reciprocated. Easygoing and talented, she was a portrait photographer. She made a bundle and she had a rep as being the nicest person in the business. I had no idea what she was doing with me, I'm a wasp to her honeybee. We met at an ad agency party, and for the life of me, my caustic wit aside, I have no idea what Laurie-Anne saw in me.

She's damn gorgeous, voluptuous as a goddess with a wild mane of blond curls and a grin to melt the ice off your heart. Meanwhile, I'm tall and bony, Wendy-Sue, a plain Jane who overcompensates with cropped purple hair and a sparkling nose ring. I've got an industrial in my left ear, along with several other piercings and I wear a uniform of faded tight high-waisted jeans and colorful sneakers with contrasting socks. Add a striped body-fitting T-shirt and that's me every day.

I work from home, using the closed-off porch as my study, weather permitting. It's a haven with a view of the street so I can keep an eye on the comings and goings of Larry the neighborhood cat and the squirrels and the blue jays and the occasional jewel-colored cardinal.

"Bummer," I said. "I thought they'd listen to you."

But I was distraught because I was, to put it mildly, noise-sensitive.

I'd been convinced that Laurie-Anne would work her magic and the toxic assault would be no more. Eight torturous months had passed. We'd both been waiting for things to calm down, for the baby to stop yowling, the pug to stop yapping and for the goddamned piano to lessen. Mrs. Grasshopper played as one would a nervous tic, scrambling frantically for hours, her arpeggios an avalanche of Nascar crashes, steel scraping the barriers.

"What can we do?" I asked Laurie-Anne, who shook her head.

"We live with it," she said, disappearing into the house. "Earplugs, I guess."

But I'd tried earplugs to no avail. I swear, I could feel the piano vibrations attacking the marrow of my bones while I floundered in a deafened sea of fury. Through my angry heartbeat, I could feel that army of disarrayed arpeggios. I couldn't escape.

And, therefore, I admit, I began to behave badly. I took up accompanying the piano with a drum set made of pots and pans. I rendered more than one frying pan unusable, forging it into a lump of unbalanced twists while being "played" by a pot.

Laurie-Anne did not enjoy my retaliatory efforts, but I couldn't help myself. As soon as the piano sounded, I started whacking my instruments. I stopped only when I hurt my wrist. I needed my job, so I couldn't afford to injure myself. No more hitting pots and pans. My wrist told me there'd no more slamming doors either.

Two years passed with me poised like a meerkat, just waiting for that first tinkle. I fired up heavy metal, dialed up to 11. I revisited my punk years. I even raised the volume on French talk shows, not understanding a word.

The yappy diaper dog died and was replaced by an even louder labradoodle who sounded like a squeaky toy caught under a 16-wheeler.

The baby girl stopped crying and started talking. And man, could that toddler chat. Nonstop. High volume.

Laurie-Anne grew increasingly on edge. Not only was there the noise but there was me, ready for action, always trying for some new retaliatory trick to bring the noise monsters under control.

Mr. Clenched Buttocks turned out to be a union negotiator. How did I know? Because he made all his calls while wandering shirtless around his garden, his speakerphone on max.

"Anyhoo," he'd say, three hours into any given call, "I'll let you go then."

I couldn't escape him. If he was talking on the front porch, I moved to my upstairs study and then, I swear to God, he went into his backyard. Was he trying to drive us out?

Things worsened between Laurie-Anne and me. The clincher for Laurie-Anne was the cigars.

"I can't stand them," she said, tears streaming down her face. "I've always hated cigars."

Because Mr. Clenched had now taken to cigar smoking—big time.

"There are bylaws," Laurie-Anne shouted at him one evening.

"It's my house," he yelled back. "I can do whatever I want." He blew a cloud of smoke in her face.

"I'm outta here," Laurie-Anne said.

"What do you mean?"

"It's your house and you won't move."

"We can't afford to live anywhere else," I said, wild with horror at the thought of her leaving.

"It doesn't matter. I'm going home," she said. "I miss my old life. It's not just you. Being here doesn't suit me. Too big-city. I want to regroup, get myself back. And, no, this hasn't helped." Laurie-Anne was a west coast girl and I knew she missed the ocean, but still? Leaving me?

"So, go then," I said although my heart was shattered in a million splintered pieces. "Go then."

She was crying when she left. She told me she loved me and that she always would and then she left.

"I'm not saying it's over forever," she said. "Just for now. I have to breathe."

I was left with nothing but bad piano playing, a cloud of cigar smoke and a broken heart.

I had no choice. I had to kill Mr. Clenched Buttocks. Get rid of him. Laurie-Anne would come back if I got our lovely lives back.

I just had to figure how to do it.

In the interim, Mrs. Grasshopper began playing ball on the sidewalk with her son. *Bounce bounce bounce.* More noise. I invested in a mouth guard to stop my jaw from clenching, and I ordered expensive earplugs, and I tried to learn to live with the feeling of bad piano playing in my marrow.

And I pushed all work aside and focused on my plan, but it's not as easy to kill someone as you might think, even if they are your neighbor. Maybe even more difficult, because you become the first suspect after the spouse.

I thought of ingratiating myself with a poisoned peace offering, but I couldn't risk harming the kids. Perhaps there was a way to poison his cigars? Tell him I'd been gifted with a box of Havanas, and lace them with cyanide? Again, too obvious.

Walk by him and stab him with a quickly dissolving drug? Where would I get a drug? And how would I get that close to him?

I stalked him online, and what a show-off he was! Mr. Macho Man taking the family camping, canoeing, paddle boarding and cycling, all while wearing a tank top, flexing his gym-boy muscles and grinning like a clown.

It's astounding the things people will share on social media.

"Worried about an upcoming doc's app," Roy The Family Man posted on Facebook. "Anyhoo, sure it'll be nothing, but thoughts and prayers, peeps please!"

Ha! A doctor's appointment. Good to know. But who was his doc, and how could I find out? I had both their phone numbers; we'd exchanged them in the early days of pretend bonhomie. Could I call him and make up a story to try to extract information?

No. I wasn't any kind of con artist. And I had to be realistic about my options. This wasn't some whacky TV show where I could make stupid shit happen out of nowhere. I had limited resources. And, speaking of limited, my funds were running out. What with Laurie-Anne gone and me focusing on my obsession, my savings were depleting fast. Not only did I have to get back to work, I also had to bring in a boarder. The horror. I'd only ever shared my space with a lover, and Laurie-Anne had been my longest one at that. Four years we'd been together.

Her status on FB had changed from "in a relationship" (with me), to "it's complicated" (not great, but better than being booted off entirely), then "single" (gulp, sob), and recently to "in a relationship."

I wanted to do die. She had moved on. I had lost her, my clients and my savings. If I didn't get my ass into gear, I'd lose my house too.

Luckily, I'm a pretty handy lady when it comes to DIY. It took a few thousand dollars and a lot of sanding, and the basement was ready. It wasn't what you'd call deluxe accommodations, but it had its own entrance, two rooms, a small shower and kitchenette. I'd done OK.

Of course, it broke my heart to be down there because the basement used to be Laurie-Anne's at-home photo studio where she did her alt-photo processing artwork. She was into carbon printing, and she was really good at it, she taught and had exhibits.

She had all kinds of lightboxes and chemicals in there, with papers hanging from the ceiling, and I had loved knowing she was down there. A moving van came the day after she left and took it all away. How had I not noticed her quietly packing things up? She must have planned her move longer than I'd thought, but I'd been busy, focusing on Mr. Clenched Buttocks, and how to get him and his noisy family to shut the frack up.

The basement had the added bonus of being soundproofed, because some former owner was a musician and he'd had it fitted up to record his stuff. So Laurie-Anne had never had to suffer the same stresses I did; she was able to escape into her own world. Meanwhile me, upstairs, had to endure six to eight hours every day of Mrs. Chopin clinking away tunelessly like Chinese water torture.

In retrospect, it couldn't have helped our relationship to have Laurie-Anne come upstairs and find me in the living room, screeching at the adjoining wall, "Shut up! You are driving me *mad*. Shut up, shut up!"

Not one of my finer moments, for sure. And now Laurie-Anne was in a new relationship with Zoey Northmore, and I was all alone in my basement, her former studio.

I needed to get a tenant I could trust, so I reached out to the only friend I had left, Jenny-Lee Anderson, a film and TV producer, and a set designer for kicks.

She knew all about Mr. Clenched Buttocks and the piano, and about how I'd lost Laurie-Anne. She'd like Laurie-Anne, too.

"Meet up for coffee?" I asked. She was stunned, not because she knows I usually drink decaf chamomile, but because I actually wanted to meet in person. It was hard to get me to leave the sanctity of my cave in the best of times, and now here I was asking her out.

"You must be desperate," she said.

It was thanks to Jenny-Lee that I'd met Laurie-Anne—she'd forced me to come to the dinner party, although why I'd agreed, I had no idea. Then, later, we discussed how she'd be my bridesmaid when Laurie-Anne and I got married but, of course, that never happened.

So, Jenny-Lee and I met up.

"Spill the beans, buttercup," she said. "Don't beat around the bush with me. What's up?"

"I need a roomie." I explained the situation.

"I've got just the guy," she said, and whipped out her phone. Guy? No way. "Guy? I need a nice quiet old lady."

She snorted and laughed. "No such thing. Most old ladies I know are batshit crazy. Trust me, you do not want an old lady. No, you want this guy. Quiet, reserved, slightly weird in the best kind of way. Won't make a noise, will help you take the garbage out blah blah. Look."

She showed me a photo of a lanky kid with his nostrils pressed up to the camera. He looked like camel. "Hard to tell anything from that," I said cautiously.

"I'll send him around," she said confidently. "You'll love him. But fugettabout that. How are you, honey? You still miss Laurie-Anne?"

The floodgates opened, coffee shop or not, and in an instant she was hugging me and I was sobbing my heart out.

She finally got me cleaned up, but I wasn't finished. "I loved her sooooooo much, and this was all his fault." And off I was, ranting about Mr. Clenched Buttocks.

"And now they've added a hot tub to the back deck and the little girl can't shut up! And they added a basketball net—more noise! And the piano!"

"Honey, I know it's hard, but you have to find a way to get over this." Jenny-Lee looked uneasy. "Look how much you've lost so far. Come on, honey. Maybe you need some therapy."

I looked at her in horror. "What the frack? No way! I'm sound of mind, anybody would be nuts about this, I swear they would. It's toxic noise. It's not just me!"

"Be that as it may, but ease off the rants when you meet Henry, OK? Let's try to get you back on track. How's work?"

"Good," I sniffed. "Really good, actually."

She let out a sigh of relief. "Great. OK, so meet Henry, tell me what you think. But honey, please, straighten up and fly right, you got me? Life's a bitch and then some, but you gotta get this mess under control. *Capisce?*"

I nodded. She was right. At this rate, I'd end up homeless or in a looney bin.

***

Jenny-Lee had been right about something else. Henry was a gem. A photographer's assistant by trade, but Henry was mainly a long, lean daydreamer with his head in the clouds. His mother had

298

kicked him out, hoping it would jump-start Henry into adult life, but I wasn't sure how successful she'd been.

He moved in with his sparse belongings. He was such a nice kid that soon I was doing his laundry, while he cooked and took out the garbage. Turned out he liked binge-watching the same sci-fi shit as me, so it all worked out well.

Apart from one thing. The piano.

It didn't take Henry long to get more than agitated by the clanking. "She's not even playing anything!" he yelled at the wall. Mild-mannered Henry! I was validated.

"Even Henry hears it," I told Jenny-Lee on the phone. "And no, I did not give him a heads-up. He came to the conclusion all by himself."

"Whatever. I'm glad you guys are hitting it off. Hey, did you see online that Laurie-Anne's back to 'It's complicated'?"

"What? No way!" I had forced myself to stop looking at her FB page. "Gotta go, Jenny-Lee, bye!" I hung up the phone and logged onto Facebook.

Yeah, baby! "Henry," I yelled, "look! Laurie-Anne's complicated!"

He came up from the basement looking worried. "If she comes back, you'll kick me out," he said, and I swear tears filled his eyes.

I grabbed him and hugged him tight. "No way! You're like family to me!" And it was true. I loved this kid. I agreed with his mother that he needed a focus, but unlike her, I knew he'd find his way. He just needed some space to figure it out. "I promise you, Henry. Besides, she'll never come back."

"She loved you, too," Henry insisted. "Jenny-Lee told me."

"She did?" The remaining embers of my heart flared up.

"But you'll give her the basement back."

"I won't," I promised. "If she comes back, she'll have to get her own studio. You have my word, Henry."

He looked cheered. "OK, then."

I gnawed at a fingernail. "But as long as we've got Mr. Clenched Buttocks living next door, Laurie-Anne won't come back."

Henry shot me a look. "You've got it all wrong," he said.

I cocked my head, confused.

"It's not Roy, it's her!"

Oh, my God. He was so right. She was the source of it all, Mrs. Grasshopper, wannabe Chopin. I mean, sure, Roy was a blight, what with his noisy bandanna-wearing labradoodle, his basketball nets, his loud speakerphone conversations and his spa pool for his kiddies, but that was just life noise. The kids were happy campers, a bit loud, but those were the sounds of summer, and Roy had taken to smoking more often in his backyard, rather than out on his front porch. Why hadn't I seen it?

"You are so right," I said slowly. Mrs. Chopin was the problem.

Henry turned on the kettle. "I don't want you to think I am a terrible person," he said.

"What? You can tell me anything! And if you have any thoughts about how to fix this, you're preaching to the choir!"

"We need to get rid of her," he said. "And not just because of the piano. Have you heard how she talks to the kids? She's horrible. So sarcastic and mean. My dad used to talk to me like that."

He was right. I took our tea tray and headed to the living room. "I've been so blinded by hatred for him that I totally overlooked the obvious," I said. "She is terrible. I've heard her, too. And one night, I heard her crying to Roy about how the kids never listen to her and how she sometimes hates them."

"You heard her?"

"Yes, I was taking a shower and when I turned it off, I heard them out in the back. It was late at night, and she was sobbing. I admit, I opened the window wider and leaned out as far as I could. I heard her say she sometimes hates them. But again, I just focused on Roy."

Henry chewed on a biscuit, his eyes thoughtful.

"But getting rid of someone isn't easy," I said. "Trust me. I had this huge vendetta against Roy, and I've thought of everything."

"Leave it with me," Henry said. "Shall we watch a *Rage Room*?" *The Rage Room* was a *Black Mirror* series based on a bestselling novel that we both loved.

"Fire it up," I said, and I relaxed. Henry would take care of everything. I somehow knew he would. Meanwhile, I'd get in touch with Laurie-Anne and put out my feelers. 'It's complicated' might just work out OK for me after all.

***

As time passed, things went well on the Laurie-Anne front. We began to communicate, and she told me that she missed me and our life together. I told her about Henry, making sure that she knew he was part of any package deal, and she seemed to be fine with that.

I hooked them up on Facebook, and they soon became fast friends.

"But what about the noise factor?" Laurie-Anne wrote on a message to Henry and me. "I can't stand it."

"I've got a plan," Henry said. "I need a few months, give or take. I'll update you when I can."

And he'd say no more than that.

***

I buried my head in my work, and Henry more or less vanished from view. When I asked him what he was up to, he mumbled something about "our project," and went out. In fact, he was hardly ever home. I began to worry. After a few months of this un-Henry-like behavior, I nabbed him.

"Henry, you need to tell me what's going on."

He sat down. "You're right. And, besides, it's time. But I have to ask you, how far are you prepared to go?"

"All the way," I said immediately. "I want Laurie-Anne back. I'm prepared to do anything, and I mean that."

"So here's the plan," he said, and laid it out. An hour later, I looked at him, eyes wide.

"You've thought of everything," I said. "You could be a private detective if you want a new career."

He laughed. "Yeah, maybe, but we both need to make sure we don't end up behind bars for this. You ready?"

"I'm ready."

The next day, Henry placed the call. "Hi, may I speak with Carla Nunce? Speaking? Thank you Carla. I'm calling from the cardiac specialists' office. You recall meeting with Dr. Clayton a few months back? Yes, right. Well, he'd like to see you to follow up on that last X-ray. Yes, I know he went through it with you and, yes, everything is fine, but there's one aspect that might have been overlooked and we just want to make sure things are all good. I know this is short notice, but could you come in this morning?"

By stalking Roy and Carla online and in person, Henry had gleaned valuable information. The doctor's appointment Roy had mentioned on Facebook hadn't been for him, but for Carla. It had struck me as odd that the man would be such a heavy cigar smoker if his health was in peril, but it really meant he didn't care about his wife. Perhaps he hated her piano playing, too.

But I was getting ahead of myself. She was the mother of his children, after all.

Both Henry and I had counted on Carla immediately rushing to the doc's office, no questions asked. He'd called her using a burner phone, making the call when he knew the kids were at school and Roy was out of town at a conference.

What else would anyone do but rush over to the doc's office? Plus, Henry was sure that Carla had no friends.

"Do you have a pen?" Henry asked Carla. "Our office has changed suites. Same address, but instead of Suite 201 on the second floor, we've moved to 105 on the ground floor. The sign in the lobby still says 201, but come to 105. We haven't updated the signage just yet."

The boy was brilliant. He'd even managed to rent an office in the same building!

He hung up the phone. "She's on her way," he said. "Are you OK to do this?"

I nodded. "You?"

"Oh, yeah."

***

I looked around. Henry had done a great job. The place was a replica of the real deal, down to the artwork on the walls. He'd visited the real office and photographed the place. The only things missing were the huge filing cabinets behind the receptionist's area but that, he assured me, was easily explained away as having been moved to the back.

"But how did you stage this so perfectly?" I asked when he first showed me the place and outlined his plan.

"Jenny-Lee!

Of course. Jenny-Lee could get her hands on anything, so setting up a doc's office would have been a piece of cake for her.

"Does she know what we're going to do?"

Henry shook his head. "Well, she might but she said 'Don't tell me nada, zip, zero. As far as I'm concerned, you're working on a music video for YouTube or some shit. Whatever.'"

Henry made a fine-looking doctor. He'd got a friend of his to act as a receptionist, telling her it was for a film project. She didn't care, a baggie of weed took care of payment and he made sure she had rehearsed her lines. He'd also told her not to mention the project in case it failed.

She had looked at him, like, *duh*! "What project?" she said. "

As for me, I had to hide in a closet in Henry's office. It had a latticed door that I could just manage to see through.

I got in position well ahead of time and hunkered down. Could we do really this? This was beyond extreme. Then I thought about Carla and her rudeness, how she stared over my head when I tried to talk to her, befriend her, make things right, appeal to her human side. And I remembered how terrible she was to her kids. And how it had been years, and she still couldn't play the piano worth a shit.

Nope, this was the right decision.

302

Henry sat quietly at his desk. I waited in the closet. I was just about to open the door and grab a breath of fresh air when I heard Henry get up from his desk.

"Mrs. Nunce, good of you to come in. Take a seat."

I heard Carla babbling on at high volume, and I heard Henry soothing her.

"Let me get you some water." He phoned though to the stoner girl who brought in the water. He then told the girl she could leave for the day.

Carla knocked back the drink.

Henry held up X-rays he'd scored from a store Jenny-Lee had put him onto. I heard him talking about a grave diagnosis, but that there was chemo and other treatments available, and she shouldn't worry.

Yep, the water was drugged, and thank God she drank it. Pretty soon she started winding down like the Energizer Bunny on dollar-store batteries.

The minute Carla slumped over, Henry called me. I jumped out of the closet.

Henry ran to the door, making sure the receptionist had gone. She'd done what he told her. Her job was to bring in the water, get out of her uniform and leave. She didn't need to be told twice.

Henry locked the door. He looked at me. "Are you ready?"

I was. We had agreed we would press the plunger of the syringe together, hand in hand.

We positioned the needle in Carla's neck and took the plunge. All for one, and one for all. Carla went from this world to the next, where she could play the piano however she liked for the rest of her eternal life.

***

Henry had rented the office for a month. Jenny-Lee arranged for trucks and a few of her mover buddies to empty the place after hours. Henry said he'd taken care of the security cameras. The boy had great potential when he put his mind to a task.

The most unpleasant part of it all was removing Carla's clothes, as we didn't want her to carry any evidence away with her. We rolled her onto a drop cloth and washed her down carefully with bleach. Sure, the task was nasty, but Henry and I worked silently, making sure we didn't miss a single spot. We even combed out her hair to make sure nothing had transferred to her from us.

We folded her body into a suitcase and wheeled it out of the building to my car. For a tall woman, she was mercifully light.

"Hollow bones," Henry muttered as he lifted the suitcase into the trunk.

"Try not to think about it," I whispered.

Henry drove Carla's car to the airport and cleaned it, while I headed north to the farmlands of Ontario. I drove for hours, eventually finding just the right ditch.

"This is on you," I said to Carla as I hauled the suitcase from my trunk. "I tried to reason with you. And if you'd been a good pianist or at least played reasonable hours at a reasonable volume, this wouldn't have happened."

Using the spray bleach I'd packed for the purpose, I carefully removed all fingerprints and other potential traces from the suitcase before hiding it under a thick mesh of bramble.

I felt a bit shaky when I drove away, but it was nothing that a visit to Tim Hortons couldn't fix. It had been a long day. Heck, it had been a long few years. I bit into my maple-glazed donut, gulped my chamomile tea, and thought about Laurie-Anne and how nice it would be to have her back.

As for Carla, no one will ever know what happened to her. Henry dumped her purse and clothes in a place they would never be found. For all intents and purposes, she had simply run away. Roy reported her as a missing person, but he didn't appear to be too distraught, and the investigation soon fizzled out.

***

Laurie-Anne came back and we got married, and Jenny-Lee was my bridesmaid. Henry joined the police force, and Roy turned out to be not such a bad guy after all. I gave Snoopy, the labradoodle, some good training and got him under control. And, heck, I even babysat the kids when Roy was out of town. It was the least I could do.

As for the piano, I have no idea what happened to it. Roy never mentioned it, and I never asked.

THE CRIMSON GRAVE

Hayley Liversidge

Hayley Liversidge is a freelance writer. Having completed a creative writing course, she has been shortlisted in both the Writing Magazine and the Crossing the Tees Short Story Competitions. Her articles have appeared in the local community newspaper, Woman Alive *magazine and most recently* MIMAzine.

She lives with her husband in the North of England. It is a wonderful place to explore the beauty of nature. It's here Hayley picked up her love of walking in the countryside, in places such as Scotland, the Lake District and the North Yorkshire Moors.

The stench of decay filled his nostrils. *Where the heck was it coming from?* Spen Bradshaw stared into the grave he'd dug only yesterday. He gently prodded the hole with his spade, scraping away the top layer of soil. Thick red liquid oozed slowly through the mud.

That was all he needed! In the year 2050, people still couldn't find a more original place to hide a body than in this pithole of a place, the cemetery.

He stiffened. Twenty years in the army had hardened him. Here was a dead person, a human being. She was fairly young, had been reasonably pretty, with blue eyes and blond hair. The woman should have had many years of life left, to live to the full. She probably had a family, maybe children. Someone would be devastated by her murder. Yet, here he was, irritated by the inconvenience of it all. Since when had he become so uncaring?

Spen pulled out his secure phone and speed-dialed the police. DI Jenkin's gaunt face appeared on the screen. His eyes were red. Worry lines were etched over his unshaven face.

"Are you OK, Mike?"

"Not really," Jenkins said. "I'll tell you over a pint at The Three-Legged Mare"

Spen frowned. More bad news.

The DI picked up his mug of black coffee and took a sip. "What's on your mind mate? Something tells me this isn't a social call."

"You'd better get your team down here. Some kind person has put a dead body in my grave."

DI Jenkins chuckled. "Isn't that what you put in graves?"

Spen sighed. Sometimes he really didn't go for his friend's sense of humor. "No, not when there's no coffin."

Mike continued to laugh. "I'll be down there shortly," he promised, finishing off his drink.

"Don't bring too many of those forensic police robots with you, either. They're more trouble than they're worth." Spen snapped the phone shut and waited. Right now he was more concerned about Mike than the dead woman. The DI just didn't look like his normal self.

There was nothing more he could do. No point in standing next to a half dug grave, just waiting for the police to arrive in their new, super-fast, electric panda vans. This might be a deprived area, but a lot of money had been put into the local police force. That and the new Apprentice Skills Scheme.

He wandered past the multitude of marble headstones. Some were shaped as trains or boats, others as houses or traditional crosses. They rose up from the ground, creating the appearance of a miniature city.

The cemetery gave way to a small park. Nothing more than grass. At its center was a small circular hut that exuded the aroma of coffee and warm chocolate.

"What do you want, Spen?" the girl asked reaching for a bamboo mug, and winking at him.

"The usual—cucumber, kale and pear, heated please," he said, trying not to wince. How he wished Sandra wasn't such a flirt. If she didn't run the only clean food establishment in the area he'd never go near the place. Our Sandra, as people affectionately called her, was the biggest gossip in town. What she didn't know about the local residents wasn't worth knowing.

"Any strangers in town yesterday?" he asked conversationally, taking a gulp of the fruity brew.

"Can't say I noticed," Sandra said, leaning across the counter. "Unless you count that snotty woman who complained about her tea yesterday. Right bitch, if you ask me. Over from the States, she said.

Well, the quicker she goes back there, the better, as far as I'm concerned."

"She wasn't youngish, with curly blond hair, blue eyes, medium height?"

Sandra laughed. "That's her, but why? You don't fancy her, do ye?"

Spen hesitated. "No, I just wondered if her face looked familiar to you."

Sandra frowned, then giggled. "Shouldn't say this, but now you mention it, she did look like a younger version of Colonel Waverley's wife, Eleanor. Can't say I go much for her, either. A right proper lady now, but in her younger days she did put it about a bit, people say. Bit of a wild 'un."

She leaned across the counter again. "Hey, you don't think there's a connection, do you? Tell all, you do work for the Colonel, after all."

Spen shrugged. He wasn't going to tell her anything. It would be all around town within the hour. "I have no idea."

Sandra grinned. "You do, and you ain't telling."

A panda van shot past them, then turned around to park. "Got to go," he said, handing her the empty bamboo cup. "Bye."

***

That evening, Spen sat in The Three-Legged Mare, drinking a pint with DI Jenkins. Only Mike wasn't having his usual. Instead he was sipping a fresh orange juice. That was odd. Normally, the DI wouldn't touch the stuff.

"OK, Mike, what was it you wanted to tell me?" Spen wiped foam from his lips and stared at his friend anxiously.

Mike coughed. Strange, he'd been doing a lot of coughing recently. "The thing is," he said, "this murder may be my last case. I want it sorted quickly. Leave things nice and tidy like."

Spen choked on his beer. "What?" he spluttered. "You're too young to retire."

The DI stared into his glass. "I'll not hang about. Thing is, I've got lung cancer. Don't know how long I've got. They said it's worth giving me some new immunotherapy treatment. Some stuff about sensitizing your white cells to the tumor so they destroy it. Much better than traditional chemotherapy. It's got a good success rate."

Spen swirled the remains of his beer in the glass. What the heck do you say at times like these, without sounding trite? "I'm sorry," he said.

Mike drained his glass. "Not half so much as me, mate."

"Is there anything I can do? One ex-soldier for another."

The DI laughed, but there was no humor in his voice. "Visit me in hospital."

"Of course I will. But I meant the investigation. I think I can be of help."

"Just how do you intend to do that?"

"This case is somehow connected with Colonel Waverley and his wife. I'm sure of it. I'm always up at the mansion. The Colonel is my line manager, so I can do some probing."

DI Jenkins stood to leave. "Look, mate," he said, "you can do what you like. At this moment, I don't care. Just be careful. We haven't identified the woman. All we know is that she was a visitor. Not that we get many of those, around these parts. From the knife wound, it could easily have been a robbery that went wrong. Seems like the most likely motive. Nobody knew her, from what we can make out. So who would have a motive to kill a stranger? Unless she had a connection with the place."

Spen quickly drank the remains of his beer and followed his friend out of the pub. "Exactly," he said. "That's what I want to find out."

The DI turned to his friend. "Look, if anyone wanted her dead, it's more likely to be another visitor to town. Perhaps someone she was traveling with. The Colonel and Mrs. Waverley are held in high regard here."

"I still think they know something."

DI Jenkins laughed. "We need a little more than that to go on. Two teenage boys were seen hanging 'round the cemetery late last night. We're trying to track who they are. There's brand new CCTV installed there with the latest technology. It only operates when movement is detected. But it's rubbish; it failed to record anything yesterday."

The automatic doors of the pub swung open. Spen frowned. He wasn't convinced the teenagers had anything to do with it. True, young people were often connected with knife crime, but that wasn't always the case.

"I'll do a bit of investigating anyway."

DI Jenkins put his hand to his mouth and coughed hard. His face turned red and his eyes glistened. "Look," he said, "do yourself a favor, leave this to the police. Yes, I want the case closed quickly, before I tell them about the big C. But let us do it. Stick to visiting the library, if you want to do some research for me."

Spen smiled cheerfully. "Oh, I'll be visiting the library all right." Jenkins didn't hear him whisper, "Amongst other things."

***

The next day, Spen Bradshaw walked into the dazzling "new look" police station. He'd been there plenty of times before, but he still had to blink every time he passed through the automatic front doors and approached the reception desk. Literally everything was a brilliant white, with the exception of five blue fabric chairs placed around a glass coffee table.

The place didn't fit with the deprived neighborhood it was situated in.

Spen was carrying a gray parrot in a metal cage. The bird did not look happy. "What a mess," it squawked, pecking at some millet. The seeds scattered everywhere. Spen set the cage on the table. He wasn't sure how this meeting would go, still it had to be done.

DI Jenkins was at the reception desk looking through some papers.

"What's that wretched pet of yours doing here?" he asked, looking up from his work.

"Mind your manners," squawked the parrot.

Spen bit his lip. Henry had this uncanny knack of answering back in a logical way.

Jenkins' lips twitched, ever so slightly. "Well mate, out with it."

"Sorry," said Spen, hurrying up to the desk. "This won't take long. The decorators are in my house, so I had to bring Henry with me."

"Oh, any excuse," said his friend grinning. "Now get on with it. What have you got?"

Bradshaw placed two small cardboard boxes onto the desk. "I suggest you do a DNA test on these. One contains hair from Eleanor Waverley, the other from her husband."

Jenkins smile faded rapidly. "How the heck did you get that? You're not police."

Spen shrugged. "I was left waiting in the hall for a meeting with the Colonel. Their jackets were on the coat stand. It was a matter of seconds to extract a few hairs from each."

Spen flicked through the icons on his secure phone, then placed it on the desk. "I think you should read this. It's an archived article from *The Chronicle* about Waverley's daughter, Claire. She went missing years ago, hasn't been seen since."

The DI picked up the phone and read the piece. "Are you saying the dead woman is their long lost daughter?"

Spen turned to check on Henry, who was shaking millet all over the floor. "You have to admit it's a possibility."

Mike put his hand to his mouth, overtaken by a fit of coughing. He handed Spen his personal case summary sheet.

Spen frowned as he perused it.

> PCS 1 Murder Investigation: Crimdon Cemetery 10-6-50.
>
> Woman aged 30-35 years. Visitor to Crimdon. Murdered.
>
> Cause of death: Knife stabbing in stomach.
>
> Time of death: Between 9-10 pm 10th June, 2050.
>
> Victim was a former drug user.
>
> Drug-related medical problems evident.
>
> No ID as yet. Awaiting results from the international DNA database.
>
> Two young men seen at the crime scene around the time of death.
>
> Witnesses? Two workers at the Healthy Food's take away. Local drug pushers?
>
> CCTV shows an additional man in his 30s walking past the cemetery at the time.
>
> No other apparent witnesses.

The DI reached for a glass of water and took a gulp. His eyes were still watering. "It's not a lot to go on," he whispered, after clearing his throat. "But we think we have a positive ID on the two men hanging around the cemetery. Some of the older cameras have given us pretty clear pictures. Both local drug pushers. We're bringing them in for questioning. It looks like a drug related murder, which should bring the case to a close in fairly short order."

Spen raised his eyebrows. "What about this other man? What about the fact that the woman looks very similar to a younger version of Eleanor Waverley?"

DI Jenkins sat down slowly on a blue chair and rubbed his unshaven face thoughtfully. "OK, mate, don't like to leave anything out. Highly irregular, but I'll have the DNA tests done. I've nothing to lose. Now get out and take that wretched bird with you."

Spen smiled, picked up the cage and left. Mike looked really bad, despite his humor. He was determined to do everything he could to help his friend close the case.

***

A few days later, Spen was back at the Colonel's house for a meeting about the local cemetery. There had always been a problem with burying several bodies in the same grave. The practice caused confusion, leading to families being unable to locate the remains of their loved ones.

The problem had supposedly been solved using technology. On each headstone there was a VDU that allowed you to see images of the people who had been buried there. It even included a brief synopsis of their lives. This IT was supposed to be robust and weatherproof, which was rubbish. There had been countless complaints from visitors.

Spen had been trying to sort out the problem, and what a waste of time that turned out to be! The Colonel's administrator let him into the hall for their meeting, then hurried back to his office. He waited in the hall until the study door opened.

Not that he minded the wait. There was a chair to sit on. Oh, yes, it was also possible to hear the conversation going on in the study. Spen was not above eaves-dropping.

Spen leaned forward in his chair to better hear the voices coming from the room. The Colonel and his wife were talking to his friend, DI Mike Jenkins.

"I was wondering if you might come and see if you recognize the lady." The DI's voice boomed through the door.

"Absolutely not," the Colonel replied.

"Might I ask why, sir?"

Spen strained to hear the muffled reply. "Dammed impudence, that's what it is."

Eleanor spoke next. "No need to get stroppy dear. Let's just explain."

There was a sound of drawers being opened and shut. "There," she said. "Our daughter's death certificate. This woman can't be her. Claire died in a road accident in Cornwall a few years ago. We were contacted by the police when they identified her. It was confirmed by DNA tests. So you see, there can be no mistake."

"You've kept this quiet a long time," Jenkins commented.

Spen stood and moved closer to the door to hear better.

"Look, we've had nothing to do with Claire since she walked out on us," the Colonel said. "Dashed embarrassing, all that press coverage years ago. We didn't want any more paparazzi hanging 'round the place, so we told no one. Easier that way."

"We're not heartless parents, Inspector," added Eleanor. "We just wanted some space to grieve in private. Now, we've no idea who this lady was, but we have no connection with her at all."

Spen heard footsteps approaching the study door. Hastily, he tiptoed back to the chair and sat down, just as the door opened and

DI Jenkins walked into the hall. His every step appeared to be an effort.

Spen jumped up. "Look," he whispered, "take some time off work. Conserve your energy."

Jenkins shook his head. "This case is going to be solved, if it's the last thing I do."

Spen shook his head. "Treatments are really effective these days. Give your body a chance. I don't want you dead. There's no need for you to push yourself."

Jenkins sighed. "Look, mate, call me stubborn if you like, but I'm going to do this my way. Working keeps my mind occupied. Now shut it. I'll join you for a beer tonight, usual place and time."

Spen nodded.

The study door opened again, and Eleanor emerged, along with the scent of lavender. "My husband will see you now," she said, walking gracefully up the stairs.

What a very composed woman she is, he thought. *Far too composed for my liking.*

***

At The Three-Legged Mare that evening, Spen sat brooding over the case, as he sipped beer with Mike.

"Sure you should be drinking that?" he asked, watching the inspector down his second pint. "I thought you were on fresh orange."

"Give over, mate, stop nannying. I'll have orange juice tomorrow." He shoved his safe phone in front of Spen. "Look, you've a clear head. Mine's too muzzy at the moment. What can you make of this?"

> PCS 2: Murder Investigation: Crimdon Cemetery Oct. 6, 1950.
>
> DNA analysis of the victim shows a possible match with Eleanor Waverley. No clear result for Colonel Waverley's DNA. Is this a false positive/negative? Is it coincidental? Eleanor Waverley has a sister living in Peru. They don't get on.
>
> Colonel and Mrs. Waverley had only one daughter, who is deceased.
>
> The murdered woman has been identified as one Ava Stillington, age 29, birth parents unknown. English originally, but now an American citizen. Lived in New York, unemployed, recovered drug addict, mental health issues.

> The third man noted on CCTV has been identified as
> Steve Hill, no known connection to Ava Stillington.
> A solicitor and ex-boyfriend of Claire Waverley. His
> statement: Went out to the local off-licence to buy six
> bottles of wine on the evening of the murder. Saw
> nothing unusual, just a white BMW driving past the
> off-licence.

Spen wiped the froth from his lips. This case seemed to be
going nowhere fast. So much for bringing it to a speedy end. "It's
difficult," he said. "No one seems to have any connection with the
woman. Could it be manslaughter?"

"Or drugs?" said Jenkins, scratching his chin. His safe phone
rang.

Spen emptied his pint.

"Yes, sergeant."

Jenkins listened, paused and smiled. He swiped the screen to
close his phone. "Things have just got a little more interesting, mate.
According to CCTV footage, our Steve Hill did meet Ava Stillington
that night, in the off-licence. They walked out together. We're
tracking him. He's headed for the airport."

"No relation to drugs then?"

Jenkins coughed, his eyes streaming. "Ava Stillington was a
recovered drug addict. Would she really fly to the UK and get in
contact with drug dealers? Oh yeah, the pathologist left a note to say
the dead woman had early stage leukemia. Don't think it's relevant,
but I wanted to mention it."

The Inspector pulled himself slowly out of his chair and
walked to the door. "Better go, but don't worry, I'll let the sergeant
bring him in. I'll question our Steve at the station. Seems he's been
lying to us."

Spen stood to leave. There were still some things he wanted
to check out.

An hour later, he was eating king prawns and rice in his
apartment. Henry was perched on the standard lamp watching the
entertainment monitor with great interest. "She's not your child,
Phil," the actress said.

"She's not your child," Henry squawked appreciatively.

Spen stopped eating. "Henry, you're a genius." He reached
for his portable computer. In army intelligence, he'd become very
adept at finding information. OK, at hacking. It was just a question
of knowing where to look. Nobody could truly hide anything of
interest. Somewhere on the internet, every important detail of every

person's life was stored, unofficially of course. Jenkins would not be impressed if he knew, but why tell him?

***

The following day Spen Bradshaw knocked on the door of the Colonel's mansion.

Eleanor answered it. "Bradshaw," she said, raising her eyebrows. "I don't believe you have an appointment."

"Quite right, but I need to speak to you and the Colonel urgently."

Without waiting for an invitation, he barged in.

Eleanor's hands clenched into fists. "What is it you want? Do I need to call the police?"

Spen laughed harshly. "You do that, lady. You won't find me objecting."

The Colonel peered out of the study. "Bradshaw, what's this all about? Dammed impudence. Get out of my house. You're sacked."

Spen smiled coldly at the couple. He was going to enjoy this encounter.

"You can certainly fire me if you wish. That's your decision. Just be aware, my next stop will be at the police station. You won't like that."

The Colonel frowned and seemed to hesitate. "Stuff and nonsense. Bravado. No idea what's got into you. What do you want?"

Spen clapped his hands together. His eyes gleamed. "That's more like it. I think we should adjourn to the study."

Eleanor glanced at her husband and followed him into the room.

The Colonel poured himself a brandy, but didn't offer a drink to anyone else. "What's this all about? Speak up, man. Why do you want my wife here?"

Spen sat on the chair closest to the door, a force of habit. "The thing is, I have information the police would be very interested in. I've set my safe phone to send it, in precisely one hour's time. It's linked to my home computer, so even if my phone is destroyed, it will still be sent."

The Colonel laughed. "What on earth has that got to do with us? Have you lost your mind?"

Spen opened his briefcase and handed them a folder. "A little research. I don't normally use hard copies, because of paper rationing. However, on this occasion, I will make an exception. This is going to the police. Read it."

Sexton Murder Case Notes: Crimdon Cemetery, May 20, 2050.

Ava Stillington: murdered, stabbed in the stomach, left in a grave at Crimdon Cemetery.

Parents of the deceased: Father, unknown. Mother: Eleanor Waverley, nee Ward. Victim believed to be the result of a brief affair.

Ava Stillington was adopted by an America couple at birth.

Adoptive parents: Meg and Stuart Stillington.

The victim became a drug addict, but recovered. Later she discovered she had developed leukemia. She had no money to pay for life-saving treatment.

Her adoptive parents were deceased, so she tracked her biological mother to the UK and spent the remains of her savings on a flight to England.

On the night of her murder, she went to Waverley Mansion to confront Eleanor Waverley about her past.

The interview did not go well. The Colonel and his wife refused to give the deceased money to pay for her cancer treatment. Stillington threatened them with a knife. The Colonel, using his army training, attempted to disarm her. In the struggle, Ava Stillington was stabbed in the stomach.

The Colonel knew a grave had just been dug at the cemetery, so he placed the body in the grave, sprinkling soil over it. In the dark, he didn't realize the grave was only half-dug. He hoped a coffin would be laid on top and the body would lay undiscovered. The Colonel drives a BMW electric sports car. A vehicle matching this description was seen leaving the scene of the murder.

Motive: Avoid blackmail or a scandal. The Colonel and Mrs. Waverley wished to protect their good reputations.

The Colonel choked on his brandy. "This is libel! I'll see you in court. It's all prefabricated rubbish and circumstantial."

Spen sighed, walked to the bar and poured himself a brandy. The Colonel had reacted exactly the way he'd expected. "Let's not waste time," he said. "I can prove the victim was Mrs. Waverley's unwanted child. I've printed the documents. The police will have forensics check out your car and house. You may have cleaned up the blood, but you can't remove it entirely. It will show up. Likewise, any fibers left from Ava Stillington's clothing found in the house or car boot. Every contact leaves a trace. However well you try to clean up, forensics will always find something."

The Colonel poured himself another brandy.

Eleanor paled. "This is all rather tiresome," she said, pretending to yawn.

"Not to worry Mrs. Waverley," Spen said. "I'm sure we can come to some arrangement."

The Colonel spluttered into his brandy. "This is blackmail!"

Spen shook his head. "No, blackmail is a horrible word. This is a business proposition, nothing more. You buy the information, so it doesn't get sent to the police. A one-off payment and all the evidence is permanently deleted from my file. Nobody else will ever know. A mere 50 million, unmarked notes, should do it."

"He's bluffing," said Eleanor. "Don't listen to him."

"That's fine." Spen picked up his secure phone, preparing to leave. "In less than an hour, all the information will be automatically sent to the authorities, unless I stop it."

"Look here," said the Colonel, trying to smile genially. "This is all a misunderstanding. If you would do us the honor of not mentioning it to anyone, I would be glad to gift you say 25 million to go toward your new house."

"No!" Eleanor shrieked.

"Shut up, woman," snapped the Colonel. "You've caused enough trouble already. I'll not have the family name dragged through the courts."

"30 million is my final offer."

"Done." The Colonel shook Spen's hand.

"You have been," a voice said. The door opened to reveal DI Jenkins and four officers. Jenkins turned to his sergeant. "Book them both."

"It's all lies!" Eleanor shouted.

"Yeah, yeah," replied DI Jenkins. "Our forensics team is waiting outside. Won't take them long to prove the point. Besides, we've recorded your conversation with the sexton. Pretty damning in itself."

The Colonel and his wife were led off, leaving Mike Jenkins and Spen Bradshaw alone in the study.

Mike thumped his friend on the back. "Great work, mate. Tell me, how did you piece it all together?"

Spen grinned. "It was Henry who gave me the final part of the puzzle. He kept repeating a sentence from a film. 'She's not your child.' Ava Stillington was Eleanor's secret child from a casual affair. Her family covered it up. The child, Ava, was adopted. She became a drug addict. She later overcame her addiction, but it meant running through her savings. She spent what was left of her money on a flight to the UK, to track down her biological mother, and to beg for finances to pay for her cancer treatment."

Jenkins rubbed his chin. "OK. What about the Colonel? How did you know he stabbed her?"

Spen cleared his throat. "That was a gamble," he admitted. "I'm ex-military, and so is the Colonel. We know how to use knives. Ava's stab wound had all the marks of an expert. Mrs. Waverley wouldn't have been able to handle a knife with such force."

"What about our Steve Hill?"

"Oh, him. He just happened to go to the off-licence for some booze and chatted up Ava. Easier not to admit that. I believe she slapped his face."

Jenkins laughed. "How did you come by that information?"

Bradshaw smiled. "Easily enough. I spoke to the shopkeeper. I know him well."

The inspector scratched his head. "Thanks. If you ever fancy a job in the force, we could do with people like you."

Spen shook his head, and followed his friend into the hall.

"You know what?" said Jenkins. "Ava and I are similar in some ways. We both were adopted and we both got cancer."

Bradshaw opened the front door and waved the Mike past. "True, but there is one big difference between you and Ava Stillington. She died. You're going to live."

Ω

BOOMTOWN SHAKEDOWN

Therese Greenwood

Therese Greenwood won the 2019 Spur Award from the Western Writers of America for "Buck's Last Ride" in Kill As You Go, *her short story collection. She is a three-time Finalist for the Arthur Ellis Award, and co-edited two short crime fiction anthologies. Her memoir of the Fort McMurray wildfire,* What You Take With You: Wildfire, Family and the Road Home, *is a Finalist for the 2020 Alberta Book Publishing Awards from The Book Publishers Association of Alberta.*

Therese's work has appeared in the Globe and Mail, *and* Queen's Quarterly. *She has a Master's degree in journalism.*

Bethany Vanderbeek was working the switchboard at the seniors' home when the spy agency telephoned. Six months earlier, she had drifted west to an oil boomtown, answered the first help wanted ad she saw, and became the home's full-time receptionist. She was still getting the lay of the land, spending her spare time in the deluxe on-site bedroom that was a perk of the job, eating low-salt, sugar-free meals in the dining room, and watching John Ford westerns in the common area with the residents. A lot of people blew oil money as fast as they made it, but Bethany was banking her pay and keeping an eye on what one of the residents called "life's rich pageant."

In a boomtown, life's pageant was really, really rich. It took Bethany two days to figure out the high-tech fixtures in her *ensuite* bathroom. The common area had a $20,000 movie projector, and every night the red sand desert of Monument Valley rolled across a state-of-the-art movie screen that took up the entire south wall. The popcorn machine was the same as the one at the Cineplex. The seniors snuck in butter from the stainless-steel-and-marble-kitchen. Some hid saltshakers in their pockets to use whenever the home's chief administrator, whom they called The Marshall, was out at one of the prime rib dinners or black-tie galas that seemed to happen every other night.

John Ford would have called it a wide-awake, wide-open town. You could get anything you wanted there. Trucks as big as Bethany's free room tried to jump the drive-through line at the Tim Hortons coffee shop, and young women flashed diamond engagement rings you could see a block away. Except at the seniors' home, everyone in town seemed to be Bethany's age, fresh out of school and wearing $500 blue jeans and white designer sunglasses. They hustled from one job to the next, bumping up a pay level with each move. New stores opened each week and construction was everywhere, 20-story apartment complexes rising up beside one-floor wooden storefronts along the main street.

The seniors liked to tell stories about the old days of dirt roads, fur trappers, and bears. The chattiest was Archie McGregor, who called her "kid," pushed the wrong buttons on the telephone extension in his room, and considered cell phones "a fucking tool of the devil." It took her a while to get used to the fact Archie considered "fuck" the perfect word, to be used as verb, noun, and adjective.

That morning she heard Archie before she saw him. He was cheerfully f-bombing his way from the corner suite he'd bagged when Henri Mercredi passed away, his curses peppered by the tapping of the cane he insisted on calling a walking stick. Archie was a cheerful man, surprising when you considered back disease was curving his spine into a C-shape and turning his walk into a scuttle. Archie had a lot of hustle for an old guy with a bum back, buying group lottery tickets, organizing whiskey tastings, and selling a fruit-basket-of-the-week that was insanely popular. The seniors swore by a naturopathic snake venom liniment he imported from China. For such a loud guy, Archie knew how to operate on the down-low, running a poker tournament in the games room when The Marshall was at her regular Wednesday Night Club dinner with local bigwigs. But still, he looked pooped that morning as he plopped himself down in one of the reception area's leather wingback chairs.

"I don't know how you do it, Archie," said Bethany. "What would you get up to if you didn't have a bad back?"

"There's nothing wrong with my fucking back, kid," said Archie, slumping sidewise in the chair. "It's just a sprain." He told her a random story about putting his money in his shoe when he went to some town named Purley, used the front desk phone to yell at his liniment supplier, and was still holding the receiver when the spy agency called.

"Hullo," he said. Bethany couldn't make out the murmur on the other end of the line, but that wasn't a problem for Archie.

"Is this the Western Star Retirement Center?" Archie said. "If it isn't, I'm in the wrong fucking place. Our most senior person? I'm the oldest wanker here. Archie McGregor, at your service."

There was more mumbling. "Who did you say you were?" Archie asked. "Uh-huh. 1400 hours. Where the hell else would I be?" He hung up the phone and asked Bethany what 1400 hours was in o'clocks.

"Who was that?" Bethany asked.

"More out-of-town newspapermen wanting to talk about the old days," said Archie. "They always want to print the legend."

Archie would talk to anyone about anything. He told Bethany three times how he and his late wife had smuggled bacon into the United Arab Emirates when he worked the Saudi oil fields. Twice he told her that last summer's student intern wore a short skirt while dancing on a table during the Seniors' Recognition Dinner at the second-best hotel in town. One afternoon there was a story, long even by Archie's standards, about a German submariner and a British sailor (Archie called him a "gob") who worked in a machine shop and became friends after discovering the German's U-boat had torpedoed the gob's ship in World War II. John Ford would've made a good movie out of it, he said.

Archie was speculating on what sort of wankers were going to show up ("I'll give 'em something to read and write about.") when Diego arrived with the weekly order of whiskey and fruit.

"*Hola*, kid," said Diego. "*Hola*, Archie."

"Diego, my friend," said Archie, using both arms to raise himself from the chair. "What have you brought this week?"

"The Okanagan cherries are incredible," said Diego, loading the baskets onto the mail cart. "*Muy deliciosa cerezas*."

"We have a cash flow situation this morning," said Archie, handing over the envelope with the weekly payment. Bethany had offered to show the residents how to bank online, but they preferred cash.

"This is less than half," said Diego, riffling through the bills.

"Fucking poker," said Archie. "I'll have the rest this afternoon."

"This is the third and last time, Archie. I have my suppliers to pay," said Diego. There was no more room on the cart, so he plopped the last basket on top of the reception desk. "It's a trickle-down economy and it trickles fast."

"No problem, my friend," said Archie.

"Where do you want the whiskey?"

"Stash it under the kid's desk," said Archie. "I'll move it before The Marshall sees it."

"That's not a good plan," Bethany said as Diego tucked the box of whiskey next to her feet.

"See you this afternoon, Archie," said Diego, as the front doors swung open with a pneumatic *whoosh*.

"I'm sorry but—" Bethany said.

"Never apologize, kid," said Archie. "It's a sign of weakness." He hustled off with the cart as the front doors swung open again and The Marshall strode in.

"What trouble is that old coot up to now?" she asked Bethany, nodding toward Archie's twisted back disappearing into the elevator.

"Trouble?" said Bethany. "There's no trouble."

"That'll be the day," said The Marshall.

"Um," said Bethany. She was always tongue-tied around The Marshall. In a town where the wealthiest women wore yoga pants, plaid flannel tunics, and fur-covered moccasins hand-crafted by First Nations artists, The Marshall dressed like a career woman in a romantic comedy. Her pastel pantsuits were paired with impossibly high heels. She had French-manicured fingernails, glossy blond hair colored weekly, and said "y'all" whenever she was speaking to more than one person. Best of all, she had a chocolate Labrador retriever she insisted was a service dog so she could bring him to work. The dog, Jack, wore a cashmere cape with "service dog" spelled out in rainbow rhinestones. He leaped on everyone he met, leaving The Marshall to shout "Jack off! Jack off!" Archie thought that was likely the reason for dog's name. Jack never jumped on Archie, and often leaned against him as if holding him up, so maybe Jack was a service dog after all.

"I have a meeting with the deputy mayor, and he's still pretending to be allergic to dogs," The Marshall said. "Could you walk Jack while I'm out?"

"Yes, ma'am," said Bethany.

The hour after lunch was always quiet, a lot of the residents took a nap, and Bethany switched the phone to auto-answer. She clipped a sparkly leash to Jack's collar, the dog leaping about so they were tangled together as the front doors swung open and they stumbled into the sunlight. They moseyed down streets lined bumper-to-bumper with parked cars, Jack stopping every few yards to sniff a newly planted tree or the titanium wheel of a luxury car.

It was quiet when they got to the downtown park. Bethany heard a song playing in the distance about a desperado refusing to come to his senses. The crew at the construction site overlooking the park was taking a late lunch, workers eating white-bread sandwiches and drinking coffee from giant thermoses as they dangled their legs over the edge of the scaffolding. A massive black bird, one of the ravens that ruled the downtown area, thumped down in front of the scaffold, snatched a bread crust, and took wing before Jack got out a bark. The dog tottered around the park, sniffing and pawing at tufts of grass and hunting non-existent squirrels, finally finishing his business so Bethany could scoop it into a plastic bag and deposit it in a garbage can.

They were ambling up the walk to the home when a white four-door sedan pulled into the last legal parking spot and a man a little older than Bethany got out. Jack jumped on him, paws scrabbling against the man's dark-blue windbreaker and knocking off his aviator sunglasses.

"Jack off!" said Bethany. "Jack off!"

The man dropped down to the dog's level and picked up his sunglasses, balancing comfortably on his heels as he rubbed Jack's ears.

"A service dog, eh?" asked the man, who was wearing tan slacks, a white-collared shirt, and shined black shoes the seniors would love. There was no insignia on his windbreaker, unusual in a town where everything was monogrammed to the limit.

"He tries," said Bethany.

"Do you work here?"

"I'm the receptionist," she said.

"Maybe you can help me. I'm a federal agent, Timothy Raite."

"Wow," said Bethany. "Thank you for not shooting Jack when he jumped on you."

"We don't carry guns," said Agent Raite. "We're not that kind of agency."

"What kind of agency are you?" asked Bethany.

"The information-gathering kind," said Agent Raite. "I have an appointment at 1400 hours with Mr. Archie McGregor."

"You're not a newspaperman?" asked Bethany. "Because you have to tell me if you're a newspaperman."

"I'm not a newspaperman," said Agent Raite. He pulled out a badge as Jack sat panting, eager to lead his new friend to the drugs cabinet and the safety-deposit boxes. The badge was in a fancy leather holder and had a photo that did great justice to Agent Raite although, Bethany thought, it would be hard to take a bad picture of that hair and smile. The badge had the logo of the national spy agency and a flashy hologram that looked hard to counterfeit.

"Mr. McGregor should be waiting for you," said Bethany, wondering what else Archie was lying about. She and the agent and the dog went through the front door with a minimum of leash tangling and stopped dead behind the reception desk.

Archie's left eye was swelling up as he looked at them over Diego's shoulder. His walking stick was broken in two and lying on the floor.

"Diego, my friend," Archie was saying, "let's work something out."

"Federal agent!" said Raite.

"Fuck!" said Archie.

Diego flipped around, knocking the fruit basket from the reception desk, spilling cherries and tiny gift-wrapped packets over the floor, and putting Archie in a chokehold with a knife at his throat.

"Easy does it," said Agent Raite, stepping out from behind the desk with his hands up. "No one has to get hurt."

"You said it," said Diego. "Archie and I are going to walk out of here and *todo es bueno*."

"Take me instead," said Agent Raite.

"Swap a gimpy old man for a trained federal agent?" said Diego. "Fat chance."

"Take me, Diego," said Bethany.

"You know this guy?" said Agent Raite.

"I won't slow you down," said Bethany. "You know he's got spinal disease."

"It's a back sprain," said Archie.

"That could work," said Diego.

"Wait a damn minute," said Agent Raite. But Diego made him get down on the floor and motioned for Bethany to come out from behind the desk. Archie took a step away from Diego, slipped on the spilled fruit and went down on his back.

Jack jumped forward and leaped on Diego, pawing at his chest and knocking away the knife. As Diego reached down for the weapon, Bethany clobbered him on the head with a whiskey bottle. The first smash just made him wobble, so she whacked him again.

Diego hit the terrazzo tile floor at the same time as the bottle, which smashed and splattered whiskey and broken glass over the spilled fruit and what Bethany hoped was organic oregano and a natural sugar substitute, but was probably the drugs that kept Archie so cheerful.

Agent Raite secured the knife and Diego, then started talking loudly into his cell phone. Jack licked Archie's face as the old man rocked and waved his arms like a turtle flipped on its back. Bethany was worried that Jack would slice his paws on the broken glass and grabbed the sparkly leash to pull him back. Jack sat at her feet and lapped at a puddle of whiskey.

"That's a fucking 12-year-old Lagavulin," said Archie. Bethany thought she saw tears in his eyes.

***

Jack did not jump on Bethany as she sat down in the pink upholstered chair in front of The Marshall's French provincial desk. The dog gave a small sigh, plopped down at her feet, and leaned against her bare leg.

"This is an impressive list of global commerce," said The Marshall, squinting at a piece of paper she was holding at arm's length. "Importation of illegal narcotics, unregulated remedies made from endangered species, untaxed foreign liquor, and some inter-provincial cannabis smuggling."

"The poker games were local," said Bethany.

"That foul-mouthed old bastard is a whirlwind," said The Marshall, pushing a box of tissues toward Bethany. "He threw you under the bus so fast I thought he'd put his back out all over again."

"Am I fired?" said Bethany.

"Yup," said The Marshall. "I run a clean outfit. Zero tolerance for alcohol and drugs."

Bethany took a tissue from the box and Jack sighed.

"It could be worse," said The Marshall. "The Deputy Mayor thinks the last thing this town needs is another scandal, the feds want the case tried in the capital city, and your spy called you a hero. Testify and consider yourself lucky."

"I don't feel lucky," said Bethany, blowing her nose into the tissue.

"I suppose not," said The Marshall.

"I'm sorry I didn't tell you what was going on."

"Sorry don't get it done, Bethany," said The Marshall. "But you learned a lesson."

"What lesson is that?"

"Not all old people are wise elders," said The Marshall. "Some are the same selfish dicks they've always been. Some can't even bother to learn your name while they run their game on you."

"I was just getting the lay of the land," said Bethany, as she took a fresh tissue. "Now what am I going to do?"

"Do you want my advice?" said The Marshall.

"Shoot," said Bethany.

"Find a handsome young man like your spy and break his heart."

"He's not my spy."

"Not yet," said The Marshall. "Take care of that, then go off to college and see what they know. Then take your learning to a town with a chance to be a fine, good place, and do your best there."

"That's probably harder than it sounds," said Bethany.

"It is," said The Marshall, "so get yourself a good dog."

At the words "good dog," Jack's thick tail thumped on the floor.

***

Bethany was headed for the front door with her suitcase and a plastic bag with a Dr Pepper, a turkey sandwich, and some John Ford DVDs when she heard a click-click coming down the corridor.

"Wait up, kid," Archie shouted. She watched him hobble toward her, leaning heavily on an aluminum walker and looking like an old man who had lost his supply of cannabis, narcotics, whiskey, and snake oil.

"Kid, I heard she was running you off," said Archie. "Best thing that ever happened to you. Get out of this fucking mausoleum. Once my back is fixed, you won't see me for dust."

"My fucking name is Bethany," she said as the front doors swung open.

Ω

THE HOUSE OF ELIZABETH DANDRIDGE

C.A. Rowland

C.A. Rowland writes historical fiction, science fiction, fantasy and a mystery novel series set in Savannah, Georgia. Her series begins with The Meter's Always Running. *Her work appears in in several volumes of* Fiction River, Pulphouse Magazine *and other anthologies.*

Ms. Rowland is also a member of Sisters-in-Crime and the Guppies. She's been a member at large with the group, a contributor to First Draft and continues to support the organization. On the local and state level, she is a member of Riverside Writers, Lake Authors and the Virginia Writer's Club. Her short story, "The History of a Fruitcake", won the Bethlehem Writer's Roundtable 2015 Short Story Award.

Marion stared out of the rain-slick window, wondering what her husband had been thinking when he'd bought the house. Sweet Jesus, she needed a cigarette.

After hours of constant rain clattering against the black 1947 Ford sedan's roof and the monotonous motion of the drive across the flatlands of Texas, the sudden stillness thundered in Marion's head. She'd never been so tired of listening to re-runs of *The Bing Crosby Show* and *The Abbott and Costello Show* droning out of the radio. But David hadn't wanted to talk about the house during the 300-mile drive.

"I want it to be a surprise," he'd said.

David had forbidden her to smoke, saying it wasn't ladylike. It was her one vice, and she limited herself to one a day, at most. Even then, she only smoked outside, and afterward, she scrubbed her hands and brushed her teeth. Marion knew it was probably a sin to deceive him, but it was one of the few areas of her life in which she had total control.

The house was an A-frame, one-story, with mottled scabs of peeling green paint in varying degrees of decay. Knee-high weeds, battered by the storm, surrounded it like a moat. Marion wrinkled her nose in anticipation of the moldy smell of a long unopened house filled with the distilled funk of the prior owners' body odors.

It mirrored the other houses on the street and subdivision. Except those were freshly painted in shades of beige and brown, with flower gardens strewn across the manicured lawns.

Bits of light had begun to peek out from the gray sky, blinding her before disappearing back behind clouds.

She opened the car door, and her black pumps touched the concrete curb. An empty beer can, bits of limp paper and other litter had taken shelter against it. She avoided them, stepping carefully out of the car.

Marion stared at what was now her new home. She knew David was proud of having found it, but a part of her resented that she hadn't been consulted in the purchase. David was usually so thoughtful. He treated her as if she were a fragile doll, to be cherished, and only occasionally played with.

Her mother had taught Marion the womanly arts so she could find a good husband. Now that Marion was married, she was looking for ways to become more assertive, a few decisions she could make on her own. Her cigarettes were one small rebellion.

She shook off the feeling, knowing that with one car and David's new job with an oil company in Midland, Texas, house-hunting had been difficult. She should feel grateful. Still, she'd thought they'd rent an apartment until she could be here and help find their new home.

"It was a bargain. Something we can really put our stamp on," David had said.

"Condemned" was the only stamp she would apply to it.

There was no getting around it—it was a done deal. Marion had been packing their small one-room apartment when David had called with the news of the purchase. He'd been afraid it would be gone if he didn't sign a contract right away. Now that they were here, she could see the house had been in no danger of being sold. Her fists curled, and she took a deep breath before unclenching them.

A last gasp of the storm whirled around her, lifting her blond curls before gently letting them fall back against her neck and the collar of her white cotton shirt. Her flowered skirt waved in the breeze, and she smoothed it as she walked up the concrete sidewalk. Just as she would if she was visiting a neighbor and wanted to look her best.

What had once been a pristine white porch was wrapped around the house. More peeling white paint decorated the hinged wooden door that yawned as it creaked open.

David took her arm, making her jump.

"Let me do that," he said, pushing the door wider so she could walk through. The entrance to their new life in this place.

Marion leaned into the warmth of his body. She did love David, even as she struggled with what her role as a wife should be. Surely she could find a way to show him she was capable of much more than cooking meals, cleaning house, and making love on Saturday nights.

"The previous owner left the furnishings," he said. "We can keep anything we want. I got it all for a song."

Marion's stomach turned over at the thought of what might be inside, even as she tried to smile. She stepped over the threshold.

She could have sworn the house trembled.

The living room was dark, and David rushed to pull back the heavy emerald green drapes, exposing the expansive front window that looked out onto the street. In the dim light, between the flecks of dust, a bright red, blue, and yellow flowered couch held court against one wall. Matching chairs dotted the room. Bolder colors than Marion would have chosen, but she had to admit whoever had furnished the place had expensive taste.

She walked through the living room to the dining room, sneezing a couple of times. A cherry table with six chairs and a matching hutch put her Formica table to shame. As she ran a hand over it, more dust rose from the smooth surface. Variegated green striped wallpaper continued from the living room. In places it was beginning to loosen and pull away from the wall as if the stripes were weeds in search of sunlight. She hoped the sneezing was due to the dust, and not the flu that her friends in their old apartment building seemed to have caught.

David's friend, Bill, would be bringing their few furniture pieces and boxes by truck the next day. They planned to unload everything into the garage until they decided what to keep and what to sell.

Marion had thought they'd be transferring things back and forth all weekend, but she could see she'd be cleaning up the dust first. Unless the bedroom was unfurnished, they didn't need to do much to be ready for the workweek.

David returned from the car with the bag holding peanut butter and grape jelly sandwiches. He placed a couple of soda cans on the table. Marion quickly pulled some napkins out of the bag and used them to wipe the tabletop.

"Our first meal." He showed her a bottle of apple cider and leaned in to give her a peck on the cheek before he opened it. "I got this to toast our new home." He smiled broadly like a kid who had hit his first home run. David's smile was the first thing that had caught Marion's eye. She couldn't help but smile back as she took sandwiches and more napkins out of the bag.

"Who did you say owned this house?"

"An old man named Robert Dandridge. He was married once. His health was deteriorating, so he moved into a nursing home. I guess the professional care helped him get better. He left the facility and spent his last years traveling abroad."

"He never came back to the house?"

"No. Said it held too many painful memories. He wanted to sell quickly and at a cheap price."

"Did his wife die here?" Marion felt goosebumps at the thought of sleeping in a bed where a woman had passed away.

"I didn't ask, but I got the impression she left him. The real estate agent wasn't clear about what happened, but he did say that at some point the neighbors realized she was gone."

Creepy. Marion hated unanswered questions. From what Marion had seen, the man had some money, and had let his wife create a home of her choice. Why would she choose to leave? What kind of man had he been?

***

Two hours later, their suitcases were in the bedroom. Marion lay on the bed, staring at the ceiling. The bedroom was lovely, although she hated the thought of sleeping on someone else's mattress. She'd ask David to replace it with their own mattress the following day, when Bill arrived.

A flicker caught her eye, and she focused on the dressing table, made of the same cherry wood as the dining set. She thought she'd seen something in the mirror. It must have been her imagination. The table was lovely, but someone had spilled perfume on it, leaving a stain and a lingering fragrance that Marion couldn't identify. Pleasant to the nose, although it wouldn't have been her choice of perfume.

Earlier, as she had brushed her hair 100 times, she'd watched stray hairs float toward the wall and stick there. Some kind of static electricity must be at play in the room. Probably because the house had been closed up for so long. That might explain how a fragrance had lingered over time.

Marion decided she would open all the doors and windows the next day to air out the place. Cobwebs, dust, and other odors would be banished by fresh air, her can of Pledge, and a bit of soap and water.

With that thought, she drifted off to sleep.

***

Marion woke feeling drained and disoriented. She couldn't remember her dreams, only that she felt like she'd been running all night. She shook off the oppressive mood, thinking that she might have the beginnings of a cold or flu.

The kitchen was stocked with cleaning products. Marion placed them on the counter, then opened the back door.

And walked into a little piece of heaven.

Although it had been neglected, the garden was bursting with greenery and flowering plants. Bursts of reds, oranges, and yellows caught Marion's eyes.

"Oh! It's just what I've always wanted."

David came up behind her, wrapping his arms around her waist as he squeezed her close. "I saved the last surprise for this morning. Do you love it?"

"Yes, oh, yes!" Marion turned to face him and planted a kiss on his lips.

David's eyes widened at her boldness, but she could see he was pleased. Maybe he would approve of her being more assertive.

"You'll have plenty of time to putter around out here. I'm sure there are lots of weeds that need pulling."

Marion grinned. Gardening was a joy. She loved the idea of making things bloom. They hadn't had space for more than a potted plant or two in the apartment. Nor the money to buy many plants. But here it was, this beautiful garden, already started and waiting for her to tend to it. She could barely control the urge to start right away.

"I'll start next week while you're at work. Right now, I need to remove some of the dust inside before we sneeze ourselves to death."

"I knew you'd love it! I'll bring in the rest of the boxes from the car. We can unpack what we need and store the rest in the garage."

Marion watched David walk away, feeling sincere gratitude. Looking at his back, she wondered if this was how Mr. Dandridge had seen his wife leave. Morbid thoughts for a sunshiny day. The garden was shimmering, after the previous day's driving rain had cleansed the world. She turned and reached for the rags and the bucket of soapy water.

***

On Monday, Marion tackled the dressing table drawers. She had delayed cleaning them out, unable to put her finger on the reason for her hesitation. The woman who had lived here was gone, so why hadn't her husband cleared out her things? Would she find a clue regarding what had happened to her predecessor?

Marion pulled out a drawer. It caught on something. She pulled on it again, this time forcing it open.

Makeup was stuffed inside. She emptied it all into a trash can.

The second drawer opened easily. It was filled with broaches and necklaces. Marion guessed this was costume jewelry, and that anything of value had been removed.

One piece caught her eye. A large red beaded flower, the petals molded so it looked almost real. It was the kind of thing she might have bought for herself. She laughed as she realized that she and Mrs. Dandridge had more in common than she had guessed.

The day's work left Marion feeling drained. She fell asleep that night as soon as her head hit the pillow.

***

More cleaning was on the schedule for Tuesday, although Marion stopped at lunchtime for a nap. When she awoke from a deep sleep, her head hurt, and she ached all over. She wasn't hot, but that didn't mean she didn't have the flu. She hoped whatever it was would pass through her system quickly.

On Tuesday night, Marion brushed her hair as she did every evening. Her usual 100 strokes felt like 1,000. Whatever bug she had picked up had left her feeling tired and wrung out. She removed the flower pin, tucking it neatly into the dresser drawer before climbing into bed, where David was already asleep.

The house was now clean. The garden was half-weeded. She hadn't needed a cigarette in days. Even the fading wallpaper seemed to be in better shape than when they'd arrived. It was as if the house appreciated her care and was responding to it. Weary but feeling gratified, she fell asleep almost immediately.

***

On Wednesday morning, Marion could hardly rise from the bed. When she did, she sat at the dressing table, staring at the mirror.

Her skin was pale, and she could barely lift her brush. On one wall, flowery paper began to shift, and a woman's face materialized.

Marion shook her head and rubbed her eyes, sure that fatigue was behind the hallucination.

"You know he killed me, don't you?" The lips were moving, but the sound seemed to emanate from all around the room.

Marion put a hand over her mouth to keep from screaming.

"This is my house, not yours. You must give it back to me," the voice continued.

"I don't know what you are talking about. Leave me alone." Marion closed her eyes and put her hands over her ears.

Malicious laughter rang out.

Terrified, Marion ran from the room. She scurried into the kitchen. Outside, she needed to be outside. Some gardening would clear her head and calm her imagination.

She prepared the same solution for dealing with weeds that her granny had made when she was a child. One gallon of white vinegar, one cup of table salt, and one tablespoon of dishwashing soap.

She carried the mixture to the garden. As she worked, her nerves calmed. Her granny would have been proud to see that Marion had remembered her lessons.

Mixing the weed killer had restored her sense of normalcy. She must have been hallucinating or dreaming in the bedroom. Maybe it was this flu she seemed to have. The voice wasn't, couldn't, be real.

Marion opted to begin at the back corner of the garden, farthest from the house. She pulled on gloves and knelt on the cool ground.

She reached for a weed under a bluebonnet, only to pull back when she saw a shimmering face in each of the petals.

"This is my favorite spot," a voice said. "At least it was. I always thought I'd kill Robert before he got me. I was wrong. Right here, in this very place, he whacked me with a shovel. I never saw it coming. Then he had the gall to stand over me and say, 'Die, Elizabeth, die.' Bet you didn't think I would follow you outside."

Marion recoiled from the vision. "You're not real."

"Sure I am. Robert buried me right here so I could be fertilizer for the garden I loved. He laughed like it was some kind of joke. But I fooled him. I made a pact with the plants. I was their fertilizer, but they gave me life through their roots."

"What are you talking about? Who are you?" Marion couldn't believe she was having this conversation, but a part of her was intrigued.

"I'm Elizabeth, Robert's long-suffering wife. I sucked his soul out of his body bit by bit, sometimes a hair, sometimes a particle of skin. Why do you think the house was so dusty? Not dirt, just particles of my murderous husband. I would've killed him, too, if he hadn't left for the nursing home. He couldn't have lasted much longer anyway. Good riddance." The face screwed up its eyes and mouth in what had to be laughter.

Marion had a sudden realization. This specter, this ghost of Elizabeth, was limited in its knowledge of events. It, or she, could only know what went on inside the house.

"Then you don't know," she said.

"What?"

"Robert lived. Sold us the house, then moved overseas."

"What? You mean you didn't buy this from his estate?" Elizabeth frowned.

Marion hesitated, wondering whether she'd said too much.

"I can always suck out some of David's soul," Elizabeth warned, "if you don't tell me what I want to know."

"Your husband is alive." Marion glowered at the ghostly face. "What have you been doing to me? Why do I feel so tired and look so pale?"

Elizabeth smirked. "Can't put one over on you, honey, can I? Feeling sick is the first stage." The face pulled back into a large laughing mouth.

"Stop it. Right now. We never hurt you."

"True. I only want to avenge myself on Robert. You and your beloved David are the only people who have been in the house long enough to allow me to draw some of your strength. I can't see letting that go right now."

Marion studied the phantom. She saw determination in Elizabeth's face.

"We could leave."

"And David give up his new house? One he got for a song?"

Marion held her breath and let it out slowly. Elizabeth was right. David wouldn't want to leave and he would never believe she'd had this conversation. "What exactly do you want from me?"

"I want your body, so I can find Robert and kill him."

Marion gasped as Elizabeth's face disappeared, leaving the bluebonnets swaying in the slight breeze.

***

On Thursday morning, the voice was back, following her from room to room. Marion finally headed out to the garden and the bluebonnets. Sure enough, Elizabeth's face appeared in the petals as she knelt beside them.

"You can't have my body." Marion had decided to hold firm and take a stand.

"You can't stop me."

Marion realized what Elizabeth said was true. She clasped her hands together to keep them from shaking. "There has to be another way."

"There isn't."

"I think you're bluffing. You can't take my body if I don't let you."

"Honey, your mama didn't raise you to have a backbone. I seriously doubt if you can keep me from doing whatever I want to do." Elizabeth punctuated this with a short laugh.

"I could find Robert and kill him. Then you wouldn't have to do this."

"No. It's my revenge. I'd never know if you did it. You don't seem like the killing kind."

"I think you're bluffing."

"Do you want to take that risk?" Elizabeth asked. "Besides, if I don't take your energy, I can take David's. I can inhabit his body. It's quite simple: yours or his. He'll never see it coming. He won't believe you if you tell him about me. Do you want to be married to David with me in control? Your choice."

Marion sat back on her heels, her breath coming quickly. "You wouldn't."

"I would."

All Marion could think of was to delay the decision. "I'll have to think about it."

"You have until tomorrow morning. Then I'll pull enough life force out of one of you to take over."

"I need time to think. Will you promise not to pull any more of my energy tonight? As a test of good faith?"

Elizabeth seemed to consider the request. "OK, one night. That's it."

Marion hung her head. She had no idea how to beat this spirit. Was Elizabeth capable of taking over one of their bodies?

***

Marion tossed and turned throughout the night. When David left for work Friday morning, she dragged herself out of bed.

Elizabeth had kept her end of the bargain. Marion felt a bit stronger. Sometime in the night, she'd realized there had never really been any choice. David was the most important thing in her life. Worth dying for if she had to.

Pulling on her gardening clothes, she reached for her purse and the pack of cigarettes. She stared at it for a moment and whispered, "David, I hope you'll forgive me."

Lighting the cigarette, she drew in a puff, felt the vapor fill her mouth, and exhaled.

She watched the end burn. That simple act gave Marion confidence she was about to take the right action.

She lay the cigarette on the cotton pillowcase, the lit end resting against the fabric.

When the pillow had started to burn, Marion headed for the kitchen.

Grabbing the plastic bottle of weed killer, she walked to the far corner of the garden, her back straight. She knelt beside the bluebonnets.

"Burning the house? A bit drastic and dramatic, don't you think?" Elizabeth said.

"I think it's just what is needed," Marion replied with a smile.

"Honey, I don't need the house. And your precious David won't forgive you for burning down his bargain."

Elizabeth wore a satisfied smile. Marion understood why Robert had hit her with a shovel.

Looking at the house, Marion couldn't see any smoke and hoped it would be some time before anyone noticed the fire. She'd had closed all the drapes before she came outside. Maybe the authorities wouldn't figure out that a cigarette had caused the fire. Then she wouldn't have to confess to David.

It was time to deal with Elizabeth.

"David will forgive me if he learns what really happened," she said. "And you're right about one thing: my mama didn't teach me to have a backbone. But my granny taught me what to do about invasive species."

Marion unscrewed the top off the plastic bottle and began to pour. "You see, this kills weeds, but if you aren't careful, it kills other plants too. Since you depend on these plants, you won't have any way to reach the house."

"No! I only wanted revenge. We can think of another way."

Marion watched Elizabeth's eyes grow wide. She could swear there was fear in them.

"I don't think so. You're not likely to forget that I bested you. And we both know you are prone to carry a grudge. Besides, David has always wanted a place to barbecue. A concrete patio right here would create a barrier you can't cross to the house. And the concrete will keep you from drawing on any plants."

Elizabeth screamed as Marion poured liquid on all the garden plants close to and around the foundation of the house. She'd need to come back and do it again, but her course of action was now clear.

As she dumped the last of the liquid, Marion whispered, "Die, Elizabeth, die."

Silence.

Marion lifted her face and drank in the air. A faint aroma of burning was coming from the house. She needed to be ready for the arrival of neighbors and firemen.

Her mother had taught her how to retrieve a memory when she needed to cry. She sent a silent thank-you to her, realizing she had learned more from her mother than she had known. She recalled her granny's funeral, and kept her tears in check as she put on her best shocked face.

A minute later, she heard the fire engines. She headed for the front yard, and stared at the house, feigning surprise at the sight of flames dancing in the windows. At the sound of glass breaking, she jumped. The shocked look on her face was now real.

Tears began to flow.

When the fire truck pulled up, she ran over to it. "Help me, please. I was in the backyard when I smelled smoke."

A fireman pulled her aside. "Ma'am, I need you to move out the way so we can try to save your house."

Marion nodded, although she hoped they were too late. She assumed David had insured the house, so they'd have money to buy a new place. One without a relentless, vindictive spirit in residence. Even if they didn't, as long as she and David were together, they could survive anything. She understood that now.

Elizabeth had taught her that she had a backbone after all. Now, she would find a way to live her life with David on her own terms. Marion would need to be gentle as he came to understand the changes she was going through. He was a good man and she loved him, after all. In time, he'd see that he had married a woman who could protect him and their family as much as he protected her.

She watched the house burn, despite the best efforts of the firemen to save it. A few neighbors came over, offering her comfort.

Looking around at the growing number of supportive neighbors, Marion thought perhaps this was a good neighborhood, despite the horror of an unwelcoming house.

She and David might want to rebuild after all.

Ω

WOMAN AGLOW

Lynne Murphy

Lynne Murphy was born in Saskatchewan and has never lost her love of its wide skies and open spaces. She worked as a journalist for print and radio news, which taught her to "write tight".

Many of her stories involve a group of elderly ladies, living in a condo building. (Write what you know). Her stories appear in all four of the Mesdames of Mayhem anthologies as well as in World Enough and Crime *(Carrick Publishing) and* The Whole She-Bang *from Sisters in Crime, Toronto.*

Crystal Berry sat on the balcony of her Panama hotel room feeling cranky. Crystal was often cranky, partly because of a physical condition which made her irritable, and partly because she had a cranky disposition.

The condition was not something she liked to talk about—it was hypohidrosis, an inability to sweat, or perspire as her mother had always said. People found it weird or even funny.

Today she had a major reason to be cranky. Her husband, Hank, had gone off for the day, leaving her to amuse herself. And after he had persuaded her to come on this trip to celebrate his 50th birthday. She had tried to ignore her own 50th birthday, a few years earlier. Well, nearly 10 years now. But Hank had been determined to mark this milestone event in style. And here she was, alone.

"You'll love Panama," Hank had said. "The Hotel Corona has all sorts of shady spots where you can sit, and the adult pool even has a shaded area where you can swim." He had stayed at the Corona the year before, on his own, and was sure it was suitable for her. She had to be so careful not to get overheated.

The hotel was all right, but not as luxurious as she would have liked. It was only a four-star and they could certainly have afforded a five.

Hank had promised her dinner at the resort's steakhouse once he got back from his jaunt to look at a bunch of old rocks. He had suggested the sushi restaurant, but Crystal had put her foot down. She didn't care for sushi.

Hank was an accountant but his passion was archeology, particularly the archeology of Latin America. Last year he had met a university professor who told him about a new dig that promised to contain wonders. And this year, Dr. Javez had invited Hank to view the site with him. "A once-in-a-lifetime opportunity," Hank had said. "Today is the only possible day Dr. Javez can take me there. I'll spend every other day at the resort with you, I promise." He had left early that morning, before she was up.

She planned to go down to the adult pool, with its shady area and swim-up bar. When she got too warm, she would just slip into the pool and cool off. Later she would have a couple of piña coladas, then lunch in the air-conditioned dining room. Then, perhaps a nap. And then another swim in the pool before dinner, with a piña colada or two at the bar.

For now, she was sitting on the balcony, as she did every morning after breakfast, waiting for her sluggish digestive system to get to work. She wouldn't use any bathroom but their own, so Hank would wait with her and catch up on the news and his messages until she was ready to go out. But today she was here alone.

Someone was moving in the room behind the balcony door. Crystal looked in through the curtains to see one of the maids moving about. But the room had already been made up when she came back from breakfast. Crystal slid the door open and said sharply, "What are you doing in there?"

The girl said, "*Con permiso, Señora*," and gestured to the mini-bar.

God, why couldn't these peasants learn English? Crystal thought. She shouted, "Go ahead," and slammed the door shut. The girl nodded and disappeared behind the curtains.

***

Fifteen minutes later, Crystal was ready to try the bathroom. She pulled on the door but it wouldn't open. At first, she thought it was stuck so she jiggled the handle several times. Then she pulled hard, but nothing happened. She banged on the door and called out, but there was no response. The truth dawned on her slowly—the stupid girl must have forgotten she was outside and locked the door.

Crystal's first reaction was anger. How could the hotel employ someone so incompetent? She would get that girl fired. Crystal hadn't paid much attention to her but she had looked taller than most of the maids. And pretty. Crystal noticed pretty women because she was not at all pretty herself.

The anger began to change to panic. Their room was on the garden side, even though they could easily have afforded the extra premium for the ocean side. Hank had explained it would be quieter here and it was. Very few people ventured out on the lawns, ten floors below. Today, a gardener was cutting the lawn, in the distance. How did you say "Help!" in Spanish? Crystal hadn't bothered to learn the language because Hank spoke it quite well. She called out to the man in English, again and again, but the noise of the mower drowned out her voice. Perhaps she could break the glass door. She tried swinging one of the plastic balcony chairs at the glass, but it just bounced off. Meanwhile, the sun was coming around to her side of the building.

Crystal wasn't used to being thwarted. Hank had catered to her all their married life. She knew he was grateful to her for the family money she had brought into their marriage—money that had allowed him to set up his own firm and indulge his passion for archeology. Before that, her parents had always given her what she wanted. They'd felt sorry because they had to stop her from various activities, such as playing tennis, after a nasty brush with sunstroke. She had been quite a good tennis player. Now her frustration made her scream.

No one heard her cries. Of course not. The balconies around her were empty. It was late morning and everyone was either at one of the pools or gone on a day trip, like Hank. And the hotel was half-empty, because it was early in the season. The sun was now edging on to the balcony. She was dressed only in shorts and a light cotton shirt, nothing to protect her. Her phone was inside on the dresser, charging. She did have her water bottle—she never went anywhere without it. She checked and it was half empty; she hadn't expected to be out here for very long. She could feel her temperature rising with the heat and panic, and she took a drink of the precious water. Her ankles were starting to swell. She screamed again, but this only made her feel hotter.

If she threw one of the chairs off the balcony, would the gardener wonder what was happening and look up to where she was? But the two chairs and little table were all she had. If she turned the chairs upside down, they would provide some shade. Before she could make up her mind, the gardener turned off his mower and

341

disappeared from the garden. The sun was now beating down on the balcony.

Crystal turned the chairs over and crawled under their shelter, with some difficulty, because she was a large woman. And she was getting muscle cramps, a result of her condition. The effort made her even hotter and her head was starting to feel fuzzy. It must be close to 11 o'clock. It would be another seven hours, at least, until Hank returned from his excursion.

One thought burned in her brain: *I hope Panama has the death penalty for that girl.*

***

It was almost dark when Hank returned to their hotel room that evening, carrying a bottle of champagne, which he had purchased at one of the bars downstairs. He took the "Do Not Disturb" sign off the door, let himself in, and put the champagne on the dresser. Then he went over to the balcony, opened the curtains and looked out. Crystal was there, lying on the floor, with two overturned chairs on top of her.

Hank opened the balcony door, stepped out and set the chairs upright. Then he half-carried and half-dragged Crystal into the air-conditioned bedroom. Every visible inch of her skin was fiery red. Hank made one brief telephone call on his cell phone, then called the desk, pleading for help. While he waited for someone to come, he ran cold water into the bathtub. When the hotel nurse arrived, he was trying to lift Crystal into the tub to cool her off.

The nurse waved Hank aside, took out her stethoscope and checked for a heartbeat, then shook her head and began CPR. While she worked, the room filled with people: the desk clerk; the hotel manager, *Señor* Paul; two security guards, several maids, and other staff members. Everyone was talking at once, in Spanish. Then Linda, the manager's secretary, appeared. She was a tall, attractive woman with the authority *Señor* Paul lacked, and she had the room cleared of onlookers in seconds. Hank threw her a grateful glance. The ambulance attendants finally arrived and took over from the nurse. In moments, Crystal was on their stretcher and was wheeled out of the room.

"How could this terrible thing happen, Mr. Berry?" *Señor* Paul asked. "It looks as though she suffered heatstroke. But how?"

"I found her lying on the balcony floor when I got back just a little while ago. She always sat on the balcony for a while after breakfast. She must have fallen asleep out there when it was still in shade. But where have they taken her? I need to be with her."

"I will have someone drive you to the hospital, Mr. Berry," the manager said. "I am so terribly sorry. Let us hope for the best."

"I can drive Mr. Berry," Linda said. "If that is all right with you, *Señor* Paul. I'll get the car and meet you at the front entrance. Mr. Berry, you may need your wife's passport at the hospital. Also your travel insurance policy. And any pills she is taking."

"Of course, Linda," *Señor* Paul said, grateful that he wouldn't have to cope with a distraught husband. He was expecting the worst.

Both men watched Linda walk away, her hips swaying. Then Hank gathered up what he would need, locked the room and they took the elevator to the ground floor.

At the hospital, the doctor was very sorry, but it had been impossible to revive the *Señora*. He understood there was a health problem. "Hypohidrosis, is that correct?" That had aggravated the effects of heatstroke, but even without it, he said, she might not have survived the exposure to the wicked sun of Panama.

"I'm surprised you chose to come here, *Señor* Berry," the doctor said. "Was the *Señora* not afraid of the heat?"

"She wanted to see the place I had enjoyed last year. She insisted, and because it was my birthday this week, I agreed to it. I wish to God I hadn't."

Señor Paul and Linda went out of their way to be helpful to Hank. They didn't want this dreadful accident to reflect on the hotel's reputation.

"Mr. Berry understands we were not at fault in any way," *Señor* Paul assured Linda after the formalities had been taken care of, and Hank was on his way back to Canada with Crystal's ashes.

"He is a real gentleman," Linda said. "And he is so appreciative of our culture."

***

A year later Hank returned to Panama, to meet with Dr. Javez again and view the recent discoveries at the archeological site. But Hank and his new wife didn't stay at the Hotel Corona.

As Linda said, "It is a nice enough hotel, but why go four-star when you can afford five?"

Ω

UNMASKED

Jane Petersen Burfield

Toronto born, Jane Petersen Burfield writes how North Toronto people have hidden depths beneath their seemingly respectable lives.

Jane's first short story, "Slow Death and Taxes", won the Bony Pete Award in 2001. She had written the story to encourage two fellow writers to enter and was gob smacked to win at the 2001 Bloody Words Conference, just two months after her husband was killed. After being one of the winners in three more Bloody Words conferences, and more recently, being shortlisted for the Arthur Ellis short story contest, Jane feels gratitude to the mystery community in Canada and around the world for their continuing support and help.

'Front line worker' was a phrase I heard too often in mid-May. Physical distancing, wearing a mask, and avoiding unnecessary contact was driven into our heads by unending media analyses. The horrors of COVID-19 were all too apparent at the hospital.

When I got home after my shift, I would strip off in the foyer of our house, turn my clothes inside out, and wash my hands before I put everything in the washing machine. And then I would shower to remove any particle of the plague from my hair and body. I saw enough death every day and didn't want to bring infection home.

Keith and I hadn't been getting along for months before the virus forced our toxic self-isolation. After his kids moved out the previous fall, I realized we'd become strangers. I was working long hours at the hospital but in the few hours I was at home, I was trying to patch our marriage. I wondered how many other marriages would be jeopardized by COVID-19.

Keith had been let go from his consulting job, but initially he seemed happy being at home. For the first few weeks, he kept the kitchen tidy, and rearranged his carefully curated ornaments in the living room. He often went down to do woodwork in the basement and kept a hand-vac nearby so he could de-sawdust himself before coming upstairs. He also decided to try painting, remote pictures with every line austere. In the early years of our marriage, he used to be sociable after a good day at work, but now, it was rare. The virus was getting to him.

Keith would sometimes have a meal ready for me when I got home. I appreciated when he made the effort as I usually hadn't eaten since breakfast. If he hadn't cooked, I would make us both sandwiches. Fuel rather than food. Then I'd listen to music or watch TV to give myself some distance from the chaos and pain of the hospital.

Keith didn't want to talk about the virus, about the people affected, or about my day at work. He said too much detail affected his ability to be calm. But I needed to talk, to describe and discard the difficult memories of that day. So much anxiety, so much sickness, so much death. We were on two different journeys, and he seemed to prefer that.

I would have let this situation continue if I could have. I had no time or energy for unprovoked action. But one night after a wrenching day, he forced me to acknowledge our distance. I got home, stripped, scrubbed and showered, dressed and went down for supper. Keith was sitting at the kitchen table, eating a pancake, my favorite comfort food. He had only made one, for himself. When he looked at me, I realized how mean-spirited and thoughtless he was. I couldn't handle more emotional upheaval. I knew I would have to find a clean way out of this relationship.

That night on the television, chirpy CBC reporters talked about handling mental stress. They suggested finding a project to work on every day like baking, writing a memoir, or gardening. Working in the garden would help me handle my stress, I thought. Increasing shortages included fresh produce so I decided I could grow our vegetables. That night I resolved to find seedlings and soil online for delivery.

My grandparents had been keen gardeners during the Second World War. They had a Victory Garden on the sloped land behind the kitchen which produced vegetables for years. I grew up eating fresh corn and strawberries and beans and enjoying my mom's homemade jams. Grandpa Bauckham also loved flowers and he spent years trying to cross-pollinate iris toward a black bloom. When he died, I inherited a shed full of tools, most antique.

I remembered watching Grandpa mark out a new bed with wooden stakes and garden twine. I mentally measured my plot, a modest 10-by-10 feet. Tomorrow, on my day off, I would have the opportunity to remove sod and dig the damp soil. I thought about asking Keith to help, but the task would be too physical and messy for him.

I tried one last time that evening to entice him into conversation. I brought him a drink, and we talked about his children. I tried to sound interested and enthusiastic, but they had never treated me as anything but an interloper. I was grateful when they had moved out. After the *National* news, I changed into lingerie, and sat beside Keith on the white sofa. He looked at me for a minute, shook his head, and turned the channel to a documentary on elephants. So, I went to bed alone again after changing into comfortable pajamas.

***

Next morning, I got up early and dressed in jeans and a soft Tee. I was grateful I wouldn't have to wear my protective hospital gown, gloves and N95 mask. My face was always sore by the end of my shift, my skin bleeding from the wire at the top. Often the mask left me breathless, although I was glad to have the protection at the hospital.

I turned the news on while having my toasted bagel and coffee. The virus was continuing to cause so much sickness and death in Toronto, with more than 400 new people infected and 19 dead in the past day. I pushed my bagel away. The garden outside looked peaceful. Rain was expected later, but for now I sat in a rectangle of sun at the kitchen table, the cat at my feet, and closed my eyes.

Keith came into the kitchen, home from his morning run. He was not wearing a mask even though I kept a supply by the front door. I never went outside without one. Asking him to wear one for the sake of other people, if not for himself, had proven fruitless. He insisted he wasn't sick and jogging in the fresh air would not cause anyone a problem. I'd hoped he would listen to advice from the medical officers of health, but he never put the daily briefing on. By late morning, he was working on his computer, reading e-mails, looking for consulting opportunities and drinking his third cup of coffee. Later, I heard him go down to the basement to take his temper out on some wood.

I didn't mind doing the necessary housework. Cleaning and washing provided me with a sense of accomplishment and safety. I loved the lemon scent of the organic cleaner. Later that morning, I sat in the sunroom listening to the rain on the glass canopy. Keith seemed annoyed by my presence while he painted blue washes on a canvas. As I drank my tea I listened to Beethoven and thought about what I would grow: green beans, corn, peas, carrots, zucchini and maybe tomatoes set in rows with the lowest-growing plants to the south where they would have full sun.

My spirit escaped into the gentler world of the garden. I would grow herbs and annuals in pots on the patio. Our cat, Midget, would enjoy catnip. I might even put in a small bed of wildflowers for the bees and butterflies. I went out to survey the old shed to get away from Keith for a bit and to inventory the tools. The spade and hoe probably needed sharpening.

At noon, Keith and I sat at the kitchen table, eating yet another cheese sandwich. He refused to go shopping when he had to wait in line and wear a mask. I thought about going that afternoon, but I was too exhausted. I couldn't nap because I would dream of people lying askew in their hospital beds, surrounded by tubes and beeping machines. But I could rest, listening to classical music to block my tumbling thoughts.

I lay in a lounge chair in the sunroom and wrote a grocery list, intending to place an order online. Then I pulled up gardening sites on my iPad. It was late in the season to start from seeds, even though I wanted to see if the old seeds I'd found in the shed would still grow. A garden center nearby would deliver plants and supplies. Keith probably wouldn't help dig my garden plot, and I lacked the strength to do it by hand. To save time I would rent a tiller at Lowe's. Plants, extra soil and supplies would be delivered on Monday, and I could pick up the power tiller the next day. I felt better for having a plan.

I wouldn't bother telling Keith about the garden. We had been arguing enough as it was. A *fait accompli* is always sweet. I settled back in the sunroom and looked at other catalogues online. Clothes, pantry staples, tires, even coffins were available. Who knew!

Keith was working again downstairs. I wondered what he was building. I called down to see if he'd like an afternoon cup of tea. His gruff response up the stairs was that he was busy. Too busy to spend time with me.

Before dinner, Keith emerged from the basement, covered in sawdust. The hand vac hadn't worked, its motor probably clogged. I doubted he had emptied it recently. He showered for the second time that day and sat at the kitchen table while I peeled vegetables. Heavy silence set in, neither one of us willing to share thoughts. Keith picked up the tablet and looked at the e-mails. A sudden exclamation meant he had found the receipts for the gardening supplies.

"What are you doing, Annie? What is all this?"

"A garden, a Victory Garden like during the war," I said. "I want to grow veggies and be outdoors."

"Why do you need to rent a gas soil tiller?" Keith asked. "Why can't you just dig?"

"Moving patients into beds has strained my back. Would you help, Keith? The garden prep has to be done quickly as it's late for planting."

"No," he said. "It could mess up my back again."

I nodded. His famous bad back prevented him from doing any serious work around the house. He wouldn't carry in groceries or push the vacuum around a room. Ever.

"That's why I'm getting a tiller, Keith. I can cut and roll up the sod and get right to it. Grandpa brought in top soil years ago. Hopefully, it will still be good enough for growing."

"It seems like an expensive activity. Why don't you try knitting instead?"

"I need physical work. It helps me forget the hospital. And we'll enjoy fresh veggies soon."

He glowered at me and stood up. Extended eye contact was rare these days. "You'll have to do it on your own. My asthma kicks in around dirt and pollen," he said.

"Could you cut some garden stakes to mark what is growing? I'll paint them white."

"I'm too busy with my current project. You'll have to figure something out, Annie."

"What are you making? May I see it?"

"It's something for a friend." Keith got up and slammed an open cupboard door on his way to the liquor cupboard. He poured a large scotch and stood by the window looking out. He was always angry now. It didn't seem to matter what he was angry at. I knew when to get away from him quickly, although he hadn't hit me for a while. I checked on the meatloaf in the oven, and began to set the table. Keith sat down at the kitchen table, putting his head in his hands. He rubbed his eyes and temples as if he had a headache.

"Don't touch your face! You know that."

"I'm inside, for God's sake, Annie. Stop nagging."

"I see people every day, Keith. Very sick people who either haven't been careful or were infected by someone. It's frustrating, I know, but we have to try. I'm fed up, too. I just want to see our friends, or shop, or go to the movies. I want our life back."

Keith moved over to the counter to pour himself another drink. I moved to the other side of the table and sat down. "What are you painting?" I asked, trying to distract him. He had been drinking more heavily during the past week or two.

"I've been trying to paint an elephant, but it's not working. I can't get it right." He swore as he spilled Scotch on the counter.

Keep talking to deescalate his temper, I told myself. "You will, Keith. Do you have any information or pictures? That would help."

"I had some books reserved at the library, but, of course, I can't get them till they open up again. For now, I'm experimenting with color. Mostly blue."

"Not pink?" He did not laugh. "Why elephants?" I asked, trying to get him talking more.

He shifted his position and reached for his glass. "I've always loved them. They're remote. They're smart, stubborn, in danger." I wondered that he didn't add, "Sort of like me."

"Like all of us right now," I said. "An interesting subject. Have you looked on Google?

"There's lot of info on them, but it's not what I want." Keith banged his glass down. "When will this bloody lockdown be over?"

"The virus isn't slowing at the hospital," I replied. "More people every day. We're only taking the sickest now."

"Is it hard working there, Annie?"

His question surprised me. He so rarely asked about me. "It's not easy," I said. "I'm always glad to get home to a more normal world here."

"This is normal? My God! You don't have any idea, Annie! It's hell here. Alone all day. No work. Even running is tough. I can't breathe through my mask, so I don't wear one."

I looked at him. "You could get sick or infect someone else. Neighbors will report you, Keith."

He grumbled and poured another scotch. "I'll wear one around my neck."

I shook my head. He had no idea how easy it was here. Yes, he should wear a mask outside but he couldn't understand how hard it was to breathe through multiple ones at the hospital. To sweat in protective gear. To watch people deteriorate, patients whose families couldn't come in to comfort them. Keith never could see beyond his own needs.

I put his meatloaf in front of him, but he looked at it and pushed it away. "I can't eat this. I need something light. Salad or cold soup," he said.

I ate a mouthful of carrots, quelling my rising irritation. "Well, you'd better get busy making some."

Keith slammed down his fist and pushed back from the table. He disappeared into the basement, loudly closing the door at the top of the stairs. I knew the whiskey bottle down there would come out, his solace. I ate in lonely peace and cleaned the kitchen. I doubted he would go pick up the tiller tomorrow. My home, my refuge, was becoming more toxic. I watched *Survivor* and went up to bed. Midget sensed my mood and lay beside my feet. I knew Keith would sleep on the sofa in the den, but I locked the bedroom door just in case.

***

On Sunday morning, I awoke feeling refreshed, for once sleeping through a night undisturbed by hellish dreams. Today, I would start my garden.

The patio called to me while I poured my ritual cup of coffee. I sat at the table outside, smelling wet soil and lilac. Looking at the garden, I imagined my vegetable plot tilled and planted. The white stakes and twine I found in the shed were old, but I could use them for marking out the boundaries since Keith refused to make new ones. I picked up the antique spade, now oiled and sharpened, and began to cut the edges of the staked garden. Thoughts of childhood bubbled up, my grandfather teaching me how to cross-pollinate and how to treat root balls with sulphur powder. I remembered my little push lawnmower, still in the shed, that had kept me out of his way. Happy thoughts.

Our new neighbor, Glen, leaned over the fence. I was glad to see he was wearing a mask to cover his lower face and dark beard.

"What are you up to, Annie?"

"Escaping reality with a new garden, a Victory garden. I really need to have something to do, something to look forward to."

"I watch you come home some nights, Annie, and I can't believe how you go back to the hospital the next day. It must be so hard."

"It was tough this week, Glen. The pressure is really getting to all of us. I yelled at a patient on Friday. And then I started to cry. I couldn't stop. They sent me home for a break."

I twisted Glen's sympathetic ear across the fence, properly distanced of course, for the next 20 minutes. When I told him about the tiller rental, he offered to pick it up for me before noon. That would get Keith's goat, I thought.

That afternoon, after removing the sod, I tilled deeply. The topsoil my grandfather had put in long ago was still workable. I dug deep so the rain would drain well beneath the roots. In one spot at the end of the plot, the tiller had excavated so deeply that I had trouble getting the machine out of the hole. I marked the spot with a spare stake to remind me to avoid stepping there. I would fill it with field stones later.

I stopped for a glass of iced tea while I admired my work. I would water the soil tonight after cutting in some peat moss from the shed. Tomorrow, I would plant the seedlings in neat rows with names written on the old white stakes. Then I would water the plants and listen to them growing. The tedium of one day sliding into the next was oddly soothing.

Keith fussed as usual about dinner. He'd been woodworking all afternoon. I'm sure he'd inhaled sawdust, not good for his already damaged lungs. This time I didn't say, "You should wear a mask." Spaghetti and salad eased his annoyance, but after dinner he started criticizing the expense and mess of the garden. And Glen.

"Why would Glen pick up the tiller for you?" he asked.

"He's a good neighbor. He moved in about four months ago and I met him at church before the lock down. You could get to know him too if you spent more time in the garden."

"You know I hate the heat. And the pollen. I'd need to be seeing pink elephants to go out there."

Pink elephants were in his future, the way he was drinking, I thought. "Well, tomorrow I'm planting the seedlings. I'd appreciate your help," I said, knowing he would rather wade through sewage. "We'll both enjoy the vegetables, Keith. And there isn't much to do after planting, although when I do go back to work, I'll need your help watering and weeding."

Keith looked at me with disdain. "Don't expect any help from me with your precious garden." He fidgeted with his glass. "I want you to stay home now, Annie. Look after me and the house. I don't want you going back to the hospital."

I moved to the back door and opened it to get fresh air. I couldn't afford to lose my temper. "That's not going to happen, Keith. We've talked about this over and over. The hospital needs everyone there. That's what I went into nursing for. I'm going back as soon as I can."

"But you don't need to work. You have your family money," Keith said. "I didn't expect to be left alone so often. For God's sake, Annie, we could use that money now. It would make such a difference."

"You knew when we married that I wanted us to live off our earnings and save that money to fund our retirement, and bequeath the bulk to the family charitable foundation. We signed a pre-nup, for goodness sake. You agreed to respect my wishes."

"Unless we divorce, or separate," he said grimly, staring at me. "And what about our kids?"

"Your kids have never had a kind word for me, Keith!"

I looked at him, seeing the child I had married. The child who had children of his own from his first marriage.

Tamping down my temper, I sat opposite him and tried again. "Keith, you've always wanted to be a painter. Why not use this time to work on it? We could set up a studio area for you on the back porch. There are classes and groups on-line. This could be a great time to experiment, to learn how to paint."

"I'm going back into consulting as soon as business picks up. Once COVID's under control." He stared at me. "I have to earn a living, remember?"

"Until then, Keith, you have to do something. Research your elephants. Write a story about them for children. You could even illustrate it yourself."

"I need to study one before I can draw it."

"The zoo has opened up drive through visits. Why not go this week? Photograph them." I got up and went back to the patio door, anxious to escape his resentment. He always could create black clouds around him.

"Right, Annie. I'll just pack up a sandwich and scoot off to the zoo, on my own."

"For Heaven's sake, Keith! Artists are supposed to have imagination." He glared at me and I could feel his anger. At times like this, I had to get away from him. As he stood, I ran past him into the garden. He followed quickly, grabbed my arm and hit my face. I cried out and twisted free. Then I ran down the lawn to the shed. Glen heard our angry voices and was looking over the fence anxiously. Keith banged the kitchen door shut, swearing. I stayed outside for over an hour, talking with Glen. As I went inside and up to bed, I put out a mask for Keith but I doubted he would wear it the next morning.

And once again, I took the precaution of locking the bedroom door.

***

When I got up Monday morning, Keith had left early. I didn't know if he was coming back. And I told myself I didn't care. After a coffee, I picked up my hat and garden gloves, and headed outside. The seedlings had been delivered early in the morning. Three hours of planting and watering got my little plants and me off to a good start. I went inside and made iced tea. Passing a mirror, I saw my blonde hair askew and my face and shoulders scarlet from the sun. The bruise on my cheek throbbed.

While sipping my tea, I searched online for elephants. I found mostly ugly statues. When I saw a pink, inflatable, seven-foot elephant with a sprinkler in its trunk, I decided to buy it. I needed it. Keith was often more able to talk after a good laugh. And we both needed him to laugh if we were going to survive. Several clicks, and I'd arranged for it to be delivered the next day.

Keith came home in the late afternoon and, after putting his token mask by the front door, looked expectantly for dinner preparation. At my request, he reluctantly washed his hands and sat at the kitchen table. He didn't apologize. I said we were ordering in chicken, a meal he reminded me was too salty for his blood pressure. I didn't care. He didn't tell me where he had been all day. In the past, Rocky's Bar would have been a good guess, but all the restaurants and bars were closed. So were libraries and most stores. When he poured himself a whiskey, I escaped out to the patio to enjoy my iced tea and the scent of my newly planted garden.

Keith had his usual evening drinks and his nightcap in the basement. I listened to music while sipping wine and starting a new mystery by my favorite author. Before bed, I looked for a clean mask for Keith, but they were all in the wash. I put the one he'd worn that morning on the door handle. He wouldn't notice. I was asleep long before he came up the basement stairs and fell asleep on the sofa in the den.

***

When I was little, I loved mornings. I still do. I was outside the next day shortly after sunrise, watering the garden. The plants looked like they had survived transplantation well. Today was going to be a scorcher. I would watch to see how they did through the heat. Outside, on the patio, I enjoyed my morning breakfast and coffee. Fragrance from the lilacs, now coming into full bloom, surrounded me and I could hear birds chirping. Such a welcome change from the intense sounds at the hospital: beeping alarms, call buttons, code-blue announcements and the rustle of hurrying people. I needed this down time. I couldn't let Keith steal any more of my peace.

He came outside an hour later, dressed for his jog, with stubbly chin and unwashed, graying hair. After brewing a coffee he sat on the edge of the patio wall, looking in bemusement at my garden.

"These plants take up so much space," he said.

"I know, but there's still lots of lawn behind. It will look nice in a week or two."

"The tiller is still here. You should take it back to save an extra charge," he said.

"I hoped you might return it later, after your run."

He looked surprised, affronted. "I have other plans. You'll have to do it yourself."

I met his eyes, and he looked away.

Maybe I would take it back while he was on his run, but first, I wanted to see where he was going every morning. He put down his cup and went inside to lace his shoes. I followed him in and put my car keys in my pocket.

"Remember to take a mask, Keith."

"My asthma is acting up."

"Maybe you shouldn't be jogging in this heat," I said.

"I need to get out, Annie. I can't just sit home all day. Like you do now."

Keith picked up his keys, took the mask from the doorknob, and left. I followed him in my car, keeping a distance and hoping he wouldn't notice.

Keith seemed to be heading further into our neighborhood, and not toward the running trails through the ravine. When he walked up a hill and turned into a driveway, I pulled over under a tree. I knew that house. His assistant lived there. I stayed an hour, watching, but he didn't come out. I drove home, picked up the tiller and returned it to Lowe's. Then, back at the house, I put in a load of laundry before I settled myself in a shady spot and watched my garden grow. When Keith returned home in the late afternoon, he was in a better mood.

Over the next two days, I followed Keith on his morning jog, which always took him to the same destination. I didn't need a private detective to confirm what was obvious. His betrayal wasn't unexpected. He had shown no interest in intimacy for a long time, but then neither had I. He disgusted me now.

That afternoon, I got out the pre-nup and read it again. If I initiated divorce proceedings, he would get half my net worth. How could I get around that?

Later that afternoon, Fedex delivered the pink elephant. I put it in the shed and watered the garden with the hose. On the far end of the plot, I almost fell into the deep hole I'd dug when I reached over to straighten a white stake. I put more decorative rocks down in that area to stabilize the ground.

***

On Friday morning, I put together the inflatable pink sprinkler. Elmer the Safety Elephant now overlooked the end of the garden near the rocks. I attached the hose and turned on the water. A lovely soft flow of droplets from his trunk drifted over the garden, satisfying my little plants. After half an hour, I turned off the hose, and went inside for an iced tea. Maybe I would make dinner tonight. I thought longingly of the many concoctions in my grandfather's old garden shed, but poisoning Keith would be too obvious.

When Keith returned home late that afternoon, he announced that he didn't want dinner. I noticed he was now shaved. When he went upstairs to shower I heard him coughing. Maybe his asthma was acting up.

After a light supper, I went outside to enjoy my garden.

"Annie," Glen called. I looked over the fence to see his smile. "Your garden looks beautiful! Well done."

"Do you like my sprinkler system?" I asked.

"Delightfully outrageous," he said. "May I come over? I'll wear my mask and sit on the other side of the patio."

I wasn't sure, but I needed some company and so did he. "Sure, Glen. Just let me get my mask on. I'll make iced tea for you." When I came out again, wearing a clean mask, he was sitting on the garden bench, on the far side of the patio, stroking Midget. I put his drink down on the edge of the table.

"How are you doing, Annie?" he asked.

"OK." I sipped my drink and thought for a minute. "That's not true. Not great, Glen. The patients in hospital are so sick, it wore me down. That's why I'm home for a week or two."

"And here at home you have your own challenges." Glen looked at the garden. "I've heard you and Keith arguing."

"I'm sorry about the disturbance," I said. "Most times, it's about nothing. We used to get along well, years ago. By the time his kids left for college we had lost too much."

"I'm sorry, Annie. In my law practice, I see a lot of discontent and divorce coming out of this lockdown."

I looked around, but Keith was inside and wouldn't be able to hear. I sighed and said, "He visits his assistant. He's having an affair with her. No distancing there, and no mask. I'm so angry at him!"

"Have you talked to him about it?" Glen asked.

"Not yet. I think, somehow, I've known for a while. He's been so distant when he talks to me." I walked back to the table and sipped on my straw. "I'll have to find the right time. He'll get upset when I confront him about it."

"Let me know if I can help, how I can help," Glen said.

I looked at him, and realized he was a good guy. One of the few. I didn't think he was over his wife's death yet. Maybe I could help him.

***

Early Saturday morning, I was surprised to find Keith sitting out on the patio, coffee in hand, waiting.

"Annie, we have to talk."

Not a good start to my day. "OK, Keith. What's up?"

"I'm concerned, upset, about your friendship with Glen. I know he's been over. Your tea glasses were out here this morning."

"You're concerned!" I said, disbelievingly. "I know you've been seeing Lucy. In the mornings. When you go jogging."

"That's just business," Keith said.

"Really?" I shrugged in disbelief. "Do you realize that she could have picked up the virus? That everyone Lucy sees is a risk to us?" I continued.

"What about Glen! He comes into the back yard. I know he delivered the tiller, and I know he was over last night!"

I walked to the edge of the garden. The pink elephant sprinkler at the far end mocked me for thinking we could share a laugh. "We distanced, and we both wore masks. We were just talking."

"What do you want to do, Annie?"

"I don't know, Keith. Talk to someone? It worked before."

"Zoom counselling? That's bizarre, Ann."

I realized I hated hearing him say my proper name. "I'm not sure I even care anymore."

We sat in silence for a while, looking at the garden.

"That elephant is so stupid!" he said. "Why would you buy that?"

"I thought it would make you laugh."

"It's just dumb," Keith said. He stood and got ready for running. I noticed he left without a mask.

I thought about our situation while I was housecleaning. We could separate, but I hated to think of him getting and wasting half of my inheritance. I thought he might get infected and bring that threat home to me. I wasn't willing to take that chance after seeing the chaos and suffering it could cause. I just couldn't.

After he left, I went downstairs to his woodworking room. Sawdust covered every surface. Misshapen boards were stacked roughly against the wall. I looked on his workbench and saw a wooden garden swing. Delighted, I moved over to admire it. When I was closer, I saw the initials L and K carved into the back.

Keith came home late in the afternoon and poured a whiskey to drink on the patio. He appeared hot and his cough shook his chest. "Should I take your temperature, Keith?"

"No. It's nothing. Stop fussing, Annie."

I shook my head and walked away.

That evening, I went out and turned the sprinkler on. The elephant's trunk spewed water across most of the garden. Glen leaned on the fence and laughed. The soil quickly absorbed the water and became very soft. Later, when I turned the water off, I realized the air holding the elephant up was starting to leak out. Duct tape would fix it, I thought.

Sunday was another tough day. Brittle conversation with Keith left me anxious and angry for most of the afternoon. After dinner, I again turned the sprinkler on, and went indoors. Keith was coughing, and not covering his mouth, so I tried to disinfect every area he'd been in. He still refused to go for testing. As I went upstairs, I heard him go outside to breathe the night air. He'd always thought it would clear his asthma. It didn't help. His hacking and wheezing were much worse.

I put on my robe and went outside. Keith was at the far end of the garden, holding the elephant's trunk. "It's starting to deflate," he said. He pulled on the trunk to try to dislodge the elephant. I saw him reach to grab the air gauge near the elephant's shoulder, but it was just out of his grasp. When he coughed, he fell, face first, into the soft ground. I realized when he didn't try to get up that he might have hit his head on one of the anchoring stones. I ran up to him.

"Keith? Keith? Can you hear me?" He grunted, and then was silent. The soft, sticky soil at the end of the plot held him in firmly.

Without thinking, I found myself pushing his face down into the soil. He struggled, but he was weak and it didn't take long. I went inside, washed my hands and made a gin and tonic before I called 9-1-1. Before long, the First Responders arrived and tried to revive Keith. When they couldn't, they took him away.

I looked at my Victory garden in the moonlight. I would have to follow the ambulance to the hospital, but there would be time afterward to sit outside, wrapped in the fragrant peace of a summer's night. I was pretty sure Keith had COVID-19 when he died. I would arrange to have him tested post-mortem, and would get myself tested as well. I'd have to quarantine myself for the next two weeks.

Glen called across the fence. "Is Keith alright, Annie? I saw the ambulance."

I wondered what else he had seen. "Unfortunately, he couldn't be revived," I said, amazed at the steadiness of my voice. "They took him to Emergency. They think he suffocated in the soil."

Later, after Glen had comforted me from a safe distance, I walked around the garden admiring the rows of plants. "I think Keith had COVID-19 when he died, so you should get tested, Glen." Midget ran up to me, purring, and I thought about the weeks of quiet ahead. Perhaps, after an appropriate period of isolation, Glen could come over for a patio dinner.

As I went inside, I thought I heard Glen say, "A Victory indeed, in the garden."

Ω

-

THE EMPTY GRAVE

Thom Bennett

Thom Bennett has authored five published plays, including Dark Rituals, *and the thrillers* Club Dead *and* Ravens Cliff. *He has also published a family fantasy,* Return to Wonderland, *and with Elizabeth Ferns, has co-authored a new production of the classic, romantic swashbuckler* The Prisoner of Zenda.

Thom's Cass Gentry thrillers include The Death Merchants *and its sequel* The Man With Hemingway's Face. *Thom is a member of the Crime Writers of Canada and the Playwrights Guild of Canada, and is a recipient of the Canada 125 Award.*

Suddenly, I was standing in the middle of a clearing, staring down at a hole in the ground. Only it wasn't a hole, but the discovery was worth it.

To be honest, the search unfolded just as the guy had suggested. If I stood in the doorway of the old concrete building, faced west and walked directly for the tree line, I'd find a barely visible pathway. Follow the path for about five to 10 minutes, and the woods would open up. I'd find it there.

And, indeed, I had. Only it wasn't a hole. It was too smooth, too evenly dug, too uniformly rectangular. I had seen far too many such holes in my lifetime not to recognize this one for what it was— a freshly dug grave.

***

One day earlier
Wednesday, July 20, 1960

After sleeping late following my weekly poker game, I was rummaging around my double apartment office on Jones Street in the Village. I'd already changed the calendar and was now at my

361

desk, unwrapping a framed picture my art dealer and friend had delivered the previous night.

My name is Cass Gentry and I'm a licensed New York City private eye. I'm also a serious art collector who specializes in original pieces that were used to illustrate old novels by writers like Dickens, Stevenson and Conan Doyle. Last year, when I was working The Death Merchants case, I'd purchased a signed copy of an original picture from Anthony Hope's 1894 classic The Prisoner of Zenda. The illustration was by Charles Dana Gibson, creator of the Gibson Girl.

My eyes lit up as I unwrapped my latest acquisition, which I must admit was a slight departure from my usual tastes. I'd just purchased an original piece of comic book art—the cover illustration for the Classics Illustrated version of Hope's swashbuckling adventure.

This work was by an artist named Henry Kiefer, and it was a fine rendering of the sword-wielding hero breaking into a dungeon to save his look-alike cousin, the prisoner of Zenda Castle. My plan was to hang the Kiefer drawing beside the Gibson print in my gallery of treasures.

"Sorry to interrupt, Mr. Gentry." A darkly handsome man stood in the doorway.

"Come in, Mr. Smith," I said. "Take a seat. You're not interrupting me."

The man crossed the carpeted floor and sat in a wingback chair near the desk. His movements were economical, liquid, almost feline. His age was difficult to gauge—anywhere between 40 and 70—but his voice was youthful, strong, assured.

"What can I do for you, Mr. Smith?" I inquired, setting aside the piece of art.

"Two things, Mr. Gentry. First, I'm going to need time off, the week after next."

"No problem, my friend. Anything I should be concerned about?"

"Nothing. It's my annual powwow. This year it's near Billings, Montana."

"Down the road from the Battle of the Little Bighorn, I presume."

"Affirmative."

"Ah, Custer's Last Stand! Give the ol' Colonel hell for me."

Willard "Zuni" Smith smiled, knowing that I sympathized with Native Americans. We had known each other for almost ten years. First, Smith had been one of my special-ops instructors following my service in Korea. Then he signed on as my man Friday when I retired from the military to set up my private practice.

But Smith, a full-blooded Zuni from New Mexico, was more than an employee; he was my mentor, business associate, live-in father figure and close friend. Honorable to a fault, he had never asked me how I could afford to live as a gentleman detective, or where my extra money came from.

"What's the second thing?" I asked.

"This note came by courier last night," Smith said. "While you were out."

"Give me the short-and-sweet version."

Smith stretched his long legs and crossed them, then settled farther into his plush leather chair. "Well, it seems that a fellow named Ryan Brady wishes to engage your services. He's suggested a sizable retainer and a very lucrative payoff if you solve the case."

"Not meaning to sound avaricious," I said, "but did he provide actual figures?"

Smith consulted the note and quoted the two numbers.

I nodded for him to continue.

"The note also states that the situation may be a matter of life and death. Therefore, he wishes to meet with you as soon as possible. He suggests a face-to-face this evening."

Leaning forward in my chair, I rested my elbows on the desk and steepled my fingers. "Please go on, Mr. Smith."

Smith consulted the note once more, and continued. "If you are interested in hearing the entire proposition, you are to meet Mr. Brady in his room at the Algonquin Hotel this evening at 7 p.m., Room 309. He'll have dinner and beverages sent up."

Straightening the wrapping paper around my new picture, I considered the information. Finally, leaning back in the desk chair, I prompted, "What do you think, Mr. Smith?"

My mentor took a deep breath and exhaled slowly as he rearranged his legs. "Rather bizarre, Mr. Gentry. On the one hand, he provides very enticing information—the matter of the life-and-death plea, and the generous fee."

"Indeed. On the other hand, no personal information is offered. Just a name, which could be bogus, and a time to meet. Anyone can rent a room at the Algonquin if they have enough money, then disappear the very next day."

"Yet, you would be left with the retainer, Mr. Gentry, instead of an empty wallet."

"I assure you, Mr. Smith, my wallet will never be empty," I said with a sly wink. "Nevertheless, the whole affair seems a little hinky to me."

"So, what are you going to do?"

"Keep the appointment, of course. Although the business appears slightly suspicious, it's definitely intriguing."

"You mean the financial aspects of the case?"

"No, my friend. The business of life and death."

"But *whose life? Whose death?*"

"That, Mr. Smith, is the intriguing part of the business."

***

At 6:55 p.m., I entered through the brass-and-glass doors of the Algonquin Hotel at 59 West 44th Street. Walking directly into the oak-paneled lobby, I carefully skirted the lobby cat napping in the middle of my path. I was about to approach the desk clerk, when a short, middle-aged man with a weather-beaten face came up to me.

"Welcome back to the Algonquin, Mr. Gentry," the man said in a chipper voice.

"Thank you, Boyd. How've you been?"

"Fabulous, sir. The missus and I just had another baby."

"How many is that, Boyd?"

"This one's number seven. Only need two more to get our baseball team."

"Wow," I joked, having known Boyd long enough to remember his desire for a large family. "I bet your wife can't wait. Maybe she'll get lucky and have twins next time."

Boyd laughed and said, "We're calling him Andy."

"After Andy Carey of the Yankees?"

"You got it! Andy goes along with the other Yankees' names we've called our kids."

"It takes all kinds, Boyd. It takes all kinds."

"Can I help you, Mr. Gentry?" the little man said. "Going to the Oak Room for dinner?"

"No, thank you, Boyd. I've got an appointment with someone on the third floor."

"Not to worry, Mr. Gentry. I'll take you up myself."

Moments later, I was knocking on the door to Room 309. It opened almost immediately, as if the man inside had been waiting with his hand on the doorknob. At a shade over six feet, he was as tall as me, sturdily built and distinguished by close-cropped, ginger hair and a neatly trimmed mustache. I figured he was slightly older than me, but he could have been any age from mid-30s to mid-40s.

After shaking hands and introducing ourselves, we settled into comfortable chairs around an occasional table. Ryan Brady suggested we order dinner and drinks, but I declined.

"I'd rather get down to the business at hand, if you don't mind," I said.

"Quite right," Brady said in a clipped, military manner. "I'm not hungry at the moment, either. Perhaps later."

"Perhaps," I nodded.

"A drink, then?" he offered. "I can order up soda water if you're not into alcohol."

I agreed to soda water. He dialed up room service and ordered the soda, along with a Chivas neat and a bowl of Spanish peanuts for himself.

"Your note mentioned a matter of life and death," I began, once Brady had placed the order. "Would you please elaborate?"

Brady took a deep breath, looked down at his folded hands, then back up at me. "It's about my wife, Mr. Gentry. She's been kidnapped and is being held for ransom. The kidnappers say that if I don't follow their instructions precisely, they will kill her. In fact, they suggest they will bury her alive."

Brady paused; I remained silent. The only sound in the room was a clock quietly ticking.

Finally, Brady continued. "She went out to the theater last Saturday night. Saw Gypsy at the Broadway Theater. Seen it before, in June. Loves the show; loves Ethel Merman."

"What's not to love? It's a great show," I said. Then, "Is that the night she disappeared?"

"No. She came home after the curtain. We're on Riverside Drive, so she took a cab. Doesn't like driving in the city at night."

Settling back into his chair, Brady continued with the story. "When she arrived home, she told me all about the show, and that Merman had three extra curtain calls. Everything was perfectly normal."

I nodded, while Brady continued speaking in a terse, unemotional manner.

"Next morning, she went off to church, while I worked in my home office. I'm an insurance lawyer, and this year's been very busy." He paused for a few seconds. Then, looking down at his hands, he said, "She never came home."

As if on some ill-timed cue, there was a knock on the hotel room door. Brady admitted a pleasant-faced young man carrying our drinks on a silver platter. The waiter, freshly scrubbed and exuding the unmistakable odor of Old Spice aftershave, set down the drinks and peanuts on the occasional table, accepted a tip from Brady, and promptly left.

Brady took a small sip of his whiskey, followed by a sip of water. Then he sat fiddling with his ring, while I took a long pull from my soda water and gently set it down.

"Did you check with the church to see if she'd arrived there?" I asked when Brady appeared ready to resume his story.

"I did, but we're not regulars, and the church is so big. The priest had no recollection of seeing anyone that matched her description."

"If you give me a picture of her, I could try asking around myself."

"No need," Brady said. "I have something better." He opened a file folder that lay on top of the table, pulled out two pieces of paper and set them on the manila folder. "The top sheet is the ransom note, while the second is a set of instructions I had to follow in order to get my wife back alive. I received both of them by courier on Monday afternoon. You can review the instructions as I explain what I was doing all day yesterday."

Taking the proffered papers from Brady, I started to scan them, as he leaned back in his chair.

"As you can see," Brady began, "the top paper says that unless I follow the instructions precisely, my wife will be killed within the week. In fact, she will be tortured…then buried alive."

He paused, twisted the wedding ring on his finger again, and appeared to be gathering his thoughts. This is the story he told me in Room 309 of the Algonquin Hotel.

***

The journey to save my wife began shortly after 10 o'clock yesterday morning. Upon crossing the George Washington Bridge into Jersey, I followed the instructions back into New York state and proceeded north along the Hudson Valley. Passing West Point Military Academy, I traveled for another hour and a half, slowing down after passing the village of Millerton. Between Millerton and the city of Kingston, I turned onto a county road with the dog tag of Cheese Factory Road.

At this point, I had to carefully consult the odometer reading, so that I didn't miss the final turnoff. At exactly 1.7 miles, I went down a long-forgotten farmer's lane that dead-ended in less than a minute. When I could go no farther, I stopped, parked my car and crossed through the trees on the driver's side, where I very soon came out onto a seemingly unending expanse of farmland. Once again, the instructions proved to be accurate.

Within minutes, I was standing on top of a knoll, surveying freshly plowed meadows and feeling a light breeze temper the noonday heat. On all sides of the knoll, the pastures extended in undulating greens, browns and yellows.

A half mile to the east, I could see a well-kept barn, noteworthy for having a glaring red door. The sun, which was high-noon bright, seemed to highlight the door's brilliance. However, the longer I stared at the barn, the less vivid the door's color seemed. A trick of the light, I told myself as I resumed my journey toward the southwest in accordance with my written instructions.

Within 10 minutes, traveling slightly downhill toward an old, wooden fence, I soon saw a deserted concrete building that the kidnappers had written about. Inside, I was supposed to find another message that would lead me to the next set of instructions.

By the time I approached the fence, I was starting to sweat and hoped the breeze would pick up or that the old building would present some cool shelter. I gingerly crossed over the ancient wooden barrier, and prepared to continue my march. At this point, the building was only several hundred yards away; all that stood between me and my goal was an area of tall grassland. I moved forward slowly.

Then the sound began.

It was faint at first. Then slowly, ever so slowly as I marched along, it gained in volume. It could have been my legs sweeping against the weeds and grasses, for when I stopped, the noise also stopped. When I moved forward, the whispering began once more, slightly louder this time, like thousands of insects buzzing indignantly at my intrusion.

I stopped again. This time, the sound continued for a second or so longer. I moved faster through the tangled growth, beginning to fear the noise that seemed to surround me. I moved faster still, acutely aware that I was starting to sweat profusely and that my heart was beating dangerously fast.

Suddenly, I was through the tall growth, and immediately started walking on close-cropped grass. Thankfully, at last, there was…silence. Only the sound of a gentle wind was audible. I stood still for a few moments, shook my head and dismissed the whole affair as the product of an overwrought imagination, brought on by the sudden disappearance of my wife. I figured the sounds were nothing more than my legs brushing against the long grass.

There before me stood the old concrete building, abandoned and desolate. It was a small structure from the previous century, made of mortar and stone. As I peered through a large opening that had no door, I could see that the interior contained a single room, measuring about 12 feet by 24 feet.

The stairs were missing in action, but it was easy to climb up inside. Once there, I looked around, but there wasn't much to see. Directly opposite the entranceway, on the east wall, was a single window minus any framework. On the far south wall, there appeared a curious-looking groove that ran the width of the building, from one wall to the opposite one. I went over to investigate.

The groove was smooth, originating when the concrete flooring was first poured. It was approximately six inches wide, and as it ended at the two walls, there appeared round openings that would have dispersed any liquid in the groove out of the building and onto the ground below. What caught my attention was an ancient frayed rope hanging directly over the groove from a rusted ceiling device. I had a disconcerting sense this might have been a slaughterhouse, where an animal's corpse would be hung over the groove and its blood carried away to the ground outside.

My mind leapfrogged to the conclusion that this might be where the kidnappers planned to torture my wife! The thought chilled my blood, and I spun around, half expecting to see them standing behind me, one with a gun, the other with a large butcher knife.

The building was empty, of course. I was alone, and as I glanced around the quiet interior, I could see nothing that would provide me with a clue as to my next set of instructions. Dejected, I headed back to the entrance, prepared to hop down to the ground and investigate the building's exterior. However, just before I jumped, I noticed fresh writing scrawled on the wall to the right of the opening.

Look out the doorway facing west. Walk to the tree line. Find the barely visible path. Follow the path to the clearing.

***

After a few seconds of silence from Brady, I piped up and asked, "Did you follow the instructions?"

"Naturally! It was the only way I could find my wife."

"And what did you discover, Mr. Brady?"

"A lot of bloody annoying trees," he said, then finished his drink in one long swallow. "Then, after struggling along the pathway for about five or 10 minutes, there was a clearing, and in the middle of the clearing was a hole in the ground."

"What kind of a hole? Round, square, smooth, jagged, how deep?"

Brady paused to think, while at the same time sliding his ring off and on his finger. Finally, he said, "About four or five feet in diameter. Not very smooth, deep enough to stick in someone's body, if he wasn't too tall."

"Is your wife tall?"

"She's medium height—about five-four."

"Was there anything else?"

Brady paused, slowly nodded and cleared his throat. "Yes. There was a stake inside the hole. Attached to it was my wife's blouse."

"Anything else?" I prompted in a flat, unemotional voice.

"There was blood on the blouse and a note, pinned to it. The note said: *Return here. Thursday. 2 p.m.*"

***

Early the next morning, I ate breakfast with Zuni Smith, gave him instructions for the day and headed north to start my assignment for Ryan Brady. By 10:45, I was driving north through New York State, along the Hudson River. I was attired in my customary black summer outfit: a Brooks Brothers tropical-weight suit, a René Lacoste polo shirt and imported Dolcis Vincenza leather slip-ons. Frankly, I have numerous sets of the same black clothing, reasoning that black is always in style, and it saves me time and worry about what the hell I'm going to wear for the day.

It was a beautiful summer morning, and I had the top down on my Jaguar XK-140. The car radio was playing the Everly Brothers' hit "Cathy's Clown," and I was just passing West Point, the military academy Brady had mentioned last night.

I was pretty familiar with the area, as I'd spent several years nearby at the Eagle Ridge military prep school, finishing my secondary education. Although I was a Canadian by birth, my father had some kind of pull and enough money to send me there, considering it to be a finishing school that would toughen me up. Indeed, it did, and I liked the States so much I decided to stay on in New York City to complete a degree at NYU. Upon graduation, I fought in the Korean War, and my stint was followed by special-ops training and service in Washington. My mother's been trying to get me to return to Canada ever since.

Elvis was whipping up a storm with "It's Now or Never" on the radio, while I reviewed the previous night's appointment with Brady at the Algonquin Hotel. As soon as I'd returned to my Jones Street residence, I'd made notes about the meeting, and tried to put my thoughts in order.

My cautionary antennae had gone up when Brady asked me to take his place for the return trip to the gravesite to receive the final set of instructions. Because of my profession and the fact I had contacts in the police force, Brady argued that I could do what was necessary to save his wife, and perhaps apprehend the villains into the bargain. To sweeten the deal, he handed over the original retainer, along with a very generous bonus. The case was an intriguing challenge, all right, and the money was definitely good, but I still felt uneasy.

My wariness prompted me to phone my gangland contact, Frank Palladino. After supplying him with some basic details, the mobster put me in touch with one of his oldest friends, a well-known Broadway producer named Charlie Silverman. Silverman, after a quick search, provided me with information confirming my growing suspicions. It didn't take me long to make a few more calls, and when I finally got what I'd been looking for, I woke up Zuni Smith and got him into the office to thrash out our strategy.

***

As Bobby Darin sang "Mack the Knife," I parked my Jag down the old farmer's lane and headed up the hill to the top of the knoll. I looked east and about a half mile away was able to see the barn with the brilliant red door. Only the door wasn't brilliant red, as Brady had described it, but a washed-out, dirty pink. It hadn't seen a lick of paint in more than half a century.

I checked my watch. I was a little early, but my plans with Zuni Smith were already in motion.

I started downhill, bearing slightly to the southwest, until I'd reached the wooden fence. Crossing over, but being careful not to snag my lightweight summer blacks, I headed to the long grass which swished and swayed, but made no threatening sounds. Again, Brady had misrepresented some detail in his story. Deliberate, to get my attention, or just careless?

Upon entering the concrete building, I found everything the way Brady had described it, right down to the groove, the frayed rope and the note on the wall.

Eight minutes later, I entered the woods and started to fight my way along the path. I had to agree with my client—the trees were bloody annoying.

Almost 10 minutes passed before I was there, standing over the hole. Only it wasn't a simple hole about four or five feet in diameter, just deep enough to stick in a short body. It was too smooth, too evenly dug, too uniformly rectangular. I recognized it as a freshly dug grave.

"What do you think?" came a voice from above me. "Do you know what it is?"

"Seen a few in my time," I said without turning around. I recognized Brady's voice and figured that he was up in a tree somewhere behind me. And most likely armed.

"Know who's going to die in it?" Brady said.

I paused for a moment, then responded, "What would you say if I suggested it would be you?"

"I'd say you'd died with a lie on your lips."

The silence of the woods was broken by the sound of a rifle bolt sliding into place.

"Son of a bitch!" Brady cried in surprise. It was not *him* who had armed a weapon.

"Actually, he's not a son of a bitch." I turned around slowly and looked up at my adversary. He was sitting in a tree and aiming a rifle of his own at my head. "He's my friend and colleague, Mr. Zuni Smith."

***

Hours later, Mr. Smith and I were sitting in the Jones Street apartment, reviewing the events of the past two days. "Twilight Time" by the Platters was playing on the living room stereo, and we were enjoying ice cold bottles of Schlitz beer.

"What was the first thing that got you on to him?" Smith asked. "You only gave me a bare-bones outline last night."

"It was a slip he made," I began. "He told me his wife had gone to see Ethel Merman in Gypsy last Saturday night."

"What was wrong with that?"

"He said she'd gone to the Broadway Theater to see it. Last Saturday night, the show was dark. It had finished its run at the Broadway on the Saturday *before*. It's supposed to reopen in August at the Imperial Theater. I'd heard about the closing, but when I got home last night, I confirmed everything with Charlie Silverman, the Broadway producer. *Gypsy* reopens on Monday, August 15. My client said that his wife had seen the show before, in June, and loved it. Logically speaking, he was already plotting this little caper last June, when the show was still at the Broadway Theater."

"That was just a small slip, Mr. Gentry," Zuni Smith said. "But there must have been lots more to trigger your skepticism."

"Indeed, there was. Specifically, the ring. He kept fiddling with his wedding ring. At first, I thought he was perhaps nervous. Then I became convinced he was uncomfortable wearing it. Finally, he slipped it off and on entirely. It was then that I noticed his ring finger was as tanned as the rest of his left hand."

"If he had been married for some time," Smith interjected, "there would have been a white patch of skin where the ring prevented any tanning!"

"Precisely. Either he was not married at all and put on the ring to make his story more plausible, or else he had just gotten married recently. If the latter was the case, you'd think he'd have mentioned it and referred to her as his bride of so many weeks or months. Regardless, it opened up the possibility that he wasn't married, and that his entire kidnapping story was bogus."

We sat in comfortable satisfaction, sipping our drinks. After a few moments, I continued my explanation, "So, last night when I got home, I proceeded to follow that line of reasoning. If it was all a lie, then why the elaborate goose chase over hill and dale? Why the hole in the woods and the suggestion of a burial site?"

"Obviously someone was going to die," Smith offered, "and someone was going to be buried there."

"And who else would that be?" I said. "There was only one other person in play at the time, and that person was me—the guy he'd asked to take his place at the empty hole the very next day after our meeting. If I was the target, that would answer a number of other questions."

"Like why would he check into the Algonquin," Smith suggested, "when he supposedly lived only five or so miles away on Riverside Drive?"

"Correct, and why would he say that he was a lawyer when clearly he was ex-military?"

"What gave that away?"

"Numerous things. His very short hair, his neatly trimmed mustache and his clipped speech when he wasn't reciting his overly dramatic tale of his travels to the empty grave site. His bearing was also fairly rigid. Clearly he's an officer, especially when he noted passing West Point Military Academy in his story to me. Normally, people might mention the town, but not so much the military academy unless there was a personal connection to it."

"Or he was a travel guide," Smith smiled and drank some of his beer.

"Further, he referred to the name of Cheese Factory Road as its *dog tag*; said that the building's stairs were *missing in action*; and used the term march instead of walk several times."

"Well done, Mr. Gentry. Please continue."

"When I reached the possibility that I was the actual victim, I made several more phone calls," Gentry said. "One was to the unlisted number in Washington we've used before in such investigations as The Death Merchants, and last autumn's case about The Man With Hemingway's Face. After a few transfers, I explained my problem to the duty officer and suggested where he might look in military records. I gave him my client's initials, his probable range of ranks, his approximate age and physical description, and the possibility he served in Korea."

"You thought there was a connection to the Korean conflict?"

"Strong probability. Based on our relative ages, it was a definite field we would have shared if he was ex-military."

"And indeed it was, as it turned out," Smith said.

"So, a little after midnight this morning, the phone rang, I had my answer from our contacts in Washington, and I woke you up. Whereupon we plotted our strategy for closing the case of the empty grave."

***

"Actually, he's not a son of a bitch," I said, slowly turning around and looking up at my adversary. He was sitting in a tree and aiming a rifle of his own at me. "He's my friend and colleague, Mr. Zuni Smith. As well as being awarded the army's Expert Marksmanship Badge with three Clasps, he's a very fine fellow, with impeccable parentage. Conclusion: no son of a bitch, but an excellent shot.

Brady scanned the trees around him before spotting Smith 20 feet down the pathway. "How the hell did you get there?" he asked.

Smith responded from his place on the trail, "I followed Mr. Gentry at a discreet distance in my own car. I parked in the farmer's lane, then headed to this rendezvous spot."

"Therefore, Colonel Robert Brennan," I continued, "I suggest you throw down your weapon, then climb out of the tree very slowly. Please note that Mr. Smith will shoot to kill."

"And I have a clean shot from here," Smith added.

"It really doesn't matter," responded Brennan, as he lowered his rifle. "I'm going to die soon, anyway. But first, tell me how you figured out my little plot."

"I'll be happy to, Colonel, but if your rifle moves even an inch, my friend will shoot you out of the tree. Understood?"

"Of course."

"To begin, after our meeting last night at the Algonquin, it soon became apparent that you were not telling the truth about your kidnapped wife. You are neither married, as far as I can tell, nor has your fictitious spouse been kidnapped. It was also apparent that you are not a lawyer, but either ex-military or still in the service."

"How did you make those conclusions, if I may ask?"

"Powers of observation and a great many slips on your part. I'd be pleased to outline all of them later. However, right now, let's concentrate on the real reason why you hired me."

"Which is?"

"To kill me and dispose of my body, of course. Now, the disposal part is obvious, but the real puzzle was why me? I'd never met you before our meeting at the Algonquin. What had I done to offend you to the extent you wanted me dead?"

"Good question." Brennan slowly rearranged his position in the tree, careful to make no threatening moves with his rifle. "But I assume you already have the answer."

"I do. But I needed some help. You were correct in assuming I have good contacts with the police. In this case, however, I used my contacts with the Army Security Agency. I gave them a list of research descriptors to see if they could ferret you out for me."

"What kind of descriptors?"

"Your physical description, age range, active service or recent retirement, possible rank ranging from major to major general, service in Korea and your initials."

"My initials?"

"Just a shot in the dark, Colonel. Many people who use aliases pick names that have the same initials…because of monogrammed clothing, jewelry, luggage and so forth. The fact that you changed your real name from Robert Brennan to Ryan Brady was a great help. As a consequence, your initials and a number of other matching descriptors helped the agency to hit pay dirt. They were able to respond to me within a few hours."

"And they came up with me!"

"Not only you, Colonel Brennan, but the fact you had come from a large Irish family, and had a brother who also fought in Korea."

"Sean," Brennan said in a quiet voice.

"Indeed, Sean. Corporal Sean Brennan of the Second Infantry Division, Charlie Company. Under the command of Captain Cass Gentry."

"Yes, you! The man who left him to die on Bloody Ridge, in the fall of '51. My baby brother!"

"I did not leave him to die, Colonel. We were under heavy fire and cut off from the rest of our unit. Sean was badly wounded, and I left him to find a medic. By the time the medic and I returned, Sean was dead. I was wounded by a KPA grenade and barely able to carry his body back down the hill."

After a moment, Brennan asked, "And you expect me to believe that?"

"Believe what you wish, Brennan. But I'm telling the truth. However, I'd like to ask you something, if you don't mind."

"Go ahead."

"Why did you decide to come after me?"

"I promised him. I stood at Sean's grave and vowed I would hunt you down and kill you."

"But why now?" I said. "Sean was killed almost nine years ago."

"I thought I might get over it, but his death and the vow kept haunting me." Brennan shifted his position slightly, but made no move with his rifle. "I thought about it, obsessed over it for a long while. I was transferred around the world, moved back home, then something happened that sealed the deal."

"What was that, Colonel?"

"Last month, I found out I had inoperable cancer. If I was going to keep my vow to Sean, I had to do it now."

"Sean was a good soldier," I said, "and I'm very sorry for your loss and your illness, Colonel. However, as trite as it sounds, you must know that killing me won't bring him back."

"Time to come down, Brennan," Zuni Smith interrupted. "But drop the weapon first, if you don't mind."

After a long silence, Brennan looked down at me, and seemed to make up his mind.

"A promise is a promise," was all he said. Then he lifted his rifle in my direction. Zuni Smith immediately fired, hitting Brennan high in the shoulder. Crying out in pain and frustration, Brennan fumbled to hold his weapon steady as he tried to aim at me. Another shot from Zuni Smith hit him in the back of the neck, and he pitched forward out of the tree.

I rushed over to Brennan, who looked up at me with wide, unseeing eyes. I didn't need a medic to tell me he was dead.

"What do we do now?" Smith asked as he joined me beside the body.

"I'll get in touch with our friends in Washington. The Agency's boys will be here in no time and clean things up. Then they'll notify the family and make sure Brennan gets a proper burial. He was misguided in coming after me, but he shouldn't be remembered for that."

"What do you intend to do with his retainer?"

I thought for a moment, then said, "How about a generous contribution to the Veterans of Foreign Wars? Perhaps in Brennan's name."

"Most appropriate, Mr. Gentry." My mentor smiled at me. "I'd expect nothing less."

Ω

THE NEIGHBORHOOD WATCH

Delee Fromm

Delee Fromm is an author, lawyer and former psychologist who grew up in Yorkton, Saskatchewan. She worked at a large psychiatric hospital in Edmonton. She switched to the practice of law in the late 80's and was a partner at McCarthy Tetrault LLP in Toronto for 16 years.

Delee lectures at Ryerson University, University of Western Ontario, York University, Rotman School of Management and the University of Toronto, Faculty of Law. She is the author of Advance Your Legal Career *and* Understanding Gender at Work *and co-authored* A Workbook for Understanding Gender at Work *with Rocca Morra Hodge.*

DAY ONE

"Can you come over for tea?"

I could hear in Judy's voice that something had happened. Something bad.

"Be there in 10." I put my phone into the back pocket of my jeans, and headed to the front hallway. "Ben," I yelled up the stairs. "I have to go and see Judy. Something has happened."

My husband's head appeared over the bannister. "I hope everything is OK."

"I hope so, too. Oh, can you remind me to have a look at the neighbor's yard? They've been doing that foundation work and left the pit on our side uncovered."

I grabbed Ted's lead from the hall closet and heard him bounding from his mat in the TV room. I smiled. He could hear the jingle of his lead anywhere in the house.

"You're a lucky boy. Two walks in one morning."

As I walked and let Ted sniff, I thought about the call. Judy had sounded distressed. Just like when her dog Riley had died. "He will have the life of Riley," her husband, Harry, had said when the puppy arrived home—so that's what they named him. I thought the cliché applied more to Harry than to the dog.

Judy lived four doors down from us in one of those modern boxes that was all glass and steel. Too cold for my taste and Judy's, but Harry loved modern architecture. To stay in the neighborhood where she had lived for 25 years, Judy had sold her house a couple of blocks away and paid way over the asking price for this one. What Harry wanted, Harry got.

Judy must have been waiting by the door. It opened before I even rang the doorbell. Still in her housecoat and pajamas, Judy looked a mess. No makeup, frizzy hair and circles under her eyes. Totally unlike her usual self.

"My dad died yesterday."

"I'm so sorry," I said, stepping into the foyer and hugging her. "I know how close you were." My dog, Ted, stood near Judy, waiting for the usual head rub. She ignored him.

"He was doing so well. His doctor told me." Judy started to sob.

"Why don't we go into the family room, and I can make us some tea," I suggested.

As the three of us made our way through the house, she stopped crying. "I didn't expect it. I mean, for a 70-year-old man with diabetes and a broken hip, he was doing so well. Even the doctors couldn't believe how well he was responding."

Judy sat down on the couch in the family room, and Ted lay at her feet.

"It must have been such a shock," I said, heading into the kitchen. I pulled out the box of tea and the teapot. After so many visits, I knew the layout of Judy's kitchen as well as my own.

She huddled farther into the couch facing the kitchen and continued. "I sat with him for a week while he rallied. When he first came in, they talked about palliative care. But I fought that." Her voice gained strength as she talked. "Dad was a fighter, and I wanted to give him a chance."

The kettle started to sing, and I quickly grabbed it. I poured the water over the leaves in the teapot as Judy continued to talk.

"I was with him the whole time. I ate there, I slept there. Harry brought me fresh clothes. Then, just when I stepped out of his room to use the bathroom, Dad dies. He was sleeping peacefully when I left. I get back and he's dead. I should have stayed with him."

"Judy, you're not responsible. You were a wonderful daughter to him," I said, setting the tray with the teacups and the pot on the coffee table in front of her. Stepping over Ted, I sat beside her.

"It's so unfair. I spent all that time with Dad, and Harry's the one with Dad when he dies. Harry knew Dad all of two years. I could have done better by him."

"He knew what a great daughter you were."

"No, I could have been better. Much better." Judy continued to cry as I hugged her. Her depression colored her perception, so it was hard for her not to blame herself. When Riley died, she had blamed herself for months, even though she had nothing to do with his death. Riley had gotten out of the yard when she wasn't home.

Ted and I stayed with Judy awhile. Judy and I drank tea, and I listened to her talk about her dad, and the fond memories she had of him. When she was finally talked out, I continued to sit quietly, thinking about everything she had said and what I knew from the past.

One thing was for certain, Judy would be well looked after. Her father had been a wealthy man. She was about to inherit a vast fortune. As Ted and I were leaving, I asked the name of her dad's doctor.

***

Ben was making lunch when I got home. His egg salad sandwiches were to die for. As he smashed the boiled eggs and added the cut-up bits of pickles and dobs of mayonnaise, I told him about my morning.

"Judy has the worst luck, doesn't she?" I knew he was referring to Riley's death six months earlier and her sister's death the previous year.

"Do you really think it's *just* bad luck?" I asked, pouring us two glasses of water.

Ben gave me a knowing look. "Your Spidey sense telling you otherwise, Mieka?"

"Yeah, it's jangling big time." I dove right in. "I think Harry's involved."

"And you *have to* investigate it, right?" he said, spreading egg salad onto pieces of bread and topping the mixture with crunchy pieces of lettuce.

I nodded. "Mom taught me well."

"You definitely inherited that Spidey sense from her." Ben put the open-faced sandwiches on plates and handed one to me. "And Judy's your friend, so you feel you have to do something."

"Yes. If anything were to happen to her, I would never forgive myself."

"I'm just concerned it could end badly." Ben put the extra egg salad into the fridge before turning to look at me. "If, and it's a big if, Harry's a psychopath, I'm warning you: don't listen to what he says. Instead watch what he does."

"I'll be careful." I took Ben's warning seriously. As a criminal lawyer he had worked with psychopaths, colleagues as well as clients. He knew firsthand what the experts say—the really smart ones never get caught.

Before we started to eat, I promised Ben, "I'll get the facts and I'll go to the police."

***

I called Kate and invited her over. Like Judy, I'd known Kate for decades. We were among the first homeowners in our subdivision. I trusted her to tell me if I had wandered into loony tunes territory.

I filled her in on what I knew while she filled up on leftover egg salad.

"Let me get this straight, Mieka. You think hotter-than-hot-Harry killed Judy's dog and her dad." Kate had given Harry that nickname when he married Judy. Not only did he look like Brad Pitt, but he had the same charming personality. Everyone seemed to like him. Everyone but me.

"Yes, and maybe Judy's sister Claire, too," I said as I started in on my second sandwich of the day. Thinking always made me extra hungry. "He had the means, motive and opportunity to kill Judy's dad. *And* Judy and Harry were staying with Claire when she died."

"You think it's for the money, right?" Kate asked.

"Yeah. Harry spends a lot of money for someone who doesn't have a job. How many sports cars does he have now?"

"Six at the latest count." Kate sat up straight in her chair. "Hold on. Wouldn't he get half of Judy's money if they divorced?"

"No, they have a prenup agreement," I explained. "Her dad insisted on it. Harry gets very little if they divorce."

"So we weren't the only ones who thought she married way too soon after Jeremy died. Maybe that's why Judy's so trusting. Her first husband was a gem."

"She told me a year ago that the prenup really bugged Harry, and that as soon as her dad died, she would get rid of it."

"Soooooo," Kate drawled, "he kills her sister, making Judy the sole beneficiary. Then he speeds up her Dad's death, so no more prenup. Starting to look *way* more suspicious." Kate finished her sandwich and pushed the plate aside. "If he were instrumental in those two deaths, and money's the motive, how does Riley's death fit in?"

"Do you remember all the jokes he made about Judy loving Riley more than him?"

"I sure do. Come to think of it, it was strange that Riley got out of the backyard. It's built like Fort Knox with all that fencing—if Fort Knox was for dogs and not gold."

Kate sat quietly, staring into space. "You think he might try to kill Judy? Is that what you are thinking, Mieka?"

"If I'm right about his motive of wanting all the money sooner rather than later, that's the next logical step." I put our plates into the dishwasher.

"He'd be pretty stupid to do it so soon."

"I agree. That means we probably have some time. If you're in that is."

"I'm in. What now?"

"Do the research. Gather the facts. Go to the police."

"I'll talk to neighbors about Riley's death when I hand out notices for tomorrow night's community meeting. I'll say I want to get a puppy and ensure that it's still alive for its first birthday. That sounds plausible, right?" She lifted the head off the cow-shaped cookie jar and reached in to grab a cookie.

"That's perfect, Kate," I said, rolling my eyes. "That won't raise any suspicions at all." I picked up my iPad. "I'll search for information on the family deaths. What did we ever do before the Internet?"

***

I Googled "Claire Evan death," mentally crossing my fingers that there had been some press coverage. I wasn't disappointed; there was a ton. Being an heiress ensured both regular media and tabloid coverage.

I learned that Harry and Judy *were* visiting at the time of Claire's death. TMZ (of course) took a picture of them getting into their Range Rover the day after the death. Judy looked distraught.

Claire, who had a history of suicide attempts, had died from an opioid overdose. Judy was the one who found her.

Then came new information. Claire Evans had been diagnosed with bipolar disorder four years before her death. I searched medical articles, and discovered that the depressive phase of this disorder is often very severe, with suicide a significant risk factor. People with bipolar disorder are more likely to attempt suicide than those with regular depression. So, based on her medical diagnosis, there would have been nothing suspicious about Claire's suicide.

I read more. Studies show that bipolar disorder runs in families. I wondered if Judy suffered from it, too, but with only the depressive aspects on display. Another article confirmed that although such a condition was rare, it did exist. So it would have been easy to target both of them for murder, and get away with it.

Next, I turned to my attention to Judy's dad, researching the morbidity rate after hip fractures. It was depressing. About 30 minutes into my research, I came across an article that summed it up nicely: "Why Hip Fractures in the Elderly are Often a Death Sentence." At 70, Judy's Dad didn't seem elderly to me, but medically he was. I guess being 65 myself distorted my view of what was young.

I made a mental note to exercise my core muscles more, and started thinking that maybe, just maybe, my Spidey sense *was* off. Judy's dad might well have died from natural causes. That meant that both of the deaths were not only probable but likely, based on their medical diagnoses. Grave diagnoses, it turned out, in both cases, but not necessarily murder.

I felt discouraged and relieved at the same time. There was just one more thing to check. I googled Dr. Sam Schultz, Judy's dad's doctor. Coincidently, I knew Sam from my years as the senior medical librarian at the university's health care center. I hoped that would make him agreeable to giving me some information. I called Sam's office number, got his voice mail and left a message. Sam returned my call around 9 p.m.

"I'm sorry to bother you, Sam. I'm a neighbor of Judy Enright, and she told me you were her dad's doctor. I was wondering if I could ask you a question."

"You know, Mieka, I can't give out patient information."

"Of course. But could you tell me if there will be an autopsy?" This was as close as I could come to telling him that I suspected something, and to find out if he did as well. I held my breath.

"There won't be one. I suggested it to Judy and her husband, but they declined. I thought it might be reassuring since his death was so sudden." There was a pregnant pause, then he added, "The circumstances *were* unusual. That's all I can say. I've probably said too much."

I thanked him, and we exchanged a few pleasantries about how I was enjoying retirement and how he would be doing the same in a few years. It was only after the call that I realized my Spidey sense was still working. But it gave me little comfort.

DAY TWO

Bright and early the next day, I took Ted to the nearby seniors' home for a visit. I was distracted. I couldn't stop thinking about Judy's situation but Ted, as always, was in top form. It was uncanny how he could intuit who wanted to pet him, who wanted to just look at him and who wanted to have nothing to do with him. It always amazed me.

We returned home just before lunch. Ted went bounding up the stairs as Ben's head appeared over the bannister.

"How was the visit?"

"You know how good Ted is." I took my jacket off. "Any calls?"

Ben knew what I meant. "Judy hasn't called, but Kate did. She sounded upset." He looked at me inquiringly.

"Probably the research she's doing."

Ben nodded knowingly. "If you need to discuss anything with me, you can. Oh, and I left BLTs in the fridge for you and Kate."

I felt a rush of gratitude. Ben was always there for me. He made sandwiches for my friends. And, most importantly, he wasn't trying to kill me.

***

I called Kate to ask her over. Then I called Judy to see how she was. The moment I hung up the phone, I heard the doorbell. Kate had arrived.

"How's Judy doing?"

"Much better. She's like a different person. It's such a relief."

We walked into the kitchen. Kate sat on a breakfast bar stool.

"She even bought a smartwatch online," I added.

Kate laughed. "If she's shopping, she's definitely feeling better!"

I retrieved the BLTs from the fridge, and placed one on the counter in front of Kate.

Kate took a sip of water but didn't reach for a sandwich. That was unusual.

"Ben said you seemed upset on the phone. What did you learn?" I asked.

"Riley didn't escape from the yard. Harry was walking him."

"So why did we think he escaped from the yard?"

"Judy told us that. Right?"

"And Harry must have told her. She wasn't around when it happened," I said.

"It would have been easy for Harry to dig a small hole under the fence. Make it look like Riley did it."

"Who told you what happened?"

"June Hubbard, who lives a block away. The woman who seldom goes out and seems to stare out the window all day."

"She didn't tell anyone when it happened?"

"Who would she tell? She lives alone and doesn't seem to have many visitors. Sad really." Kate took another sip of water. The sandwiches remained untouched.

"What did June say?"

Kate put her glass down. "That she saw Harry take the lead off Riley, then throw something into the street just before a car drove by."

"What!" I cried.

"Yeah, in broad daylight. Crazy risky."

"OMG! He thought he would get away with it?"

"Well this is suburbia and the neighborhood's pretty quiet on weekdays. And unless you knew about June…"

We sat in silence for a good minute before I said, "My research wasn't quite as conclusive." I told Kate what I'd found.

"So we don't have anything concrete to take to the police," she said.

"Except for Riley's death."

"Unfortunately, canine murder's not yet a major crime," Kate said, finally reaching for a sandwich.

"It should be. Maybe we can work on that," I said, grabbing one too.

"I thought I would never say this," Kate said between mouthfuls of sandwich, "and please don't ever quote me, but after this conversation, I'm looking forward to tonight's boring community meeting."

***

"What about the rapist?" The question came in the middle of a tedious discussion about recycling, raised by an older woman seated at the front. It had the effect of making everyone talk at once, and the noise was deafening. Since I was running that part of the meeting, I stood up and asked for quiet. Then I asked the woman for more details.

"My son's a policeman in Mississauga, and he tells me there's a rapist in the area. They're calling him the Lakeside Rapist."

The meeting quickly descended into noise and chaos again.

"The police have a duty to warn us about crimes like this," someone yelled from the back of the room.

"They have a nickname *already*, and they haven't told us about him?" yelled another.

"Please, if I can have everyone's attention," I shouted. The room became quiet. "Kate and I will phone the police tonight to find out more. As soon as we know something, we'll let you know. We're just as concerned as you are. That's all for tonight's meeting."

The noise in the gym slowly abated as people got up and left. Kate and I went over to the woman who had asked about the rapist to see if we could get more details. Unfortunately, she didn't have anything to add, so I asked her to provide me with contact info for herself and her son.

Kate and I walked out into the chilly night. "Well, Mieka, that sure was a boring way to end the day."

I started to laugh. Not in the fun ha-ha way, but in the hysterical won't-be-able-to-stop way.

"This whole day has been frigging bizarre," Kate continued. "Why didn't the police tell us about a rapist?"

"We're on the Peel/Halton border, so two different police forces. Likely a lack of communication," I said, "But they did have time to come up with a nickname for him."

"Maybe the Peel police just figured out today that they were dealing with a serial rapist, and a rookie cop wanted to make sure his mother knew," Kate replied.

"I'll call the Halton police when I get home. We need some answers."

"I agree. The sooner, the better."

As we approached my street, I could see flashing lights. *What now?* I wondered.

"There's an ambulance at Judy's house," Kate exclaimed, just as I spotted it.

The flashing lights lit up the darkness and were reflected off the glass and steel. I could see Judy being wheeled out of the house on a stretcher. She looked unconscious. Harry was at her side.

We both started running toward the ambulance.

"What the hell happened?" Kate demanded when we arrived. Harry looked up, a bit shocked by both the question and Kate's tone.

"She took too many sleeping pills. I found her in the bathtub."

The news sent shivers through me. Not about the suicide attempt, that was bad enough, but about the bath. Judy had a phobia about standing water. Her fear was so acute that she only showered. She wouldn't even go near swimming pools.

The attendant pushed the gurney into the ambulance and clicked it in place. Harry jumped up into the space beside her. Seeing that jolted me awake.

"I'm going to the hospital," I said.

"Best to come in the morning," Harry replied, "once she's awake."

As the paramedic opened the driver's door of the ambulance, I overheard her say to her colleague, "Wasn't it amazing that her smartwatch called 911? Saved her life. Technology's so awesome."

"Her smartwatch called 911? Can it do that, Kate?" I asked.

"I think so. One of the doctors I know has one. She passed out in the shower, and woke with paramedics there thanks to her watch. Embarrassed but grateful."

"Harry told us he found her, but he didn't. I don't think Judy's safe in the hospital."

"I agree," Kate replied. "Let's take shifts."

DAY THREE

Kate came into Judy's room at around 9 o'clock the next morning. Judy was still asleep.

"How is she?" Kate whispered.

I yawned and stretched. "She was awake on and off during the night," I whispered back.

"Did she say anything?"

"Nothing that was clear. She's still pretty groggy. She did say she doesn't think she took any pills, but can't be sure."

"Poor soul."

"She told me why she got a smartwatch," I said, squelching another yawn.

"Why?"

"Dr. Sam Schultz suggested it."

"Her dad's doctor. That's odd, right?"

"For sure. I think it's time to talk to the police."

***

Kate stayed with Judy while I went to the police station. I spoke to Detective Sergeant Stephanie Fryer. She listened patiently while I told her about Harry, Judy and my suspicions.

"I appreciate your concern, Mieka," she said when I'd finished, "but you don't have any solid evidence. Without that, we can't start an investigation. I'm sorry."

I had expected that, but still felt deflated and tired. As Detective Fryer handed me her card, I remembered the Lakeside Rapist, and asked her about it.

"Robocalls are going out today to warn people," she said as she escorted me to the door.

Walking to my car, I couldn't get Harry out of my mind. He was clever but a risk-taker. That was his weakness. And that was how we would get him.

***

Back at the hospital, I told Kate about my plan. At first, she refused to be involved. But soon she realized how few options we had now that the police were a no-go, so she agreed to help. On one condition: Ben had to be on board.

Before we left the hospital, we called friends to take turns sitting with Judy. When the first one arrived, we headed over to my place. The plan had to be tight and, given how little sleep the two of us had had in the past 24 hours, there was no certainty it wouldn't have some holes.

***

It was really late when I went to see Harry. By then I had managed to get a few hours of sleep so I was feeling sort of OK. Not crackerjack, but OK. I had loaded a recording app onto my iPhone, and checked three times before leaving home that it was recording. I had my jogging shoes on just in case a quick getaway was required. I had some doubts about my plan, and hoped it would not prove conclusively that I was too stupid to live.

Harry looked surprised when he opened the door. "It's you."

"Expecting someone else?" I said flippantly. "Can I come in?"

"What are you doing here? Where's Ben?"

"He left for a golfing trip today. I just got back from the hospital and thought I would see how you were doing."

"Oh." He sounded surprised. "Well, come in."

As we walked through the house to the family room, he became the perfect host. "Do you want a drink?"

"Sure."

"Wine, whiskey, gin, beer?"

"Whatever you're having."

He picked up a glass from the coffee table and said, "Whiskey it is." He headed to the kitchen.

He's been drinking. Good, I thought. I needed every advantage I could get.

"Judy seems much better," I said, sitting down. I placed my phone on the coffee table face down.

"You've been such a good friend to her," he said, setting the drink in front of me. "Thanks for that." He was good at sounding sincere.

I decided to get to the point. "Amazing how Judy's smartwatch called 911."

"I'm so glad it did. I was in the garage working on my new car. Didn't think to check on her since she seemed to be feeling better. Depression can be tricky."

It was a medical diagnosis that would let him get away with murder. I kept talking, hoping to goad him into dropping his mask.

"Weird about the water, wasn't it?" I said. "She has a standing water phobia, right?" I took a sip of my drink, thought better of it, and immediately put it back down.

"Yeah, I was surprised by that, too. Didn't make any sense, but then with her disease..."

So that would be his mantra when she died. Her disease.

"It's been an unlucky time since you married Judy. Her sister, then her dad."

"Yeah, it's been a rocky time."

"And there's Riley, too."

He looked at me with interest. "Too bad he got out of the yard."

"A neighbor seems to think you were walking him that day."

He shifted slightly in his seat, but his voice was casual. "I wasn't even home. I was at a car rally. Judy walked him. When she wears my green hoodie, we look alike."

It was true that Judy sometimes wore his hoodie. And she did look like him from behind with the hoodie up. Had I been looking at this the wrong way? I quickly tried to rearrange the facts to put Judy at the center. Judy as the killer. Had she been setting up her husband? Was Judy the one who killed her dad and her sister? Means, motive and opportunity. Did she want all of her dad's money? But what about Riley? Why make it look like Harry killed Riley? That made no sense.

"And what about your friend Kate?" Harry said with a smirk. "Do you think you can trust her? I love her nickname for me, by the way."

My mind was scrambling. Kate? Had I been so focused on righting wrongs that I missed what was really going on. The world felt like it was spinning. Kate had been so eager to go along with all of my ideas. Was the Riley information wrong? Did I have any correct information? Then it hit me: I was in deep trouble. Kate knew the plan.

Suddenly Harry was standing in front of me. My heart was pounding. *Don't listen to what they say, watch what they do.* He calmly picked up my phone, turned it over and turned off the recording app.

"I think we're done here," he said calmly. Too calmly. I had all but accused him of murder. Two murders. What was *his* plan?

I grabbed my phone and got up, leaning into the furniture to avoid getting near him. He seemed to enjoy my fear. As I walked rapidly to the door, I could hear him behind me. *Please be open, please be open,* I said to myself all the way down the hall.

I swung open the front door and started power walking. I could hear Harry rummaging in the coat closet. What was he doing?

I started striding down the drive. My heart was racing. The street was silent and dark. Would people hear me if I screamed? The news of a rapist in the area was keeping people indoors. And this was suburbia; everyone would be streaming TV shows in their family rooms.

I couldn't hear anything behind me, so I turned to look. Big mistake. Harry barreled out of the house carrying a package and wearing a balaclava. *Don't listen to what they say, watch what they do.*

Adrenaline kicked in. I starting running full-out. The frontages seemed endless. Just two more houses. Harry was gaining. I could hear his breathing and his footfalls.

"You are going to regret this. No one plays me and gets away with it," he called out.

He was getting closer. Too close. I could feel his breath on my back. I spun into our neighbor's driveway and ran full speed. I reached the garage doors and kept going through the gate to their backyard. I felt Harry grab my shoulder, making me stumble. *Oh no, oh no!*

I used my last bit of strength and adrenaline to straighten myself up and leap to the right. I slammed into a wooden fence. I felt the air whoosh behind me and heard a *thud*. Like a heavyweight falling on wet mud.

I clung to the fence, my feet balanced precariously on a ledge, and my fingers barely catching purchase through the lattice. I felt strong hands grab my shoulders and secure me.

"Are you OK?" Ben whispered from the other side of the fence. I could hear feet pounding on the driveway. I turned my head. Kate stood in the gateway, looking relieved to see me. I was ecstatic to see her.

"That was very close," she whispered, even though the neighbors weren't home. They were returning the next day from a golf tournament.

My breathing slowed and I relaxed. The plan had worked.

Kate shone her flashlight into the pit and I looked over my shoulder. Harry, with the balaclava still covering his face, lay impaled on the metal stakes at the bottom. It was a gruesome sight.

With Ben's help, I climbed carefully over the fence into our backyard. Kate headed home. None of us knew what the next day would bring. All we knew was that Judy was safe.

DAY FOUR

Our neighbors pulled into their drive at around 10 the next morning. Thirty minutes later, two Halton Regional Police vehicles pulled up, followed by an ambulance. No lights or sirens. Our phone started ringing around 11:30. Phone call after phone call from neighbors.

"Did you hear? Harry's dead. And right beside your house!"

"Fell into the hole on your neighbor's property. You were right about that hole—an accident waiting to happen. Don't know how they could leave it open like that."

"I feel bad for Judy. So much loss in such a short period of time."

***

In the early afternoon, Kate and I headed to the hospital to be with Judy. As we arrived, Detective Fryer was coming out of her room. The detective saw me and stopped. "Can we speak privately?"

I tried to look relaxed. Kate eyed me nervously before disappearing into Judy's room.

"I want to apologize for dismissing your concerns yesterday," Detective Fryer said. "Harry Enright did need looking into."

"Why do you say that?"

"We found him at your neighbors' place—in the large hole. You probably saw us there. We think he may have been coming for you. Did you tell him you went to the police?"

"No, I didn't."

"OK, good. This is still confidential, but we found Harry with a pack containing the items we associate with the Lakeside Rapist."

My knees went weak. I leaned against the wall. I had told Harry that Ben was away.

"Are you OK?" she asked.

I straightened up. "Yeah, I'm fine, just tired. Have you told Judy?"

"Just that her husband is dead. We'll wait with the other news until she is out of the hospital."

"OK, thanks for telling me."

I walked into the room to find Kate sitting by the bed, holding Judy's hand. Judy looked surprisingly well.

"How are you doing?" I asked.

Judy looked from me to Kate. "Is it awful to say I'm relieved?"

Kate and I exchanged glances.

"What do you mean, Judy?" Kate asked.

"I don't know if I should say." She pulled her hands away from Kate and looked at the window.

"Do you feel safer?" I asked, hoping she did.

"Yes, much safer."

"Did you think Harry was going to hurt you?" Kate asked.

"Yes," Judy said, looking down at her hands. "I finally confronted him. About the deaths in my family, and about his going out in the middle of the night. It was the day I…" Judy hesitated.

"The day you came to the hospital," I finished for her.

"Yes. I told Harry I saw him standing by Dad's IV when I returned to the room. Just before I found Dad dead and called the nurses. I asked him what he did to Dad."

"What did he say?" Kate asked.

Judy took a deep breath. "That I was confused from being on all those meds for my illness. He wanted me to think I was crazy. Like I couldn't remember things. He made me feel the same way when money went missing from our joint account." She looked up at us. "But the two of you taking shifts to be here with me, that's what made me realize I wasn't crazy."

"Oh, Judy, it must have been so awful," Kate said sympathetically.

Judy continued talking as if she hadn't heard Kate. "And then there was Claire's death. The doctors were puzzled when she died. Just like with Dad. Claire had been doing so well. She was on new meds that were working beautifully. She was herself for the first time in four years. And just when I got her back, I lost her again."

Tears rolled down Judy's cheeks and she wiped them away with the back of her hand. "I'm sorry. I really have been feeling so much better here. Better than I have in a while."

"So you think Harry was involved in Claire's death?" I said.

"Yes, but I don't have absolute proof. Harry was always too smart for that. There were too many odd things. The afternoon Claire died, Dad was out. Claire went up to her bedroom after lunch and I went to watch TV in the media room. I passed out for four hours, something I never do. I woke up to the sound of police in the house."

"So Harry made sure he was alone with Claire that afternoon?" Kate asked.

"That's what I think," Judy replied. "And her overdosing on opioids was strange too. Claire never took that kind of drug. I am positive about that. Harry, on the other hand, had a lot of friends who used them."

We sat in silence for a few minutes. I had been keen to ask Judy about something she had said earlier, and now was my chance. "What did Harry say about his late-night activity when you confronted him?"

"That he was working on his car. Or rather cars. But I know for a fact he was leaving the house. Our security system *dings* when a door opens. I heard it *ding* twice—going and coming—since I'm a light sleeper. This has been going on for a long time."

Kate and I sat with Judy throughout the long afternoon. We knew she would soon find out exactly what Harry had been up to late at night. It would be difficult for her, but we would be there to see her through.

Finally, we said our goodbyes, telling Judy we would be back the following day. We silently walked to the hospital parking garage. It had been a long four days, and we had done what had to be done.

It had been worth it. The neighborhood was safe again.

Ω

THE RED CORD

Rob McCartney

Rob McCartney's interest in crime fiction stems from his days as a reporter covering the police beat at The Sun Times *daily newspaper in Owen Sound, Ontario.*

Rob has studied novel, screenplay, TV and comedy writing through various workshops at George Brown College, Raindance Canada, The Second City *and Start Writing in Toronto. He is also a graduate from* The Second City *improvisation program. "The Red Cord" is his first published short story and he dedicates it to his friend, Fi. He is working on his first crime novel,* Bury the Lede, *set in Toronto.*

For the life of me, I can't remember where I left my gold earrings. The ones Arthur gave me for our 25th anniversary. Shaped like dolphins jumping out of the water, they remind me of our annual winter pilgrimages to Anna Maria Island in Florida. That seems so long ago.

I hope Arthur visits me today. One of the ladies who works here and wears a dowdy pink polyester pantsuit tells me he comes every afternoon at 3 p.m., but I don't think that's true. I'd remember if he did. I'm ticked off with him these days. I think he's fooling around with another woman while I sit in this hotel room. I don't understand why I'm even here.

Arthur finally shows up in my doorway and sings out a chirpy *hello*. It's about time! I was worried sick, and I let him know immediately. He just leans over my wheelchair and gently kisses my forehead. How romantic! If he thinks that's gonna let him off the hook, he's got another think coming.

"Is it cold outside?" I ask.

Arthur stomps his feet like a giant. "It certainly is," he says. "Just look out your window."

I look out the big window, and I see that it's snowing. Flakes are covering the tall pine tree just beyond my window. It looks pretty, but I don't understand why it's snowing at this time of year. It's July, after all. If it really was winter, we'd be on the beach at Anna Maria.

"Arthur, I can't find my gold earrings," I say. "The ones you gave me for our 25th."

He goes over to the jewelry box I keep on my dresser. He pulls out a variety of gold and silver chains, a purple broach and several pairs of earrings, some loops and others studs.

"I don't see your gold earrings in here, honey," he says gently. "Are you sure you put them in here?"

"I dunno." I shoot him a dirty look. I'm annoyed that he's insinuating I did something with the earrings. I hate it when he does that.

Arthur starts rifling through my dresser drawers, lifting out panties I rarely wear. (I wear diapers now. Isn't that silly?) He pulls out sweaters and runs his hand along the inside of one of the dresser drawers.

"What the hell are you doing?" I ask.

"I'm looking for your gold earrings, dear," he tells me. The next thing I know, he's bent over fishing through my plastic wastebasket. The basket is mostly full of snotty old tissues.

Arthur stands up and sighs. "Damn it, I can't find them anywhere."

"Find what?" I ask.

"Your gold earrings, dear. I'm looking for your gold earrings."

I don't know what the hell he's talking about. "What gold earrings?"

"Honey, the gold earrings I bought you for our 25th. I knew I should have taken them home."

He seems annoyed, but he changes the topic. "Did you do your exercises this morning?"

"What exercises?" I don't remember doing any exercises. "Where the hell have you been, anyway? You're late."

"No sweetie. I come every day at 3 p.m."

I give him the cold shoulder. He looks nervous, and he should be. I dunno why the hell he put me in this place and why I can't go home. He tries to explain it to me but it sounds like a bunch of

malarkey. I wheel over to my dresser and start taking swe
the top drawer and putting them on my bed.

"What are you doing, dear?" Arthur asks.

"What does it look like I'm doing? I'm packing. I'm
staying here any longer."

"No, Lu, you're safe here and you can get all the help you
need. I can't take care of you at home by myself. If you fell, I
wouldn't be able to lift you back up. And if something happened to
me, you'd be up the creek."

I have to go to the washroom.

"Pull the red cord," he tells me.

"What red cord?"

"There's a red cord beside the toilet. There's another one
beside your bed. Just remember, *pull the red cord*, and one of the
personal support workers will come and help you."

"I don't need any help."

"Yes, Lu, I'm afraid you do need some help."

"I don't want to bother them." I have no intention of pulling a
cord and bugging busy people.

Arthur finally walks over to my bed and pulls the red cord
that is hanging down the wall with the bottom end clipped to my
pillow. I hear *beep, beep, beep* outside my door. I really have to go
the bathroom.

A young lady in a pink suit comes into the room.

"Hello, Lu. You have to go the washroom, hon?" she asks.

I nod, and she wheels me into the bathroom and closes the
door. When I come back out, Arthur is going through all my
drawers.

"What the hell are you doing?" I ask.

He looks at the young lady and says, "We can't find her gold
earrings. They're shaped like dolphins."

"Oh, no," she says. "We'll keep our eyes open for them and
tell the room cleaner. Patients sometimes get confused and, well,
take things."

She puts the brake on my wheelchair. "We told you it would
be better if you kept your wife's jewelry at home," she says to
Arthur.

"Lu insists on having it with her," Arthur explains.

"That's right," I say. "I can take care of my own damn
jewelry!"

The pink lady leaves, and Arthur slumps into the yellow
armchair in the corner of the room. "D'you want to go down to the
lobby for a coffee?" he asks.

I don't know what the hell he's talking about, but I say yes, as long as he pushes me there. He takes me to an elevator, and we ride downstairs. When we get there, I'm surprised to see that this lobby has a lounge with tables and chairs, and a woman working behind a counter. She must be the bartender.

"Do you want a coffee and a cookie?" Arthur asks.

"I'd like a gin and tonic," I say.

"I'm sorry, dear, they don't serve alcohol here, but wouldn't a coffee be nice?"

What kind of cheapskate hotel has Arthur put me in? I shrug and nod, and he goes over to the counter. I think he's flirting with that lady. She's smiling at him like a crocodile at an ibis. It makes me angry as hell.

There's an old bag sitting at the table next to me who smells of baby poop. Arthur returns with coffees in brown paper cups. He sits beside me and puts an arm around my shoulder. The coffee is bitter, and I tell Arthur to get me more sugar. He should know better. Honestly.

He pours a packet of sugar into my coffee and mixes it up with a plastic stir stick. He sits back down and taps his fingers on the table. We just sit there sipping our coffee, saying nothing.

I'm worried that I'll miss dinner, so I tell Arthur to take me back to the room.

"We've got lots of time, sweetie," he says.

"I want to go now. I have to be ready for when they come and get me."

***

Dinner is boneless pork riblets, but mine are all mashed up like stew. I pick at that and a ball of mashed potatoes. There's also some Brussels sprouts, but I don't like them. After dinner, one of the ladies wheels me down a hallway and into a room with photographs on the walls. They're pictures of Arthur, my son and daughter, and some young kids. They must be my grandchildren. I'll have to ask Arthur about them.

"OK, Lu, time to get ready for bed," the girl says. She holds up two sets of pajamas. "Do you want the green ones or the gray ones tonight?"

I point to the gray ones, and she starts pulling off my sweater and pants. I scooch into the pajama bottoms, and she lifts me slightly to get them past my bum. She lifts me gently out of the wheelchair and sits me on the bed. She must think I'm like a bag of flour that might explode if I'm not handled with care. She swivels my feet up onto the bed so that I'm on my back, and she pulls the blankets up to my neck.

"Where's Arthur?" I ask.

"He's gone home for the night, Lu, but he'll be back to see you tomorrow."

I don't know why Arthur won't sleep with me in here. He says he's not allowed, but I think he's just full of baloney.

***

Something wakes me in the night—a *thump*. It's dark in the hotel room, but I see a silhouette beside my dresser. I'm scared, so I lay still and pretend I'm asleep. I hear a funny sound, like a mouse scurrying around in my jewelry box. After a while, the shadow retreats back out my door. I hear the door click shut. I'll have to mention this to the ladies tomorrow. I'm frightened, but I fall back to sleep. I'm old. I'm tired.

***

Arthur is helping me play Bingo because my hands don't work so good. But we aren't winning anything. We finish the last game. I needed a B-14 to win, but I didn't get it. Arthur pushes me back to a room where I must be staying.

"What time is it?" I want to know.

"It's 4:30," Arthur says. "Let me get your watch and we'll put it on your wrist."

Arthur starts fumbling through my jewelry box while I look out my window, watching cars and trucks zipping along the highway. Arthur groans.

"What is it?" I ask.

"I can't find your watch."

"Check in my purse."

He picks my purse off the floor and sits down, placing it on his lap. He unzips it and shuffles stuff around. He pulls out a brush, a comb, some lip balm and my change purse.

"It's not in here," he says.

"What's not in there?"

"Your watch," he mumbles. He starts rooting through my wastebasket, opens dresser drawers and even looks under the bed.

Arthur looks perturbed and worried. He turns on the television set, and we start watching *Ellen*. One of the gals in pink comes into the room. "Time for your medication, Lu," she says. She sticks a spoon of apple sauce in my mouth and hands me a small plastic cup with a chocolate protein drink and a bendy straw.

"Drink that up, Lu," she says. "We'll be by shortly to take you to dinner."

Arthur stretches and says, "Guess I'll get going."

"Aren't you staying for dinner?" I ask, miffed.

"Luanne, I stay for dinner every Saturday night and today is only Friday."

He kisses me on the forehead and hugs me gently so I don't snap in two.

"Fine," I bark. "If you're going, go already."

Dinner is goulash. It's soggy, but I eat a good bit of it, and I wash it down with cranberry juice. One of the ladies takes off my bib and wheels me back to my hotel room. She leaves me there. Later, she is back to help me get into my pajamas. She gets me into bed and turns off the light.

"Sweet dreams, Lu," she whispers.

***

I'm dreaming about Arthur running around with another woman, but I wake up when I hear my door click open. I open one eye and see a big shadow moving in the darkness. I listen as something scratches around over by my dresser. I'm afraid, and I try not to move.

From somewhere in my mind, an idea pops up: *Pull the red cord, pull the red cord.*

I slowly reach my left arm above my head and fish around in the dark for the red cord. I fumble about until I touch the plastic strip. I grab it and tug it hard. It makes a clicking sound, and the shadow freezes. I hear *beep, beep, beep* outside.

I hear the door open, and a sliver of light enters my room.

"Stevie, what were you doing in Lu's room?" a lady asks in the hallway.

"Just checking to see if she was asleep," a male voice replies.

"What do you have in your hand, Stevie?" she asks.

"Oh, nothing…"

"Open your hand."

"No, it's nothing, really."

"Give it here," she says. "Oh, Stevie, how could you?"

I don't know who Stevie is or what he has in his hand, but I get the feeling he's in trouble. Then I hear a second lady's voice. "I'll check on Lu," she says.

The lights in my room go on and hurt my eyes. "Lu, you pulled the cord! That was great! Are you OK?"

"I'm fine," I say. Then I must have fallen back to sleep.

***

It's Saturday and Arthur arrives at 4 o'clock. He's late, but he's also staying longer so we can eat dinner together in the dining room. He's all smiles today, and he's holding something in his hand.

"Look, Lu! Your gold earrings, your watch, and a broach," he says. "We found them."

He pulls the chair up in front of me and grabs the wheels of my wheelchair. "I'm sorry I doubted you, honey. Someone was sneaking into your room and stealing your jewelry, but they caught him. Found all your stuff in his locker. And he doesn't work here anymore."

Arthur leans toward me. "Turn your head to the side, Lu," he says. He grabs my earlobe and feeds an earring into it. I turn my head the other way and he puts in the other earring.

"Hold up your wrist," he says.

I hold up my wrist, and Arthur straps on my gold watch. I ask him to push me to the bathroom door so I can go inside and put on some lipstick. I don't want to go out on a date without lipstick.

"Do you want to use the toilet before we head out, honey?" Arthur asks.

"Yes," I say. I wheel myself into the washroom and pull the red cord.

Ω

HYPOCHONDRIACS NEVER GET THIS

Kevin P. Thornton

Kevin P. Thornton was born in Kenya, and has lived or worked in New Zealand, Namibia, South Africa, Swaziland, England, Dubai, Afghanistan, Ontario and now Northern Alberta. He has been a soldier, a rugby player, a contractor for the Canadian military, a logistics consultant, a columnist and writer, and a magazine editor.

A seven-time finalist for the Arthur Ellis Crime Writers of Canada awards, his short stories and poetry have appeared in several publications. He is a member or former member of most crime writing organizations, and is also a member of the KEYS, the writers group founded by Ronald Knox and G.K. Chesterton.

Enock Powlle was driving his wife, Portia, mad, as he procrastinated from writing his next opus. He hadn't had a book published in nearly three years, and that one had gone from the publisher to the remainder bin at warp speed. In truth, he didn't really want to write crime fiction anymore. What he wanted was to be a crime solver, here in Fort Clearwater, the gleaming armpit of Alberta. He hoped the phone would ring and he would be transported away to a jolly good murder, which did happen on occasion.

The phone was silent. Enock rustled into the kitchen, trying to sound busy as he walked.

"Here, read this," he said to Portia. "Tell me what you think."

Portia suppressed a sigh. She had been married to a writer long enough to realize that "Here, read this" meant *please praise me*, and "Tell me what you think" was code for *please praise me to the highest heavens.* She took the page from Enock and looked it over. It didn't take long.

> Project for the Fort Clearwater Heritage Society's Bingo and Taffy Pull, celebrating the 120th anniversary of the community.
>
> Fort Clearwater is an anomaly. An ore-mining town in a land of oil, it is 150 miles northwest of Fort McMurray on the edge of the Athabasca Oil Sands. On the same latitude but 31 miles west of Fort Chipewyan, it came into being as an accidental offshoot of the Klondike mining frenzy of 1896. Unlike the Cree and Dene nations farther east who found fresh water, good hunting and a comfortable life on the shores of Lake Athabasca, the 13 families who laid claim to Fort Clearwater at the turn of the 20th century, did so because they discovered gold. This made their lives richer, but not necessarily better.

"It's a bit short," said Portia, trying to find something positive to say. "Incomplete even. How many words do they want?"

"About 5,000."

"Due?" she asked, sounding like a teacher who wished corporal punishment was still on the table.

"Er, yesterday."

"Enock. Madeleine Burfield-Murphy is my cousin, as well as the treasurer of the Founding Families Fellowship. I'll never hear the end of it if you don't finish this job."

"Madeleine Burfy-Murphy is an evil woman who does not deserve my work."

"Except she paid you in advance didn't she?" said Portia. "So in fact she does. What are you going to do?"

At which point the phone rang and Enock snatched it up. He listened, did a little dance, said, "Of course I am," and hung up.

"What am I going to do? I am going to solve a murder. Sergeant Ramsbottom is on his way."

"Well, do try and be home for supper. It's chicken parm, and you know you don't like it if it's dried up." But she said this to an empty room.

***

Enock was a much better amateur detective in his head than in reality. He had only one fan of his investigative prowess, Inspector Maffini, who was in command of the Fort Clearwater Royal Canadian Mounted Police outpost. Maffini had delusions of literary, criminous pretension. He involved the town's formerly famous crime writer in investigations because it made him happy. Maffini thought of the two of them as a detecting duo. Maffini & Powlle. Like Holmes and Watson; or Spenser and Hawk.

"Maybe Batman and Robin," he mused, "or Lewis and Morse."

He finally settled on his ideal pairing. "Walt Longmire and Henry Standing Bear."

The thought satisfied him. Maffini had never actually read any of Craig Johnson's books, but he owned the DVDs of the television show and he felt there were distinct similarities. In this he allowed himself a break from reality. Robert Taylor, the actor who played Longmire, was tall, rangy and Australian, while Maffini was short, walked with a waddle, and Canadian. Enock Powlle had nothing of the haunting handsomeness of Lou Diamond Philips; instead he had the pasty look of a chinless WASP. As a detecting team, they left a lot to be desired. Although Powlle's fleeting glimpse of fame had been in the mystery-suspense genre, it had fluttered by on the winds of whimsy because his books had been neither suspenseful nor mysterious. Inspector Maffini was alone in his awe of Enock Powlle's fame as a writer. Despite this, Maffini's fanciful dreams meant that Enock was invited to peruse the occasional crime scene and voice his multitudinous opinions. Not to the inspector, mind, who had never seen an investigation he wanted to work. No, Inspector Maffini left such exertions to his underlings. Powlle was almost always foisted onto Sergeant Hector Hugh Munro Ramsbottom.

This did not make Ramsbottom's life easy. He was the senior and only investigator of the unit, the outpost, the community and indeed the entire area in a 31-mile radius. He was often stuck with Enock because, although Inspector Maffini liked the idea of a writerly sleuth attached to the team, he didn't like it enough to go to an actual crime scene with Powlle and put up with him as Sergeant Ramsbottom did.

"Take Enock with you," he would tell Ramsbottom, "he has good eyes." Generally, this instruction would be given over his shoulder as the inspector rushed off to a civic function at the hotel where the Rotarians met, or to a presentation lunch at the golf club, both of which had generous and well-stocked bars.

Still, Ramsbottom put up with Powlle because it meant he would be allowed to run his investigations as he saw fit. It was a price he was willing to pay.

But dear Lord, Powlle could babble on like a convention of PR consultants and make just as much sense. It was he who had been so convinced that a stab wound was the result of a fantastical gun that could shoot blades 40 yards across a back garden, all the while not noticing the blood under the wife's nails and discounting the kitchen knife in the dishwasher that matched her wounds. It was also Enock Powlle who had proclaimed all of his last four forays into the field to be locked-room murders. One had indeed been a murder, but in a room without a door. The other three had been an assault in a public park, a robbery in front of seven witnesses, and a complicated fraud that had largely taken place on the internet.

Honestly, if Sergeant Ramsbottom never heard the phrase locked-room murder again in his life, it would still be too soon.

But there was also that one occasion in which Powlle's encyclopedic knowledge of arcane mystery plots had helped to solve a murder and put a killer in jail. Who else would have known that dry ice could be a murder weapon?

***

Powlle was vibrating with excitement as he climbed into Ramsbottom's truck. The sergeant sighed. Powlle was like a beagle, constantly quivering in anticipation of the next morsel of food.

"What do we got?" he said, and Ramsbottom winced at his grammatical insouciance.

"What we have," he said, "is the late Bert MacDonald. He lives, lived rather, with his niece, Gina, and when he didn't come down from his study for breakfast, she tried his door, then called us."

"And?" asked Powlle, who was polishing the passenger seat as he wriggled in excitement. "We have another one, don't we? Oh, say it, say it, sayitsayitsayit SAY IT!"

"We have what appears to be a locked-room mystery," said Ramsbottom, already regretting his decision to get up that morning.

"Bert MacDonald was the last survivor of the second generation of the Thirteen Families, the founders of Fort Clearwater," said Powlle, as Ramsbottom drove up the hill to where all the old money lived. "He must have been nearly 90."

"91," said Ramsbottom.

"Thank you," said Powlle. "He was one of the profligate children of the original gold miners, and his hobbies included expensive whiskey, fast cars and tawdry women who helped him achieve a life of excess." Powlle looked at his phone and continued. "About 30 years ago he had a come-to-Jesus moment when he went from living fast to wanting to live forever. Since then he has been to every specialist, quack, loony medical charlatan and nouveau treatment center in the entire western world. I wouldn't be at all surprised if he had a cryogenics setup in his basement." He clicked off his phone and put it away.

"You have access to a lot of information," said Ramsbottom. "I looked him up before I left and I didn't see a quarter of that on Google."

"It's from Portia, for an article I'm writing about the history of Fort Clearwater. Her family, the Powlles, are one of the Thirteen."

"So when you married Portia, you took her name?" said Ramsbottom.

"It seemed to be an appropriate defiance against the conjugal slavery that men have forced on woman over the centuries."

"That was indeed very noble of you," said Ramsbottom.

"That, and my last name was Stittsenfahrts."

"German," said Ramsbottom.

"And difficult, growing up. I became Fits-and-starts in the first grade, which wasn't too horrendous, given what came next. By fifth grade, I'd become Shits-and-farts, then it was just Shits. That stuck with me and I couldn't make it go away. Imagine, my prom date called me that all evening because, like the rest of them, she didn't know my real name."

For the first time, Ramsbottom saw Enock Powlle as more than just a burden, and he felt for him.

"I, too, am cursed by my name."

"Hector Hugh Munro? All that shows is your parents had good taste in short stories."

"Thank you," said the sergeant, "but I was referring to Ramsbottom. It is most unfortunate, given my lifestyle."

"I don't understand," said Powlle.

"I'm gay."

It took a moment, then Powlle hooted with laughter. It was such a contagious sound that the sergeant joined in.

Eventually they stopped and Powlle, wiping his eyes, said "Oh, boy, what a pair of detectives. Stittsenfahrts and Ramsbottom. I don't see a TV series in it anywhere."

"That's because you're saying it wrong," said the sergeant. "It works better as Ramsbottom and Stittsenfahrts."

It was another five minutes before they stopped laughing.

***

Constable Alison Campbell was leaning against her cruiser writing up her notes when they arrived. She walked into the house with them. It was a modern, ungainly McMansion that might as well have had a plaque by the door that proclaimed: "We built this because we are rich and tasteless."

"The deceased's niece called us when she couldn't get an answer from her uncle," said Campbell. "She didn't want to kick the door in because Bert had a temper."

"I see you had no such worries," said Ramsbottom, looking with approval at the study entrance. The door hung off its hinges and partially obscured the opening. "Tell me what you found."

"Bert, Mr. MacDonald, was sitting at his desk in front of his laptop, with his head slumped forward. Pending the coroner, who is on his way, it looks like a natural enough death. There is no evidence of an assault, no visible damage to his body, nothing appears to be taken. The windows are closed and latched, and I looked around outside. The gardens and flower beds are undisturbed, so there appears to be no entry or egress. And then there is the door itself. There is a deadbolt which locks from within the room as well as out, and a drop lock from the inside which Ms. MacDonald said he always engaged." Constable Campbell paused. "It appeared he liked his security."

"Which you think is suspicious," said Enock. "You are not alone. Now, when you entered the room was there a smell of almonds? Strychnine? Neurotoxins?"

"Nothing like that Mr. Powlle," said Campbell. She wasn't too sure what a neurotoxin was or whether it had a smell, and she didn't really want to find out.

"Thank you," said Ramsbottom. He wanted to keep Powlle upstairs away from the witness, but that wouldn't be fair to the constable, who was relatively new in her role. Also there had been constant warnings from Staff Sergeant Mel Bruce, the last of which had been, "I don't care what deal you have made with the inspector. I'll not have civilians involved with my police. If you have to have Powlle traipsing along, at least keep that corkwit away from my uniformed officers."

As Bruce was also a Methodist lay minister in her off-hours, the dual derogatory had borne much emphasis.

Sighing, he signaled to Powlle to follow him. "Constable, carry on your investigation up here," he said. "I'll go and talk to Ms. MacDonald."

***

"To be honest, I've been expecting this for a while." Gina MacDonald sat at the kitchen table drinking expensive-smelling coffee without offering any to them. "The old bugger was 90 and apoplectic at least twice a day. He'd had heart troubles for years."

"Ninety-one," said Ramsbottom. "What medication did he take?"

"I think the question should be what did he not take?" She pulled over a pill box the size of a safety deposit box and opened the lid. There were 12 compartments per level, each holding an assortment of pills.

"Is that for the week?" said Ramsbottom.

"Each tray is for a day. I used to make this up for him, and he'd take it into his office with a carafe of water."

"Did he take them all?"

"I assume so. The tray was always empty in the evening, and he was quite structured about his health."

"Structured?" asked Powlle.

"Rigid. Bert MacDonald went from being a wild, carousing man to someone who never did a spontaneous thing. His medications ruled his day. I swear the man was trying to live forever."

"Quite," said Ramsbottom, not following how that was linked to Bert's death. "Could you please explain exactly what you mean?"

Gina MacDonald sighed and pushed a strand of loose dark hair back from her face. She was in her early 40s and looked as if life had passed her by. Ramsbottom sensed a sadness in her, and he thought she looked like a sexy librarian, albeit one about to shush the room.

"Bert was an eternal bachelor. He never settled down, never married, was always looking for the next thrill, following the in-crowd to St. Tropez, the Alps, the Caymans. He was in a party of skiers when one of those famous people died, I can't remember which one."

"Natasha Richardson?" Powlle asked.

"No."

"Sonny Bono?"

'No.'

"Michael Kennedy?"

"No."

"Michel Trudeau?"

"No, and hush your mouth. We don't mention the T word in Alberta. It was some foreign royalty. The Count of Monte Cristo, the Duke of Plaza-Toro, some such."

Powlle had more questions, but Ramsbottom shook his head. Apart from displaying a disturbing knowledge of famous dead skiers, his line of questioning had not been helpful.

"How did the death affect him?"

"He was much shaken by it. Apparently, it was a close call for him as well and he nearly died with his friend. He damaged his heart somehow, and was in the hospital for quite some time. I remember having to make him a get-well card at school, fourth grade, I think. When he finally came home, that was the start of his strict medical regimen."

"I heard it was an obsession," said Powlle.

"It was more than that. He thought that conventional medicine wasn't answering all his questions, so he followed every alternative health regime he could find. There were many and he had lots of money, always a serendipitous pairing." She pointed at the pill trays. "I don't even know what this stuff is. He gave them to me in bags with labels attached for scheduling them. Some of them smell and looked a bit dodgy. At least two came from Africa by mail."

"He seemed very security conscious," said Ramsbottom. "His study is very…locked-up."

"You noticed, did you?" said Gina. "I wish he'd treated his paranoia first instead of all his other ailments." The way she said the last left it hanging, and Sergeant Ramsbottom let it hang. He knew that an awkward silence sometimes produces interesting answers.

Sadly, Enock Powlle did not seem to know this.

"Do you think he was a hypochondriac?" Powlle asked. "They're often paranoid, aren't they? They'd have to be because hypochondria is such a silly thing."

Sergeant Ramsbottom repressed the urge to ease the tension from his shoulders by beating the blabbering writer. It was no wonder his books didn't sell; the man didn't have the slightest idea of how to build tension.

"How did you happen to work for your uncle, Ms. MacDonald?"

"I used to work at the mine, but it was only part-time. I left to write for the newspaper. That doesn't pay much, so about 10 years ago when Uncle Bert needed some help, I came over."

"So it was a paid position," said Ramsbottom.

"It was more like indentured labor. He paid little and expected a lot." She paused for a second. "Look, I may as well tell you. There was no love lost between the two of us, but that wasn't uncommon. Bert MacDonald was a miserable man. Miserly, niggardly, and just downright mean. There was a joke some years back when the theatre group did Dickens' A *Christmas Carol*. They said he'd have been perfect for the part of Ebenezer Scrooge, up to the point where Scrooge recants. Bert wasn't that good an actor."

Gina MacDonald smiled a little, a wan smile, lacking in warmth. "Nobody liked him, and I only stayed on because he was family. He was so cantankerous nobody else would see to him."

"What do you know about his will?" Ramsbottom asked.

"It's the other reason I stuck it out. He promised he'd look after me."

"Do you know what he left you?" Powlle asked.

"That depends on how cranky he was feeling. For all I've put up with, it had better be a lot."

As they went back upstairs Powlle said, "Poor Gina. She should have moved on with her life."

"Maybe she will now."

***

Constable Campbell had been busy. The study was notable for its lack of bookshelves, a waste of good wall space in Powlle's opinion. However, Campbell had found the keys to a cabinet under the window and had just finished emptying it onto the desk.

"Look at this," she said. The book titles varied, but all were on a theme. Among them were *Overcoming Health Anxiety; Hypochondria – Woe is me; Hypochondria – the only ailment I do not have*; and *F**K Anxiety*.

Powlle did a little dance. "Nailed it," he said. "I told you he was a hypo."

Powlle looked through the books and pondered the last title. Did the asterisks help the sales? Did pious people feel safer or was it a false front, like pasties in a strip club? Did people look at a book title like *F**k Anxiety* and think, "It's not swearing, there are asterisks," just like, "She's not naked, she's wearing pasties?"

Powlle felt himself drifting off on a flight of fancy, and reluctantly pulled himself back. There was something about these books. To the astonishment of Sergeant Hector Hugh Munro Ramsbottom and Constable Alison Offiah Campbell, he picked up a book and sniffed it, then he did the same to another. He gently fanned the pages of the third one.

"They're all new," he said. "Not only have they never been read, they've never been opened. Why would he have these books?"

"Maybe he intended to read them," said Campbell.

"No, because the one disorder hypochondriacs never have is hypochondria."

"What do you mean? Also how do you know so much about the topic?" asked Ramsbottom.

"I know a little bit because I was going to use it in a story, but it never worked out. Hypochondria is one of those ailments that is very difficult to understand and, from my point of view, not of much use as a plot point. I was trying to work out how you would kill someone using hypochondria, and there wasn't enough agreement in the literature about how to go about it. Hypochondria seemed like a pseudo-science, so I gave up and strangled my character instead."

"Judging by these books, it still is a pseudo-science," said Ramsbottom.

"And that's my point. If Bert bought these books, why are they unread? But it's unlikely he bought them. The hardest thing for a hypochondriac to do is admit his problem. What are the odds that after 30 years, he suddenly had a Road-to-Damascus moment?"

"Not very high," said Ramsbottom. "Constable, take all the industrial-sized pillboxes in the kitchen to a pharmacist, and see if he can identify their contents. We also need to see Bert MacDonald's will. I'll find out which lawyers he used and arrange for them to have a copy ready for you to pick up."

Campbell started to leave.

"Wait," said Ramsbottom. He was examining the door. "Constable Campbell, you broke the door down on the hinge side, right?"

"Yes. Ms. MacDonald said the door was double-locked. Quite often the hinges are not made to the same standard, so they are easier to break through."

"Did you touch either of the locks?"

"No, I left them for any forensic work. Why?"

"I can see where the locked deadbolt ripped through its mountings. If the drop lock had been engaged, we'd see similar damage, but there's none."

"But Ms. Mac Donald said he always locked it."

"How would she know?" said Powlle. "Does she have an omniscient point of view?"

"What?" said Ramsbottom.

"It's a writing technique. It means that the writer is writing from up on high, able to see all aspects of the story and impart information whenever and wherever he wishes. Unlike a first-person narrative, which sees everything through the eyes of the main character. My point is, how does she know that he locked it all the time when he was inside? She wasn't in there with him. She's just guessing. Or maybe she just made her first mistake."

As they left the room Campbell said, "What about second person point of view?"

"Nobody can write in the second person," said Powlle. "Only weak writers do as it creates suspense in place of a non-existent plot. It is a sign of a bad writer. Second-person writing has no value."

"There's one type of writing where the second-person-singular voice excels," said Ramsbottom.

"Where?" said Powlle.

"I'll tell you later."

***

Later that afternoon, Ramsbottom and Campbell met Powlle at the coffee shop. Against his instincts, the sergeant was forced to admit that what had started out as a death by natural causes had turned into a humdinger of a murder. And he had Powlle to thank for that.

"So there is no doubt she did it?" Powlle asked. "Gina MacDonald killed her uncle?"

"I'm almost certain of it," said Ramsbottom, "but whether I can prove it or not is another matter."

Constable Campbell was ecstatic that she'd been kept on the investigation. She'd heard of senior police officers who wouldn't do the work but would take the glory. Hector Ramsbottom didn't seem to be one of them.

"The coroner's preliminary report says myocardial infarction," she said, "with no evidence of anything else. She also said he could have gone at any time. His heart was a sieve, and she was surprised it still worked at all. She said only his medication was keeping it ticking. As for the will, apart from a few bequests, he left the bulk of his estate and his shares in the family goldmine to Gina, which no doubt will piss off the rest of the nephews and nieces, all of whom have alibis. None live here anymore, and they can all be accounted for. If it's murder, it's Gina."

"So why would she kill him?" asked Powlle. "She'd been patient for 10 years, and he was 90 years old."

"Ninety-one," said Ramsbottom. "And I don't know, yet."

"Why now?" Powlle asked. "It's not even a proper locked-room mystery. Where are the other suspects? When are we going to gather them together for the grand dénouement? As plots go, this is as bad as a Mickey Spillane."

"Who?" said Campbell.

Powlle sighed.

"Well, that's just it," said Ramsbottom. "This isn't a complicated Agatha Christie, it is real life. There only is one suspect, and if you want someone to blame, try yourself."

"Me?" said Powlle.

"Yes," said Ramsbottom. "The books, all new, all untouched. You noticed that, and that got me wondering. Who would set up Bert MacDonald's study like that? Only someone who had access."

"Someone who overthought this a bit. Hinting at hypochondria was her way of trying to lead us away from the possibility that he died because of her."

"But she said he had the only key," said Powlle.

"People have been known to lie," said Ramsbottom. "If she had a spare key made, and she must have had the opportunity in her years of working for him, then she would have been able to get in and out of his office, read his will, maybe even read his new draft, if it existed. It's the only explanation. She was setting him up to look like someone who had been worrying himself to death."

"And," said Campbell, "it explains how she knew that he used the deadbolt. You need a key to find out."

Both the men looked puzzled.

"Gina MacDonald is not a criminal mastermind," said Campbell, "and everything doesn't wrap up nice and easy, like a cozy mystery book. She mentioned the second bolt on the door, the drop lock, by mistake, when she spoke to us. She knew he used it because she had tried the door with her key at some point when he was in there and found he also drop-locked himself inside. She didn't need to mention it, and by doing so she led us back to herself when we noticed it wasn't engaged."

"Still," said Powlle, "if she was going to inherit everything, why do all this now?"

"Alison?" said Ramsbottom.

"The law firm said that they had been called by Bert only last month," she said. "He was thinking of changing his will."

"To what?" said Powlle.

"They don't know," said Ramsbottom. "But Bert MacDonald was cantankerous, and if you believe you are getting everything, then any changes can only mean you are getting less. And there's more."

"Oh, this is getting to be fun," said Powlle. "What now?"

"I took the pills to the pharmacy," said Campbell. "Some of them are placebos, common practice if a doctor suspects hypochondria. Others are holistic, harmless but expensive, and one of the African capsules smelled like it had feces in it. But a couple of them were important, including this heart medicine, as we found out from the medical examiner." She held up a two-part capsule. "The pharmacist corroborated what the medical examiner said. Judging from the dosage, he surmised that these pills were critical to Bert's health and life."

With a flourish, Campbell took the capsule apart, and turned both sides upside down. It was empty.

"Oh, my," said Powlle. "That looks to be premeditated."

"And one more thing," said Campbell. "Guess which favorite niece collected these from the pharmacy for her uncle?"

"Gina MacDonald has been a naughty girl," said Enock Powlle. "She knew enough to identify the heart medication. Identify it and doctor it."

"Indeed," said Ramsbottom. "Constable Campbell, your theory please?"

Alison Campbell closed her eyes and appeared to gather her thoughts. "I think that Bert MacDonald was not a nice person to care for, but the promise of being the beneficiary of his will kept Gina coming to work every day. He was a mean old man. Maybe one day Gina placed his coffee cup down the wrong way and he told her he was cutting her out of the will, or maybe she heard the lawyer's phone message." She opened her eyes and was startled to see her audience of two drinking in her words.

"Carry on," said Hector. "You're doing fine."

"Maybe she just wanted him to drop dead, and maybe she decided to hasten his death by emptying the most important capsules. Making him more susceptible to heart failure."

"Maybe she hid in his office," said Powlle, "and jumped out wearing *A Nightmare on Elm Street* mask, scaring him to death."

Ramsbottom sighed. Campbell looked perplexed.

"No?" said Powlle. "It's what I'd do. Anyway, why the hypochondria books?"

"I think she thought it would strengthen her case," said Campbell. "Make it look like an expected death."

"Instead of murder by fright," said Powlle, never one to give up an idea.

"What she actually did was lead us back to herself. The books gave us our first clue that all was not what it seemed. How could she know that we'd have a book whisperer on the team?"

Ramsbottom closed his eyes, and groaned silently. He opened one eye, ever so slightly. Powlle was grinning like the Cheshire Cat.

"It was a silly idea," said Powlle. "But as you said, she's not a criminal genius."

"And it doesn't really matter," said Ramsbottom, "because even though we can guess what happened, we can't prove anything. The empty capsules will be useless as evidence in the hands of any competent defense attorney. I need her to confess, and she won't do that."

"She's seen enough TV," said Powlle, "to know that all she has to do is keep quiet. There's no real evidence that she did anything wrong. It's all conjecture and how do you prove the heart attack was a setup? Bert MacDonald was 90 years old."

"Ninety-one," said Ramsbottom.

"I wish you would stop being so precise," said Powlle. Then there was a sudden change in his demeanor. "That thing you do," he said to Ramsbottom, "where you are pedantic, and annoying, and righteous. Is that an act? Can you do it while bluffing?"

"What do you mean?" asked Ramsbottom, intrigued despite the insulting way Powlle was going about this.

"You doubted my suggestion that Gina MacDonald scared old Bert to death because it sounds so unlikely. But does it? And how would she react if you confronted her with evidence and looked really confident that you had her bang to rights?"

"But we have no evidence," said Campbell.

"I know where we can get some," said Powlle.

***

Ramsbottom was alone when he returned to the crime scene. He had a wireless microphone under his tie, and Enock and Alison were listening in the car outside.

Gina MacDonald was sitting in the kitchen, looking as if she hadn't moved in the intervening hours.

Ramsbottom sat down across from her. "Just a few more questions, Ms. MacDonald." He dug into his jacket pocket and pulled out some short cables attached to small, black plastic boxes. "Now, do you know when your Uncle Bert had these installed? Or did he put them in himself?"

"What are they?" asked Gina.

But the sergeant saw the look in her eyes, and he knew. He had her.

"They are surveillance cameras. They broadcast wirelessly to a security company. We don't know which one, but we'll have the files soon. He had two in his office and one outside looking at the door. Didn't he tell you?"

"No," she said, biting the nail on her index finger.

"Ms. MacDonald, it will go better for you if you cooperate now. There is still time for a lighter sentence. Once we get the tapes, they'll stand on their own as evidence and you'll be tried on what the jury can see."

***

"You're good," Powlle said. He and Ramsbottom were back at the coffee shop. "I can't believe it worked. Nothing I suggest ever works properly. There are so many ways this could have gone bad. The cameras looked brand new, not as if they'd been mounted on a wall. She never thought how a 90-year-old man—I beg your pardon, a 91-year-old man—would be able to install them and connect them, or have it done without her knowing. This shouldn't have worked."

"It was almost exactly as we hoped it would go down," said Ramsbottom. "She bought the books on hypochondria to point the police toward a false cause of death. As she was confessing to me, she seemed to realize the books had been a mistake, compounded by her mentioning the drop lock. She'd stopped his heart medicine three days before, and she was panicking that he was still alive and that he'd live long enough to change his will."

"And she knew that he planned to change his will."

"You heard what she told me. He'd been talking on the phone about changes he wanted to make to his will, and she was furious. She did have a key to the office; he fell asleep with the door open one day, so she took an impression and made a copy in the workshop. On the day he died, she went up before him and hid in the closet. When he came in and sat down, she ran out, stood behind him, touched him on his head, and shouted *waughghghghghgh* in his ear. The effect, she said, was instantaneous. Uncle Bert's heart stopped right then."

"I'm not surprised," said Enock. "I nearly had a heart attack right now when you shouted *waughghghghghgh*. By the way, where's Constable Campbell?"

"We received a phone call from the lawyers. There was an e-mail with an attachment from Bert. Apparently, he'd sent off his amendments but they were lost in the electronic world until a couple of hours ago. Ah, here she is now."

Campbell was quivering as she sat down. "They only let me have a printed copy."

"And?" asked Ramsbottom. "What were the changes?"

"He had left some small bequests to eight people, former staff and friends. It turned out he'd outlived them all, so he was cancelling them in favor of Gina MacDonald. She was getting the lot."

Ramsbottom buried his head in his hands, and Powlle muttered, "Oh, Jeez, I want to be there and see the look on her face when you tell her."

415

***

Portia was in bed when Enock arrived home. A Jamie Oliver book was opened on the recipe stand in the kitchen, her hint as to what she'd had for supper and what was waiting for him to reheat.

He texted Ramsbottom, "Recipe Books."

"What?"

"The only time the second-person voice is useful."

"Well done. Good night Enock."

"Good night Hector."

There was a note on the fridge door. "Check your e-mail." He did. Portia had taken his scratchings for the heritage society, and turned it into a terrific article on the history of the community.

Enock heaved a sigh of relief. He could eat and go to bed. Madeleine Burfield-Murphy had been appeased, and Portia had once again circumvented the family ructions

He opened the fridge and took out his dinner. There was a note on the cover.

"You owe me."

Yes I do, he thought. *I certainly do.*

Ω

CRIMINALS LIKE US

Rosalind Place

Rosalind Place was a Brit until she was five years old, when her entire family emigrated to Canada. She grew up in Toronto, Ontario. She now makes her home on a quiet rural road in southern Ontario.

Rosalind has had a number of short stories and poetry published over the years and recently completed her first book, a tale of magic and discovery set on a rural Ontario farm in the 1960s. Her stories appear in: In the Key of 13, The County Wave, *and* 13 Claws.

If they think you want it, they will never let you go. All her mother's stories. All those years ago.

Dee checked the clasp on her one suitcase, slipping the ticket into the innermost pocket. All those stories, all those years ago. She closed the flat door, walked down the long, dimly lit corridor to the front entrance, put her key in the locked box and stepped out into the rainy, frantic afternoon. Cars were backed up for blocks, horns blared, there was the distant sound of sirens. The streetcar she needed sat trapped and empty in the middle of it. She would have to walk.

Six months on, two months off, they'd told her at the Ministry of Rural Affairs, slapping her ticket down on the chipped Formica countertop. The farms nearly run themselves now, but we don't want anyone out there too long on their own. They had no idea what she'd done to get this assignment. Years spent searching through websites, libraries, archives, all illegal, looking for anything that would prove it was true, then removing any trace of her searching. Changing her name had been the easy part, creating a new identity, harder. Hacking into medical records, looking for the genetic markers that would make her ineligible—if they ever found out what she'd done to get here, she would be in prison for the rest of her life.

"It's not a train you're taking." The guard at the rail station shook his head impatiently and pointed to an escalator further down the platform. "The Pod. There are no signs, just show them your ticket at the desk."

Dee could hear the subways roaring above her. She assumed she would be going by train. Her mother had gone by train. Not a pod.

Pods were fast but small and claustrophobic. One person per pod and no windows. She would see nothing until she got there. Twenty-five years since they gated the cities. She had no memories of a time when the roads leading to the farms were open. In a few minutes she would be outside the city walls. She tightened the straps, felt the *thunk* of gears as the pod was released, the pulse of its engines as it picked up speed.

If they think you want it, they will never let you go. A phrase her mother repeated over and over again in those last days. They had closed the farms to everyone but the technicians long before Dee was born. Hadn't it all been explained to them in grade school? After The Wars, with Wild's Disease decimating the population, they had destroyed what was left of the wilderness they claimed the disease came from, brought most of the people into the cities and established the farms.

The farms were there still, beyond the city walls, stretching mile after mile after mile until they touched the outskirts of another city. They were a necessary evil, like the birds that darkened the city skies twice a year. And, like the birds, most people feared them. Wild's killed Stephen, her little brother, then her father. Dee had never questioned it. A representative from the Ministry of Health had stood in the hospital corridor, shaking his head. The damage was done a long time ago, he'd said, and we are still reaping the consequences. Dee's mother, shook her head as well, watching him walk down the hall. It wasn't the wilderness that killed them, she whispered. Hadn't they all been born in The Junction, the new site on the edge of the city, constructed over one of the demolished arms factories left over from The Wars?

Dee's father and brother had died quickly, their bodies shutting down without ravaging their minds. But her mother had lingered long past any predictions of survival. Her mind failed her first, and as it failed her, she no longer kept her secrets.

Her story had seemed unbelievable at first; a life Dee had never known existed. *The wilderness is not what you think, Dee. I was there. I know. Oh, long before you were born, darling. I worked on the farms for years...the flights we took, Dee. The things we saw! We would walk for miles...*

She was delusional surely, hallucinating, talking, at times, in a language so unfamiliar that Dee had to stop her to ask her to define words, to explain. Open skies as far as one could see, massive trees, green pastures, breezes and bird song. *Why it sounded just like music, music from the old days, light and sweet. The mornings were the best, Dee. A little concert just for me.* Nights so dark you could see nothing but stars, countless stars. And the animals: deer, wild horses, caribou. Creatures Dee knew to be long extinct. They were there, outside the cities, moving in herds across the open fields.

If they think you want it, they will never let you go. The longing in her mother's voice. The images caught in Dee's brain and stayed there long after her mother was gone. The stories wouldn't leave her alone. She couldn't sleep, stood for hours looking out the small window in the flat, the images of the unknown, brilliant world filling her mind.

Eventually she had understood what she must do. There was nothing to anchor her anymore—no family; no close friends; a meaningless job; this small, dark room. The only certainty, growing stronger as the months went by, was that she must find out if any of it was real.

***

It was a long time to lie, unmoving, in a single pod, hurtling through the tunnels. What would it actually be like when the doors opened at the end? All those months at the training center learning the complicated web of technology, the robotics that kept the farms productive. And they had never shown her what the farms actually looked like. They described the monitoring stations, the huge linked lighthouses with their rotating observation rooms, explained the staffing—one technician for every 10 houses, the pilots who monitored the furthest drones and would check in once a month for supplies and occasional repairs. You won't be entirely alone out there, they said. We will always be in contact.

Dee didn't want contact. She didn't want anyone checking in, checking on. It didn't matter that they said the houses were entirely self-sufficient and she could monitor everything from within. She wanted only to step outside and into the world her mother's stories had shown her, to see those fields, feel those breezes, hear the songs of birds. She had seen enough, hacking her way through the farthest

419

reaches of the dark web, to know that some of it, at least, might once have been true.

***

What had she been thinking? So *stupid.* Dee slammed her fist against the shiny white walls. There was no way out of the lighthouse except the pod to the next one or back to the city. Weeks of searching and nothing. No way out. She couldn't even find the pilots' entrance, not that it would have helped her. She pushed the button for the elevator, ascending quickly to the observation room. Observation room? Glimpses of nothing as the sections of the lighthouse tower rotated, the screens sliding across the windows, section by section as it moved. It could be paused apparently, but only on the authority of one of the managers and only if there was some kind of an emergency. Any problems and they would just shut down the lighthouse and send you along to the next one. Or home. There was nothing to see, to feel, to hear, to smell—no sky, no wind, no birdsong, just glimpses of green below the white film of covers protecting the crops from the sun, row upon row upon row of them, stretching to the horizon in all directions. The lighthouse hummed and vibrated as loudly as the city at night. There was no darkness: lights were controlled automatically from the central station and never entirely turned off. Within days, she understood that her mother's stories had been just what she thought they were the first time she heard them—hallucinations, delusions, the ramblings of a dying woman. Dee had bought a very expensive ticket, costing years of her life.

Walking down the few steps into her tiny living quarters below the observation room, turning on the set that kept her in touch with news from the city she had escaped, she wanted only to return to the life she had lived before. The months stretched ahead of her, months sitting at screens, watching the dim, grainy video feeds from the security cameras, or repairing the software glitches that plagued the drones. Meetings with the central monitors came weekly, unreliable images and robotic voices. Much better to just be left alone to count the days to the end of this terrible mistake.

It was on the last day of her second month at the lighthouse, when the pilot came. Engrossed in untangling the software of a misfiring drone, she'd looked up to release a kink in her neck, and was shocked to see a free flying pod gliding in to land below her. There was a faint grinding noise then the hum of the elevator and finally, the *swoosh* of its opening door. A tall, athletic, gray-haired man stepped onto the deck and stood, staring at her, saying nothing. She got up and walked over to him, extending her hand.

420

"Lisa Carr. Nice to meet you."

He didn't immediately respond, just stood there, staring.

Dee let her hand drop. She had been told the pilots could be a little eccentric. Many of them had been on the job for years and stayed out far longer on their own than the lighthouse technicians.

"Lisa, is it?"

"Yes. Hi." She stepped back as he brushed past her, walking into the center of the room, looking, it seemed, at the bank of computer screens, Dee's workstation.

"Stan." He turned back again suddenly, extending a hand.

He was far older than Lisa had expected. His hair close cropped, clearly whiter than gray; his face lined. His handshake was strong and confident.

"You in the middle of something?" He nodded toward the screens.

"Nothing that can't wait." Dee felt herself smiling, at the same time thinking what an odd interaction this was. Rudeness, then warmth. She had been so intent on marking off the days until her return to the city that she had almost forgotten the pilots' existence, focused entirely on her work and how to get back to the life she had torn to pieces.

"Hmm." He smiled, looked a little embarrassed. "You wouldn't have any tea?"

He would always ask her this, over the weeks that followed. He flew in at least once a week, sometimes more often, he said, to deal with recurring mechanical issues with the pod. It required the use of the equipment stored in the lighthouse and, occasionally, contact with the control center mechanics. She would see the pod landing or hear the hum of the elevator, and go into the galley, surprisingly content to take a break to make tea and conversation with this gentle, and as it turned out, thoughtful man. He had such a quiet, steady way about him, listening seriously to what she had to say. There was a sadness in him as well, and she wondered at the loneliness the pilots must feel, out here for so long and so far away, but he seemed as reticent as she was to talk about personal things. If, sometimes, looking up from making tea, she caught him staring at her, she had to remind herself that he might not be who he seemed. There were different ways of monitoring those who worked outside the cities, and she had far too much at stake.

Yet he never questioned her, never gave her any reason to think he was anyone other than who he appeared to be. They shared their frustrations about the knotty mechanics of mis-firing drones and undependable pods, even shared stories of their sometimes bizarre interactions with the monitors. He talked, occasionally, about the other technicians and pilots he had known over the years. It was easy to relax in his company. She even found herself wanting to confide in him—to tell him about her lost family, her search for the truth about the farms, all the things she had done to get here—until the day came when she realized she had made another terrible mistake.

They had been working together on a tricky software issue that had been plaguing the station for weeks. She'd first noticed it as a distortion on the video feeds from the furthest drones. It looked as though shadows were passing in front of the cameras, almost as if something was moving along the rows directly below them. It frightened her at first, because the fleeting gray shadows appeared almost human. But when she showed the feed to Stan, he had told her it could be the first sign of a more serious software problem here on the station. It might be what was causing the short outs, he told her. One of the drones had even caught fire in the repair bay. Stan had been there at the time and put it out quickly, but the short outs remained a dangerous problem.

They had spent the day running a new software program, working late into what passed for evening in the lighthouse, and Dee offered to make dinner for them both. She was in the galley, chopping vegetables. He was at her workstation watching the final check on the software fix, running the screens when he suddenly turned to her and asked her straight out what had brought her to the lighthouses. He just stood there, looking at her and she felt all the affection she had for him drain away.

"I've told you already." She could hear the coldness in her voice.

"No. I don't believe you did." He didn't move, was clearly waiting for her answer.

Fine, she thought, *I'll give you an answer.* She had a story ready, nothing anywhere near the truth, but well-rehearsed, in case she ever needed it. Even so, she found it oddly difficult to lie to him.

"I see," he said, when she'd finished, shrugging and looking away. "Well, I've got secrets of my own, I guess."

"What do you mean? I don't have any secrets, Stan." What had she said? Her anxiety was rising. She tapped her fingers on the galley table, had to force herself to stop.

"That pod of mine, for example." He ignored her question, turned back to her. "There's really nothing wrong with it. I kept breaking it down so I could come back here to fix it."

"You sabotaged your own pod?" She was now entirely confused. No one would do such a thing, let alone admit to it. It would mean years in prison. He was an old man already. He would die there.

"That's right, Dee. You can turn me in if you want to."

She heard the knife she was holding clatter to the floor. She had no idea she had let go of it. Her heart was pounding so quickly that she had to hold onto the table for support. She looked at the half-chopped vegetables, the teapot, the empty mugs. *Liar!* He was a monitor, not a pilot at all. She tried to laugh at him, make it look like she didn't understand.

"What did you just call me?"

"By your name. Don't worry," he said, nodding toward the screens. "I'm not one of them."

"It's *not* my name."

He didn't respond, just walked over to her.

"I recognized you the moment I saw you, Dee. I knew your mother a long, long time ago."

***

It was so beautiful there. You must find a way to get back, Dee. The sun shines there in a different way, and the clouds...There's nothing to fear. There was never anything to fear...

Dee opened her eyes. Was it a dream or a memory? She got out of bed, dressed quickly, walked over to the galley to get breakfast. Stan would be here soon, but she wouldn't be offering him tea.

She had told him to get out and he hadn't returned since, but yesterday she'd had no choice but to call him back in. The monitors wanted to know if they needed to close down the station. The gray shadows were of no importance, they told her. Shadows on screens are just shadows on screens, but they needed to know that the drones were safe.

When he stepped off the elevator, she ignored him. They had to finish running scripts first. As soon as they were set to run, she stood, pushing her chair away from the screens, and walked into the center of the room.

"You knew my mother?" If he was a monitor, let him arrest her. It would all soon be over anyway.

"Yes. I did." He looked so calm, held her gaze until she had to look away.

"How did you know my name?" She looked back at him.

He shrugged in that half-embarrassed way he had. "You're not the only one who knows how to hack a database, Dee."

"How long have you been lying to me?"

He walked over to her then, reached out but didn't touch her, the sadness in his voice telling her everything. "About as long as you've been lying to me."

So she gave him the truth—about the deaths of her father and brother, her mother's slow decline. "I couldn't sleep," she told him. "Mum was describing a place so... unimaginable. And she wanted me to go there. I wanted to go there. I had to find out if any of it was true. We were never close, you see, until the end. I didn't really know her at all. Whatever she wanted for me, it just isn't here, is it? There's nothing outside those windows. Whatever she was talking about, if it ever existed, is gone."

He stood, listening, never looking away. It was only at the end that he seemed to react, shaking his head ever so slightly, then walking over to her workstation, to the furthest of the screens, the ones that controlled the inner workings of the lighthouse. He sat down, tapped away for a few seconds and the panels stopped moving.

"What are you doing?" It was disorienting to see them suddenly go still. She had just revealed everything to him and he had simply walked away from her to do something entirely reckless that would bring the monitors down upon them both.

"What are you doing?" she asked him again. "How are you going to explain this?"

"Don't worry about it. Come. Look."

"Don't worry about it? And I already know what's out there." She was angry now. "I've been watching those panels move across those windows every single day. There is nothing to see but the crops, row after row after row, just like the video feeds." She walked over to the one uncovered window.

"Yes, the farms are out there." He ignored her question. "What's beyond the farms?"

"Cities of course. But I can't see those from here!"

"It's hard to see when the panels are moving. Look at the furthest horizon there. Ignore everything else."

"It's green. I just see green. Another row of crops."

"It isn't another row of crops, Dee. You're seeing what you expect to see. Look!"

It was a different shade of green. The thinnest line, right at the horizon—darker, higher maybe.

"What is it?"

"It's what your mother's stories are made of, Dee. It's the wilderness."

"It can't be." She squinted at the thin green line, then turned away from the window. "There isn't any wilderness."

"So they say, Dee. So they say."

So they say. That was Stan's answer any time she challenged him.

"This is BS, Stan."

"No, it's not. You want to see for yourself?"

"And just how would I do that?"

"With me. Just pause the monitors for..."

"*Pause* the monitors? Is this some kind of a trick?"

"It's no trick, Dee. You can do it. You're a genius at these systems. Your mother was too."

***

It was the tiniest line in the wall. Stan slid his keycard into it and the door opened. The walls of the corridor that led to the landing pad were almost opaque. She could barely make out the shape of the lighthouse girders, but that was all. As the pod hummed to life and she squeezed herself into the emergency hold, attached snugly to the main body, she was suddenly terrified. The pod lifted up and away.

The flights we took Dee. The things we saw! We would walk for miles.

She had trusted Stan with her story that day and he had trusted her with his. He spoke about the farms of his youth—they had just started building the lighthouses back then, he said, so there were lots of workers and small stations out in the fields and far fewer monitors. Most of them eventually moved back to the cities.

A few, like him, like her mother, had stayed longer, unwilling to leave the land to the hands of others. The farms expanded, the lighthouses were raised and the drones were introduced. The pilots moved off the land and into the skies above it. Her mother stayed longer than most. Before the monitors, before the lighthouses and the drones, you could still get to the wilderness they claimed didn't exist. He and her mother would go there, slipping out again and again to walk through its fields and its forests.

"All your mother's stories," he told her, "everything she told you, all of it was true."

It didn't take long, listening to the familiar longing in his gentle voice, for Dee to understand that Stan had been in love with her mother, that he loved her still.

"We kept in touch for a time, mailings here and there, when we could. I shouldn't have said that about finding your name in a database. She told me about you, about Stephen and Dan. Then her

425

mailings suddenly stopped. It had been harder and harder to get past the monitors. I assumed she just couldn't get through anymore."

Dee felt the pod beginning to slow. She was so terrified that she couldn't think straight. What if everything Stan had told her had been a lie? What a story he had created! Lost loves and secret communications. The hatch doors would open and she would find herself back in the city behind prison walls. He had played her. He had never known her mother. Yeah, I saw what I expected to see, what you *told* me to see.

The hatch door started to hum, sliding back slowly on its track. She closed her eyes.

There was a scent—like the paths, years ago, she and her mother had taken through the parks, the sweetest scent, earth, grass perhaps. She opened her eyes. Blue. Blue sky.

Stan reached in, leaning over to unbuckle the safety harness. She pushed herself up and out of the hatch to stand beside him.

She had never seen anything so beautiful. It was difficult to breathe, and she reached for his hand. The sky was immense above them; white clouds moving slowly across it. They were standing in a green field, dotted with what must be wildflowers. It stretched before them to what must be a forest. Trees so massive that their branches seemed to touch the sky. She stepped forward. It seemed like the earth was a living thing beneath her feet. The very air was alive as well, with sound, movement and scents she couldn't recognize. She felt as if her legs were going to give way. She knelt, unsteady, pushed her hands into the grass, her fingers into the earth, more scents rose up and almost overwhelmed her.

"Look!" Stan touched her shoulder, then pointed toward the trees on the edge of the forest. A large, slender, pale gray bird rose up out of the branches, stretching its wings, tucking its long legs beneath it as it gained height. Dee watched, transfixed, as it glided directly above them, then out into the open pasture.

"But they're extinct!" She stood, turning to him. He was watching it too, shading his eyes from the bright sun.

"So they say, Dee. So they say."

They must have walked for miles, first through the fields, then into the cool, sun-dappled forest. They were there, the creatures of her mother's stories, birds and animals Dee had seen only in the pages of illegal books. Only as the sun brought the day toward evening did they return to the fields and the waiting pod.

"We'll come back again, I promise you," Stan told her.

***

Even through the dense walls of the escape hatch, Dee could hear the alarms. She felt the pod shudder for a moment as Stan banked it, hard. She had found a way to pause everything. A pause that wasn't really a pause, a ruse that made it look like all was functioning as normal, that she was there, sitting in front of the screens. The ruse was a loop that repeated again and again with enough slight variations that even if she and Stan were late returning, it would simply begin again. The only thing that she hadn't anticipated was an alarm.

They weren't landing on the pad. She could feel the lurch as Stan taxied over uneven ground. She could feel the heat too, unnatural heat. As the hatch dropped and the door opened, she saw that the lighthouse was on fire.

"No, Stan! No!" She started to run toward it but he caught up quickly, grabbed her, pulling her back and holding her tight.

It must have been one of the drones she'd been working on in the repair bay. It must have shorted out again. It appeared that the fire had started there, on the lower deck, but it had already moved upward, flames licking at the lower levels of the tower.

There was no way to explain away a fire. The monitors, watching their banks of screens would see multiple warnings flashing but all they would see coming from her station at the lighthouse was her repeating loop. She would be arrested, charged, imprisoned. She would never see Stan again, never listen to his gentle voice, never fly with him again to the beautiful world beyond the farms. She would never see the wilderness again. It seemed to her then that it was the wilderness itself she was watching burn, turning to ashes, disappearing before her eyes.

"Dee! Dee!" Stan had his hands on her shoulders, was shaking her, hard. "We have to go back, Dee. Now. There's no other option." When he had her attention he let her go, and started walking quickly back to the pod, gesturing to her to follow him.

"Back to the city." Of course, there was no other choice. Since there was no possible way to explain it, best to go back and turn herself in. If she could just think clearly. It felt like her body was frozen, her thoughts sliding into incoherence.

"Wait!" She stopped. "What do you mean we have to go back? You don't have to go back, Stan. You don't have to admit to anything. They don't have to know you were ever here. It could—"

"I don't mean go back to the city, Dee. No."

"But where? I don't understand. There's nothing..."

"I'll have to leave you there for a bit. I don't want them searching for a missing pod."

"What are you talking about?"

He wasn't even listening to her. She caught up to him, grabbed his arm, forcing him to slow down. He stopped, turning to her as she let go.

"We have to go back, Dee. Now. We have to go back where we came from."

"*What?* You mean back to the wilderness? We can't survive out there." She was crying now. This was madness.

"Sure we can, Dee."

"How? How can we possibly survive out there, alone in the wilderness?"

"We won't be alone."

He wasn't making any sense. None of this was making sense.

"The criminals will help us." He took her arm, started guiding her gently toward the pod.

"What are you talking about? Criminals?"

"Yes, Dee, that's right. A good thing to be, don't you think?" He let go of her arm, stepping away to open the door of the hatch. "A whole village of criminals in the forest, not so very far from where we walked today."

Shadows on screens.

"A whole village of them." Stan repeated, smiling. "Young. Old. All kinds. And all of them criminals. Just like us."

***

"All this time and I never asked you what you thought," Dee said.

They were walking in the forest, in and out of shadow, as a breeze moved the branches above them. They were together for the first time in months, certain at last that no one was searching for them. "About the Governors. About what they did, gating the cities, taking all the wilderness. Even the idea of it."

"You're asking the wrong person." Stan paused. "I can tell you what your mother thought, though. That they were afraid, especially after The Wars, afraid of what they couldn't control."

"The wilderness."

"Yes. And the people. They will destroy it one day, your mother said. Their fear will destroy us all unless we stop them." He laughed then, shaking his head. "She was quite the radical back then."

They walked on, in silence. As they neared the village, Dee led them down to one of the rough benches, near the downward path.

The afternoon was cooling into evening, but she wouldn't wait any longer.

"You have never asked me about Wild's Disease. I'm 30 years old. No one gets to 30 without symptoms." She put her arm through his, felt the tension there. "Fathers always pass Wild's Disease to their children."

Stan was looking down, wouldn't raise his head.

"They would never have given me a ticket. I'd already changed my name, my history, but I knew that when they looked at the genetics, they'd see the markers. I got into the database. I thought I could manipulate my record somehow. Only I didn't have to. The markers weren't there." She squeezed his arm, felt him relax beside her.

"Because he wasn't your father."

"Yes. He wasn't my father. You are."

***

During all the years that came after, Dee would often think back to those days, when she found her father, when she found herself. Her children, then her grandchildren, grew up learning the stories her mother had told her. And when she told them her own tales, of the lighthouses, of the drones and the pods and the first people to come to the wilderness, she would always end by laughing.

"It's not a word we use in this way now, but back then they were called criminals, the people who lived outside the cities. And those who came later, who ungated the cities and protected the wilderness, who opened the farms and founded the villages beyond them, they were called criminals too. But the meaning had changed. 'Criminal' means those who honor the wilderness and the creatures who live there, who live, always, in harmony with them.

"Criminals, all of them. Just like us."

THE REFERRAL

Linda Cahill

Linda Cahill writes crime fiction because it lets her play with characters in crisis, and the lingering possibility of redemption. She honed her affection for the crime and justice genre after covering riots, the police blotter, and the courts as a reporter for the Montreal Gazette *and* The Montreal Star.

Linda has lived and worked in Canada, the United Kingdom, and Israel as a reporter, editor, government policy analyst, and writer. Her professional background includes the CBC, CTV News, BBC Radio *and an Ontario government agency. These experiences flavor her stories of individuals at a turning point in their lives.*

Dr. William Osbourne, MD, CFPC, stood at his polished mahogany desk in a starchy white lab coat. Dr. Osbourne never sat when he could stand. Now, he flipped through the afternoon's patient charts, preparing for the onslaught of the sick, the bored, the tedious, and the lonely. Karol, Keith, Kilbride. So far, so good. His new secretary knew the alphabet, at least. Kilbride, Lewis, Loring, Drinkwater. … Drinkwater? That was plain sloppy. Drinkwater should come before Karol.

Dr. Osbourne glared at the files. Nancy Moore wasn't exactly working out. Frowning, he grabbed the offending folder and paced to the window, opened slightly to air the place. Eight stories down, fat snowflakes drifted from a leaden sky onto his newly purchased Jag XKE. His square jaw softened into a smile. Admiring the sports car's red enamel finish put him into a better mood. A bit ostentatious for a family physician, maybe. But, thanks to Aunt Celia, it was all his.

Osbourne looked at the files again. Not much new there, except for a letter from the Ministry introducing him to Jeremy

Melrose Drinkwater, 34. Another new referral from the Ministry? He had told Nancy to say no to new patients. Just what he didn't need, with that filthy Coronavirus driving mask-wearing hysterics into his office to be swabbed, and in a few unlucky cases, to be shoveled off to hospital to take their chances on ventilators.

Picking up the Ministry's unwanted intrusion on his Christmas preparations, Osbourne swept through the door between his roomy office and Nancy's cubicle. "The appointments are out of order!" His white coat brushed against the garish green plastic garland and holly berries she had stapled to the doorframe.

Nancy gaped up at him, eyes wide under her frizzy hair. "Sorry. They came up late from central filing."

Dr. Osbourne opened a meaty hand. "And what's this?" The Drinkwater letter fluttered onto her desk. "No new patients. Remember?"

Nancy reached for her reading glasses. "New rule from the Ministry." She picked up the paper and read aloud: "Being of sound mind, suffering untreatable pain, the usual …." She paused, then handed the letter back to her boss. "Besides, you have to take these requests. You've been on TV. People ask for you." Her voice trailed off.

"He wants this *now*? Right *now*? Right before Christmas?"

She shrugged. "It's his *right*." Then she smiled, pleased at her little joke. She tapped her computer to bring up the December schedule. "Mr. Scorsi just cancelled to go to his kid's concert. And Mrs. Frame can't make her appointment, either. That gives you a window early tomorrow."

Osbourne paced the floor. Crap. What a thing to look forward to. He glanced out the window. He could see the Jag's beautiful lines disappearing under a crystalline layer of snow. Good thing he had put up the soft-top. Maybe he would leave early, have time for a workout before dinner. His girlfriend expected him to keep trim. No pudgy docs for her. Then an early Christmas getaway tomorrow.

"Haven't got the time," he said, hoping that would do the trick. "I would have to conduct an interview, take a history, and do the paperwork. Then the procedure. No time."

Moore took off her glasses. "You have to make time. You can speak with him this afternoon and I'll book the room for first thing tomorrow."

He frowned.

"Hey, no big deal. You'll be free for our Christmas Eve lunch. Pepperoni with extra cheese?"

"Look, Nancy, can't we put him off until after New Year's? I wanted to get away early tomorrow, without any drama."

"No can do." She dangled her glasses from one hand. "He has rights. You'll miss the 'timeliness' window, and the Ministry will be on your case. Again."

Osbourne snorted. The extra fees the Ministry paid for this particular service were helping with the mortgage on the Florida beach house, but he didn't need this one job, two days before Christmas. "Tell him I have a conflict."

"You don't. There's a two-hour window, Dr. Osbourne."

"Not that kind of conflict," Osbourne snapped. "It's just damned sudden and inconvenient. Refer him to the holiday clinic. One of the new grads can do it."

She shook her head. "The clinic is overbooked."

Osbourne sighed. "Oh, for God's sake! You win. Get him in here for a consult today after my last patient." This crap wouldn't happen if he had gone into anesthesiology. Or dentistry. And this receptionist had to go.

***

Late that afternoon, Nancy nodded at a poorly dressed man in the waiting room. "Dr. Osbourne will see you now."

"OK Nancy, you may as well call it a day." Osbourne stood to welcome the patient as Nancy reached for her coat.

"Thank you, Doctor," she said. "See you tomorrow."

He heard the office door close behind her, and the reassuring click that told him she'd turned the lock.

As the patient approached his desk, Osbourne bawled out, "Social distancing, please. No handshakes. Grab a chair."

Osbourne's nose twitched. Jeremy Melrose Drinkwater's running shoes were sodden with snow. Soiled cargo pants hung from his skinny hips and dragged at the heels. His damp leather jacket carried just a whiff of mold. Then Osbourne took a closer look.

"Well, well, Mr. Jeremy Melrose Drinkwater. What can I do for you, Mr. Melrose Drinkwater?"

Jeremy Patrice Lassonde settled his skinny frame onto the chair across from the doctor. "Sorry about that. It's my mother's maiden name." Lassonde stared past Osbourne at a painting of a fishing scene on the wall. "You're the only one I know who does this." His voice quavered. "I was afraid you wouldn't give me an appointment. And I need the service. I don't have much to live for since your sister died."

"Cut the crap, Jeremy." Osbourne rolled his eyes. "Lianne may be dead, but you're the picture of health."

433

"Not anymore." Jeremy's voice trembled. "You...you owe me big time. I quit my job to nurse your sister when she had breast cancer. My doctor says I have PTSD."

"I don't owe you squat. I supported you and Lianne for years before she died."

Jeremy nodded slowly. "True. You let us live in your basement apartment because you needed help with Aunt Celia in her last years. We played a lot of bridge with her at the country club." He leaned across the desk and stared into Osbourne's eyes. "After Lianne passed away, Celia took sick. When she died, you kicked me out!

"Garden flat." Osbourne dismissed the complaint with a wave of his hand. "It's a garden flat, not a basement." He shrugged. "I needed the space."

Jeremy eyed his brother-in-law. "Yeah, space. To build a garage for that fancy car you bought after Celia died. She passed away quite suddenly, wouldn't you say?"

"The old dear had a brain tumor." Osbourne's voice was cool. "She could have gone any time."

"So you say. There was no autopsy." Jeremy leaped to his feet. "Celia promised me a legacy; she was going to split the estate." He faced the older man. "But later she told me she had to change her will, or you would cut off her pain medication! Two days later she had a heart attack and died, leaving everything to you!"

Osbourne flushed. He jumped up, put a beefy hand on Jeremy's throat, and began to squeeze.

Jeremy gagged. "Stop! I won't say a word. Just give me the needle. That's all I want now. There's nothing left for me here." He rubbed his throat, where the doctor's grip had left an angry red blotch.

Osbourne sank into his chair and eyed his dead sister's husband. "You're crazy, Jeremy! Crazy doesn't meet the criteria."

Jeremy stopped rubbing his neck. "I can't go on. I have no partner, no family, no money, nowhere to live."

Osbourne grunted. Jeremy was indeed a loser. "So, what are your symptoms?"

Jeremy took a shaky breath. "Depression. Terrible depression. Ever since Lianne died, I've been looking for an out. I tried to get my own doctor to do it. He wouldn't, he's morally opposed to medically assisted death. He referred me to the clinic. But that will take weeks, months. I need something now."

"Depression is a treatable condition." Osbourne grabbed a prescription pad. "I'll give you some meds."

"No! I can't take the pain anymore. I want to die!"

Osbourne rolled his eyes. Always the drama queen. He decided to call Jeremy's bluff. "All right, you want to die." He scribbled a note and tossed it on the desk. "So die. There's your referral to the clinic. I'll do the paperwork later." He waved Jeremy to the door.

Jeremy grimaced. "No! I checked. The wait is too long. Half the new doctors put in their required three months and quit. Now, it takes forever to get appointments. And Christmas is here."

Osbourne shrugged. "There's always an uptick before the holidays. People see everyone getting together, and the lonely ones, the ones without family, the losers, get depressed. You'll just have to wait your turn."

"No." Jeremy clasped his hands together, squeezing them white. "You have to help me yourself!"

Osbourne glanced at the clock. Would this whining never end? His girlfriend would be annoyed. "I'm sorry, Jeremy, but I can't treat my sister's husband. It wouldn't be ethical. That's my final word."

Jeremy stood and stepped over to the open window. Far below, the Jag was covered with snow. He turned back to his brother-in-law. "Will, I'm begging you. You're my only hope. If you won't, I'll take the window." With a push, he threw it open.

Dr. Osbourne stared, looked at the clock again, contemplated the scandal, then threw in the towel.

"OK, OK. Calm down." He rummaged through a desk drawer, until he found the bulky freezer bag. He took it out, unzipped it, and extracted a bottle of dark liquid and a handful of capsules. "My emergency kit. Not legal. Not ethical. Not pleasant. But effective. Faster than the clinic."

Jeremy stared at the meds with a thin-lipped smile.

With a grimace, Osbourne pushed the bottle and pills across the desk. "You can do it yourself. Take the capsules first, so you don't vomit the liquid. Ten minutes later, empty the bottle into a glass with a lot of whiskey. A lot. Drink it all and you'll never have another hangover."

Jeremy pocketed the meds, and with a nod of satisfaction, he squared his thin shoulders. "Thanks. That should work. It worked for Aunt Celia, didn't it?"

Osbourne jumped to his feet. "You bastard!" He darted around the desk and threw himself at Jeremy.

But this time, Jeremy wasn't playing the weakling. He pushed Osbourne back with a wiry shove, throwing him against the buffed mahogany, scattering files and paper to the floor.

Osbourne barely kept his feet. "You can't prove a thing!"

"Oh, no?" Jeremy laughed. "I fished a bottle like this one out of the wastebasket in Celia's room after she died."

Osbourne shrank back. "I do you a favor, and this is what I get? Screw you!"

"Not this time." Jeremy stepped toward the exit. "You're not screwing me this time. The cops are suspicious when a rich old person dies suddenly after changing their will. And I've got a copy of Celia's previous will, which splits the estate between us. That should pique their interest. And it won't be difficult to get an exhumation order."

He paused under the plastic holly, and glanced back at Osbourne. "Merry Christmas."

Ω

DAYS WITHOUT NAME

Sylvia Maultash Warsh

Sylvia Maultash Warsh was born in Germany to Holocaust survivors and emigrated to Canada as a child. She graduated from U of T with a MA in Linguistics. She is the author of the Dr. Rebecca Temple series. To Die in Spring, Find Me Again *and* Season of Iron *were all winners or finalists for prominent Awards. Project Bookmark Canada chose* The Queen of Unforgetting, *an historical novel, for a plaque installation in Little Lake Park in Midland, Ontario. Her novella,* Best Girl, *came out in 2012.*

Sylvia lives in Toronto with her husband, Jerry, a psychiatrist and sometime resource for her medical sleuth. She has two grown children and two grandchildren. She also teaches writing to seniors.

After only 45 minutes on the single-engine turboprop, Lou landed in Punta Gorda, a sleepy little fishing town at the end of the Southern Highway. Eighteen months earlier, in another life, she had been a broke student and could only afford the six-hour bus ride south from Belize City. It had been her last excavation at the ruins before walking away from her Ph.D. studies. She was already dating Cary, but their conflicting schedules only allowed contact every few weeks, making each meeting a tease. He was a police detective, tall, confident, with the knowledge of darkness in his eyes. He said she wouldn't believe all the horrors he had seen. It wasn't till after they were married that she realized the darkness emanated from within.

Grabbing her backpack, she ran to catch the local bus to the village of Indian Creek, an hour's drive away.

She sat across from a woman holding a live chicken in a cage, probably holiday dinner. It was nearly Easter weekend, coinciding with *Wayeb,* the inauspicious five-day month in the Mayan calendar. The ancient Maya had developed a solar calendar of 18 months with

20 days each, but since that only added up to 360 days, they had tacked on a period of five days which were considered ill-fated, days without names, without souls. Even today, villagers considered it a dangerous time of the year, when the portals between humankind and the underworld dissolved, letting evil spirits cross over and cause calamity. Maybe that was why the woman with the chicken looked around nervously and wouldn't meet Lou's eye. She felt particularly unlucky coming back now, though without reason, as Cary had agreed to a trial separation.

His handsome, deceptively boyish face loomed before her, reminding her why she had fallen in love with him. His eyebrows had a way of tilting together as if he were in pain and that had pulled at her heartstrings. Once she got to know him, she realized it wasn't pain at all, but contempt. He stood apart, judging the world and finding it wanting. Judging *her*. Nothing she did could please him.

The bus stopped abruptly at the side of the highway. After descending from it, she turned to walk down the dirt road leading to Nim Li Punit, the ruins accidentally discovered nearly 20 years earlier in 1976 by oil prospectors. She knew the way in her sleep, though when she was last here in the winter of 1993, she drove Dr. de Waal's jeep down the road to Punta Gorda for supplies.

The ruins sat atop a steep hill, making for a sweaty climb with a backpack in the late afternoon heat. She loved the ruckus of the rainforest, the unbridled thrumming and croaking of invisible birds and insects and howler monkeys. Something leaped at her feet, making her yelp. She looked down to see a cane toad, a brown warty thing that grew to a length of nine inches, huge for a toad. She'd been astonished by their size at first, but they were plentiful in the region and she'd gotten used to them. They weren't harmless though, with their sacs of venom behind their eyes.

The dirt road, hacked out of the jungle, finally opened into a clearing where the visitors' center stood at the top of a long flight of wide stairs. She stopped, winded, yet relieved to see the familiar wood and glass building, a wildly optimistic project in the middle of the bush. The site attracted few visitors.

She climbed the stairs tentatively. She had timed it so the students would be gone after their term, retreating to their respective universities. De Waal would still be there finishing up, but she also would be gone in a week or two. Lou would offer to stay on during the rainy season, when the digs stopped, to continue work on the tomb she had discovered in December of '93. Besides, it only rained one or two hours in the afternoon from May to November.

She opened the wooden door of the visitors' center. Nothing had changed. Down the middle of the room lay twin long frames containing two gigantic stone stelae discovered on the site. Lou dropped her backpack on the floor, wiping her sweaty face with a hanky, and gazed down at the carvings on the stone that described life during the Classic Maya period. De Waal had helped translate them.

Down the hall, the office door flew open. A woman marched out in khakis and an embroidered Maya blouse. Lou squinted, trying to make out who she was, because it sure didn't look like Dr. de Waal. Last time she'd seen her professor, de Waal had been tall and stately despite excess baggage around the middle and a frizzy topknot of gray-blond hair. This woman had a real waist but a slight stoop, as if the effort of holding up her body was too much. The tight curls made her head look small but intimidating, her power visible. Her face had been sculpted down to cheekbones and eyes.

She had opened her mouth to chastise the intruder but stopped, her brown eyes taking Lou in.

"Dr. de Waal?" Lou couldn't help staring.

"Put your eyes back in your head, Louise," said the familiar voice. "I've had a makeover. You like it? It's the latest thing, styled by cancer."

Lou deflated. Of all the possibilities, she had not foreseen this. "You look…great!"

"Don't be ridiculous." De Waal brought her hand up to her hair self-consciously. "What the hell are you doing here?"

Lou had hoped for a warmer welcome, that after a year and a half the professor would have forgiven her.

"I must look a mess," Lou said, embarrassed, trying to smooth her dark ponytail. "Been travelling all day."

De Waal put a hand on her hip, waiting.

"I'm sorry I didn't keep in touch."

"I don't give a shit about that. Be sorry you ditched your Ph.D. Because you've got a brain. At least you had one. Maybe it's been sucked out…"

Lou smiled ruefully. "I got married. Not a lobotomy."

"Same thing."

Lou took a breath. "It was a mistake and…I'm back. The university says I can finish my research if the department gives me an extension."

"Your supervisor has to agree to that."

Lou hesitated. "So, *do* you?"

"You left me in the lurch! How can I trust you to finish?" De Waal settled her arms across her chest. "Won't your husband object, you leaving him for months at a time?"

"We're…separated. Giving it some time."

"Hubby didn't meet expectations?" De Waal tilted her chin toward her.

What could she say? "He's a very…negative man. He sees no good in the world. Maybe it's because he's a cop, but he thinks everyone's a crook out to get you."

"That seems like an abstract reason to separate."

"After a while I was starting to think like him, and I hated myself."

De Waal continued to wait.

"He had some version of a wife in his head that I couldn't be. He expected me to have dinner waiting for him every night, make apple pie in my spare time. He didn't understand my work. Didn't *consider* it work. He made me disappear."

"Well, I'm sorry things didn't turn out. But you should've made arrangements with the university first. It's after term, as you know, and not convenient for you to be here now—"

"I could get a head start on my work during the rainy season. I won't bother anyone." Lou cleared her throat. "I could stay on after you leave."

"You can't."

"Why not?"

"Because I'm not leaving."

"Well then, we can work together."

"I won't be working."

Lou pondered this. "I'm not asking for money."

"I don't want anyone here when…"

"I won't get in your way."

"…when I die."

That stopped Lou in her tracks. "You…you're dying?" She had no experience with death.

"I have leukemia. Doctors can't say how long I've got. Could be a month. Could be a year."

She motioned with her head for Lou to follow her into the office. Lou collapsed on a chair in front of the desk while de Waal retrieved a bottle and two plastic cups from a drawer. After pouring a generous amount into both cups, she handed one to Lou. Her tequila was legendary—the students all knew the professor liked a nip in the evenings.

De Waal pulled up a chair beside her. "It'll be bad at the end." She took a long swallow.

Lou felt uncomfortable with this private revelation. They had never exchanged personal information in the time they had worked together. She took a swig, felt it go right to her head after the rigors of the trip.

"But you look fine now." The professor's stoop was less noticeable when she sat and she did look good, what with the lost weight and the tamed hair. Maybe a bit pale. Lou didn't know what else to say. She'd never known anyone who was dying before.

De Waal shook her head. "I've always been in control of my life. I've decided to take control of my death. I have no family. I'm going to take my last breath here."

"Well, maybe I could help you."

"I don't want you to get into trouble. I need to be alone when I do it."

Lou stared at her, horrified. "You mean you're going to—"

De Waal downed her tequila and looked pointedly at her. "You're young and healthy. You can't understand. I've seen what happens to people at the end—bedridden, incontinent, pitiful. I won't go like that."

Lou blinked. "How are you—?"

"Bufotoxin."

"Toad venom?" She knew the villagers milked the poison from the toad. They dried and smoked it to see visions during their rituals. They warned the few hippie tourists who came to trip to smoke only small amounts and not swallow the stuff. From time to time, someone accidentally ingested enough of it to kill them. The toxin brought on arrhythmia, then cardiac arrest.

De Waal looked past Lou to some spot over her shoulder. "The shaman prepared some for me. I'm going to put it into my tequila on Sunday."

Lou gaped at her. "*This* Sunday?" It was Thursday.

De Waal leaned back, suddenly looking small in her chair.

"But—you said you might have a year. Why the rush?"

"I have no one to take care of me when I get sick. I can't take the uncertainty. I need to get it over with."

Lou took in a gulp of air. "Well, *I'm* here. I can take care of you."

She heard herself saying it, but wasn't sure she believed it. De Waal was right, she couldn't understand. But what she did understand was that her mentor had morphed into someone unrecognizable. Lou had idolized her, still did. Now the two of them were a pair, each so changed from the last time they'd been together. Lou owed it to her.

De Waal was watching her intently. "I appreciate the offer. Really. But I can't let you do that. You can't imagine what it'll be like."

***

A half hour later Lou stepped out the back of the visitors' center to climb the trail leading to the ruins. A smaller building near the center held more artifacts and a room with a cot where de Waal slept. Lou followed the path past logwood trees, palms and scrub, reaching the open plaza of grass clipped by hired villagers. Moss-covered piles of stones lay at the edges, ancient buildings that had collapsed over the years. She passed a ruined temple, its crumbling stairs leading up to nowhere. With determined steps, she headed to the southwest corner of the site where she had done her excavation. After a year and a half spent dreaming of the place, her heart quickened to finally be there again.

At last she came to it: a square hole in the ground lined with flat sandstones, the rubble that had been removed beside it, the whole marked off by a half dozen sticks with orange ties. Other students had continued to dig after she left. She had discovered the tomb in her third year, along with eight pots, some jade, numerous shells, and the skeletons of four people. The headdresses on the man and child meant they were a noble family, the two teenaged boys probably slaves.

The priest had slain them in a ritual sacrifice to appease the gods, with the community watching. It wasn't cruel, scholars insisted, because the ceremony was carried out in the belief that life was cyclical and those sacrificed would be born again, pure. Life was difficult in the forest, and they had to feed the gods with their life force in order to continue living. Without this payment of blood, the world would end. The man had most likely offered up his child, something Lou could not fathom. She loathed this violence, couldn't reconcile it with an otherwise intelligent and artistic culture. But after Cary, she almost understood. It was the paradox of the heart. Love and malice in the same body, the same breath.

She had told Cary about her discovery when she came back, showed him her diagrams of the excavation, where the bodies were buried, she joked. He barely pretended interest, didn't care about the bewildering number of Mayan gods or their bloodthirst. He was busy chasing drug dealers, which was clearly more important than distant phantoms who had lived 1,000 years ago.

***

Lou stayed on, with no further objection from de Waal. On Friday afternoon she joined the professor at a low wooden table in the yard beside the visitors' center. They had finished eating dishes of rice and beans and small meat pies, washed down with Coca-Cola. Now they sat back in their sling chairs listening to the jungle symphony. On Wednesday the villagers had brought de Waal enough prepared food to see her through the weekend, because they abstained from making fires during *Wayeb*. There would be no cooking while evil spirits roamed who could engulf their houses in flames. Indeed, the villagers would stay at home during the five days, lest disaster befell them outside.

Lou had never been there during *Wayeb* and she noticed the absence of people around. No villagers working on the grounds or making deliveries. She didn't believe in evil spirits, but a sizzle of anxiety had started up in her temple.

It wasn't till late Saturday at the same table that Lou dared broach the subject that weighed on her mind.

"What if a doctor discovers a cure in the next three months? It'll be too late if you go through with it."

"Cures don't come so quickly. I've read enough about the current research."

She tried another tack. "You could continue your work longer…"

"I've done enough. There are young people like you waiting to take my place."

Lou ignored the dig. "Everyone respects you. What you've done."

"Nobody really cares about me. I'll be a footnote in their day. *Oh, the old battle axe is finally gone, is she?* Then they'll finish their coffee."

"I care."

She gave Lou a crooked smile. "You have to say that since you're here. Eating my last meals."

Lou chuckled uneasily. "Really, you shouldn't make important decisions when you're depressed."

"Don't presume to know me."

"I just think you should wait. I don't see why—"

"You don't know anything! I'm *scared*, damn you!"

Her eyes blazed at Lou, as if she had purposefully pulled the confession from de Waal's lips. Then she covered her eyes with a hand to hide the tears.

Lou was stunned. Who was this person? Not the exalted Dr. de Waal who intimidated even her superiors.

Lou stood and came to kneel beside her chair. She wanted to say something helpful, but all she could think of were platitudes: *Everything will be OK. You'll feel better tomorrow*. None of it was true. She carefully reached out and took her professor's free hand.

De Waal uncovered her face, stared at their joined hands but didn't move. She closed her eyes and dozed off.

***

Sunday arrived, the last day of *Wayeb*. Lou fought the feeling of impending doom. Maybe de Waal had changed her mind. Maybe Lou had convinced her to wait. She spent the morning in a cubicle off the visitors' center going over the pots and stingray spines found in "her" tomb by other students. The spines were used for bloodletting, another Mayan ritual to feed their hungry unrelenting gods.

De Waal hadn't yet arrived at her office and for a terrible moment Lou was afraid she had already done the deed. She was about to jump up and check the professor's room, when she heard de Waal's slow footsteps enter the visitors' center. Lou gave her a minute to reach her office before exiting the cubicle.

She found her prof at her desk emptying powder from a small packet into a plastic glass of tequila. The plastic was opaque, hiding the danger. Lou's stomach churned.

"You shouldn't be here," said de Waal. "I've arranged with a villager to call the police when he finds my body tomorrow."

Lou gasped, her breath gone. She hadn't really believed this moment would come. A well of emotion rose in her, then burst from her throat. She sobbed into her hands, unable to control it.

De Waal came around her desk and took Lou in her arms. "Silly girl. Everyone dies."

Lou quieted down, comforted by the motherly warmth, out of character for de Waal. Her own mother had never embraced her or given her a kind word. She had sided with Cary about the separation.

A noise came from the visitors' center. Someone had entered. "Anyone here?"

Lou's head jerked up. She swiped the tears from her face and stepped away from de Waal. A moment later Cary poked his head through the doorway.

"There you are!" His boyish face looked at them suspiciously, as if he had come across a crime scene.

"What are you doing here?" Lou asked, her heart racing.

444

"Is that how you greet your husband?" He stepped toward her with arms outstretched.

She stepped back. "You're not supposed to be here."

His arms dropped to his sides. "I missed you." His brows fell together, but she wasn't fooled by them.

"We agreed to a trial separation."

"It's been five days, babe. I thought you'd go to your mother's. Not some godforsaken hole in the middle of nowhere."

De Waal moved back toward the desk.

"This is where my work is."

He made a show of looking around, unimpressed. "You don't need to work. I make enough money to support you."

"You're not listening. This is what I want to do. I don't need you to support me."

"How much will you make here? You used to complain how poor you were."

"Some things are more important than money."

"Nothing's more important than us, babe. Come home with me."

"You're forgetting our agreement."

"I changed my mind. Don't you love me anymore?"

Lou and de Waal exchanged glances.

"I'm not ready. I need more time."

"I was hoping you wouldn't say that." He pulled a gun from the back of his pants.

Lou stared at it. "Are you crazy?"

"I love you. It's just to persuade you."

"It persuades me that you're crazy."

"Stop saying that. If I'm crazy, it's your fault, because you left me. I can't live without you."

De Waal took a step closer. "I'm Kay de Waal, Lou's prof. I'm so glad to meet you." She put her hand out toward him.

He stared at it, then placed the gun in his other hand so he could shake hers.

"I don't want to get in the middle of a lovers' spat, but Lou, you didn't tell me how handsome your husband was." She gave him a wide smile. "You let him loose now, some other girl will snap him up. Maybe it's time for you to go home."

"Now there's a smart lady," he said.

Lou glared at de Waal. What was wrong with the woman? Then she realized the professor was trying to get rid of her. Pushing her out the door with a madman aiming a gun at her. "How can you say that?"

"Just thinking about what's best for you."

Not true. "What about my work?"

"Give yourself some time with your husband. You can start again in October, in the new term."

Lou's pulse raced. She couldn't believe de Waal had so misread her relationship with Cary. The gun should've told her something was very wrong. It had been a constant presence at home, though never aimed at her before. An escalation of their conflict. She considered trying to knock the gun from his hand, but worried it might go off, a stray bullet hitting de Waal.

"So it's settled?" de Waal asked.

Lou glared at her but nodded. She would have to figure out another way to escape from him.

"You can put the gun down now," de Waal said. "You got what you want."

"I knew you'd see reason, Lou." Cary returned the gun to the back of his pants. "Thank you, ma'am."

He pulled Lou into an embrace. She stiffened.

"Well, this calls for a drink!" de Waal said. "Let's celebrate. I have some very good tequila."

She returned to her desk and poured two more plastic glasses of the liquor. Then stepping toward him, she stretched out her arm, about to hand Cary the drink she had prepared for herself. She looked pointedly at Lou, a question in her eyes. Lou blinked in disbelief. De Waal had understood after all. And she was asking her for permission to—

Lou opened her mouth but nothing came out. Here it was, the paradox of the human heart. Love and malice in the same breath. Except Cary had supplanted them both with fear.

Had she nodded? Because de Waal was giving him the drink.

"To the happy couple," she said, raising her glass.

"To us." He lifted his, while grinning at Lou.

She could still have saved him, pushed the glass away from his mouth.

Instead, heart on fire, she watched as he gulped down the contents.

The jungle noise stopped as she waited. Everything stopped, except for the reedy laughter of the gods.

Ω

Acknowledgements

No book, especially an anthology of this volume and diversity, can go to press without the help of so many people.

During this challenging year of the pandemic, 2020, this fact is even more relevant.

While those who offered help, support and a trained eye are too numerous to mention, I would like to take this opportunity to thank a few by name.

My undying gratitude and respect goes out to Rosemary McCracken, author of the popular Pat Tierney mystery series, for her many hours of hard work and her exceptional skills as a seasoned copy-editor. I'd also like to thank M.H. (Madeleine) Callway, for helping to organize the launch, and for her work behind the scenes. My personal thanks to Marian Misters of Sleuth of Baker Street bookstore in Toronto, for her lifetime of support for Canadian crime writers, as well as to Joan O'Callaghan, for her friendship and advice on the layout of these stories.

Finally, my love and thanks go out to my husband and partner, Alex Carrick, and our children, Tom, Ted and Tammy, for their support during the months of work.

Made in the USA
Monee, IL
27 January 2021